FORT SUICIDE AND THE BRAVE RIFLES

ALSO BY GORDON D. SHIRREFFS

Range Rebel and Code of the Gun
Slaughter at Broken Bow and Southwest Drifter
Roanoke Raiders and Powder Boy of the Monitor
Barranca and Blood Justice
Last Man Alive and Now He is Legend
Too Tough to Die and Valiant Bugles
Gunswift and Voice of the Gun
Arizona Justice and The Lonely Gun
Last Train from Gun Hill and The Border Guidon
Rio Desperado and Top Gun
Rio Diablo and The Proud Gun
Renegade Lawman and The Lone Rifle
Jack of Spades and Ambush on the Mesa
Action Front! and The Grey Sea Raiders
Fort Vengeance and Shadow Valley
Judas Gun and Hangin' Pards
Ride A Lone Trail and Massacre Creek
Rio Bravo and Bugles On The Prairie

FORT SUICIDE AND THE BRAVE RIFLES

Two Full Length Western Novels

GORDON D. SHIRREFFS

WOLFPACK
PUBLISHING
— EST 2013 —

Fort Suicide and The Brave Rifles
Paperback Edition
Copyright © 2023 (As Revised) Gordon D. Shirreffs

Wolfpack Publishing
9850 S. Maryland Parkway, Suite A-5 #323
Las Vegas, Nevada 89183

wolfpackpublishing.com

Paperback ISBN 978-1-63977-994-9
eBook ISBN 978-1-63977-594-1

FORT SUICIDE

CHAPTER ONE

Travis Walter squatted in the hot shade of a rock outcropping high on the side of a mesa that thrust itself up from the flat floor of the New Mexican desert. Far below him, he could see the winding ruts of the old military road which led to Fort Joslyn. The desert and mesa seemed empty of human life, but instinct and long experience in the Southwest warned him that this was the very time to look for Apache. They would watch and wait until the right time for an ambush occurred; then, and then only, would they be seen by their intended victims.

The metal of his Sharps carbine was almost too hot for his hands, so he set it aside after checking the cap on the nipple. The rock at his feet burned through the thin soles of his worn boots. The long miles from the valley of the San Pedro down across the border into Sonora, then across the Continental Divide which separated Sonora from Chihuahua, had played hell with his horse and with him.

He had crossed over from Chihuahua into New Mexico Territory before dawn that morning, knowing he would strike the Fort Joslyn road north of Big Hatchet Peak. It would have been easier for him to strike north up the valley of the San Pedro and reach the old Butter-field Trail, but in the early summer of 1861, all Federal troops had abandoned their posts and stations in Arizona to retreat to the Rio Grande, leaving eastern Arizona and western New Mexico open to the ravages of Cochise and his Chiricahuas and Mangas Colorado and his Mimbrenos. So Travis Walker, Captain of United States Cavalry, had taken the longest but safest way around to report for duty at Fort Craig on the Rio Grande.

Travis eyed the flapping toe of his left boot. He pulled his dirty bandanna from about his throat and bound it about the boot toe. He had done more walking over rough country in the past week than he had done in the eight years of his service in the Southwest.

He waited with the patience of an Apache until the long shadows fell across the slopes of the mesa. Travis shook his canteen and was about to swill his remaining water when he thought of his horse. It took all the will he had to carry the canteen to where he had picketed his rangy bay. Boots softly whinnied when he saw Travis. He shoved his nose against Travis' dusty shirt and rubbed at it.

Travis grinned. "Look, hardhead," he said, "I'll be wearing a uniform again in a few days."

Travis took off his hat and poured the remaining water into it. He held the hat toward the horse, and Boots drank. Travis put on his hat, grateful for the temporary coolness of the wet fabric. He led his bay to the rock outcropping, then attached his carbine to the snap ring on the saddle.

The darkening desert was still deserted. He led the horse down the long slope, taking advantage of every scrap of cover. A velvety darkness had fallen when he reached the desert floor. A cool wind fingered about him as he struck off for the dim bulk of Big Hatchet Peak.

There was one thought in Travis Walker's mind as he plodded toward the peak - to get back to the Army and fight against the Confederacy. He had entered West Point at the age of eighteen and had graduated nineteenth in the Class of 1849. Since then, *U.S.* had been branded on his lean flank just as it had been on the flanks of the cavalry company he had commanded at Fort Yuma until April of '61. He had missed the Mexican War, but from all reports, this new war promised to outdo that recent affair by far, and Travis Walker meant to get into it.

There would be no moon this night, but Big Hatchet Peak would be his beacon. He crossed the Fort Joslyn road, and as his boots sank into the deep ruts, he thought again that perhaps Fort Joslyn had been abandoned as so many other Southwestern posts had been. Perhaps the Confederates had come up from Texas and had occupied it.

Travis led the bay half a mile beyond the road, then mounted him. He placed his carbine across his thighs and loosened his Navy Colt in its holster. He rode steadily, with his gray eyes sweeping the terrain all about him. Apache didn't like night fighting, for a warrior killed at night might wander forever trying to find The House of Spirits, speaking through the melancholy voice of Bu, the owl. Still, if he blundered into some of them, they'd fight like the skilled warriors they were.

It was midnight by his watch when he called a halt high on the slopes of the Hatchet Mountains. The big bay was tired. He picketed Boots in a draw that afforded the horse some sparse grazing. He himself gnawed at some dried venison he had purchased from a Mexican ranchero. The man had thrown in a bottle of Baconora mezcal for good measure. Travis finished his frugal meal and allowed himself two dollops of mezcal. The potent liquor seemed to put new life into him.

He looked to the north, up the valley between the Hatchets and the dim Cedar Mountains. Suddenly he saw a spurt of yellow light on the valley floor; then, it was gone as quickly as it had come. There was life down there.

"What kind of life?" he asked himself aloud.

Fort Joslyn was down there somewhere. Maybe a sentry had risked taking a smoke on duty. If it wasn't a member of the garrison, who had struck that light, then it could only be an Apache.

He looked to the east. He was at least a hundred miles from the Rio Grande. There was plenty of water between him and the river. The only trouble was that the water was contained in waterholes, many miles apart, and every one of those waterholes was known to the Apache like the palms of their greasy hands. There was good water at Fort Joslyn and at the little *placita* of Santa Theresa some miles north of the outpost. But, if Fort Joslyn had been abandoned, that would also mean that Santa Theresa would be a ghost town, haunted by the predatory Mimbrenos.

Travis unbuckled his cantle pack and removed his uniform from it. He shook his head as he eyed the wrinkles in the good material. He'd be a helluva-looking yellow leg when he rode onto the first occupied post he could find. Travis spread the blanket on the ground and lay flat on it, with his Sharps between his right arm and his body. He looked down into the dark valley as though he could penetrate the darkness with his eyes. Travis fell asleep with an uneasiness that refused to leave him.

———

THE BAY WHINNIED SOFTLY, and Travis was awake in an instant. He got to his feet and snatched up his carbine. He padded down the slope to the bay and spoke softly to it. He was ready to cut off its wind instantly if the bay tried to whinny again.

There was a faint trace of light in the eastern sky, but he wasn't sure if it was the new moon or the coming of the false dawn. He waited there with a trickle of cold sweat working its way down from each armpit.

The bay raised its head, and Travis clamped a big hand on its windpipe. The bay shied a little. Travis looked down the slope. There was movement in the darkness. Dim mounted figures materialized from among the brush. There were six of them looking up the slope toward Travis. Then suddenly, they were gone as quickly as they had come. No troopers nor Mexican travelers could move as silently as those mysterious horsemen had done.

Travis backed away from the bay and went to his camp. Swiftly he rolled his cantle pack and took it back to the bay. He buckled it in place and then walked away from the horse to listen. The wind moaned softly through the brush. The thudding of his heart interfered with his listening. Mentally he calculated the risk. If there were only six of them, he had a chance of holding off a rush. But there were some alternatives. They could wait until he went down into the valley and then ambush him or close in on him. They could surround his camp and hold him there until thirst and heat softened him for the kill.

The night had been quiet before, but now it seemed alive with a myriad of soft and indistinguishable sounds. The wind sighed, and the brush rubbed against rocks. Something scuttled for cover down the western slope. Travis wet his cracked lips. They could move as noiselessly as cats. He had once been on patrol from Fort Yuma into the brooding Kofas. They had found three prospectors dead in their bloodstained blankets, with sightless eyes staring at the dawn sky. Their throats had been slashed from ear to ear. Their horses, mules, and equipment had been taken, and all the Cocopah scouts had found were the tracks of only one warrior about the camp. Probably none of the three murdered men had had a chance to awaken for their last living breath.

Now the brush seemed alive with prowling figures, razor-edged *besh* in their strong hands, closing in on Travis Walker.

He fought down the slimy green panic which tried to flow over his mind. His bowels seemed to churn within him.

The eastern sky was lighter now, and he could distinguish the distant peaks. In a short time, he would be exposed to a carefully aimed rifle shot, a crippling shot that would leave him helpless in the hands of the Apache. They would have their sport before they finished him off.

Boots moved restlessly. His hoofs clashed on the rock, causing a cold sweat to break out on Travis' forehead. A white man could have heard the din half a mile off. Boots raised his head, then shied and blew. There was a devil's ring closing in on the hilltop. Dawn was the time for killing.

Travis swung up on the bay and laid the steel into his flanks. The bay reared and plunged, then shot down the dim slope. A rifle shot shattered the quietness not fifty feet behind Travis. He bent low in the saddle and spurred for his life. He saw the ledge just in time to lift the bay over it. Boots came down hard, lost his stride, then crashed pell-mell through a clinging thicket of catclaw, which raked through Travis' trousers like red-hot needles.

An ululating cry broke out behind Travis, driven up from the Apache's diaphragm and pistoned out of his squared mouth. Travis did not dare look back as he made his breakneck descent of the treacherous slope, gripping the reins with his left and his Sharps with his right hand. Rifles popped behind him, and he felt something pluck at his hat.

Boots hit the level ground and broke into his long swinging stride. There were great coils of power in the haunches of the big cavalry gelding, coupled with a sure eye for holes and loose stones, and Travis knew the bay could outrun most Apache mounts for a time. But they would try to wear down the bay. Travis dared to look back. The bucks had broken into the clear too. Half a dozen of them, driving their wiry mounts as though they had been born part of them. The pursuers separated. Four of them stayed behind Travis while the other two began to forge ahead at top speed, one on each flank, forming the dread pursuit crescent.

The strategy was old. Travis had seen Cocopah and Yuma run down rabbits the same way by keeping some of the runners behind the quarry while others came up alongside it, driving it to its utmost frantic speed, forcing it from one side to the other so that it covered more ground than its pursuers, while the rear party kept up the steady pressure behind it.

Travis cocked his Sharps. He dropped the reins on Boots' neck and swung in his saddle. He raised his carbine and led the left hand buck a little, then lowered the muzzle to get a bead on the buck's wiry claybank. He squeezed off. The Sharps jerked back against his shoulder, and he saw the claybank go down, pitching his rider far in front of him. The Apache hit the ground running.

There was no time to reload the Sharps. Travis snapped it to its sling and then freed his Navy Colt. The Fort Joslyn road trended from the west. He spurred the bay until he was racing down the high center of the road. Boots kept up his steady pace, but he was tossing at the bit. The rear party was gaining steadily. The right flank warrior closed in. He leveled his rifle and fired but missed. Travis looked for the warrior to draw a hand gun, but instead, he whipped a war club up from where it hung at his waist. The rear warriors began to fire to rattle Travis.

The hard-riding warrior was twenty feet from Travis now. "Trying to make a blasted hero of himself," said Travis aloud. Travis fired, but the warrior threw himself on the far side of his dun, leaving exposed only a moccasined foot hooked on the near side of the dun and a hand gripping the shaggy mane. Still, he gained on Travis.

Travis looked ahead. There was something on the valley floor. It looked like a handful of children's blocks. He knew it for Fort Joslyn, but there was no sign of life there. He passed the burned remains of three wagons. Three bloated horses lay to one side, with strips of flesh hacked from them. There wasn't much doubt in Travis' mind about it being Apache work, and that done within sight of the fort. It was a sure sign that the fort had been abandoned.

Boots' head was outstretched. His breath was rasping. Foam from the weakening bay's mouth struck Travis' face. The warrior lanced in for the kill, drawing his war club back for a smashing blow at man or horse. Travis switched his Colt to his left hand, dropped the reins, and whipped his saber free from its sheath. He caught the surprised warrior with a backhand stroke that sheared through the tough handle of the war club and struck hard against the warrior's head. He went down as though poleaxed.

A rifle cracked from behind. Boots faltered in his stride. He'd never make it to the shelter of the post walls. Travis shot a glance back at his pursuers. They were sixty yards behind him and gaining fast. There was no sign of life at the fort as Travis turned to look at it. There was only one thing to do, his last drawing card in the swift game of death. He freed his left foot from its stirrup, sheathed his saber, and gripped the forward edge of his saddle with his free hand. Then he fired the Navy Colt inches from the rear of Boots' head. As the big bay went down, Travis leaped from the saddle to clear the horse. Boots smashed against the ground, jerked a little, and then lay still.

Travis dropped behind the dead horse and rested his right hand on the bay to steady his aim. He had four shots left. He gripped his right wrist with his left hand

and sighted over the hammer notch. A brown chest swam into view, and he squeezed off. Smoke blew back into his face as he cocked the big hand gun, but through it, he saw the Apache fall.

The last three bucks swerved aside, throwing themselves on the far side of their horses. They raced to the west, trailing a cloud of dust behind them.

Travis rested his head on the sweaty body of the bay. The reaction from the fight flooded over him. He forced himself to free his carbine from the bay and load it. The warriors were out of sight in the thick brush, but a scarf of dust revealed their passage. Travis loaded his Colt and then bent to get his gear lose from the bay. His head jerked back as he heard the familiar notes of a big infantry G bugle break the valley quiet, to be instantly followed by the brazen notes of a cavalry C trumpet.

Travis turned slowly. He was no more than a quarter of a mile from the adobe buildings of Fort Joslyn. The post stood out clearly in the dawn light, and even as he watched, he saw lamplight brighten the windows. A shower of sparks shot out of a chimney, followed by a puff of smoke that trailed off in a streamer before the shifting dawn wind. The wind had been blowing directly toward the fort, and surely, if a sleepy sentry hadn't seen the fighting on the road, he would have heard the shooting.

Travis raised his carbine and fired it; the report flatted off. A moment later, he saw a man come out from between two buildings and look toward him. He reloaded and fired again. Then he sat down on the dead bay.

———

IT WAS twenty minutes after Travis had been seen that a squad of horsemen broke from the fort and trotted toward him through the thick brush until they reached the road. An officer led them with a drawn saber in his hand.

Travis stood up as the officer halted his squad fifty yards away. "Who are you?" called out the officer.

"Captain Travis Walker, United States Army."

"What are you doing out here?"

"Looking at the Goddamned scenery!" roared Travis. "Come over here, mister! I'm not in the mood to make conversation across fifty yards of space!"

The officer rode forward, followed by his squad. The bare shoulder straps of a second lieutenant were on his shoulders. He stared at Travis and then at the dead bay. "I'm Second Lieutenant Nerval DeSantis," he said. "Second United States Dragoons on detached duty here at Fort Joslyn."

Despite his anger, Travis felt relieved that Fort Joslyn was still occupied by United States troops. "You must be wide awake, Mr. DeSantis," he snapped. "Six Apache chased me this far from those hills, shooting at me and getting shot at, and not a soul stirred in your precious fort."

DeSantis flushed. He sheathed his fine saber. "I have just your word on that, sir," he said hotly.

Travis thudded his carbine butt against the ground. "You'll see a downed Apache twenty yards up the road if you'll look," he said.

DeSantis spurred forward, then reined his fine black in sharply as he saw the buck lying in the brush. He swung down quickly and walked toward the warrior. He was five feet from the Apache when the warrior came to swift, violent life. A knife flashed upward in his hand. DeSantis jumped back, caught a spur in a root, and went down. The Apache jumped up and raised his knife. Travis freed his Colt from its sheath and fired twice. The warrior spun about and went down, clawing at the ground.

Travis hurdled his dead horse and raced toward

DeSantis. The warrior was still thrashing on the ground. He turned his head to look at Travis and began to sing his death song in a husky voice. *"O ha lei O hale..."* The crashing report of the Colt cut short his song. The bullet had hit him squarely between the eyes.

Travis blew the smoke from his Colt.

"For God's sake!" husked DeSantis. "You never gave him a chance! We could have taken him prisoner!"

Travis grinned crookedly. "How long have you been out on the frontier, mister?"

"Three months."

Travis holstered his Colt and nodded. "Still wet behind the ears, too. No experienced soldier would have walked up on a buck like that. They're experts at playing possum, and the wounded ones won't surrender. What were you looking for? A brevet for bringing in a live Apache?"

DeSantis flushed as the barbed verbal shaft drove home. An intense hatred of the sunburned, whiskered man before him was conceived at that instant.

A corporal cantered up. He saluted Travis. "We've got your saddle and equipment, sir," he said. He looked down at the dead warrior and then at DeSantis. "The captain sure saved your life, sir. You didn't have a chance."

DeSantis got up and dusted off his fine broadcloth uniform. He waited until a trooper rode up and gave his horse to Travis. Travis mounted, and the trooper slogged back through the sand to mount behind one of his mates. Travis and DeSantis rode to the squad. DeSantis took his place at the head of the detail and rode toward the fort. The corporal looked at Travis. "You had a close call, sir," he said.

"Does your commanding officer allow Apache to raid within half a mile of the post?"

The corporal shrugged. "Major Lester has his problems, sir."

"What about those three wagons back there on the road?"

The corporal shrugged. "Those were Mex wagons being driven to Santa Theresa. Cuchillo Rojo struck them three days ago while the garrison was standing retreat. We heard the shooting and saw the smoke. We buried five Mex men in the post cemetery. One of them lived long enough to tell us there had been two women and a fifteen-year-old girl with the wagons. The captain knows what probably happened to them."

Travis placed a hand on his cantle and looked back down the road. "How many Apache did the garrison get?"

The noncom laughed harshly. "We didn't go out until the Apache were gone. The only trace we found of them was fresh horse manure. Maybe someday we'll run across the bodies of those three Mex women. I hope I *never* see them."

Travis looked ahead as the detail skirted the fort and turned in toward the gate, which was nothing more than a wide space between two buildings. What kind of a commanding officer was Major Lester to let those three wagons get shot up and burned within eyesight of the post and do nothing about it?

"Cuchillo Rojo," he said. "Mimbreno?"

The corporal nodded. "One of Mangas Colorado's fighting chiefs. One of the best-damned guerrillas and raiders in this God-forsaken part of the Southwest."

Travis looked at the hills, now being lit by the rays of the rising sun. Cuchillo Rojo...Red Knife. There was no need to ask how he had earned his name.

CHAPTER TWO

Fort Joslyn could hardly be called more than a military camp. The post was formed by a rectangle of adobe and fieldstone buildings in poor repair. Troopers and infantrymen looked curiously at Travis as he swung down from his horse and slapped the dust from his clothing with his battered Kossuth hat. The rising sun shone on the barrel of a stubby brass howitzer that stood near the warped flagpole.

Norval DeSantis saluted Travis. "The major is in his quarters," he said.

"I'll wait for him in his office, mister."

DeSantis hesitated. "The major hasn't been feeling well," he said with a faint tinge of sarcasm in his voice. "He'll probably want to see you in his quarters."

Travis nodded. The young lieutenant led the way to a large adobe structure and opened the door for Travis. Travis walked into a dim hallway, and his nose was instantly assailed by the pungent odor of some kind of medicine or ointment. DeSantis wrinkled his nose as he opened another door and ushered Travis in ahead of him.

The medicinal odor in the big hot room made Travis' eyes water. A pudgy man wearing a thick flannel night-gown sat on a rumpled bed, his feet immersed in a steaming pan of water. A fire blazed in a whitewashed beehive fireplace in one corner of the room. A trooper was busily rubbing the pudgy man's neck and shoulders.

"Well, DeSantis," snapped the pudgy man. "What is it? What is it?"

DeSantis saluted. "One of our sentries heard firing south of the fort. Captain Cass sent me out to investigate. I found this man out there. His horse had been downed, and he had driven off an Apache attack. He says he is Captain Travis Walker of the United States Army."

Travis saluted. "I assume you are Major Lester, sir?"

The man nodded. "Major Enos Lester, Corps of Quartermasters, officer commanding Fort Joslyn, Department of New Mexico."

Travis eyed the man. Even in a uniform, Major Enos Lester would not be imposing. His skull was bald and pink, with a ruff of grayish-white hair standing up about it. His pale blue eyes were weak and watery.

"You have proof that you are an army officer?" demanded Lester. "Shut that damned door, DeSantis! Do you want me to catch my death of cold?" He looked back over his shoulder. "Rub harder, Kelligan!"

"Yes, sir!"

Travis took out his orders and silently passed them to Enos Lester. The major took a pair of brass-bound spectacles from a table and adjusted them on his pulpy nose. He peered at the orders. "On special detached duty in Arizona, eh? Well then, sir! What are you doing here?"

Travis raised his head. The man sounded like a pettish old woman who had been disturbed while feeding her cat, "If the major will read the attached sheet, he will see that my orders, at the completion of my mission, are to report to the commanding officer of the Department of New Mexico. I did not care to risk traveling to New Mexico via the Butterfield Trail, so I passed into Sonora, then east to Chihuahua, thence north here to Fort Joslyn. I traveled in civilian clothing to avoid suspicion. However, I brought my uniform with me."

Lester folded the orders and tapped on them with a blunt forefinger. "What was the nature of your special detached duty?"

Travis looked at the orderly and then at DeSantis. "It is of a confidential nature, sir."

Lester waved a hand. "Out with the both of you!" he snapped. He waited until the door closed behind DeSantis and Kelligan. "Well, Walker?"

Travis loosened his collar a little. Sweat was pouring from his body. The temperature in the room was at least ninety degrees. "We received information at Fort Yuma that certain Regular Army officers, still in our uniform, were traveling through Arizona, inciting enlisted men to desert and join the Confederacy. We also heard that there were certain citizens of some prominence in Arizona who were planning to give aid and comfort to the enemy should they invade that territory. My orders were to track some of them down and gather the necessary information on them to have them brought to trial for treason."

"And you succeeded?"

"To some extent."

"Show me your information."

"It is memorized, sir. Certain incriminating papers have been cached near Tucson to be repossessed when Federal troops return there to take control of the territory again."

Lester snorted. "That will take some time. We have heard that Confederate troops are forming in Texas to invade New Mexico. At the present time, the department commander is strengthening Fort Craig on the Rio Grande for the purpose of stopping a Texan invasion of the Rio Grande Valley. My post, sir, is the only post still under the United States flag between the Rio Grande and Colorado."

"A tough assignment," said Travis.

"It is, indeed, sir." Lester shrugged his damp night-gown up about his shoulders and swilled medicine from a square black bottle. "I am a sick man, Captain Walker, with almost forty years of service behind me. I have been more or less abandoned here in the Apache country with inadequate supplies, outmoded weapons, a ragtag and bobtail set of officers and enlisted men, and with no one to give me advice but God himself. And I may add, sir, my prayers have not been too successful!"

"I hope they will be, sir. Now, with your permission, I'll draw a horse from your quartermaster officer and continue on to the Rio Grande."

Lester stood up. "Put some more wood on that damned fire so that I can dress in comfort."

Travis did as he was bid. Lester peeled off his gown, revealing a potbelly and bandy legs. He pulled on long underwear and then dressed in full uniform, buckling on his sword belt. He hastily brushed back his muff of hair and placed a velvet-trimmed Kossuth hat on his head. He pulled the brim down over his eyes. "An officer on frontier duty must always look smart in front of his men," he said.

My God, thought Travis, the look of an eagle. The heat of a summer day in that country was enough to fell a man wearing a flannel shirt.

"You have had much frontier service?" asked Lester.

"Eight years, sir. Class of '49, then duty in New Mexico, Texas, and Arizona ever since."

"In eight years, you've made a captaincy? Surely it is a brevet rank?"

"No, sir."

Enos Lester shook his head. "And me with forty years of service behind me and still a major. Incrimination, sir. Politicking by desk officers in Washington. I had hoped to get my brigade if my health improved. The drums of war are fine music to my ears, Captain."

"I have no doubt about that, Major," said Travis politely.

"Eight years' frontier service and a captain at your age. I could use you here, sir."

"I have my orders, Major Lester."

"So you do, and I have *mine*. Suppose we go to my office and talk things over?"

Travis looked suspiciously at the bumbling little man as he opened the door and waited until Lester passed into the hallway. There was something in Lester's tone that Travis didn't like.

The outer air, warm though it was, struck Travis like a cool draft after leaving Lester's room. Half a dozen ramshackle wagons were grouped at one end of the post quadrangle. As Travis eyed them, he saw a buxom woman step over the tailgate of one of them, revealing a long expanse of shapely legs clad in red-and-white striped stockings. A passing trooper whistled. The woman turned and giggled. Another woman eyed the trooper and flirted her hips at him. Some civilian men squatted beside a building, drinking from tin mugs. A line of wash was strung from one wagon to another, and women's underwear waved in the warm breeze.

Major Lester pointed at the wagons. "Refugees," he said offhand. "I have given them protection here. They are awaiting a chance to make the Rio Grande."

"A rough-looking lot," observed Travis.

"Perhaps. But they *are* United States citizens. It is my duty to protect them."

Travis nodded. With women like that, on a crowded post surrounded by women-starved troopers, the post took on an air of a powder keg with someone waving a lighted cigar over it. He had experienced situations like this before during Indian scares.

Some of the troopers saluted Lester as he passed, and Travis was sure he caught a glint of amusement in their eyes. The more he saw of Fort Joslyn, the more he wished he was watering his horse in the Rio Grande.

Lester paraded pompously into his office and hung his Kossuth hat on a hook. "Sit down, Walker," he invited.

Travis sat down. Lester shoved a box of cigars toward him. "Help yourself. They do my sinuses no good."

Travis lit up one of the dry cigars. He eyed a picture of General Winfield Scott, which hung on the wall behind Lester's desk. Lester glanced up at it. Thinking he had resembled Old Fuss and Feathers in his younger days filled him with pride.

"Now about *your* orders," said Lester. "I'm afraid they have been superseded; shall we say?"

Travis shot a look at the major. "Superseded? By whom? They came directly from Santa Fe last June."

Lester waved a pudgy hand. "I know that, Walker. I saw the signature and date at the bottom. But times have changed in the department. Not a month ago, I received an order, a blanket order, shall we say, which certainly supersedes those you have."

There was a cold feeling in Travis' gut. The pompous little rooster wasn't joking. Joking was probably something Enos Lester never did. It might deflate the dignity of forty years' service and the gold oak leaf on his shoulder strap.

Drill Call sounded out on the parade ground as Lester fumbled through a stack of papers in a basket on his desk. Then, with a triumphant air, he withdrew a sheet. "Read this," he said with a tight little smile.

Travis scanned through it. It was an order to the effect that all officers and enlisted men, who had no definite assignment and were separated from other commands, would report to the nearest camp, post, or station of the United States Army for such duty as would be prescribed by the commanding officer of any such camp, post, or station until orders were received from the department commander ordering them elsewhere.

Travis looked up at Enos Lester. "This can't apply to me," he said quietly.

"No? Are you a guardhouse lawyer, sir?"

Travis bit his lip, holding back a retort that would sting the pudgy little man like a giant Sonoran ant, "My orders were to report to the department commander at Santa Fe when I had completed my mission. My mission has been completed, and I am on my way to the Rio Grande."

"So?" Lester steepled his fingers and rested his wrists on his chest. He leaned back in his chair and idly swung it back and forth. He seemed perfectly at home in his swivel chair. Travis wondered whether he'd be as much at home in a McClellan saddle, leading his hoped-for brigade. "You were driven here by Apache. The country between here and the Rio Grande is probably swarming with more of them."

"I can get through by traveling at night."

"Alone? I can't spare you a squad, sir!"

Travis waved a big hand. "A company couldn't get through perhaps, but one man, traveling as I do, has a good chance of doing so."

"What makes you think so?"

Travis smiled faintly. "I rode alone from Fort Yuma to Tucson, from there to the Sonoran border, then to Fort Joslyn."

Lester dropped his hands to his sides and let his chair swing him upward. He smashed a hand down on the desk with the obvious intention of startling Travis, but he had mistaken his man. Travis relit his cigar and eyed Lester through the bluish smoke. "You will remain here under my orders, sir!" snapped the major. His voice broke a little.

"And if I don't, sir?"

Lester extended a forefinger. "I will *prevent* you from leaving."

The little puffed-up toad had Travis by the short hairs, and he knew it.

Travis leaned back in his chair. There would come a day when Major Enos Lester, Quartermaster Corps, commanding Fort Joslyn, Department of New Mexico, would have to face his commanding officer and explain how he had countermanded his superior officer's orders. Until that time, Travis Walker would sweat out the days, weeks, and perhaps months under Enos Lester's command. It wasn't a pleasant prospect to look forward to, for Travis had learned plenty about Fort Joslyn and Enos Lester in the short experience he had had with both of them.

Lester smiled. "I'm sorry I have to be so abrupt," he said, "but I am in dire straits here, and I could use a man of your experience."

Travis nodded.

"I have sixty men and five officers here. The men are a mixture of infantry, quartermaster, dragoons, and cavalry. I have one gun section composed of dragoons to man my one mountain howitzer. Captain Charles Cass commands the infantry; First Lieutenant Clinton Vaughn is post quartermaster; First Lieutenant Kenneth Carlie commands the mounted men with Second Lieutenant Norval DeSantis as his second in command, also in charge of the howitzer section; Second Lieutenant Martin Newkirk is my adjutant."

"That makes seven officers for sixty men. Quite a large percentage, isn't it, sir, for a one-company post, while officers are needed to command units which may have to fight battles against the Confederate States Army?"

Lester flushed. "By Heaven, sir, you try me! I have this post to defend as well as protecting the people of Santa Theresa. My post of command is vital to the peace of New Mexico Territory, and don't you ever forget it, sir!"

Travis bowed his head. "I apologize, Major."

"Apology accepted!" snapped Lester. "You will act as my executive officer. The sergeant-major will make out the order. You will see Mr. Vaughn in regards to quarters and equipment. You will present yourself in uniform at the officer's mess for the midday meal to meet your fellow officers."

Travis stood up. "Yes, sir."

Then the little man went through one of his surprising changes. He stood up and extended his hand. "Glad to have you with us, Walker."

Travis gripped the soft damp hand. "Glad to be with you, sir."

Travis walked outside and looked at the cigar in his hand. He threw it on the ground and stamped on it, then walked toward the quartermaster warehouse to find Lieutenant Vaughn. The post looked sloppy, and the men down-at-the-heels. There was a general air of decay and low morale about Fort Joslyn. It was nothing specific, but Travis had learned in eight years to sense the inner feelings of men and frontier posts, and this God-forsaken collection of sagging adobes and cracking fieldstone buildings was the worst, by far, he had ever experienced. God help the United States Army in New Mexico if this was representative of their strength.

CHAPTER THREE

The quartermaster warehouse of Fort Joslyn was a long, sagging adobe. Seeds had caught root on the thick roof, and the building had a curiously shaggy effect from the wild growths there. Travis shook his head. A detail should have cleaned off that mess of a roof long ago, but the appearance of the warehouse was in keeping with the rest of the post.

"Looking for someone, Captain?" a low-throated feminine voice asked from behind Travis.

Travis turned. The woman was so close behind him he almost bumped into her. He stepped back. She was in her early twenties and well formed, almost too well formed. Her bold green eyes studied Travis from head to foot.

"I was just about to enter the warehouse," said Travis.

She smiled. "I thought I could help you."

Travis looked past the woman. Two troopers were polishing the little brass mountain howitzer and eying Travis and the woman with obvious delight.

"I'm Maggie Gillis," she said. "You're new here, ain't you?"

Travis nodded.

"You staying here awhile?"

"Until I can leave for the Rio Grande."

She tucked away a strand of her reddish-blonde hair. "You going alone to the Rio Grande?"

"I hope to."

"It's a lonely trip for a man."

"I prefer it that way, ma'am."

"*Ma'am?*" She raised her eyebrows in surprise, then laughed. "Thanks, soldier!"

"You're from the post?"

"God forbid! I came in with a wagon train from the west and have been stuck here ever since. What a hole!"

"I'll agree to that."

Travis felt a little uncomfortable. She was as bold as a jay and quite unconcerned about anyone watching her. "Sure is dead around here. Old Enos Lester tries to keep us, civilians, around our own camp, but it ain't easy with handsome officers walking about. A girl has to have *some* social life."

I'll bet you do, thought Travis. There was a strong aura of sweat and cheap perfume clinging about the young woman. He looked past her to see a tall, lean civilian watching them from the shade of a wagon. The man was paring his nails with a thin-bladed knife, but his eyes were more on Travis than they were on his fingernails.

Travis touched the brim of his hat. "Good morning to you, ma'am," he said.

She pouted. "Ain't I good enough for you to talk to?"

"If that's your husband watching us from over there, you'd better get about your business."

She glanced at the lean civilian. "Him? That's Ben Joad, and he *ain't* my husband."

Travis turned on a heel. "You'd better stay out of the sun," he said over his shoulder. "It does strange things to the mind."

She planted her hands on her full hips. "Damn you!" she said.

Travis grinned as he walked into the warehouse. His grin faded as he heard the two troopers guffaw.

An officer looked up from a littered desk. "Morning, sir," he said.

"You're Clinton Vaughn?"

"Yes." Vaughn stood up.

"Captain Travis Walker. Major Lester has ordered me to stay here on temporary duty. You are to issue me quarters and any equipment I may need." Travis gripped Vaughn's hand.

Vaughn's gray eyes studied Travis. "I have a feeling you won't like it here, Captain."

"That's neither here nor there, mister."

The quartermaster smiled. "No. What will you need in the way of equipment?"

"Nothing much. My horse was killed in my attempt to get to the post. I have my uniform. It needs mending and pressing, but it will do."

"One of the women will attend to that. Maggie Gillis is a good seamstress when she wants to be."

Travis shot a hard look at Vaughn. He had a feeling the man was laughing at him.

Vaughn filled his pipe. "I saw her talking to you outside, sir."

"So?"

"She's a bold one. She seems to take a perverse delight in badgering officers, particularly those she thinks are real men."

Vaughn lit his pipe. He eyed Travis through the smoke. "That was a helluva fight you put up getting here, sir. Corporal Cole told me about it. Major Lester doesn't think much of having patrols out; as a result, the Mimbrenos raid right up to within gunshot of the post. We're practically in a stage of siege here. In a way, it can't be helped. We're the only garrison between here and the Colorado, from what I've heard."

"You're right."

"You probably want to clean up. About quarters... Captain Cass is married and has his wife here; Ken Carlie has a small room in the officer's barracks, while DeSantis and Newkirk bunk together. I have a large double room with an extra cot in it. If it's all right with you, you can bunk with me. If not, I'll move in with Carlie and let you have the room by yourself."

Travis waved a hand. "I don't want to put you out, Vaughn."

Vaughn put on his forage cap and slanted it to one side. "There's one other alternative; Major Lester occupies one part of a double set of quarters. The quarters across the hall are not used." The gray eyes studied Travis.

Travis shook his head. "I'm used to bunking with someone else. I'd rather have it that way."

Vaughn nodded. "It's just as well. Major Lester has his furniture, spare clothing, books, and other gear in the quarters across from him. It's quite full, I assure you."

"I can imagine."

Vaughn looked about his crowded warehouse. Dust motes danced in the rays of sunlight that came through the little high windows. "Quite a store," he said.

"You seem well supplied."

Vaughn grinned. "Weevilly hardtack, wormy embalmed beef, bacon as hard as lignum vitae, ammunition issued right after the Mexican War. Jennifer and Grimsley saddles with cracked forks and rotting leather. Chicopee sabers pitted with rust. As far as I know, we're the only troops in the department still carrying muzzle loading Enfield carbines."

Travis raised his head. "You have no breechloaders?"

"A few. In fact, the Mimbrenos are armed mostly with good Sharps carbines, better equipment than we have."

"A nice situation."

Vaughn nodded. "Let's go to my quarters. Get cleaned

up and tell me what equipment you need, and I'll have it brought over later."

They left the warehouse. A buxom woman planted herself in front of Vaughn. "You did not send over a carpenter, Mr. Vaughn! My front door is sagging on its hinges, and my back door won't open."

Vaughn held up a hand. "Now, Mrs. Reilly! I told your husband he could have the use of all the tools he needed to do the job."

Mrs. Reilly thrust out her chin. "And poor Pat down with a misery in his back? Are we not as good people as the Army people?"

"I'm sure you are, Mrs. Reilly."

"Then you'll see to it a man comes at once?"

Vaughn shrugged. "All right."

Mrs. Reilly stamped off. Vaughn shook his head. *"Poor* Pat is as healthy as a hog. These civilians have been nothing but trouble since they been staying here."

"Quartermasters are a sorry lot, Clint."

Vaughn nodded. "Sore-tailed from sitting on a hard seat in a dusty warehouse, listening to the drilling of the weevils in the hardtack. Storekeeper, plumber, architect, clerk, wagon master, chaplain, and target for every inspecting officer. I wish I was a private in the rear rank of a fighting infantry company."

Ben Joad was leaning against a wagon watching them. Maggie Gillis sat on a keg beside the man, her bedraggled dress open as far down as frontier modesty would permit

"Who is Ben Joad?" asked Travis.

"Border scum. He claims he's a trapper and scout. Personally, I believe what I've heard about him. They say he was a scalp hunter and raider with Mexican bandits. Men walk quietly around Ben Joad. I never could stand a man who fought with a knife instead of a pistol. I suppose it doesn't really make any difference. After all, it's a means to an end."

"True enough," said Travis dryly.

Vaughn opened the door of his quarters and ushered Travis in ahead of him. The quarters were spacious, with a large beehive fireplace in one corner. Two bunks were neatly made up. Gear hung from pegs driven into the walls, and a shelf of books hung over a desk. An Apache lance hung over the fireplace. Travis touched it. "You've done much Indian fighting?" he asked.

"Enough to dislike it. I got that fighting near Cook's Peak. A rather curious thing. The blade is made from an old French saber. I often wondered where the buck got it from."

"How many of the other officers have had experience in fighting Indians?"

"Captain Cass has had some. Ken Carlie did some fighting against Lipan's and Comanches in Texas. DeSantis is as green as grass. Marty Newkirk just came out from the East before the war started."

"And the major?"

Vaughn knocked out his pipe and felt for his tobacco pouch.

"Well?"

"The major talks a lot about his forty years' service. He knows his regulations."

"You didn't answer my question."

Vaughn turned and looked Travis full in the face. "He claims he has fought Seminoles."

"But that was twenty-five years ago!"

"The captain is getting the idea."

"But he has seen quite a bit of frontier service, hasn't he?"

Vaughn lit his pipe. "As I said, Major Lester knows his regulations. His health hasn't been too good for some years. He was originally an infantryman, but most of his service has been in the Quartermaster Corps and in various staff and paperwork assignments. He wasn't allowed to accompany his regiment to Mexico with Scott's command. Ill health was given as the reason.

Captain Cass thinks differently. Cass says every time pressure is put on Lester; he becomes ill."

"A nice situation."

"Has he given you an assignment?"

"Executive officer."

"Thank God for that."

"Why do you say so?"

Vaughn walked to the window and looked out upon the sunlit parade ground. "You've had considerable service, Captain, from your looks and actions. You haven't been here long, but I can tell by your eyes and words how you feel about Fort Joslyn and the garrison here. We're sitting out here on the edge of Apache country, facing hundreds of Mimbrenos and Chiricahuas led by two of the greatest Apache chieftains, Mangas Colorado and Cochise. Cuchillo Rojo keeps us under constant pressure. He's a real bronco, a rim-rock Apache who gets the very breath of life from raiding and killing."

"Major Lester fears Cuchillo Rojo as though he were the very devil himself. I feel sorry for the old man, but it's his responsibilities which bother me more. If Cuchillo Rojo strikes in force, Major Lester will crack up. We have a leavening of Regulars, old veterans, mixed throughout this inadequate command. The rest of the men are green and frightened. As soldiers fighting alone against the Apache, we might have a chance if we were properly led, but we have the civilians here, as well as the responsibility of protecting the people of Santa Theresa."

Vaughn turned. "I'm sorry that you were not allowed to keep on to the Rio Grande, and I wish to God I would have been able to go with you on your journey there, but, as long as you've been ordered to stay here, I'm glad. For you see, Captain, we need a strong hand here if we are to survive."

"It's as bad as all that?"

"You *know* it is, sir."

Travis felt as though he was in a cage with invisible

bars, bars composed of the Apache threat and the peremptory orders of an inadequate and frightened old man who was making a poor pretense at commanding a frontier outpost

"Fort Perilous," said Travis quietly.

Vaughn nodded. "I'll have water brought in for your bath. The tub is in that alcove back there. I'll have your gear brought in, too. The major will expect you at noon mess."

When Vaughn had left, Travis stripped to the buff and swabbed down his sweating body with his filthy shirt. He found a bottle and filled a glass. He dropped on his cot and sipped the strong liquor. In a short time, he felt the power of the alcohol seeping through his tired body.

An orderly bustled in with Travis' gear and placed it on a chair. "Is there anything I can do for the captain?" he asked.

"I'll need some water."

"I'll bring it right away, sir."

"Can you have my uniform mended and pressed before noon mess?"

The orderly grinned. "That's one thing we do have here at Joslyn, sir, plenty of seamstresses and washerwomen."

"So I noticed," said Travis dryly.

The orderly eyed the liquor bottle. "Some of the women are right sociable too, sir."

Travis looked up at the trooper. "Get out of here!"

"Sorry, sir." The orderly flushed as he beat a hasty retreat.

———

RECALL SOUNDED across the post as Travis finished dressing. He buckled on his belt and slid his Colt into the holster. He slapped the dust from his cap and then settled it over one eye. Travis looked at himself in the flyspecked mirror on the wall. He had lost weight on his rough trip to New Mexico. There were hollows in his cheeks, and his nose looked bigger because of the hollows. Somehow his eyes looked harder than usual. Travis took a last drag at his cigar, then threw it into the fireplace. "Here goes," he said aloud.

All of the officers were in the mess, with the exception of Major Lester. Clinton Vaughn did the honors. Captain Charles Cass was a big, solidly fleshed man with a sort of ruddy handsomeness, but his eyes were too small to suit Travis. First Lieutenant Kenneth Carlie was a slim-hipped man with broad shoulders. The man's rakish good looks almost concealed the hardness that Travis instinctively felt as soon as he spoke to the officer. Second Lieutenant Martin Newkirk was a mild-looking man who wore spectacles and spoke with an assured polish. Travis placed him as a born gentleman. DeSantis nodded shortly to Travis and then applied himself to a whiskey bottle on the sideboard. His face was already a little flushed.

"Attention!" bawled out Captain Cass.

Enos Lester bustled into the mess. "Sit down, gentlemen. You've already met Captain Walker, I'm sure."

There was only small talk during the poor meal. The beef was tough and stringy, and the beans had been cooked too long. The coffee was strong enough to stand a spoon in. DeSantis toyed with his food, and twice during the meal, he filled his whiskey glass, ignoring the sharp looks of his commanding officer. Enos Lester, for all his talk of ill health, helped himself to three servings, gnawing away at the beef as though his very life depended on it.

When the table had been cleared, the orderly brought out a box of dry cigars and placed a liqueur bottle on the table. Travis looked curiously at the bottle. Lester waved his cigar. "We believe in the amenities here at Fort Joslyn, Captain Walker. No need to go on a Spartan regime merely because we are facing the enemy at our very doorsteps."

"I see," said Travis quietly.

Lester sucked at his cigar. "Now to business," he said. "Captain Walker will relieve Captain Cass as executive officer. Captain Cass will, of course, still remain in command of the infantry section. Mr. Vaughn will remain as quartermaster. Mr. Carlie will command the cavalry section as before, while Mr. DeSantis will act as his second in command, also in charge of the howitzer section. Mr. Newkirk will remain as adjutant."

Charles Cass raised his leonine head. "I would like to know Captain Walker's date of rank."

Travis looked quickly at the man. Their eyes met like thrust and riposte. "April twelfth, eighteen-sixty," said Travis quietly.

Cass flushed.

Enos Lester flicked the ashes from his cigar. "I know my regulations, Captain Cass, sir! I would not have placed Captain Walker as I did without knowing that he ranked you."

Cass nodded, then toyed with his glass. "I hope Captain Walker has plenty of experience in fighting Apache."

Clinton Vaughn smiled. "He proved that by coming up from the Hatchet Mountains right through Cuchillo Rojo's patrols."

The thin-stemmed liqueur glass snapped in Charles Cass's big hand. DeSantis giggled, and Cass shot him a look of hate. He slowly wiped the blood from his fingers, then filled the fresh glass brought to him by the orderly.

"I'll make a post inspection this afternoon to start off," said Travis.

Enos Lester worked his cigar back and forth in his loose mouth. "Fine! That's the spirit! Perhaps we had better talk about building breastworks between the buildings for defensive purposes."

DeSantis emptied his glass. "I thought the purpose of cavalry was to attack rather than to defend."

Lester stared at the young officer. "Get thoughts of glory out of your head, Mr. DeSantis. I have a great responsibility here, sir. This post might have to stand a siege."

Cass looked up. "Indians aren't much for siege work," he said.

Martin Newkirk folded his napkin and threaded it through his napkin ring. "We're practically under siege right now, Captain."

Lester stood up. "I have no fear of that. Our howitzer section will drive them off in fine shape. Drill those gunners of yours, Mr. DeSantis. Smartly! Smartly!"

The officers stood up. Major Lester relit his cigar. "Now, gentlemen, the affairs of a post commander take up a great deal of time. Come to me with any problems you have. Good afternoon, gentlemen." Lester bustled out.

"The damned old fool," a voice said from the end of the table.

Travis turned to look at Charles Cass. "You're in the presence of junior officers, Captain Cass," he said.

"They know what I mean."

"You'll keep your opinions to yourself."

Cass picked up his cap and placed it on his head. Without a word, he stalked from the mess.

"You've made a great friend there," said Clinton Vaughn.

"A great loss," said Ken Carlie.

Travis looked from one to the other of them. "I want all sections paraded in front of their barracks in one hour. Jump to it, gentlemen."

Later, as Travis walked to his quarters with Clinton Vaughn, he looked out toward the quiet desert. "How much pressure has Cuchillo Rojo put on this place, Clint?"

"Raids. Runs off a horse or mule now and then. Fires into the post at night. Watches the roads to see that we get no reinforcements for supplies. Major Lester sent out two couriers a week ago, twenty-four hours apart. We haven't seen them since."

"You have a civilian scout here?"

"Yes. A man named Baconora."

"From the Mexican town or from the mezcal?"

Clint grinned. "From the mezcal."

"Send him to me."

"Right."

They walked into their quarters. Vaughn filled two glasses. "You have nothing against an after-dinner drink?"

"After that slop, I need a good drink."

"Yes."

"Where do you get the cigars and liqueurs?"

"James Morris, the *alcalde* of Santa Theresa, sends them to us now and then."

"An Anglo is *alcalde* of Santa Theresa?"

Clint nodded. "He lived here before the American Occupation and stayed on. The Mexicans love and respect him. He has a great deal of influence in this part of the country."

"He should have abandoned Santa Theresa long before this time."

"You'll learn why he didn't when you meet him."

"I'd like to meet him."

"I'm going into Santa Theresa tomorrow to buy supplies. Perhaps you'd like to go along?"

"I will. As long as Major Lester feels responsible for the town, I'll have to see what they can do to help themselves, for it doesn't look to me as though this command can help them too much."

"Amen."

Clint dropped onto his bunk. "Charlie Cass certainly didn't like your taking over exec," he said.

"I'm worried."

"Lester has always been afraid of Charlie Cass. Cass thinks he's quite the soldier. I've heard it said he got his captaincy so quickly because of relatives in Washington. But you know how those stories spread around the latrines."

"What's your personal opinion?"

"I'd rather not say."

"As long as every officer on this post is so damned outspoken about everyone else, you might as well tell me."

"He fancies himself quite a stud. He used to spend a lot of time in the *cantinas* of Santa Theresa until Morris complained to Lester that Cass was bothering Morris' granddaughter Theresa."

"What did Mrs. Cass think about that?"

Clint raised his glass and studied the contents. "That's right," he said, "you haven't yet met Mrs. Cass."

"No."

Clint downed his drink and rolled over to face Travis. "Evelyn Cass is quite a woman. In fact, she's *all* woman, with most of the faults and few of the virtues, but she can still turn the eye of every man on this post except two."

"What two?"

Vaughn grinned. "Charlie, her dearly beloved, and Major Lester. Oh, she's quite the girl, is Ewie."

"Fort Joslyn is quite the place, from what you've been saying."

Vaughn refilled his glass, corked the bottle, and tossed it over to Travis. "Fort Joslyn is the rectum of the universe. The cesspool and catch all of the Department of New Mexico."

"You're the first officer who has been here in months to whom I've been able to talk without hating his guts."

Travis downed his drink and refilled his glass. He corked the bottle and placed it on the table. "You've had quite enough to drink, Clint. Perhaps in a few days, you'll classify me with the others."

Vaughn shook his head. "I had resigned myself to this sinkhole, waiting for Cuchillo Rojo to take it over with knife and fire. Now I've suddenly felt that I've received a reprieve." He got up and put on his cap. "I'll send Baconora over to you."

Travis shook his head as the quartermaster left. He emptied his glass, reached for the bottle, then slowly withdrew his hand. It would be too easy to try to find a way out of this stinking mess through the neck of a bottle.

In a few minutes, someone tapped on the door. "Come in!" Travis called out.

The door opened, and a man walked in silently. Travis sat up on his cot.

"Baconora," said the man.

"Travis Walker."

"My pleasure, Captain."

Baconora was a man of medium height and build, without a surplus ounce of flesh on his lean body. His eyes were reddish brown, and so was his lank hair. His nose had been smashed by a terrific blow sometime in his past. A heavy, tobacco-stained mustache hung down on each side of his thin-lipped mouth. He wore faded and dirty trail clothing, with elaborately carved but worn Mexican boots on his feet. A Navy Colt hung low at his left side for a sidearm draw. It was balanced on the right side by a heavy knife in a wide, fringed sheath.

"Sit down, Baconora," said Travis. "What's the rest of your name?"

"The name is Baconora, sir."

"I see. Drink?"

The scout glanced at the bottle. "Bourbon?"

"Rye."

Baconora shrugged. "It'll do."

"Look in my left saddlebag on the chair there."

The scout drew out Travis' bottle of mezcal. "This is more like it."

Baconora poured a drink and sat down on Vaughn's bunk. "What can I do for you?"

"How bad is this Apache situation?"

"About as bad as it can be."

"How many warriors does Cuchillo Rojo have?"

"*Quién sabe?* Some say a hundred; others say more. Right now, he's the big man among the Mimbreno under Mangas Colorado. Mangas is getting old. Cochise is no spring chicken. The Mimbreno and Chiricahua like young leaders like Cuchillo. The young men of both tribes will follow him to hell and back."

"I was afraid of that."

"You know the Apache?" asked the scout.

"Yes."

"You've fought against them?"

"Mohave-Apache, Tonto, White Mountain, Chiricahua, Mimbreno and Jicarilla."

Baconora grinned crookedly. "You haven't left many of them out."

"I wish I could have at times."

"Hawww! That's good. Hawww!"

The scout downed his drink and refilled his glass. He felt inside his shirt for pipe and tobacco, then filled the pipe. He lit it and leaned back against the wall. "What's on your mind?" he asked.

Travis sat on his chair and tilted it back against the wall. "I've been told two couriers vanished a week or so ago."

The reddish eyes held Travis' and then looked away. "Yeah. Damned fool thing to send them out."

"Why didn't you go?"

"I ain't loco."

"I see. Will you go?"

Baconora shrugged. "What good will it do? Old Lester won't get any reinforcements. From what I've learned, the rebels are planning a big buffalo hunt in West Texas."

"So?"

"It ain't no buffalo hunt. Old John R. Baylor is supposed to lead that hunt. He's a colonel in the Provisional Army of the Confederacy. Right now, Old John is sitting at Fort Bliss with three or four hundred Texas Mounted Rifles, and they ain't waiting there to hunt buffaloes. They're getting ready to sweep up the Valley of the Rio Grande like a dose of salts and kick the Federals right out of New Mexico."

"You seem to know a lot about the military situation, Baconora."

"I do. That's why it won't do any good for Old Man Lester to try and get reinforcements here from the Rio Grande. We're here, sink or swim, live or die, and all alone, Captain. You can bet your commission on that. Cuchillo Rojo knows that, too. He'll squat out in them hills, watching and waiting, stopping couriers and supply trains at his will. When the time comes, he'll take Fort Joslyn and Santa Theresa, too."

A cold feeling crept over Travis. The man was so sure of himself. "Maybe we can do something about that," Travis said quietly.

The scout puffed at his stinking pipe. "Maybe...maybe not. You want me to take a *pasear* into those hills tonight and see what Cuchillo is up to?"

"Can you make it?"

Baconora grinned, revealing even yellow teeth. "I ain't lived in 'Pache country for all these years without being able to get about."

"*Bueno!* Draw anything you need. Report back in three days."

Baconora stood up. He glanced at the bottle.

"Go ahead," said Travis.

"*Gracias.*" Baconora drank deeply and then wiped his

mouth with the back of a sleeve. "See you around, Captain."

Travis walked to the window and watched the lean scout walk across the parade ground. He passed the troops who were forming for the inspection and headed for the civilian camp at the south end of the post. Travis shrugged. The man must have more than his share of skill and guts to go up into those hills alone.

CHAPTER FOUR

R etreat was over, and the sun was low over the Hatchet Mountains. Travis Walker sat at his desk in headquarters, looking over the results of the afternoon's inspection. The sweat dripped from his face and spattered the inspection sheets. Finally, he pushed back the papers and looked at First Sergeant Mack Ellis. "It's a mess," said Travis.

Mack Ellis was a man about as wide as he was high, with hard blue eyes and a mahogany complexion. He had the unmistakable stamp of the old cavalry regular upon him. "The garrison needed new gear and weapons when the war started. Nothing came through from Fort Union. We've had to get by with what we have, sir."

"I appreciate that, Sergeant. But muzzle loading Enfield musketoons for the cavalry! Ye gods! What do they think we're fighting out here? Diggers and Paiutes?"

Mack Ellis shrugged. "Seems as though all the supplies are going to Fort Craig, sir, where the department commander is concentrating regulars, volunteers, and militia to stop the threatened rebel advance up the valley of the Rio Grande."

"Wouldn't it be just fine if the rebels swung west to

strike into Arizona and found just us at Fort Joslyn to stop them?"

"For this, we are soldiers, Captain."

Travis nodded. "By Act of Congress, out of necessity."

Ellis grinned. "Forgotten by our sires and mistreated by our mothers."

"How are the horses?"

"Not too good. We had fine mounts up until a month or so ago. Then we lost all of them and had to get second-rate remounts."

"How were they lost?"

"Epidemic glanders, sir. We lost forty-five mounts. Had to shoot most of them. Had to destroy the old stables."

"I see. Just another bead in the necklace of unfortunate circumstances."

"The captain has a fine way of putting orders."

Travis smashed a hand down on the desk. "Those blasted musketoons are too muzzle-heavy. I want you to have your ordnance artificer remove the butt plates and drill a hole in the buttstock large enough to take about eight ounces of lead. That should awake the deference."

There was a look of admiration in Ellis' eyes. "I should have thought of that, Captain."

Travis stood up. "Have him work on two or three at a time. We can't take chances on men being unarmed."

"I'll see to it right away, sir."

Travis wiped the sweat from his face. Major Lester was taking his siesta, which Travis had been told took place between Retreat and evening mess. The old man, despite his fears, made sure nothing disturbed the routine of forty years' service.

"I want target practice tomorrow morning, Sergeant," said Travis over his shoulder, "each man to fire twenty rounds with the weapon he is armed with. The infantry will fire the first relays, which should allow enough time for the ordnance artificer to have the musketoons weighted and ready for the mounted troops to fire in the afternoon. Do you have butts set up?"

"There is a low ridge to the west of the fort which will serve the purpose."

"Good! Officers, not noncommissioned officers, will be in charge of the firing of their respective units. When each unit is through firing, they will prepare enough cartridges to replace those they have expended. Quartermaster Vaughn tells me there is enough cartridge paper, bar lead, and powder for the purpose. It might be best if the troops expended their older cartridges in order that they have fresh rounds in case of an attack."

"Yes, sir."

"Jump to it then."

It was dusk when Travis left headquarters and stood outside beneath the ramada to get a breath of fresh air. The mingled odors of cooking beef and beans hung over the post in the windless air. Travis walked toward his quarters and was even with a low adobe fronted by a ramada when he suddenly became aware of a woman standing beneath the ramada.

Travis turned to look at her. She came to the front of the ramada and placed a hand against one of the posts. "Captain Walker?" she asked in a low voice.

"Yes."

"I am Evelyn Cass. I haven't had the pleasure of meeting you."

Travis eyed her. She was fairly tall and very well formed. Her dark hair was parted in the middle and drawn back into a large cluster at the nape of her shapely neck. A fine Mexican comb had been thrust through the cluster. Her skin had not been exposed to the blazing suns of New Mexico, and even in the dimness, Travis could see that it was milky white. Her eyes were exceptionally large and set wide apart. Her mouth drew Travis' attention. It was wide and full lipped, with a sensuous quality about it.

Travis took off his forage cap and bowed. "A pleasure to make your acquaintance, Mrs. Cass."

She came forward. "I stay in the quarters to avoid the heat of the day," she said. "I love the starlit nights of New Mexico."

The faint odor of jasmine came to Travis. She wore a clinging gown which revealed her full breasts and hips. "Charles has spoken of you," she said.

"I am honored."

There was a subtle look in her dark eyes. "You are the first new officer we have had here in quite some time. One gets tired of the same faces and worn-out conversations. You must honor us by having dinner with us."

"I'd appreciate it, Mrs. Cass."

She looked him up and down. "You've had some interesting adventures getting here," she said.

"More dangerous than interesting, I'm afraid."

She pressed her body back against one of the ramada posts and hooked her hands together behind it. It had the effect of extending her full breasts toward Travis. "Do you expect to go on to the Rio Grande?"

He smiled ruefully. "I had intended to, but Major Lester stopped that."

"I hope we all may leave soon. I had hopes Charles would be assigned to the staff at Santa Fe. It's so gay there."

"It might not be if the rebels advance up the Valley."

She shrugged. "Anything would be better than being penned here at Fort Joslyn. *Fort* Joslyn...it isn't anything but a run-down outpost."

Boots thudded against the hard caliche of the parade ground, and the tall figure of Charles Cass appeared. He stopped short as he saw them. Evelyn Cass smiled. "I have been passing the time of day with Captain Walker, Charles," she said.

"So I see."

"You didn't find time to introduce me, so I introduced myself."

Cass nodded. He looked at Travis. "What's this about target practice tomorrow?"

"The orders will be posted this evening."

"It's a waste of time."

"When was the last time you had practice?"

Cass waved a big hand. "Some months ago. If the Apache hear us firing, they'll get excited. You might have an attack on the men firing."

"Then they'll get some real practice, won't they, Captain?"

Cass flushed. "We haven't too many cartridges."

"There are plenty of materials to make more."

"The major might not think so."

"Then he can stop the practice."

Cass drew in his broad chin and bent his head forward. His big hands half closed, then opened again. He looked almost as though he meant to rush Travis.

"Dinner is on the table, Charles," said Evelyn Cass quickly.

Charles nodded. But he kept his eyes on Travis.

Travis bowed to Evelyn. "Good evening, Mrs. Cass," he said. He walked a few feet and then turned to look at Cass. "I'm riding into Santa Theresa in the morning," he said. "You'll take over in my place until I return."

"I've got plenty work of my own to do, Captain Walker."

Travis smiled thinly. "I've already given my orders; all you have to do is make sure they're carried out." He walked away.

"Damn him!" grated Charles Cass.

Evelyn Cass laughed. "Just look at you! He certainly slipped the bit into your mouth, Charles."

He gripped her by the arm and pushed her ahead of him into the dark interior of their quarters. "You're hurting me," she said.

He shoved her back against the wall and slapped her face so that her head snapped back against the plastered adobe. "Don't ever laugh at me like that again!" he snarled.

She touched her bruised mouth and looked at him with hate in her big eyes. "You never could stand to be laughed at."

"In any case, *you* won't laugh at me."

Her right hand dropped to her side and gripped a bottle that stood on the table beside her. "And you won't strike me again," she said coldly.

He stood there and stared at her, then turned on a heel and walked away. "I'll put Travis Walker in his place. You'll see."

She released the bottle, and a cynical smile curved her bleeding lips. She had been looking for a long time to find a way to get rid of Charles Cass and leave Fort Joslyn. She knew now, if she played her cards right, she might make it. She also knew she had the right cards to play. She stroked her full body with her slim hands.

———

TRAVIS WALKER LAY on his cot, stripped to his drawers, feeling the cool fingers of the night breeze touch his hot body. Evelyn Cass was quite a woman, especially to a man penned up on a two-bit post like Fort Joslyn. Travis had been thinking of her ever since he had talked with her. Clint Vaughn had said she was quite a woman, with most of the faults and few of the virtues of her sex. He had also said she could still turn the eye of every man except two on the post, Charles Cass and Enos Lester. Clint had been exactly correct when he had made his statement.

Travis stood up and walked to the window that looked out on the parade ground. Faint moonlight gave the parade ground a silvery hue. The reflection of flames from a big fire down at the civilian camp danced on the walls of the farrier shop. The civilians had been making a lot of noise ever since the evening meal. Now and then, the shrill laughter of a woman broke out over the low voices of the men.

Bottles were being passed around. It had been in Clint's mind to ask Major Lester to stop the civilians from drinking too much, but, as Clint had told Travis, the major had refused to do so. The result was a nightly drinking party, and more than once in the past week, there had been several bloody fights among the men and some skirmishing among the women.

The major had given orders that the soldiers were not to mingle with the civilians during these affairs, but it wasn't easy to stop them. Several times the guard had turned troopers and women out of the hay piles behind the long stables.

Clint Vaughn came across the parade ground. He stopped to look at the big fire, then shrugged and came on toward the quarters. Be came into the dark room.

"Some racket down there," said Travis over his shoulder.

Clint scaled his hat at a peg and then stripped off his gun belt and shirt. "The major seems to think it keeps up the morale."

"It doesn't help the morale of the garrison."

Clint dropped onto his bunk. "No."

"Who is officer of the guard tonight?"

"DeSantis."

"Well, he'd better have them quiet down before Taps, or he'll answer to me."

Clint lay back on his bunk. "Drink?"

"No."

"I agree. It just seems *to* make you heat up more."

Travis sat down and tilted the chair back against the wall to feel the cross draft of air against his body. "You were told about firing practice tomorrow?"

"Yes. Corporal Covello will issue cartridge paper, lead,

and powder for fresh cartridges. Sergeant Hoeffie will have bullet molds ready."

"What time do we leave tomorrow?"

"Early. The major didn't object?"

"No. He was eager to have me go."

"It'll be a big change for me, not that Santa Theresa has much to offer in the way of amusement other than strong liquor and loose women."

"That should add up to something."

"Wait until you taste the liquor and see the women."

"I met Evelyn Cass this evening."

"So?"

"You analyzed her quite well."

Clint laughed. "I've been looking at her with more than the eyes of friendship for some time."

"Cass wasn't too happy about the firing tomorrow."

"He might have to stay out in the sun for a while. He's putting on weight, and he suffers from the heat quite a bit."

"He'll suffer a hell of a lot more from the heat in hell if we don't have target practice."

Clint nodded. "Charlie is lazy. He'll do anything to get out of exerting himself, with a few exceptions."

"Such as?"

"Lifting a schooner of beer and having a tumble in bed with any woman he can get to lie with him."

"With the wife he has?"

Clint raised himself on an elbow. "In my opinion, they hate each other's guts. I'll bet they have some good go-arounds when they're alone, and I don't mean it the way you're thinking right now."

Travis pulled on his trousers and then his boots.

"Where are you going?" asked Clint.

"Out for some air."

"Stay within the post quadrangle."

Travis shrugged into his shirt and buckled his gun belt about his slim waist. "I know better than to go beyond the post at night. How close in do the Mimbreno come?"

Clint held his hands about two inches apart. "You'll hear them talking to each other out there."

Travis picked up his cap and put it on his head. He drew his Colt and twirled the cylinder to see that each nipple was capped. "See you," he said.

There were only two lights showing on the post, a lamp in the guardhouse and the bright fire of the civilians. Travis walked to the gate and stood beside the sentry. "How is it tonight?" asked Travis.

The sentry shrugged. "You can hear the Mimbrenos out there once in a while. If it wasn't for all that noise at the fire, we'd be able to hear the Apache better, sir."

"Step back behind the buttress of the building, soldier. You're silhouetted against that fire."

The sentry nodded and moved behind the buttress. Travis turned. If anyone walked between the fire and the darkness of the desert, he'd be a fair shot for an Apache marksman.

"Listen," said the sentry.

A night bird had called not fifty yards beyond the gate. A moment later, another bird answered the first a hundred yards to the west.

"It's them," said the sentry.

Suddenly a coyote's shrieking laugh split the momentary quiet, then died away. The wind shifted a little and carried the melancholy howling of another coyote from a low ridge west of the fort.

"Fair gives a man the shivers, sir," said the sentry.

Travis nodded. He never had quite got used to the cry of a coyote as imitated by an Indian, while, on the contrary, he had always sensed a melancholy sort of enjoyment from the true cry of the scavenging animals.

A woman laughed near the fire. A bottle smashed. Travis cut swiftly across the gap of the gate to the next building and walked down the west side of the quadrangle. Fifty feet from the fire, he walked between two buildings and stood in the dimness of a building ell to look west. Then he saw what he was looking for. The firelight had glistened for a fraction of a second on something moist out there—something like a bright amber bead.

Travis drew in his breath. The Mimbreno was no more than fifty yards from the closest building.

Travis walked back to the quadrangle toward the fire. A trooper stood up and scuttled for cover. Two men and three women sat by the fire. One of them was Ben Joad. Travis scooped up a bucketful of foul-smelling water from a fire barrel placed at one corner of the quartermaster warehouse. He walked quickly to the fire and cast the water over it.

"What the hell!" roared Joad as he leaped to his feet. His trousers had been soaked. Steam rose from the fire.

Maggie Gillis giggled. "It's the good-lookin' officer who just came in."

"I'll fix his good looks!" snarled Joad. He whipped his hand back for his knife. The other man staggered drunkenly in between Joad and Travis. Travis drew his Colt and slapped the heavy octagonal barrel against the drunk's head, driving him down to his knees. The woman beside Maggie Gillis screamed.

"Corporal of the guard! Post Number Four!" yelled a sentry.

Joad kicked the drunk flat, then came at Travis with his knife lying flat in his right hand, at waist level. Travis jumped back and stumbled over a bottle. The knife tip slashed through his left sleeve, and he winced as the metal sliced into his forearm.

"I'll teach yuh, brass bounder!" yelled Joad.

The woman who had screamed snatched up the bucket Travis had dropped and swung it in a wild arc toward Travis' head, but Maggie Gillis was too quick. She stepped forward and fended the bucket off with her left forearm. Then she drove in a hard right jab that connected neatly with the enraged woman's jaw and sprawled her backward over the prostrate drunk with a wild show of dirty petticoats.

Joad closed in as he heard the tramping of feet as the guard approached the south end of the fort. He thrust in at Travis with the knife. Travis leaped sideways, switching the Colt from his right hand to his left. He gripped Joad's right wrist and pulled him off balance at the same time. Travis struck swiftly at the base of the civilian's neck with the barrel of the six-shooter. Joad fell down into the hot ashes of the fire and lay still. Travis gripped Joad by his ankles and dragged him from the ashes. He hooked a boot under the man and rolled him over.

The guard stopped behind Travis. "Jesus, lookit," said a trooper. He pointed at Joad's ash-smeared face. Joad's short beard was smoldering, and the embers beneath the bed of ashes had seared the left side of his face.

Travis holstered his Colt. As he did so, he heard the sound of a shot west of the post. The slug struck a trooper with the sound of a stick being whipped into thick mud. The trooper folded over, dropping his musketoon with a clatter. "Scatter!" roared Travis.

They scattered behind buildings and wagons. There was silence for a few moments; then, suddenly, a demoniac cry came from the darkness west of the post. It was diabolical, more like an animal's cry than a man's. The bloodcurdling cry came again, then died away. Then, faintly, the sound of hoofbeats came from the sandy ridges to the west.

Travis knelt by the shot trooper and rolled him over. Sightless eyes stared up at him. Travis wiped the blood from his hands and stood up. "Corporal," he called out. "Throw Joad and those other two into the guardhouse. Have the medical orderly dress Joad's face and examine the other two." He looked for Maggie Gillis. She was leaning against a wagon, holding her left forearm. Travis walked to her. "Are you hurt?" he asked quietly.

She laughed. "Just a bruise. How's your arm?"

He took his bandanna from his neck and bound it about the slash. "I'll be all right. You've got quite a wallop in that right hand, Miss Gillis."

"Maggie!"

"All right...Maggie then. That bucket might have cracked my skull."

She shrugged. "I like a fair fight," she said. She looked up at him. "You've marked Ben Joad for life, Captain. He won't never forget it. You look out for him."

"Thanks. I will."

She brushed back a strand of her straggling hair. "You sure got a direct way about you."

He smiled. "It works."

"It'll keep on working if you live long enough to talk about it."

The guard carried the trooper off. Travis watched them. "A good man died tonight because of the foolishness here."

"What will you do with Ben and the others?"

"Ben can sit in the guardhouse a day or two. When the others are sober, they will be freed. What is Ben to you, Maggie?"

She straightened up and thrust out her chin. "Not a damned thing, and don't you forget it!"

He shrugged as she walked away into the darkness.

Maggie walked to her quarters. A trooper sidled up out of the darkness. "How about messing around tonight, Mag?" he asked.

"Get out of here, Scully."

He gripped her by the arm and whirled her about. Maggie timed it perfectly. Her open right hand smacked loudly against his face. "I told you to get out of here!" she cried.

Scully watched her walk into her quarters. He felt his

stinging face. "Now I wonder what's got into her?" he asked aloud.

Travis walked over to the guardhouse. "Where's Mr. DeSantis?" he asked a trooper.

The trooper pointed to DeSantis' quarters. "He's been in there for some time."

Travis crossed the parade ground *to* DeSantis' quarters. He opened the door and walked in. He could see two men asleep on their cots in the dimness. One of them sat up. "Who is it?" he asked.

"Walker, Newkirk!"

Travis gripped DeSantis by the shoulder and shook him. DeSantis sat up. "What the hell is this?" he asked.

"You're officer of the guard. What are you doing in bed?"

DeSantis slid his legs out from beneath the covers. "I told the sergeant of the guard to awaken me at midnight for my rounds."

"Get into your uniform and double-time down to the guardhouse. Didn't you hear the noise out there?"

The young officer shook his head.

Travis stepped back and hooked his thumbs over his gun belt. "The mesquite is thick with Apache. Ben Joad and his cronies had a hell of a fire going, and they were making enough noise to awaken the dead. Joad came after me with a knife. One of the members of the guard was killed by a sharpshooting buck. You were supposed to be alert, mister. Now get out there and keep up your rounds all night. Every hour on the hour! I want no fires and no noise!"

DeSantis dressed hurriedly. Newkirk lit a lamp. His serious face studied Travis. "I've been expecting something like this," he said quietly. "You should have stayed at the guardhouse as I suggested, Norval."

"Shut up, you pen pusher!"

Newkirk flushed. DeSantis buckled his gun belt and

hooked his saber to it. He jammed his hat onto his head and stamped from the room.

Martin Newkirk shook his head. "We've been sloppy here, Captain Walker. Too sloppy. I'm glad you're here to tighten up this post."

"I can't say that I am."

The young lieutenant stood up. "I've been afraid of what might happen here, sir. But with you as executive officer, I'm sure we are at least strengthened against our many enemies."

"I didn't have much choice in the matter, Newkirk. My orders were superseded by those of Major Lester's. My duty is here now, and I'm going to see to it that it is done to the best of my ability."

"I'm sure it will be. You said, sir, that Major Lester's orders superseded yours. May I ask how?"

"Simply enough. I was ordered to report to the commanding officer of the department when I had completed my mission in Arizona. I arrived here to learn that, since then, other orders had been issued, holding me here."

"Specifically, sir?"

Travis looked quickly at the serious-faced young soldier. "What do you mean, mister?"

"Did the orders *name* you?"

"No. It was a so-called blanket order."

Newkirk nodded. "I thought so."

"What are you driving at, mister?"

"I assume your orders were important to the defense of the Southwest by the United States Army. I cannot fathom why Major Lester would force you to remain here knowing how important your mission was."

"I saw and read the order stating that all officers and men, who had no definite assignment and were separated from their commands, would report to the nearest camp, post or station of the United States Army for such duty as would be prescribed by the commanding officer of any such camp, post or station until orders were received from the department commander ordering them elsewhere." Travis smiled. "And so on and so on."

Newkirk nodded. "I know the usual verbiage. Major Lester, if you'll pardon me for saying so, is a very frightened old man who has developed imaginary ills to cover up his fright. He needs you, but you are really more valuable elsewhere."

Travis shrugged. "I'm here now, and here I'll stay because if I don't, I'll be put under arrest by Major Lester. Good night, Mr. Newkirk." Travis left the quarters.

Martin Newkirk walked to the window and watched Travis stride off. "Odd," he said quietly. "Very odd indeed."

CHAPTER FIVE

Clinton Vaughn drew in his horse and felt inside his shell jacket for his cigar case. He looked at Travis Walker. "Let's give the horses a breather."

Travis slanted his hat low over his eyes and looked at the salmon-colored hills. The mesquite and sage stippled them like cloves in a ham. There wasn't a breath of air moving across the baking desert. Far across the dune sands, a wind devil rose to towering height and swept toward the hills in a wild, whirling dance.

Clint passed a cigar to Travis. "The town is beyond those hills."

Travis lit up. "I wonder why those people didn't leave? Some parts of Arizona are practically deserted. Once thriving communities are now ghost towns."

"You haven't yet met James Morris, the *alcalde*."

"He must be quite a man to keep these people here."

Clint lit his cigar and blew out a puff of bluish smoke. "James Morris is practically a legend around this part of the country. Mexicans and Anglos look up to him as though he was the prophet, Moses."

"Wandering in the wilderness."

Clint nodded. "It's too late for them to leave now. There are no United States troops between here and the

Colorado to protect them if they move that way. North there are nothing but mountains and deserted towns. South into Mexico is a wilderness of burned ranches and deserted *Placitas*. The Apache are hammering on the gates of Durango. Between here and the Rio Grande there is nothing but painted death for travelers."

Travis nodded. Suddenly he took the cigar from his mouth.

"There seems to be a little painted death near here right now."

A puff of smoke had shot up from a hill not more than two miles away from them. It was quickly followed by two more.

Clinton Vaughn swallowed. "We'd better get on into Santa Theresa," he said quickly. "I feel as though I suddenly need a drink, two, in fact."

They rode swiftly on toward Santa Theresa. There was a place where low sand ridges closed in on the rutted road, and they kept their eyes on the brushy slopes, riding with carbines loaded and cocked across their thighs.

Smoke drifted up ahead of them. Travis drew in his sorrel a little, but Clint waved him on. "The town," he said.

Santa Theresa seemed to sleep in the sun on a wide stretch of sand. Trees showed the course of a stream. Wisps of smoke rose from chimneys. On a hill behind the town, the mine workings could be seen, but there seemed to be no activity about the workings. The town itself was typical of that part of the country. The adobes and jacals formed a square about a dusty littered plaza. Pigs, chickens, dogs, and cats scattered from in front of the two cantering horses as Travis and Clint reached the edge of the plaza. The adobes were well and solidly built, but some of them were badly in need of plastering. Vegetation had sprouted on some of the sagging roofs. Doors and windows were tightly closed, and there was a brooding air about the little town.

Across the plaza, Travis saw a two-storied *torre*, or defensive tower, obviously built generations ago as protection against marauding Apache. There were great cracks in the round tower. Other than the little church, the only building in the whole assembly that looked as though it had been taken care of was a low rambling structure situated on a low knoll at the west side of the plaza. The doors had been freshly painted in pale blue, while the shutters were faint pink. Ollas hung from the ramada beams, and bright flowers cascaded from the ollas.

"That's the *alcalde's* house," said Clint pointing to the low building with his cigar. "Old man Morris keeps it looking nice. The rest of the people here just don't give a damn since the Apache threat. They just sit around and brood, waiting for something to happen, and, by God, if they don't get out of here one way or another, something disastrous *will* happen."

They swung down from their horses in front of a yellow-painted *cantina*. Great scabrous flakes of plaster and paint littered the ground along the walls. The door sagged on its great leather hinges.

"The house of Jonas Simpson," said Clint. "The place stinks, but not as bad as some of the Mex *cantinas*. Come on; I'll buy you a drink."

They walked into the dim interior. Half a dozen men sat at tables, drinking and playing monte. "Here comes the soldier boys," said a man with an English accent.

"'Bout time they did somethin' about them 'Paches," said a little man who was half concealed under a battered Mexican steeple hat encrusted with coin-silver filigree work. Despite the heat of the day, he wore a gay but filthy-looking serape over his narrow shoulders.

"Shut up, Vince!" roared a man from behind the bar.

Flies buzzed up from the liquor slopped on the zinc-topped bar as Clint and Travis stopped in front of it. A huge man stood behind the bar, mopping it with a filthy rag. His bald head glistened with droplets of sweat. A bright blue eye surveyed Travis from the right socket; the left eye was long gone, leaving a puckered, evil-looking hole.

"Mr. Jonas Simpson," Clinton Vaughn said to Travis with an air, as though he was introducing royalty. "Captain Travis Walker, new executive officer at Fort Joslyn."

Simpson extended a thick arm from which depended a massive paw of a hand. He gripped Travis' hand. "Pleased, I'm sure," he rumbled. "What's your pleasure, gents? On the house."

"*Aguardiente*," said Travis.

"The same, mine host," said Clint.

Vince called out, "That include us, Jonas?"

"You ain't paid me for the last three drinks you had, Vince," Jonas said sourly.

Vince cackled. "What the hell difference does it make? The 'Paches will soon take over, Jonas."

Jonas picked up an empty bottle and hurled it across the room. It smashed just over Vince's head, splattering him with glass. "Get out, you buzzard!" yelled Jonas.

Vince grinned. He threw down his cards, brushed the glass from serape and hat brim, and stood up, sweeping the hat from his head, and bowing low, then sauntering to the door. "I'll take my business elsewhere," he said over his shoulder.

"Good riddance," said Jonas. He placed a bottle and two glasses before the two officers.

"How does it go?" asked Clint.

"Rotten," said the *cantina* keeper. "Oh, there's enough drinking, more than usual if the truth be known, but most of it is jawbone. No work around here. No pay. So it goes. I carry these chiselers on jawbone, and I ain't so sure old Cuchillo Rojo won't wipe out them tabs when he makes up his mind to take the town—and the fort, too, if the truth be known."

"Now, Jonas," chided Clint as he filled the glasses.

"Well, it's plain as the nose on your face, Mr. Vaughn."

"Maybe so."

"You know it is!"

Clint grinned. He looked at Travis. "Jonas is the fount of all gossip in Santa Theresa. The oracle of this part of New Mexico. An old soldier, scarred by honorable wounds."

Jonas placed a hand across his gaping eye socket. "Lost it at Chapultepec under Old Rough and Ready, General Zachary Taylor, God rest his soul."

Travis looked quickly at Jonas and then at Clint. Clint kicked Travis' right ankle. The quartermaster downed his drink and refilled his glass. "How is the old man?" he asked.

Jonas shook his head. "Somehow, he just doesn't seem to understand how bad it really is. Says he's weathered many an Apache scare hereabouts."

"We didn't see any guards about the town."

"Yeh, 'cause they're all sitting in *cantinas* swilling rotgut. Cuchillo could go through here like a dose of salts if he had a mind to."

"The *torre* was supposed to be repaired."

Jonas laughed without humor. "That damned old wreck? We'd be better off if we tore it down and built a new one, but there ain't anyone around here who'll sweat out in that sun to do it."

"So, what is Morris doing?"

Jonas shrugged. "Sitting in his chair with his cane of office across his lap, listening to the poor, sick, and needy like he always does. Now and then, he calls a meeting of the head men of the town and talks about cleaning out the well, painting the 'dobes, keeping the animals off the plaza grass."

"What grass?"

Jonas tilted his head to one side. "He still thinks we have grass." He took a drink himself. "Sometimes I can talk some of the boys into standing guard at evening and at dawn when there ain't no sun. The rest of the time, they sit around and drink. *Jesusita!*"

Travis emptied his glass and waved Jonas' hand back as he started to refill the glass. "We're going to see the *alcalde*," he said.

Jonas filled the glass. "Then you'll need this, Captain."

Clint nodded. They finished their drinks and walked outside. "Come back after you're done!" roared Jonas.

"Quite a character," said Travis. "Wounded at Chapultepec with Old Rough and Ready, eh? Quite a feat that. Considering Zach Taylor was never there."

Clint grinned. "Lost his eye in a barroom brawl in Mesilla, but he likes to talk about being at Chapultepec. We all have our little lies, Travis."

"Yes. He doesn't seem too happy about the conditions here. Are they as bad as he says?"

"Probably worse. I'm afraid James Morris lives pretty much in the past."

They led their mounts over to the *alcalde's* house. "Nice place," observed Travis.

Clint tethered his horse to the rail. "The old man has been here for a long time. He's a fixture here. Made his money in trading. Used to take *vagonetas* of trading goods down into Chihuahua and sometimes beyond. He's a man who had position and wealth back in the States but forsook all of it to come out here when he was a young man. He's almost more of a Mexican than he is an Anglo. He has two loves left in his life."

"Two—at *his* age?"

"I meant his granddaughter Theresa and the town here. She was named after the patron saint of the town. She is the issue of the old man's only son Theodore and a Mexican woman who was probably part Indian. When you see Theresa, you'll know what I mean."

A shout echoed throughout the plaza. They turned to see two men tumble out of an open doorway and roll over and over in the dust, biting, kicking, and clawing at each other. Half a dozen men came out to watch the brawl. A slatternly woman whose brown breasts hung half over the top of a ragged gown came out to join them. "Gut him, Frank!" she screamed.

Doors opened, and people came out to watch fee cursing, sweating combatants. One of the men got to his feet. The other man started to get up, but a boot connected against his jaw, the cruel Mexican spur roweling his bearded face. The droplets of bright blood splattered the caliche beneath him. Once again, the tall man booted his vanquished opponent.

The woman ran to the tall man and drew a knife from her bosom. She thrust it toward the man. "Go on!" she screamed. "Gut him. The pig called me a *puta*!"

The tell man shoved her back, wiped a bloody nose, and staggered into the *cantina*, followed by the other men, who slapped him on the back. The woman hurled the knife at the door.

"Nice town," said Travis dryly. "Reminds me of last night at the post."

"There really isn't any law here. Morris does what he can. Now and then, he calls for soldiers from Joslyn, but lately, Major Lester has refused him."

Travis walked up onto the warped wooden porch. Between Fort Joslyn and Santa Theresa, he would have his hands more than full. The lonely feeling swept over him again. The whole country was girding for war, North and South getting ready for a bloody fracas, while he was standing on the edge of a gulf in western New Mexico—a gulf of hate, peopled by the tigers of the human species, the Apache. There was no one to pull him back from that gulf nor anyone to catch him if he fell.

Clinton Vaughn hammered on the great bolt-studded door of the *casa*. "This is probably the only house in Santa

Theresa that could stand any kind of a siege," he said over his shoulder.

Travis nodded. The walls were thick. He could see that by the deepness of the door embrasure. The roof supports that extended from the upper front wall just beneath the thatched ramada were of great size, and they had been carved by some crude sculptor. The shade of the ramada was a relief after the blazing heat of the morning sun. The shutters were thick and in good condition, and Travis figured that they and the doors must have sheet iron sandwiched in between layers of thick wood to hold back arrows and bullets. James Morris had built well.

The door opened a crack. "*Quién es?*" a woman called shrilly.

"It is Lieutenant Vaughn from Fort Joslyn with Captain Travis Walker."

"*Si! Si!* The smiling lieutenant!"

The great door creaked open, and a flood of cool air poured about the two sweating officers. A dumpy Mexican woman ushered them in. "You're getting prettier every day, Angelique," said Clint. "Be careful. I'm looking for a woman to clean up my quarters and make me happy."

Angelique tittered. She flapped her apron up and down. "I cannot leave the *alcalde*," she said.

Clint shrugged sorrowfully. "I thought as much. Well, he is a fine-looking man with many *pesos*. I do not have a chance with the pretty *senoritas* with him around."

Travis shook his head. Angelique closed and bolted the huge door, then led the way up a tiled corridor. The walls were hung with Indian and Mexican blankets.

Angelique opened a massive door at the end of the corridor and ushered Travis and Clint in. They entered a large, low-ceilinged room. The windows were sealed by shutters, and the room was lit by sweet-smelling candles held in large silver candelabra. The candlelight reflected from the whitewashed walls of the room and from the polished wood of the heavy furniture. A small candle in a red glass guttered before a carved wooden *Santo* placed in a deep wall-niche.

A tall man sat in a great carved chair. His lower limbs were swathed in a thick Navajo blanket. His strong gnarled hands clasped a silver-knobbed ebony cane that lay across his thighs. His face was long and strong, with a well-trimmed mustache and short white beard. A shock of thick white hair was carefully brushed. It was his eyes that held Travis' attention. They were light blue, steady, and thoughtful, and they seemed to reveal the deep inner peace of the old man.

"*Buenos dias, señor alcalde,*" said Clint.

"*Buenos Dias, Teniente Vaughn,*" answered the old man. "*Como ha estado?*"

The *alcalde* waved a hand. "*Regular; lo mismo.*"

"*Tengo el gusto de presentarle al Capitán Travis Walker.*"

The old man extended a hand. "*Gusto en conocerle, Capitán Walker.*"

Travis gripped the proffered hand and was surprised at the powerful grip of the old man. "My pleasure, sir," he said.

"Do you speak Spanish, Captain?"

Travis smiled. "*Mas o meno, señor alcalde.*"

"If you prefer, sir, we will speak in English."

"I would prefer it, sir. My Spanish is of the cow-pen variety."

The old man smiled gently. "I speak it almost as much as I do English. It is a beautiful language that sometimes lends itself to nuances that are not quite the same in English. You must understand I have spent many years with my adopted people here in the Southwest."

"I understand, sir."

"My house is yours, *señor Capitan.* Do sit down."

Travis and Clint drew up chairs before the old man. James Morris reached to the table and tinkled a small bell. Angelique appeared almost instantly. "We will have wine, Angelique," said James Morris.

"Yes, *señor mayor*."

James Morris smiled at Travis. "You are new here in our country, are you not?"

"I have just arrived. I will serve at Fort Joslyn for a time."

"That is good. You must come and have dinner with me. You are from the States?"

"No. From Fort Yuma on the Colorado."

"I see. How are conditions there?"

"Fort Yuma is strongly held by a good garrison. I wish I could say the same about the rest of the Southwest."

"These are hard times. Brother against brother and father against son."

Clinton Vaughn leaned forward. "The captain has come with me to talk about the protection of Santa Theresa."

"We will take care of ourselves. We have strong men here, well-armed, who do not fear the Apache."

Travis leaned back in his chair. The old man was living in a fool's paradise, from what Travis had seen both at Fort Joslyn and Santa Theresa.

"The mines are not being worked," said Clint, "nor is there any trading going on."

James Morris smiled. "We have lived through bad times and good. In the language of my adopted people, *'No hay mal que por no bien venga!'*"

Travis looked at Clint. Clint shrugged and held out his hands, palms upward. Travis shot an angry glance at Clint. His action was rude beyond belief. The old man had said that there is no evil which may not be turned into good. But James Morris seemed to be unaffected by Clint's rude gesture.

Clint felt for a cigar. He took one out and handed it to Travis. Then he leaned forward and handed one to James Morris. The old man placed it in his mouth, drew out a lucifer, and lit the cigar. "I do not often get the cigars," he said with satisfaction. "Theresa seems to think they affect my health."

Travis and Clint lit up. Travis eyed the old man. There was something odd about James Morris, but he could not put his finger on it.

Angelique bustled in and placed a bottle and three glasses upon the table. James Morris reached for the bottle and took out the cork. He filled the three glasses. "Help yourselves, gentlemen," he said.

Travis took his glass and sipped the wine. It seemed to have the sun and wind in it, the smell of the sage, and the warmth of the Southwestern sun, in a subtle sort of a way. He put his glass on the table. "Mr. Morris," he said, "Major Lester has appointed me his executive officer, and because of that, I have come here to Santa Theresa to investigate conditions. I find here an undefended town with people drinking during the day and morale at a very low ebb. The hills are thick with Apache, just waiting for a chance to strike against your *placita*.

"The garrison at Fort Joslyn is small, but part of our responsibility is the safety of Santa Theresa."

James Morris raised a hand as though in protest. *"Las aparencias enganan."*

Travis felt a surge of anger within him. "I *know* appearances are deceptive, but the fact remains that you are here in a practically undefended town. You have NO reliable defenses, *señor mayor*."

"We have the *torreon*. It has done us good services in past years."

"This is a brutal question, Mayor Morris, but have you seen your *torreon* lately?"

James Morris swung out his ebony cane and thudded its tip against the tiled floor. "I have no need to do so! My people know their responsibilities as laid down by their mayor! Some weeks ago, I ordered them to reinforce that tower; I feel sure they have done so."

Travis ignored a quick gesture by Clinton Vaughn. "The fact is this, *señor mayor*, the *torre* has *not* been repaired. There *are* no guards watching those hills. The garrison at Fort Joslyn is hardly able to take care of itself."

Clint shot an angry glance at Travis. Travis waved a hand at him. "I would like an estimate of the situation from you, *señor mayor*."

James Morris's big hands clenched and then relaxed. "Who *is* this man, Lieutenant Vaughn?"

Clinton Vaughn emptied his glass. "The man who is probably capable of saving all of us, *señor mayor*."

"I am not accustomed to be bearded in such a manner, Lieutenant Vaughn."

Clint shrugged. "The very esteemed Captain Walker may be speaking the truth, *señor mayor*."

The *alcalde* gripped his cane. "This man you have brought here is a *Yaqui*!"

Clinton Vaughn shrugged in an elaborate gesture. "Yes, *mi mayor*, but he speaks the truth."

The door swung open, and a young woman entered the room. She closed the door behind her. Travis turned to look fully at her, and his breath caught in his throat. She was little more than twenty years of age, but her figure was that of a perfectly developed woman. "Are you all right, Grandfather?" she asked in a soft voice that was slightly accented.

Travis could not take his eyes from her. She seemed to be an amalgamation of the better qualities of Anglo, Mexican and Indian; her face had a cameo-like beauty which would catch and hold any man's attention, be the hot-blooded young buck or almost senile oldster. She was a woman in the very essence of the word, with all the good and bad that is woman itself in her expression. She walked to her grandfather and slid a smooth arm about his wrinkled neck. Travis was fascinated by her, and it took a hidden kick from Clinton

Vaughn for Travis to remember his manners. He stood up.

"This is my granddaughter, Captain Walker," said James Morris with quiet pride.

Theresa Morris extended a slim hand to Travis. The touch of her cool flesh did strange things to him. She smiled at Clinton. "How are you today, Clinton Vaughn?"

"Just fine, Theresa. You are more lovely than ever."

She flushed a little as he tilted his head to one side and studied her. She walked back to her grandfather and stood beside his great chair, one slim hand on his shoulder.

James Morris placed a gnarled hand atop hers, hiding it from view. "Captain Walker seems to think we of Santa Theresa cannot defend ourselves, Granddaughter."

She smiled a little. "These are hard times, Grandfather. There has never been anything like this before. If the captain offers his help, I am sure he knows we need it. We should be grateful."

The *alcalde* opened his mouth, but she interrupted him swiftly. "Remember, Grandfather, that the country is at war. There are few troops available to help us. Cuchillo Rojo rides the hills with many warriors. The people here are frightened. They cannot leave now. We stay here and fight for our homes. Only fools would turn away offers of help."

Clint turned his head to hide a grin. He winked at Travis. James Morris cleared his throat. "Well, perhaps I was too hasty, Captain Walker. I am a man who has always taken care of myself and my people. Please do what you can to help us. Tell me what measures you require for the defense of the town, and I will see that they are carried through."

"Thank you, Mayor Morris."

"It is we who should thank you, Captain Walker," said Theresa quietly.

Travis looked at her in a different light now. There

was strength in the young woman, a far greater strength than he had realized. The candlelight seemed to bring out the soft tones of her flesh and accentuate the darkness of her hair. It served, too, to give Travis the vague impression that he was looking at a full-length oil painting by one of the masters.

Travis picked up his hat. "If you'll excuse me, sir, and you, Miss Morris, I'd like to inspect the town with Mr. Vaughn."

The mayor nodded. "A man of quick action. That is good. There are too many young men these days who are not men of action, as I once was."

"You still are, Grandfather," said Theresa Morris. She pulled the serape higher on his legs. "I'll escort these gentlemen to the door."

Travis opened the door, and Clint Vaughn stood aside to let her pass. She was taller than Travis had realized. A faint, almost indistinguishable odor of perfume came to him. Travis glanced at the old man as he closed the door. James Morris sat in his great chair, bolt upright, his strong hands clasping his ebony and silver cane. He was looking straight at Travis. Travis nodded, but the old man did not move. It was almost as though he were a figure without life. It gave Travis an eerie feeling.

Theresa Morris smiled up at Travis. "He is old," she said, "and sometimes set in his ways. But he loves the people of Santa Theresa and the town itself. It is not easy for him to realize that his life's work may be wiped out in one Apache attack."

"It won't be!" said Clint heartily.

Travis glanced at the quartermaster. Clint was whistling in the dark. Theresa stopped at the front door. She placed a hand on Clint's arm. "You don't have to worry about me, Clint. I know what might happen."

"You should have left here long ago," said Travis angrily.

She shook her dark head. "My grandfather would not

leave, nor will I as long as he remains. We have only the two of us. Each gives strength to the other in many ways."

Clint opened the great door. The outer light struck against Theresa's face, and again Travis realized how beautiful she was. In candlelight or sunlight, her beauty was the same. Travis and Clint walked out beneath the ramada. "If there is anything you want done, Captain Walker," she said, "you have only to tell me, and I'll see that it is done."

Clint grinned. "You are now the *alcalde*, Theresa?"

"No. But there are many things I can do to help him. Good morning, gentlemen."

They both bowed. The door clicked shut behind them. Travis was silent as he walked out into the brilliant sunlight. They walked toward the sagging *torreon*. Clint lit a cigar. "Say," he said, offhand, "you never did tell me if you were married."

"I'm not."

Clint nodded. "I can usually tell."

"What's bothering you, Clint?"

The quartermaster looked back at the house. "Nothing. I'm just the second son of a second son, Travis."

"So?"

"I can foresee things."

"You better foresee the Apache attack."

Travis stopped in front of the *torreon*. He looked back at the rambling house they had just left. He had a feeling he had left part of himself back there, something he would never fully possess again as long as he lived.

Travis bent his head to walk into the *torreon*. He stood in the center of the littered floor and looked at the sunlight streaming through the great cracks. A rack of rusty *escopetas* stood to one side. Spiders had made their homes about the old weapons. A rickety ladder rose to enter a trap door in the second floor. Travis tested it with his feet. The bottom rung snapped off. "Jesus," said

Travis. "Can't the old man see the condition this town is in for defense?"

"No."

"Is he that bullheaded or just plain stupid?"

"No. Didn't you notice anything about him?"

"He's a cripple."

"In more ways than one. He's also stone blind, Travis."

Travis turned to look at the quartermaster. "What?"

"I meant to tell you."

Travis shook his head. "A fort commanded by a bumbling old fool, a town falling apart, a crippled and blind *alcalde*. What next, I wonder?"

"Cuchillo Rojo," said Clint quietly.

They looked at each other. "Well," Travis said dryly, "I always wanted to be a soldier."

Clint nodded. "Me, too."

"Then we'd better play the part, *amigo*."

"Yes. What do we do now?"

"Get some of these lazy *paisanos* to get to work on this ramshackle *torreon*. Find out how they're fixed for weapons and ammunition. Get a squad or two to help garrison the place."

"The *torreon* can be patched up, and if they need weapons, we can draw them from my stores. As far as letting Major Lester allow troops to be garrisoned here—well, I think you'll have a hell of a time convincing him of that."

"If I had my way, I'd move these people to the fort or else move the garrison here."

Clint shrugged. "Sure. Sure. But you don't have your way at all. It's going to take a lot of convincing talk to allow me to issue weapons to these people."

They walked out into the sunlight. A drunk lay atop a pile of straw in the hot shade of the *torreon*. From a nearby *cantina* came the soft strumming of a guitar. Two men sat in the shade of a crude thatched shelter industriously playing monte. A peon walked across the plaza carrying a fighting cock under his left arm. The town looked as though there was only peace in New Mexico.

A scarf of signal smoke drifted up from a hill far behind the town, staining the clear blue sky. A deadly warning of danger for anyone to see, but Santa Theresa slept in the hot sun and dreamed of nothing but peace.

Travis placed a hand on Clint's shoulder. "Go about your business," he said. "I'll look around. How long will it take you?"

"No more than half an hour."

"Get moving then."

Clint Vaughn strode off toward the south end of town. Travis walked about, eying the houses. Some of them could be put into shape for defense. He looked at the rambling adobe of lames Morris. There were several outbuildings in good repair behind it. Perhaps the towns-people could use the house as a citadel while others defended the *torreon*. There was a good field of crossfire possible between them if one old sagging adobe was leveled. The great house likely had a large cistern in it.

Travis walked along the row of *cantinas*. Bold women eyed him as he passed. Some of them flirted their well-padded hips at him. He could hear men laughing and talking in the *cantinas*.

Clint came to meet Travis. "Do you have a note-book?" asked Travis.

"Yes."

"*Bueno!* Now write these instructions down for the mayor—I want the *torreon* reinforced and repaired as much as possible; the ladders are to be replaced; every cistern in town must be filled to the brim; I want that old adobe between the *torreon* and the mayor's house leveled so that there is no defilade between both buildings; every man in town is to clean and furbish his weapons.

"I'll try to get some troops here. Their Commanding officer will be responsible for seeing that toe weapons are ready in case they are needed. He will also inspect tile cisterns to see that they are full and will make sure that adobe is torn down."

Clint wrote rapidly and then looked up. "Anything else?"

"No. Wait—you might add that if these conditions are not met within the next few days, I will ask Major Lester to declare martial law."

"These people won't like that."

"To hell with that! We're trying to save their lives!"

Clint nodded. "What do I do with this memorandum?"

"Send it to the mayor."

Clint got a small boy to deliver the message. The two officers mounted their horses and rode from the town, followed by the cynical eyes of the gamblers beneath the brush shelter. One of them laughed aloud. It was the little man, Vince.

CHAPTER SIX

There was no sound of musketry as Travis and Clint approached Fort Joslyn. As they entered the fort quadrangle, they saw a line of troopers, under the charge of Sergeant Ellis, practicing with their heavy Chicopee sabers. Thrusts and parries, right and left moulinets, were being done by the sweating cavalrymen. "Sergeant Ellis!" called out Travis.

The big noncom approached Travis, then saluted him with his saber. "Yes, *sir?*"

"Surely you haven't finished target practice?"

"We didn't even start, sir. Captain Cass instructed us to practice with the saber."

"A hell of a lot of good that will do us," muttered Clint Vaughn.

Travis looked up at the brilliant sun. It would have been hot enough on the target range, but this was sheer idiocy—men swinging those heavy blades in blasting summer heat. "Give them a ten-minute rest," said Travis. "I'll have further orders for you in a few minutes."

"Yes, sir!"

Travis swung down from his horse. An orderly led it off. Clint rode to his quartermaster warehouse and looked back at Travis. He shrugged as he dismounted.

Travis entered headquarters. Major Lester was seated at his desk, poring over a sheaf of papers. He looked up and returned Travis' salute. "Well?" he asked.

Travis leaned forward. "My instructions for the garrison were for them to have target practice this morning, sir."

Lester nodded. "I know. I countermanded them on the suggestion of Captain Cass."

"May I ask why, sir?"

"We cannot afford to waste ammunition, Captain."

"We'll be wasting a great deal of ammunition in an Apache attack if the men do not get practice."

Lester smiled thinly. "Our troopers can ride them down with the *arme blanche* and the pistol. The saber and handgun are all a good trooper needs to attack with."

"Perhaps. But what of the infantry, sir?"

"They have other duties at present."

Futile anger swept over Travis. The man before him lived in a little world of his own with boundaries he had set up for himself, playing at being a field soldier, afraid of the responsibility of command, yet determined that he be recognized as the final authority on all matters.

Enos Lester did not seem to notice Travis' anger. "What did you learn in Santa Theresa?" he asked.

"The town is practically unprotected. The people seem to be torn between their fear of the Apache and their love of comfort. The *cantinas* are doing a rushing business. It seems to me that the people have turned to amusement to throw a temporary shield between them and inevitable disaster."

Enos Lester smiled. "Come, come, Captain Walker, it can't be as bad as that. A soldier must be an optimist, not a dismal pessimist."

"I have promised to send some troops into the town. I have left orders for the cisterns to be filled. The old *torreon* is to be repaired. Weapons are to be cleaned and readied for a possible attack."

"The town is not under martial law, sir! We have no right to interfere in civil government."

"There doesn't seem to be much civil government there. James Morris is a cripple and blind to boot. He knows little of the condition of the town's defenses."

"He is a capable man, well beloved by all." Lester steepled his pudgy fingers on his chest. "You said you promised troops? By whose authority, sir?"

"I assumed you would send them, sir."

Lester sat bolt upright. "You *assumed*? By what *right* do you assume? *I* am in command here, sir!"

God help us all, thought Travis.

There was an angry flush on Lester's face. Any time his authority was questioned, he seemed to lose his reason.

"Sir," said Travis patiently, "if Santa Theresa is attacked, the blame will be placed upon you. It is part of the major's district of command. Mayor Morris is well known and respected throughout New Mexico. If anything happens to him and his town, the finger of guilt will point at one man—Major Enos Lester."

Lester sagged a little in his chair. Travis' opening shot had struck home.

Travis continued. "There are two alternatives, other than sending a detail to Santa Theresa, sir—the first is to evacuate the townspeople and bring them here under your protection; the second is to move the garrison to Santa Theresa, abandoning Fort Joslyn!"

Lester waved a hand. "Both of them are impossible. I have no authority to command the evacuation of Santa Theresa. Then again, we have no room for those people here. Our water supply is not sufficient. I cannot abandon this post."

"Then we must send troops to help the people of Santa Theresa."

Lester fiddled with his pen. He yawned and looked

out of the window. He scratched his throat. "How many men?"

"At least two squads under the command of an officer."

Lester cracked his knuckles.

"Well, Major?"

The major looked up. "Very well. Send Captain Cass in command of the detail."

"Rather a high rank to command two squads."

"It requires more ability than just the command of two squads. It requires enough rank to make those people listen and obey. I'm sure that Captain Cass will have the qualities to deal with them."

"Very well, sir."

"Is there anything else?"

"I would like to send some couriers to the closest fort on the Rio Grande."

"That would be Fort Craig. That is about one hundred and fifty miles from here."

"We can pick the men, sir. I'd suggest sending three of them by different routes."

"Even if they *do* get through, they will accomplish nothing. No troops will be dispatched to us."

"That was not my thought, sir. I think the major should request authority to abandon this post and to evacuate Santa Theresa. If we get that authority, we can travel in column to the Rio Grande."

"Too dangerous, sir!"

"Is it possibly any more dangerous than staying *here*?"

Enos Lester wet his purplish lips. Then he eyed Travis. "Very well, Captain. Pick your men and send them out. God help them."

"There is nothing else we can do, Major."

"Get to it then."

Travis left headquarters. Major Lester walked to the window. "They'll never make it, Captain Walker," he said quietly. He laughed, a crafty look in his pale eyes.

THE THREE TROOPERS stood by their horses, listening to Travis' final instructions. It was dusk, and lamplight gleamed in the windows of the buildings. "I asked you men to volunteer," said Travis, "because I wanted the men who went to know what they were up against. It is a dangerous mission."

"No more dangerous than it is here, sir," said Ames Corby, a lanky Vermonter.

"Perhaps," said Travis.

"I'm sick of sitting around here waiting for Cuchillo to swoop down on us," said John Nolan, a quiet Pennsylvanian.

"I'm with you, John," said the third courier, Benson Duryea, a squat trooper from Kentucky.

"You three will ride together until you reach the vicinity of Red Mountain," said Travis. "Then you separate. Corby will trend north toward Cooks Peak, then skirt the mountains and continue north to about the vicinity of Fort Craig, thence east to Fort Craig."

"Nolan will ride toward Good Sight Peak, skirt it to the east, thence past Sunday Cone, thence up the west bank of the Rio Grande to Fort Craig."

"Duryea, you will head east to Massacre Peak, thence toward Sierra de las Uvas, skirting them to the north, thence crossing the Rio Grande to follow the Jorado del Muerte north to the vicinity of the Lava Flow. You'll have to ford the Rio Grande at Valverde, north of the fort and return south down the west bank of the Rio."

"The long way around for Benson," said Corby, with a wide grin.

"Hole up during the day," said Travis. "Travel from dusk until just before dawn. Don't wear out your mounts. You'll have to travel slowly to conserve them. You've been told of the water holes and have sketch maps. You have your extra canteens and pistols?"

The men nodded.

"Good!" Travis shook each of them by the hand. "Remember—the lives of many people and your fellow soldiers may depend upon you. I'll promise two stripes to each of you if you're successful."

"Or a wooden cross and a pat in the face with a shovel," said Nolan quietly.

"On your way," said Travis.

He walked to the gate with them and watched as they led their mounts quietly into the wash that traversed the desert in a northeasterly direction. They had muffled their horse's hoofs with soft leather boots. In a few minutes, there was no sight nor sound of them.

"We'll never see those three again," a sentry said.

"Shut up," said a corporal.

Far out across the desert to the west, a coyote gave voice. The howl died away, echoing faintly in the hills.

Charles Cass had formed his detail near the gate. They were to travel in two wagons, and Travis had ordered that they travel at night to avoid detection by the Apache. It wasn't likely that the keen-eared Mimbreno would miss hearing the passage of the wagons, but it was a chance that had to be taken.

Cass looked at Travis. "I'll leave now," he said.

Travis nodded. "Report to James Morris. You'll have to be quartered in the town. Perhaps the mayor will take you in."

Cass wet his lips. "I'll see to that."

"You have your instructions. If you want to say goodbye to your wife, go ahead and do it."

Cass laughed. "Her? She doesn't give a damn *where* I go."

"Move out then."

The wagons had been prepared for the trip. Axles dripped with grease, and rags had been wound between the wheels and the axles to deaden sound. Harness chains, too, had been wrapped to prevent their jingling.

Leather boots had been wrapped about the horse's hoofs.

The two wagons rolled softly out onto the road and vanished from sight. Travis stood there for a time, listening to the soughing of the night wind through the brush, half expecting to hear a burst of gunfire, but it did not come. So far, so good.

Travis made his rounds. He had ordered that all outward-facing windows be shuttered. No lights were to be shown an hour after dusk. Here and there, lights blinked out as he walked about the quiet post. He checked the sentries, then walked to the high-walled corral. Two sentries stood at the corral gate. They had orders that one of them must patrol the outer walls of the corral every hour. The civilians were quiet enough. Travis' treatment of Ben Joad and his two drunken companions had had a sobering effect on them.

It was after nine o'clock when Travis finished his thorough inspection. He walked to his quarters, glancing at the quartermaster warehouse. Clint was hard at work on his accounts and would be for some hours. Travis opened the door, then closed it behind him. He slid the bar across. He had experienced Apache sneak raids before. At one post, two officers had been found dead in their beds with slashed throats because they had been foolish enough to leave their outer doors open for the night breeze.

Travis unbuckled his gun belt and hung it over a chair. He stripped off his shirt and undershirt and threw them in a corner. He wiped his upper body with a towel then reached for a bottle. Something scraped in the rear of the big room. He snatched his Colt free from its holster and cocked it as a figure took shape in the darkness. His finger drew up the trigger slack, and then he noticed the strong odor of jasmine.

"I've been waiting for you, Travis," said Evelyn Cass. She came closer. The muzzle of the big Colt touched her soft belly. Cold sweat broke out on Travis. He lowered the Colt and let down the hammer. "For God's sake!" he said huskily. "That was a foolish thing to do!"

"I'm sorry I startled you, Travis," she said softly.

"What do you want?"

She smiled in the dimness. "I wanted to ask you about Santa Theresa. It's been some time since I've been there."

Travis shrugged. "It's just the same, I imagine."

"At least there is some life there."

"You're safer here."

"Why Charles will defend the town, won't he?" There was veiled sarcasm in her voice.

Travis threw his Colt onto his cot and reached for a fresh shirt. He drew it over his head and buttoned it. "You'd better get out of here," he said quietly.

She tilted her head to one side. "Why? Do I make you nervous?"

"No. But you know post rules. If anyone should find you in here, there would be some nasty talk resulting from it."

"I'm worried. Clint won't be here for hours. Major Lester is already in bed. The other officers are playing poker in the mess."

"You made sure of everything before you came here, then?"

She laughed. "I hadn't thought of a rendezvous, Travis."

He stuffed his shirttails into his trousers. "Leave by the back door," he said.

"I'd like a drink."

"No."

She reached for the bottle and tilted it to her full lips. She drank deeply then placed the bottle on the table. "Do I shock you, Captain Walker?"

"Get out of here."

"Your virtue is safe enough."

"Damn you!"

She swayed a little, and then Travis realized she had been doing considerable drinking. She gripped his left arm and tried to pull him close to her. Then, suddenly, she threw her arms about his neck and drew him close, searching for his lips with hers. She found them and crushed him to her. Her full body pressed hard against his, and he knew damned well she had nothing on beneath her thin summer gown. Her mouth tasted of liquor as she forced it against his, bruising his lips.

Travis pulled her arms from around his neck and pushed her back. "Go!" he said.

She staggered a little as she reached for the bottle. He took it away from her then walked to the back door. He threw it open. For a moment, she stared at him, and then she smoothed down her dark hair. "All right," she said thickly. She brushed heavily against him as she walked outside. Then she turned and looked at him. "Sir Galahad," she said sarcastically. She softly laughed as she walked unsteadily toward her own quarters.

Travis closed and barred the door. He whistled softly. She was a bundle of woman, all right. He picked up the bottle and drank deeply. It seemed to him as though he could taste her mouth from the rim of the bottle.

A woman came from the sanitary sinks at the far end of the quarter's row. She watched Evelyn Cass stagger a little as she walked up on the rear porch of her quarters. The woman smiled thinly, then hurried toward the civilian quarters. It was the woman who had been mixed up in the drunken brawl when Travis had disarmed and beaten Ben Joad.

———

EVELYN CASS WALKED into her stifling bedroom and picked up a cutglass decanter. She drank from it, then hurled it into the beehive fireplace. The decanter smashed, filling the room with the pungent odor of strong brandy. She stripped herself and threw herself on the damp bed. She passed her hands over her full body. "Damn him," she said drunkenly.

———

TRAVIS PULLED off his shirt and boots and sat by the window for a breath of fresh night air. Now and then, he sipped at the bottle. It had been quite some time since he had been with a woman, and she hadn't been in a class with Evelyn.

He almost wished he had sent some other officer to Santa Theresa, but in a way, he was glad to get rid of Charlie Cass. He wondered if Evelyn would find another officer on the post willing to tumble with her.

Travis was still sitting there when Clint Vaughn came to the quarters. Clint pulled off his damp shirt and undershirt and reached for the bottle. "I feel like I've been in a Turkish bath," he said.

Travis nodded.

"What's bothering you?"

"Nothing."

Clint eyed Travis. Then he raised his head. "Damned if I don't think I smell jasmine," he said.

"You're loco."

"The hell I am!"

"Take a drink and forget it."

Clint took another drink. He stood up and walked to the washstand at the rear of the room. He lit a candle and poured water into a basin. Then he saw something lying on the stand, and he picked it up. It was a filmy handkerchief. He raised it to his nostrils and inhaled. Then he looked over his shoulder at Travis. "I'll be damned!" he said.

"What's wrong now?" asked Travis.

Clint stuffed the handkerchief into a drawer. "Bugs in the water," he said quickly.

Travis grinned. "Just taking a cooling swim, Clint?"

"Yeah. Yeah."

Clint washed himself and opened the rear door to pitch out the water. "The musketoons have been weighted as you ordered," he said.

"At least that's one thing I accomplished."

Clint closed the door and glanced at the drawer into which he had stuffed the perfumed handkerchief. "Yeah," he said softly.

Later, as they lay on their cots, Clint raised himself on an elbow and looked at Travis. "I've heard Charlie Cass was more than willing to go to Santa Theresa."

"He seemed happy enough about it."

Clint lay back on his cot. "Charlie will have a time for himself. He likes his liquor and his women. I told you that before. I remember you wondered about that with the woman he has already."

"So?"

"Nothing."

Travis looked through the darkness toward Clint. Then he rested his head on his hot pillow and closed his eyes. He listened to the night sounds, the soft whispering of the wind about the quarters; the bawling of a mule from the corral; the fluttering of the flag halyards against the warped pole; the tread of a sentry making his rounds. He tried to think of lovely Theresa Morris, but the oval face of Evelyn Cass seemed always to get in between Travis and the face of Theresa.

CHAPTER SEVEN

The roar of a rifle snapped Travis Walker into wakefulness. He sat up, pulled on trousers and shirt, then yanked on his boots. Clint was alert, dressing swiftly. "Came from near the corral!" he said.

They buckled on their gun belts and rushed out onto the dim parade ground. It was almost dawn. A trooper darted between two buildings, raised his musketoon, and fired into the darkness. The thud of hoofs came back on the wind, and a derisive yell floated back with the sounds of the hoofs.

Travis cocked his Colt and headed for the corral.

"Corporal of the Guard! Post Number Six!" roared a sentry.

Travis saw something lying on the ground at one side of the corral. It was a trooper. His chest had a curiously flattened look. The corral gate was sagging on one hinge, and the bitter smell of dust was mingled with the acrid odor of burn gunpowder. The guard came up on the double. "What is it, Cassidy?" yelled the corporal.

Cassidy grounded his musketoon. "Me and Fletcher was in front of the corral gate. Fletch hears a noise. He goes to open the gate when all of a sudden, the damned gate crashes open. A horse comes racing out with an

Apache on his back. Poor Fletch gets run down. I snapped a shot at the red devil, but he was in the clear, he was."

"What shall we do, sir?" asked the corporal.

"Stay where you are!"

Travis walked into the corral. The horses and mules milled about, whinnying and braying. Dust was thick in the air. Travis looked at the gate. The thick leather hinges had been slit by a knife until they were hanging by a mere half-inch of leather. That last half inch had been ripped through.

Travis edged past the excited animals until he reached the rear wall. A rawhide rope hung down from the top of the wall. Clint Vaughn came up behind Travis. "What happened, do you think?"

Travis eased down his pistol hammer and holstered the Colt. "Simple enough. A buck came over the wall, slashed the gate hinges until they were hanging by a thread, then picked out the best mount he could find and crashed it through the gate."

"But why one horse?"

Travis turned. "To show us what they can do if they want to. Psychology, Clint. Damned diabolical psychology."

"'Twas Cuchillo Rojo on the horse," said Cassidy.

"You're sure?" asked Clint.

"Certainly, sir! I know his face, the dirty, murderin' bastard!"

Travis walked to the gate of the corral. "You made your rounds, Cassidy?"

"Yes, sir!"

Clint shook his head. "I don't see how he did it," he said.

"He waited until the sentry went past, then threw over his rope. Perfect timing."

"Shall we turn out the post?"

"They'll all be awake now. There's nothing more we can do."

Clint looked down at the dead trooper. "Poor bastard," he said. "He probably never knew what happened."

"It's just the beginning," said Travis quietly. "From now on, he'll whittle at us until he's ready to strike for keeps."

———

TENSION SEEMED to settle about Fort Joslyn that day. The sentries stared at the surrounding hills until their eyes ached. Each wind devil that arose on the flats was eyed narrowly, as though the dust were rising from the hoofs of Apache mounts. But there was no sign of the Mimbrenos. No smoke stained the clear sky. Cuchillo Rojo had done his work well. He had the garrison on edge now, and he would keep it that way.

At noon mess Norval DeSantis seemed restless. He toyed with his food. "What's bothering you, De?" asked Ken Carlie.

"Those damned Apache! I'd like to take a patrol up into the hills and run Cuchillo to earth."

Carlie laughed. "You wouldn't see one of them until they opened fire and cut you to pieces."

"I'm not afraid to go."

"No one said you were."

DeSantis looked down the table. "I'd like to ask the major's permission to patrol the hills west of here," he said.

"Absolutely not!" snapped Lester as he helped himself to more stew.

DeSantis emptied his coffee cup. "Are we to sit here like roosting chickens and get knocked off our perches without a fight?"

"You may get all the fight you want without leaving here," said Travis dryly.

There was a sneer on DeSantis' face. "United States Army soldiers sitting here behind walls, letting a pack of half-naked savages put the fear of God into us. Two troopers shot down without a fight, and we still sit here!"

"That is enough, Mr. DeSantis," Lester said, with his mouth full. His jaws worked steadily on his food.

"It sickens me," said DeSantis.

Travis looked up. "Run your gun crew through drill this afternoon. That'll take some of the disgust out of you," he said coldly.

DeSantis opened his mouth, then closed it as he looked into Travis' hard eyes. He looked at Enos Lester, who was forking more food into his mouth. Then he stood up. "I'd like to be excused, Major," he said.

Lester waved his fork. "Granted," he said thickly.

DeSantis left the mess. Martin Newkirk filled his cup. "The young eagle wants to try his wings."

"He'll get them clipped quickly enough," said Clint Vaughn.

"The boy is hot-blooded," said the major as he ladled jam onto a piece of bread. "I was that way myself once. One good bloodletting, and he'll cool off."

Travis looked at the major. He wondered if Enos Lester had ever seen a good bloodletting. Travis was willing to bet the old man would crack completely and let Travis take command if an attack occurred, but until he cracked, he'd probably raise hell with the morale of the already shaky garrison.

A trooper came to the door. "Captain Travis," he said, "Baconora is back."

"I'll see him in my quarters."

Lester jerked his head. "He'll report here," he said. "We'd all like to hear what he has to say."

Travis nodded to the trooper. "Tell him to come in here."

Baconora padded into the room, bringing with him a strong aura of stale sweat and rank tobacco. He touched his hat brim with his right hand.

Major Lester turned in his seat. "Well?" he asked.

Baconora squatted on his heels and wiped his ragged mustache both ways. "Cuchillo had a big palaver in the hills night before last. Mimbrenos mostly, with some Chiricahuas, but all top warriors."

"Chiricahuas?" asked Lester. "It isn't likely they'd be over here. You were probably mistaken, sir."

Baconora's reddish eyes surveyed the major. "I said they *was* Chiricahuas there."

"Bosh! How could you tell? They all look alike."

Baconora spat into a spittoon. The metal rang softly with the impact of the tobacco juice. "Not to anyone what knows them, they don't."

Lester sniffed. He filled his coffee cup and slopped a little of the coffee down his chin as he drank.

"Go on, Baconora," urged Travis.

"Well, it seems as though Cuchillo is talking big about having Fort Joslyn and Santa Theresa under his greasy thumb. Looks like he's rallying as many warriors as he can."

"They'll sit out there in the hills," said Lester. "They won't dare attack."

"No," said the scout quietly. "When they meet and palaver and then begin to gather, they got plans on their minds. They ain't like white men, who'll keep up a force for weeks and months and then strike. When they start gathering, you know damned well they mean to attack, for they can't keep together for long periods of time like we can."

"How many warriors do you think he can muster?" asked Travis.

"I saw about fifty or sixty in the hills."

Major Lester laughed. "We can handle them."

Baconora shifted his chew. "I said I *saw* fifty or sixty.

Cuchillo has warriors watching this fort and others watching Santa Theresa. He has war parties raiding as far east as the Rio Grande and other parties raiding down into Chihuahua. When the time comes, he'll have enough warriors for his purpose."

Major Lester paled a little. His eyes seemed to dart about the table. "Well, gentlemen, we must keep a stiff upper lip and gird our loins. I want no fear amongst you."

The officers looked at him. There was some fear in each of them in varying quantities, for none of them were fools, but each of them knew that Enos Lester was more afraid by far than any of them.

The major stood up. "To work, gentlemen." He left the mess. Travis walked outside, followed by Baconora. They walked over to Travis' quarters. Travis handed the scout a bottle of mezcal. "I don't know how you got close enough to Cuchillo's camp to learn what you did," he said, "but it's worth a bottle of mezcal to me."

Baconora grinned crookedly. "I just use Apache methods," he said.

Travis nodded. "Take it easy for a day, and then report to me. Don't leave the post."

Baconora patted the bottle. "Not with this to keep me company, I won't."

"I have three couriers out trying for the Rio Grande."

The scout's head jerked. "When did they leave?"

"Last evening."

"They'll never make it."

"We had to take the risk."

"Ain't no risk in it; the throw of the dice was against them before they left. You won't see those men again. Not alive, anyways."

"You seem pretty sure."

"I am."

"We'll wait three days. At the end of that time, I want you to trail them to see if they got out of this country."

"Yeah. I'll do it. Won't do any good, though. You'll

see. Maybe even before I go." Baconora walked to the door, saluted Travis carelessly, then left the quarters, leaving a feeling of deep apprehension hovering within Travis.

Travis went to the window and watched DeSantis drilling his men on the use of the howitzer. The sun glinted from the highly polished brass piece. It wouldn't be of much value as a killing instrument, but cannon had always had a terrifying effect on Indians. They hated the wagon guns worse than anything. The howitzer might be of value in a defense, but on the offensive, it would be impractical because the Apache certainly would never allow it to get within effective shooting range. The howitzer was one of Enos Lester's pet projects at Fort Joslyn. The bumbling major, with all his years of quarter-mastering and paperwork, seemed to think he was commanding a force of the three arms of the service—infantry, cavalry, and artillery. It wasn't a force in any sense; it was hardly a representation of the three arms.

Travis shook his head. Perhaps the major had dreams of leading cavalry, infantry, and artillery in some minia-ture battle, preparatory to taking command of his ambi-tion, the combat brigade.

A lean man walked past the drilling gunners. It was Ben Joad, his face swathed in bandages. No charges had been pressed against him because Major Lester didn't want the civilians to take up Ben load's fight with the military. There was enough friction already at Fort Joslyn. Travis had known men of load's stamp before. The man would never forget or forgive Travis for what he had done.

Travis walked outside and walked past the corral. He stopped fifty yards from the corral and looked about. He had ideas of having a redoubt built to protect the fort because the fort was such in name only, hardly able to be defended by the small garrison.

There was a low knoll a hundred yards from the fort.

It overlooked the Santa Theresa road and was some fifteen feet higher than the site of the fort. Rifle fire from the knoll could effectively cover the corral, preventing the Apache from attacking it. A redoubt would also be able to afford a sweeping fire along the west and south sides of the fort.

Travis went back to the post and got an axe and several short lengths of boards. He returned to the knoll and paced off an area about fifty feet square. He hammered in stakes for boundary markers, planning an octagonal redoubt. Perhaps he could persuade the major to have the howitzer mounted in the planned redoubt on a plank platform. Grape or canister fired from the small artillery piece could sweep the western and southern approaches to the fort. Such redoubts had already been started at Fort Yuma before he had left there.

Clint Vaughn approached Travis. "What are you doing?" he asked. "Staking out a claim?"

Travis grinned. "Certainly. This is a solid mound of silver."

Clint lit a cigar and eyed the stakes. "A redoubt?"

"You guessed it."

"You think the major will allow you to have it built?"

"He'd better."

"I wouldn't bet on it."

"Why?"

"He doesn't believe in pick and shovel work. He thinks the United States Army is far too valorous to hide behind heaps of dirt."

Travis wiped the sweat from his face. "If Cuchillo Rojo is the tactician I think he is, he'd see the military value of the knoll at once. He could place a dozen good marksmen on here and pepper hell out of us at will."

"You forget the major has his inestimable howitzer. With it, he thinks he is invincible."

"He'd have to roll it out into the open to get a clear

field of fire. By the time the gun was in battery, the gunners would all be shot down by fire from this knoll."

"You won't convince him of that, Travis."

Travis hurled the axe at one of his stakes. The axe struck true and hard, splitting the stake. "The man is an utter fool!"

Clint waved a hand in warning and jerked his head toward the fort. Major Lester was walking toward them through the brush. "Gentlemen! Gentlemen!" he called. "What are you doing out here?"

"This is your chance, Travis," said Clint *sotto voce*.

The major puffed up the slope and returned their salutes. "What is this? Are you planning a garden here?"

Travis shook his head. "We need a redoubt here, sir. We can put the howitzer into position here and cover the western and southern sides of the post, as well as the corral, with howitzer and rifle fire."

The major shook his head. "It will not be necessary to exhaust the men by digging under this hot sun. I have already made plans for an effective defense of the fort."

"Yes, sir?" asked Travis.

Lester nodded complacently. "We will place the howitzer on the roof of the quartermaster warehouse."

Clint Vaughn looked away. He relit his cigar. His shoulders seemed to be shaking a little.

Travis looked at the warehouse. "It might not be possible to depress the howitzer enough to sweep the area close into the fort, sir."

"I do not intend to let the enemy approach *that* close, Captain. When the time comes, we will meet them with saber and pistol. Our infantry can defend the buildings and, if necessary, attack the enemy on foot."

"But if they do manage to get close to the buildings, sir," said Travis patiently, "the howitzer will be of no value whatsoever."

Major Lester shook his head. "You know cavalry tactics, I am sure, sir, but you must leave the proper handling of other arms to me. We can raise the trail of the howitzer with blocks and fire close to the buildings. Simple, is it not?"

"Very simple," said Travis dryly.

The major nodded in satisfaction. "You see my wisdom then."

"Quite, sir. But I still believe this knoll, if in our hands, would be the key to the defense of the fort. On the other hand, if the Apache gain possession of it, they will have a fine field of fire into the fort."

"But the howitzer will drive them from the knoll, will it not?"

"The gunners will be almost completely exposed up on that roof, sir. Besides, the shock of recoil might weaken the roof to such an extent that it will collapse."

Enos Lester waved a hand. "The roof will hold, sir. I do not like to hear talk of defense. As a junior officer with a career ahead of him in the cavalry, you should think of *offense* rather than *defense*."

It was no use, thought Travis. The man was hidebound and would brook no arguments against his plans. His very lack of fighting experience had probably convinced him he could do no wrong. A veteran soldier would have examined and evaluated all possibilities of an enemy coup, but not Enos Lester.

Major Lester placed a hand on Travis' shoulder. "Remember, Captain, that I too have studied Vauban. I know all about parapets, epaulements, redans, redoubts, glacis and chevaux-de-frise. But you are not an engineer, and neither am I. We are field soldiers, and, I might add, *fighting* soldiers, not men who put their trust in heaps of earth and in the defensive. Remember that well. Now, there is work to be done. Mr. Vaughn, your post of duty is in the quartermaster warehouse. Captain Walker, I'm sure you have many details to superintend. To work, gentlemen, to work!"

Major Lester bustled off down the hill with the brim

of his Kossuth hat flopping at every stride. At the base of the hill, he clenched the hilt of his sword with his left hand and balled his right hand. He shook it vigorously toward the hazy hills. "Cuchillo!" he cried. "Just match swords' points with Major Enos Lester. Just try!" Then he hurried past the corral and vanished from sight.

Clint Vaughn took his cigar from his mouth. "Well, I'll be damned," he said.

Travis picked up the axe and hefted it. "It seems as though we are, Clint, *seems as though we are*."

They walked down the low hillock together.

———

MAJOR LESTER, a far cry from the man who spent much time doctoring himself and soaking his feet in mustard baths, spent the long hot afternoon supervising the placing of the howitzer atop the quartermaster warehouse. Sergeant Ellis, a jack of all trades, rigged shear poles to hoist the barrel and carriage of the stubby little weapon to its position on the flat roof of the large building.

Norval DeSantis said hardly a word all afternoon, other than those which were necessary for commands. Major Lester was quite pleased with himself and spent much time in asides to any officer and enlisted man who got within earshot, explaining the brilliance of his stratagem in placing the cannon in such a position. He saw to it that shot, grape, and canister, with the necessary powder and friction tubes, were hauled up to the roof and placed in a wooden structure Corporal Covello had fabricated. A trooper, temporarily assigned to the artillery detail, was to stand guard beside the howitzer. Major Lester ordered the preparation of heavy wooden blocks, which could be placed beneath the trail of the gun in such a way as to elevate the trail and thus depress the barrel for close-in shooting.

Clint Vaughn walked about inside his stuffy warehouse among the piles of boxes, sacks, and barrels, eying the roof over his head. Now and then, bits of adobe pattered down upon the stores.

Travis kept himself busy with the myriad of details an executive officer is responsible for, but, now and then, he couldn't help viewing the progress of Major Lester's brainchild. Travis only hoped that Charles Cass was as energetic as the major in seeing to the defenses of Santa Theresa, according to the instructions laid down by Travis. God help Santa Theresa if the major went there and used his wild reasoning in the preparation of the town's defenses.

A mild sort of madness seemed to have come over Enos Lester, as though, by his intense supervision of activities, he could forestall the mysterious movements of Cuchillo Rojo. But there was no sign of the Apache. No smoke against the clear skies, no dust rising from the desert floor, no sight of lone Apache scouts on the distant hill slopes. It was as though the Mimbrenos and their Chiricahua allies had completely vanished from the area.

When night came, it was as silent as the grave; an apt simile thought Travis Walker grimly as he made his evening rounds. The sentries were alert. There was too much tension at Fort Joslyn for them to be otherwise.

The moon had not yet risen when Travis left his quarters. Ken Carlie was officer of the guard. Travis knew the man was capable and conscientious, but the responsibility for the safety of the fort really rested on Travis. He walked toward the corral and heard the sharp challenge of the sentry. He looked up toward the roof of the warehouse and saw the trooper on guard pacing back and forth near his charge, the little brass howitzer. Travis walked toward the gate. The moon was beginning to tint the eastern heights.

The gate sentry was standing behind a buttress of the

guardhouse, staring out into the darkness beyond the gate. He turned to see Travis. "I thought I heard something out there," he said.

Travis stared into the darkness. He could vaguely make out the indistinct outlines of clumps of brush. It was a job he planned to order soon—the cutting of all brush within at least a hundred yards of the post.

The sentry leaned forward. "There *is* something out there, sir," he whispered hoarsely. "Something that don't look quite right to me."

"You've got good eyes, soldier."

Ken Carlie came up behind them. "What is it, sir?" he asked.

"I don't know," said Travis. "We'll wait until the moon rises."

The long minutes dragged past as the moon slowly rose over the eastern heights, gradually silvering the desert.

"Turn out the guard, Mr. Carlie," said Travis. "No noise, mind!"

Carlie turned out the guard. The men stood in the dimness, fingering their rifles, trying to probe the mysterious darkness with their eyes.

"There!" said the sentry. "You see it, sir?"

A hundred yards from the post, right in the center of the Santa Theresa road, a strange growth seemed to have sprouted up since daylight had gone. It was in the shape of a thick cross, some feet higher than a man's head. Travis eyed it until his eyes played tricks on him, but the keen-eyed sentry turned away. "There's a man hanging from that cross," he said in a thick voice.

The moon was higher now, and Travis knew the sentry was right. A man was hanging from the cross. He was naked, and his head had been pulled back and lashed to the upright of the cross. The body didn't move.

"Good God," said Ken Carlie.

"Who put it there?" asked a young trooper.

"'Paches, I'll bet," said a corporal.

The desert was flooding with moonlight, bringing out each detail of the terrain and illuminating the crucified man. There was no sign of human life on the sands nor in the thick brush.

Travis looked at the corporal. "Get a shovel," he said.

The noncom hurried off and was back in a few minutes with the tool. Travis placed a hand on Carlie's shoulder.

"Station two men on each roof to cover me. You stay here with two men. Corporal, follow me with two men."

Travis took the shovel in his left hand and drew his Colt with his right. He cocked it and walked out into the open, followed by the three enlisted men. Gun hammers clicked back. Travis' boots made little noise on the soft sand. Now and then, he stopped to look and listen, but there was nothing to be seen, and the only sound was the noise of the wind sighing through the brush.

Travis stopped in front of the cross. He looked up into the set face of Amos Corby, the lanky Vermonter whom he had sent out with Troopers John Nolan and Benson Duryea. Amos Corby's sightless eyes stared at the fort.

"No sign of anything," the corporal said huskily.

Travis holstered his Colt and attacked the sand at the base of the cross. The cross tilted as he dug. Travis and the corporal dragged at the cross until it was loose enough to be pulled free from the sand. Corby had been lashed to the cross with rawhide thongs. The corporal cut the tight bonds loose, and they rolled the stiff body to one side. Travis took the corporal's knife and cut through the lashings which held the crossbar to the upright. He carried the two pieces of heavy wood into the brush and hurled the lashings after them. He picked up the body of the courier and walked toward the fort. The three enlisted men walked behind him, holding their weapons at the ready and turning their heads quickly from side to side, waiting for a possible pantherlike rush of Mimbrenos from the brush.

Travis felt a wave of relief pour over him as he passed into the quadrangle. Ken Carlie helped him lower the body to the ground. "Jesus," he said. "Look at the back of his head."

The skull had been smashed by a murderous blow, but there were no other marks on the naked body. Corby had probably been caught asleep and killed before he had awakened. Travis could visualize what had happened. Corby had made his hidden camp for the day, sure that he was unseen by the Apache. They had allowed the tired courier time to drop to sleep. Then, at dawn, their favorite time of action in an attack, they had closed in on silent feet to strike hard and sure.

"Christ in the Desert," said an enlisted man.

Travis stood up. "Wrap him in a blanket. Keep him in the guardhouse until daylight. See if you can find an old uniform for him so he can be buried properly as a soldier."

There was no use telling the enlisted men to forget what they had seen on the road. The gruesome story would be all over the post by morning mess.

Travis walked toward his quarters. He wanted to forget Amos Corby, who had said that his mission was no more dangerous than staying on duty at Fort Joslyn. Travis walked behind his quarters and looked to the east. Somewhere out there, the other two couriers might be well on the way to Fort Craig, or they might have suffered the same fate as Corby. But Cuchillo Rojo had played his hand well. The chief was a master at psychological warfare. The real game had just begun, and so far, Cuchillo held all the aces.

CHAPTER EIGHT

Morning mess was a quiet affair. None of the officers, with the exception of Major Lester, were very hungry. Everyone knew of the fate of Trooper Corby.

"It is beyond me, Mr. Carlie," said Enos Lester, around a mouthful of bacon, "how your sentries could allow the enemy to approach to within one hundred yards of the post and place the body of Trooper Corby right in the center of the road. Carelessness, Mr. Carlie, pure carelessness. Pass the bread, Mr. Newkirk. I'll thank you for the jam, Mr. DeSantis."

Ken Carlie bit his lip. The major was ready for one of his long and windy diatribes.

The major flourished his fork. "Continual alertness is the only safeguard we have at the present time, Mr. Carlie. You young officers are apt to be lackadaisical in such matters. In my forty years of service, I have learned the ways of the red man, but perhaps I forget that you gentlemen are of a different generation and will not spend the time in learning your business—for, after all, we *are* in a business. I remember one time when I was post quartermaster at Fort Duncan in Texas. The Lipan's had been harrying the surrounding countryside, and our post commander, although I hesitate to say so, not being in the habit of criticizing my superior officers as you gentlemen so often do, allowed the garrison to become careless, despite my repeated warnings." Here the major paused to let his words sink in and also to lay a thick layer of jam on a slice of bread.

The door swung open, and Sergeant Ellis appeared. "Sir, there is a messenger here from Santa Theresa."

"We are dining, sergeant."

"I'm sorry, sir, but the man says his message is urgent."

"Bid him enter then," said Lester testily.

A Mexican came into the mess room and took off his steeple hat. He hesitated, looking from one to the other of the officers.

"Speak up, my man," said Lester, turning in his seat. He sank his yellow teeth into his bread and jam and began to chew steadily.

"A woman is missing from the town, Major," the man said in good English.

"So?"

"It is said she left with her man to try and reach Chihuahua."

"Continue."

"It is thought that they might have been attacked by the Apache, sir."

Major Lester finished his bread and jam. He wiped his mouth. "What am I to do, sir?"

The man shrugged. "The *alcalde* requests that troops be sent to try and find the woman and her man."

"I have no troops to spare. Is not Captain Cass there in Santa Theresa? That is under his temporary jurisdiction."

The man swallowed. "The captain is not feeling well, Major."

"I am sorry to hear that."

Travis stood up. "I had thought of going into the

town to see the progress of the work I ordered done, with your permission, Major Lester."

The major drummed on the table with stubby fingers. "There is work for you here, Captain. However, Santa Theresa is part of my responsibility. Go then and see what you can do."

"I'll take Sergeant Ellis and Baconora with me."

"That will be satisfactory. But no risks, mind! I cannot afford to lose you, Captain Walker."

Travis saluted and left the mess. In ten minutes, he was on the road with Ellis, Baconora, and the Mexican. "The woman must have been loco," opined Baconora.

The Mexican shrugged. "She was headstrong. A fine woman in looks, but headstrong, as I said. Her man did not want to go, but she said she would find a real man to take her if he refused to accompany her. They left last night sometime."

"Nice," said Sergeant Ellis. "She'll find some real men among the Mimbrenos if she lives to talk about it."

The Mexican crossed himself. "Mother of God," he said.

———

Santa Theresa was quiet under the morning sun. Men and women stood at the corners, talking quietly among themselves. "Where are the rest of the soldiers, Captain?" called out an American.

"You have soldiers stationed here," answered Travis.

A man laughed. "Yeah," he said sarcastically.

Travis swung down from his horse and tethered it to the rail in front of James Morris' house. He glanced at the *torreon*. It looked just the same as the last time he had seen it, and the old adobe which he had ordered torn down was still standing as it had been. A surge of anger raced through Travis. Cass had had plenty of time to get the work done.

Travis rapped on the big door. Theresa opened it. There was a worried look on her oval face, but she managed a smile. "It is good to see you," she said.

"Is Captain Cass here, Miss Morris?"

She hesitated. "Yes."

"Please tell him I would like to see him."

"He is in his room. My grandfather insisted that he be quartered here." She led the way down the hall and then out into the patio, a lovely place of blooming flowers and shapely shade trees. A bird sipped at the water in a pool. Theresa stopped at a door. "This is his room," she said.

Travis rapped on the door, but there was no answer. He opened the door and walked inside. He wrinkled his nose at the thick, cloying aura of sweat and sour liquor slops that filled the big room. Charles Cass lay on his belly on the large bed, stripped to his drawers. An empty bottle was on the chair beside the bed. His uniform was scattered across the floor. Travis pulled the door shut behind him. "Cass!" he said.

The big officer did not move.

"Cass! Damn it, wake up, man!"

The officer rolled over and threw an arm across his eyes. "That you, Dorner?" he said thickly. "Get me some black coffee."

Travis did not answer. He walked to the window and undid the shutters, throwing them back. Sunlight poured into the room. Charles Cass sat up and blinked at Travis. "Oh, it's *you*. What brings you here?"

Travis drew in a breath of fresh air from the open window. "You sleep late, Captain Cass," he said coldly.

Cass reached for a pitcher and poured the water over his tousled blond hair. He hiccupped. "Jesus," he said thickly.

"Did you know a woman and a man of this town left here last night?"

"What am I supposed to do?"

"No one was to leave town. The hills are thick with Apache."

"I know that."

"Damn it, man, don't you realize what might have happened to them?"

"If they're loco enough to leave town, I can't be responsible."

"You don't seem to be responsible for anything! Why haven't you obeyed orders? The *torreon* hasn't been repaired. That old adobe is still standing. I didn't see a work party or a single sentry on the streets."

Cass wiped the water from his face. He looked at Travis with bloodshot eyes. "I only have sixteen men and those the dregs of the Fort Joslyn garrison—snowbirds, skrimshankers, and drunks."

Travis looked at the bottle. "You've been doing a little drinking yourself, Captain."

"I did it off duty."

"You're on duty twenty-four hours a day here until things clear up."

Cass laughed. "Until things clear up? When will that be, Captain Walker?"

"Get dressed. Report to me in ten minutes. I'll issue you orders once more, and by God, Cass, you'd better see to them!"

The big officer stood up. He swayed a little. For a moment, Travis thought Cass would rush him. The man was mad clear through. Travis almost hoped he would try it. It would be a pleasure to skin his knuckles on Cass's bristly jaws.

Travis walked outside, shutting the door behind him. Theresa stood by the pool. She was quite a picture as she stood there in the dappled shade, wearing a flaring dress and a thin blouse that exposed her smooth white shoulders. She wore moccasins on her small feet. Travis walked to her. "This is a beautiful and quiet place," he said.

"Yes. Grandfather planned it for my grandmother.

She spent her last days here, feeding the birds. They would come to her without fear and flutter about her."

Travis leaned against one of the porch supports. "How is your grandfather?"

"Well enough."

"Who was the woman who left here?"

"Maria Diaz. She once worked for us, but she was wild and flighty. Since that time, she took up with Teodoro Vaca. It was she who shamed *him* into taking her from the town."

"But why?"

Theresa shrugged. "She has relatives in Durango. It was her thought to go to them."

"Didn't she realize that the Apache are watching the town?"

"Teodoro has traveled much. It is said he meant to travel at night and hide during the day. But it is a long way to Durango. A way of peril. Pray to God that she is safe."

Travis looked away. "The odds are against it, Theresa."

"Yes...I know. I liked her. She was so pretty and popular. If Teodoro had not taken her, she would have talked some other fool into doing so."

"How old was she?"

"Nineteen, Captain. There was no one in Santa Theresa who could dance like her, and she sang like a bird."

"The soldiers have not worked here?"

She shook her dark head.

"They have been drinking?"

"I don't want to talk about it, Captain."

"It doesn't matter. I know."

She looked across the sunlit patio at Charles Cass's door. "I do not like him," she said.

"Has he bothered you?"

She looked away. "No," she said quietly.

Travis knew she was lying. Charlie Cass wasn't the type of man who would be around Theresa Morris, or any other good-looking young woman, without trying his hand at her. Cass had been made an officer by Act of Congress, but they hadn't been able to make him a gentleman, in the smallest sense of the word, by legislation. Evelyn Cass was a fit mate for her husband. Travis wondered how the two of them had ever mated.

Cass opened his door and walked out into the sunlight. The bright rays must have lanced deep into his throbbing skull because he winced and pulled down his hat brim.

Travis looked at the girl. "I'll see what I can do about Maria and Teodoro," he said.

Charles Cass smiled sarcastically. "All we've got here is two squads of infantry," he said. "You figure on chasing out into the desert with them?"

Travis turned quickly. "No. Your job is to get to work on the details I outlined for you. I'll go after those two."

Cass smiled again. "Do," he said dryly. He looked at Theresa, not missing those of her charms he could see and mentally stripping her to view the rest of her charms in his mind's eye. The man was a born lecher, thought Travis.

"There is breakfast for you, Captain Cass," said Theresa.

"Thank you, Theresa."

"Forget it," said Travis. "Come with me, Cass."

"I haven't eaten yet."

"You've got all day."

"You have no right..." The officer's voice trailed off as he saw the icy look in Travis's eyes.

"Come on!"

Theresa led the way into the house and up the long hallway to the door. Cass wet his lips as he looked at her hips. He glanced at Travis and then looked away. There was a sly grin on his flushed face.

"Good morning, Theresa," said Travis. "You will come back to have coffee with Grandfather?" "Perhaps. I want to see if I can find Maria." The big door closed behind the two officers. "A nice bit of fluff," said Cass as he glanced back at the door. "Mixed blood seems to make them prettier and develops them earlier." "So? You're an expert on the subject?" Cass grinned. "I've been around," he said. "You'd better get around this town. Hop to it. I'm going out into the desert."

Cass nodded. He watched Travis mount his horse. Travis was followed by Sergeant Ellis, Baconora, and the Mexican who had come to Fort Joslyn. "You ramrod-backed son of a bitch," said Cass aloud. "I hope Cuchillo nails you good."

———

JORGE, the Mexican, drew rein just short of the low foothills and looked back at Travis. "They rode burros," he said. "We know this because they were missing from the corral of Señor Morris."

Baconora cast about, riding slowly, with his eyes fixed on the ground. He waved them on. "Here," he said. "Two burros crossed this wash." He swung down and raked quick fingers through some droppings. "Fresh. Not more than eight hours old." He wiped his hands on the seat of his filthy trousers.

Sergeant Ellis nodded. "Damned fools," he said.

They went on. The hills were quiet, brooding in the late morning sun. "Look," said Jorge quickly.

High overhead, three *zopilotes*, the great land buzzards of the Southwest, wheeled like scraps of charred paper caught in an updraft. Lower and lower, they swung until they passed beyond a cone-shaped hill.

The four men did not talk as they rode toward the bill, but carbines were placed across thighs, and Colts were loosened in their sheaths.

The obscene birds rose heavily and reluctantly from the brush as they heard the approach of the horses. The four men drew rein and looked about from beneath their hat-brims. There was no sign of Apache, but right in front of them, in the soft sand, were the marks of many horses' hoofs. To one side lay a rusty *escopeta*, which had evidently been smashed over a rock. "Teodoro's, I think," said Jorge softly.

Farther on, they saw a steeple hat lying beneath a clump of mesquite. Travis held up an arm. They dismounted and led their horses forward through the tangled mess of brush and shattered rocks. The sun beat down on them like the heat from a baker's oven.

"Look," said Sergeant Ellis.

The man had been roped to an upright finger of rock. The sun shone on his naked body. They had had their fun with Teodoro Vaca before he had been allowed the blessedness of death. Knives had changed him from the likeness of God into something indescribably horrid. Only his face had not been touched, but his staring, sightless eyes still mirrored the horrors he had seen and experienced.

"Christ," said Ellis.

Baconora spat. "There she is," he said, without emotion.

Maria Diaz would never dance and sing again for the *bravos* of Santa Theresa, nor anyone else. Teodoro Vaca had probably seen what had happened to his lady love, and his mind might have snapped at the sight. At least Travis hoped it had, for the foulness of the thing would have cracked most men's minds.

Her pitiful rags of finery had been ripped from her body as she fought a hopeless fight with nails and feet against her assaulters. Sergeant Ellis took a blanket from his cantle and threw it over the poor relic which lay on the hot sands, with broken-nailed fingers dug deep into the earth in final agony.

Baconora spat out his wad of sweet chewing tobacco and cut another chew. "Must'a been at least seven or eight of 'em," he said. He stowed the fresh wad into his mouth and began to work it into pliability.

Jorge crossed himself. "She was like a bird," he said softly, "always singing and fluttering about."

"Cut Teodoro loose," said Travis. "Let's get out of here!"

They placed the bodies on horses and lashed them into position. "Might just as well have left them out here," said the scout. He looked up at the wheeling *zopilotes*. "Them boys would soon take care of them," he said.

"Mother of Jesus!" said Jorge. "Have you no feelings?"

"Coldblooded bastard," said Mack Ellis.

There were tears in Jorge's brown eyes as he drew the blanket down about Maria. "There was a time," he said brokenly, "when she almost became my wife. It was months ago. I did not have enough money."

"Forget it, my friend," said Travis quietly.

They rode slowly toward the road. The *zopilotes* followed them for a time and then flew off in search of other prey.

———

THEY BURIED them in a common grave in the little walled cemetery of Santa Theresa, and most of the townspeople were there. They knew now that there was no chance for any of them to escape. They were in a prison without bars, with the executioners biding their time in the hazy hills.

Captain Cass had his men working on the *torreon*, aided by some of the men of the town, while others had started the task of leveling the old adobe. Two-wheeled *carretas* creaked and groaned between the spring and the various cisterns in town, filling them to capacity. A corporal, helped by one of his squad, worked on the shabby weapons of the townspeople. Several women had been assigned to rolling cartridges under the direction of a trooper. Another corporal had formed some of the able-bodied men of the town into a volunteer militia to augment the small force commanded by Charles Cass.

Sergeant Ellis was a tower of strength to Travis. The big noncom rawhided the men who tried to shirk, and under the whiplash of his tongue, the work progressed swiftly. But Captain Cass kept away from Travis. He stood in the meager shade of the *torreon*, puffing at a cigar, while his head pounded like an Apache tom-tom.

A servant came from the house of James Morris to invite Travis for dinner. Travis was in no hurry to get back to Fort Joslyn and under the thumb of Enos Lester, so he accepted the invitation. He sent Baconora and Sergeant Ellis back to the post in the middle of the afternoon.

———

A VELVETY DUSK settled over the great valley, and candlelight shone through the cracks in the shutters of Santa Theresa. The *torreon* had been reinforced as well as it could be, and the old adobe was leveled. Sentries, both civilian and military, paced the dark streets of the little *placita*. Travis cleaned up in the backroom of Jonas Simpson's *cantina* and then stopped at the bar for a drink.

Jonas Simpson eyed Travis with his one good eye. It had a strange effect, as though the one good eye had much more penetrating power than two good ones. "You think all your preparations will do any good for us, Captain?" he asked.

Travis shrugged. "We do the best we can," he said.

Jonas nodded. "Yeah...*you* did. All that bastard Cass did was sit around and swill *aguardiente*, with both eyes, peeled for a likely-looking woman. Well, he run off the best of the lot. You saw what happened to her."

Travis straightened up. "What do you mean?"

"You mean you didn't hear about it? Hell, it's common gossip that Cass was after Maria Diaz. He was trying to run the town like one of them feudal lords, or whatever you call 'em. Maria was scared to death of him. She talks that poor lovesick Teodoro into going with her. He was more scairt than she was, but he goes. You know the rest."

Travis emptied his glass. "Just what did Cass do to Maria?"

"Well, she was helping out a little at the Morris *casa* to make a little money. Cass traps her one day in his room. It was old Angelique who hears her. From what she said, Cass was really giving Maria a going over, and Angelique got there just in time. It wasn't until she threatened to tell the *alcalde* that Cass let the girl go. By that time, he had had his way with her. Chihuahua! There's a lot of the beast in that man."

Travis refilled his glass. A picture formed in his mind —the sight of Maria Diaz lying out there under the hot sun, ravaged and torn by the tigers of the human species under the tortured eyes of her Teodoro. He tightened his right hand. Suddenly the glass shattered in his grip, and he felt a sharp sensation of pain. *Aguardiente* and blood trickled from his hand as he opened it.

"*Jesusita!*" said Simpson.

Travis let the broken glass drop to the sanded floor. He bound his handkerchief about the hand and drew the knot tight with his teeth. Jonas Simpson looked at Travis' eyes, then looked quickly away, for he did not like what he saw there.

"Maybe I talk too much," said Jonas.

"No. Just enough."

Jonas wiped the bar. "I got a feelin' you aim to have a talk with Charlie Cass."

"I will."

The *cantina* owner looked up. "I ain't no angel. I got one foot in hell and the other on a pool of grease, but I don't like Charlie Cass, and I did like Maria. Oh, she was a little wild at times, but she was no *puta*. She would have settled down and made a good wife and mother. This I know. I never heard of any man making her in this *placita*, and there ain't much I miss around here. I'll bet my *cantina* against that hat of yours that Charlie Cass was the first man who got her."

Travis walked to the door. "He wasn't the last. There were at least eight or nine Mimbrenos in at the death, and it wasn't a quick, clean death, Jonas. Good night."

Jonas Simpson wiped the sweat from his bald head. "God help Good-time Charlie Cass when that cold-eyed bastard Travis Walker reckons with him."

———

TRAVIS LIT a half of a cigar he had been saving and leaned against the base of the *torreon*. Now and then, he saw the shadowy figure of a sentry pace along the plaza. The night wind swept in from the cooling desert, bringing with it the mingled odors of sage and mesquite. Here and there, in the dark blue blanket of the sky, an ice-chip star winked forth. The faint cry of a coyote drifted to him from the hills.

A slim young woman appeared around the *torreon*. "The *Capitan* is lonely this night?" she asked softly.

"No."

She sidled up to him. "I am."

"Go home, little one."

"Do you not like me?"

"I do not know you."

"I am Rafaela."

"It is a pretty name."

"Do I not have more than the pretty name?"

"You are very pretty, Rafaela."

"Come with me then."

"I dine with the *alcalde* tonight."

She laughed. "You will get nothing from Saint Theresa."

"Close your beak, little bird."

She leaned back against the warm wall of the tower. "My house is the second one beyond this tower. The *Capitan* with the yellow hair has already been with me. Ask him. He will tell you of my charms."

"I'm sure he can."

She laughed again. "What a bull that one is. But I do not sleep with the common soldiers—only the officers."

"A real lady," said Travis dryly.

"You will come then later tonight? I will wait."

"No."

"Before God!" she said angrily. "Are you a man of stone?"

He shook his head and looked down at her. "I was the man who brought in the bodies of Maria and Teodoro. Did you see Maria, Rafaela?"

She shivered. "I did not, but I have heard of what happened to her."

"Now you know why I will not come. Good night, Rafaela."

"Good night, *Capitan*."

She vanished silently into the darkness. The odor of her cheap perfume seemed to spoil the taste of his cigar. He hurled it to the ground and walked toward the big house of James Morris.

It was Angelique who admitted Travis. She started to usher him into the house, but he took her by the arm and drew her outside. "What is this I hear about Captain Cass and Maria?" he asked.

"It was a terrible thing. She was to help me here in the house. I sent her to make the captain's bed. I did not know he was still in it. Miss Theresa was shopping, and the *alcalde* was in his study. He cannot hear too well. Only Esteban was in the house, and he is old and cannot hear at all. I heard Maria scream and hurried to the room." She stopped and looked away.

"Go on!" he said fiercely.

"It was terrible, *Capitan*. He is like the mad bull with a woman. She was such a child. He threw me aside, but I am strong and came right back. He was going to strike me when I told him I would tell the *alcalde*. Then he laughed and told me to get her out of the house. He threw money at us as we left. I am afraid of him, and I am afraid for Miss Theresa with him in the house."

"Don't worry about her."

She slid a hand inside her dress and drew out a slim-bladed *cuchillo*. "He will not touch her while I am here, *Capitan*."

They went into the house, and she led him to the dining room. James Morris sat in his great chair. Theresa sat near the fireplace. She wore a black dress trimmed with exquisite lace. There was a comb in her dark hair, and she had drawn a filmy mantilla over it. It covered her bare shoulders, but their whiteness could be seen through the fine mesh of the lace. Travis' breath seemed to catch in his throat. She could have been sitting there waiting for one of the great masters to paint her in immortal oils.

The huge table was spread with a heavy white cloth, and the candlelight glistened softly on the heavy silver service. James Morris was evidently a man of great wealth.

"Good evening, *alcalde*," said Travis.

"Good evening to you, Captain Walker."

Theresa came forward. "You have hurt your hand," she exclaimed.

Travis nodded. There seemed to be more than just concern for an injured friend in her low voice. "It is nothing," he said.

"She has some skill in such matters," said the mayor. "Let her examine it."

Travis smiled. "Before dinner?"

"She is strong, Captain, much as my wife was."

Theresa took Travis' bandaged hand in her soft ones. She removed the bandage. "It must be disinfected," she said. "How did you do it?"

"A glass broke in my hand."

Her dark eyes studied him. "It must have broken very hard to inflict such cuts."

"Yes."

"Come with me, Captain."

She led the way into another room and took out bandages and antiseptic from a cabinet. She poured water into a basin then bathed the wound. He winced a little as she applied the carbolic. She bandaged the hand swiftly and neatly.

He looked down at her dark hair and at the smooth white shoulders, now exposed where her mantilla had fallen back, and there was a great desire within him to pass his free hand across that delightful flesh. She looked up at him, and there was an odd look in her eyes as though she had read his mind. But she did not release his hand.

"Gracias," he said.

"You must be more careful, Captain."

"The name is Travis, Theresa."

"Travis, then."

Her tone of voice broke the halter on Travis' restraint. He drew her close, and she made no effort to pull away. He tilted back her head and kissed her softly. For a moment, she hesitated, and then she slid an arm about his neck and drew him close, kissing him again and again. Then she broke away, passed a hand across her mouth, and walked quickly to the door. "Grandfather will wonder what has become of us," she said.

"I'm wondering what will become of us."

Her dark eyes held his. "I think I know," she said, and then she was gone.

Travis touched the bandage. He had thought he had

been in love before. He had known many women of all kinds and bore the invisible scars of what he thought had been lost loves on his soul, but now he knew for sure he had never really been in love as he was now.

Travis entered the great room. Theresa stood beside her grandfather as before, but there was a difference in her now as she looked at Travis.

Angelique bustled in to serve the meal, aided by aged Esteban. The door swung open, and Charles Cass came in. "You might as well set four places, Angelique," he said.

The serving woman shot him a look of hate, then looked at Theresa. Theresa looked away, but her grandfather spoke up. "Captain Cass, is it not? You are welcome, sir."

Cass had been drinking again. He lounged over to the sideboard and helped himself to a glass of wine. Travis clenched his hands so hard his right hand began to bleed afresh. Theresa shook her head at him and then looked down at James Morris. Travis nodded. He helped her push the old man's chair up to the head of the table. Cass emptied his glass and filled it again. "You have a way of getting things done, Walker," he said.

"Thanks."

"Don't mention it. You've got a great future in the service if you live to see it."

Theresa flushed. James Morris looked toward Cass. "You sound melancholy, Captain Cass," he said quietly.

"These are melancholy times, sir."

"I agree, but we will survive them as we have so many others."

"I hope so."

The dinner was good, and the conversation was at a minimum. Now and then, Travis dared to look deep into Theresa's eyes to read the message he wanted to read again and again. After a time, Charles Cass began to notice the two of them. It must be damned apparent, thought Travis.

Cass drank steadily, spending more time with the bottle than he did with the food. After a time, his eyes darted, again and again, to study Theresa, particularly where the cleft of her firm breasts showed in her low-cut bodice. Travis suddenly lost his appetite. The man was an outright lecher.

Angelique served coffee and liqueurs after the meal. Charlie Cass drank everything placed in front of him, with frequent trips to the sideboard, and his speech became thicker. Only the aged mayor didn't seem to notice anything out of the ordinary, but Travis felt sure that James Morris knew that the officer was getting drunk.

Finally, Travis could stand no more. "I'd like to talk to you privately, Cass," he said quietly.

The captain emptied his glass. "We're with friends, Walker," he said. "They can hear anything you have to say."

"I'd rather speak with you alone."

"I'm not through here yet."

Travis felt a growing rage, but he did not dare show it. Impulse demanded that he cross the room and drag the big man outside, but cold reason bridled his anger.

James Morris yawned slightly. "It is getting late," he said.

Cass refilled his glass. "Maybe Captain Walker would like to speak with Miss Morris alone, too," he suggested.

"What do you mean, sir?" asked the *alcalde*.

Cass grinned. "Anyone who has eyes can see what I mean, *alcalde*."

The old man looked toward Travis. "I don't understand him, sir."

Travis stood up. "Captain Cass has been drinking. His duties have him worried, and he is trying to relax."

Cass laughed loudly. "By God, that's good, Walker! I didn't think you had a sense of humor at all."

"What does this man mean, sir?" persisted Morris.

Theresa placed a hand on the old man's shoulder. "Please don't excite yourself."

"What is going on here?"

Travis looked Cass full in the eye. "Excuse yourself," he said coldly. "I'll see you on the patio."

Charlie Cass wanted to show Theresa he wasn't afraid of Travis; he wanted to show her so badly it hurt deep inside, but the cold rage in Travis' eyes was too much for even him. He bowed to Theresa. "Good night, Miss Morris. Good night, Mayor Morris." He weaved a little as he walked toward the door. He turned as he opened it, eyed Theresa, and Travis, then left the room. His laugh came back to them.

James Morris looked toward Travis, "Well, sir!"

Theresa slid an arm about the old man's gnarled neck. "It is very simple, Grandfather. I am in love with Captain Walker, and he is in love with me."

"Mother of God!"

"It's true, sir," said Travis quietly.

Morris raised his heavy cane and shook it. "You come to Santa Theresa to help us, and you connive behind my back to delude this child into such things. If I could stand up, sir, I'd thrash you. If I could see, I would invite you out."

Theresa took the cane from his big hands. "How old was Grandmother when you married her?"

"What has that to do with it?"

"*How old,* Grandfather?"

"Eighteen."

"She was *sixteen,* grandfather. I remember the stories you used to tell of eloping with her and how her three brothers pursued you for two days and of how she rode like a *vaquero* beside you, never complaining until you were safe."

"That was long ago. Such things are not done now."

"My mother was but eighteen when your own son married her. It is said you raised hell to use the proper term because my mother didn't meet your requirements for a daughter-in-law."

"She was but a child!"

Theresa shook her pretty head. "That was not the reason at all. It was because she was not Anglo, nor even of pure Spanish blood. She was half Opata and proud of it, but you didn't like the thought of mixed blood in the family."

The old man bowed his head. She had struck home. "I'm sorry about that, Granddaughter. It was long ago. I have learned a great deal of tolerance since those days. You are all I have left and are as dear to me as my son was. You must forgive an old man, Theresa, and you too, Captain Walker."

"Forget it, sir."

The sightless eyes raised to look directly at Travis, and he again had the feeling that the old man could see him plainly. "My granddaughter is not the type of frontier woman who will throw herself at a man. Did you approach her first, sir?"

Travis looked at the young woman. She nodded. Travis came closer to the old man. "I think it was mutual, sir."

"You'll marry her then?"

"No."

"What do you mean, sir! *What do you mean?*"

"There is a war on us, sir. Fort Joslyn and Santa Theresa are in desperate straits. I'm a soldier on duty here. The odds are high against us; there's no use in deluding you on that point. If we survive this mess, I intend to ask Theresa to be my wife."

Her eyes held his as though she'd never let him go.

The old man nodded. "You are a man of honor, Captain Walker. But I must request you to see Theresa only by our customs. With her *duenna*, and only when I give permission."

"Agreed."

Theresa laughed softly. "But, Grandfather, I have no *duenna*."

"Angelique will serve as such." The old man held out his right hand, and Travis gripped it. "Go now, Captain," said James Morris. "I wish to speak privately with Theresa."

Travis touched her cheek with his left hand then walked to the door. He turned to look at her, and then he left the room.

Charlie Cass was in the patio, leaning against an upright. Travis walked to him. "You certainly conducted yourself like a damned fool in there," he said.

"Save the lecture."

"As your senior officer, I request you to conduct yourself like an officer and a gentleman."

Cass yawned. "There's a helluva lot of seniority between us, Walker. Get off your high horse."

"I'm warning you just once."

"You come in out of the desert from where God alone knows. You bull Enos Lester into thinking you're something special. You move in on the old man in there and make him think you're the Angel Gabriel come to save his Goddamned two-bit *placita*. Then you grab off his granddaughter. How was it, Walker? Worth the effort?"

Travis swung his left hand, and the hard open palm snapped the officer's head back against the post. Cass raised his right hand to his stinging face, then dropped it to his gun butt. "You like your whores high class, eh, Walker?"

Travis closed his injured right hand and hit Cass neatly on the jaw. The big man went down hard, groveling on the tiles. Travis stood over him. "I warned you," he said thinly. "Now listen to me again; you'll do your duty here as a soldier. If you so much as bother Theresa, I'll hunt you down and kill you." He turned on a heel and walked toward the hallway.

Cass gripped his Colt butt. "You'll pay for this," he

yelled. Travis disappeared from sight. Cass pulled himself to his feet. "By God, you'll pay for it, you brass-bound son of a bitch," he said quietly.

Travis walked toward the outer door. Theresa stepped from her room and looked up at him. He drew her close and kissed her. She laughed softly. "My *duenna* isn't here," she protested.

Travis raised her head. "There's one thing I haven't said to you yet. I love you, Theresa Morris, with all my heart and soul. Somehow I'll take you away from here."

"I know that," she said simply. "I seemed to know it the first time I saw you."

When Travis was out into the moonlit plaza, he wondered at the mystery of it all. He had found the woman he loved...the only woman he would ever love. He had made a deadly enemy of Charles Cass, a man who would never forget what Travis had done to smash his superego.

CHAPTER NINE

The moon was up high as Travis rode the Santa Theresa–Fort Joslyn road. Now and then, he drew rein to sit his saddle and listen to the night sounds. The Apache rarely attacked at night, but a bold warrior, safe in ambush, might risk a sure killing shot to get a lone rider.

He was a mile from the fort when he turned his horse aside to enter the brush. If the Mimbrenos were watching the post, they would keep warriors along the moonlit road to guard the approaches.

He was a quarter of a mile from the fort when he saw the moonlight glistening on something in a clearing. It lay on a low mound of sand from which the tussocks had been pulled away and cast in a pile to one side. Travis dismounted and led his horse toward the mound. Then he stopped short. What he saw was a complete skeleton, the moonbeams shining on the creamy-yellow bones. Beside the ankle and wrist bones, he saw pegs driven into the sand, with rawhide thongs lying loosely about the wrists and ankles, or at least where they had been.

Travis dropped the reins and drew his Sharps free from the saddle. He cocked and capped it, then moved to the base of the low mound, not ten feet from the grisly relic of a man. Tiny black objects moved busily about the skeleton. Sonoran ants are black, venomous, and voracious. He had not known they existed in the deserts of New Mexico, but he had seen them in the Sonoran deserts in the country of the fierce and predatory Yaqui, blood cousins of the equally vicious Apache.

The man had been stripped and bound over the ant mound. There was no telling who or what he had been. The ants could strip the flesh from a man in twelve hours because they worked busily by day and night. Travis ascended the mound and looked about. There was no sign of life. He drew his knife out and cut away the loose rawhide thongs. As he did so, one of the ants got at his left hand. It was like the jabbing of a hatpin almost to the bone. He jerked back his hand, feeling the quick poison of the voracious insect burning in his blood.

Travis slid down the slope. He glanced back at the skeleton. The ants were cleaning up the last fragments of flesh. Only the gristle ligaments would be left by dawn, holding the bones together. In time the bones would turn white and drop away from each other as the ligaments rotted apart.

Then he saw the battered hat hanging from a mesquite branch. It was a Kossuth hat such as he wore, but it had been an enlisted man's headgear, as he could tell by the quality of the wool and the half-inch ribbed grosgrain ribbon, originally black, which had faded to a funereal purple from exposure to the elements. Travis turned the hat upside down and turned down the wide leather sweatband. The name J. Nolan had been lettered inside the band.

Travis glanced at the remains of John Nolan, the quiet Pennsylvanian. He had said that he was sick of waiting for Cuchillo Rojo to swoop down on Fort Joslyn.

"Two gone and one to go," said Travis aloud. Corby and Nolan had never made Fort Craig. That left Benson Duryea, the courier who had been ordered by Travis, to go the long way around to Fort Craig. Where was he? Would he show up as Corby and Nolan had done? Cuchillo Rojo had made sure that Nolan would be identified by leaving the dead trooper's hat near his remains.

Travis mounted and rode toward the fort with his carbine across his thighs and Nolan's hat hooked to his belt.

The moon shone on the adobe walls of the fort. There was a sentry standing just beyond the gate. "Halt! Who goes there?"

"Officer of the garrison!"

"Advance to be recognized!"

Travis raised his hand and spurred the horse forward.

The sentry lowered his rifle. "Captain Walker! The captain is taking his life in his hands riding in the desert alone."

Travis swung down. "How has it been?"

"Quiet, sir. Too damned quiet."

"Any sign of the Apache?"

"A little smoke in the hills."

Travis nodded. He led his horse past the sentry into the moonlit quadrangle. Sergeant Ellis appeared. "I'll take your horse, sir. The major wishes to see you. He left orders you were to report to him in his quarters as soon as you returned."

"Thanks, Ellis."

"Everything all right in town, sir?"

"As well as can be expected."

"I gave those two corporals a little living hell about their laxity before I left, sir."

"You can't put all the blame on them."

"What does the captain mean?"

"Nothing. Ellis, I have a job for you tonight."

"Yes, sir?"

"Half a mile from here, on the east side of the road, you'll find all that's left of John Nolan."

"Jesus!" blurted Ellis. "Him, too?"

"Him too."

Ellis shook his head. "Poor Johnny. I thought he'd make it if any of us could. What about Duryea?"

"I don't know, Sergeant. Take two or three good men. Go and get Nolan. Don't let anyone see him as he is."

"Is it that bad?"

"Yes," said Travis quietly. "Wrap him in canvas and sew it up. A saddler can do it. I want no one to see him as he is. You understand?"

"Yes, sir."

"Wrap him up yourself and then bring him back. You will not say that it is Nolan. Just an unidentified body."

"I understand, sir."

"Keep your mouth shut."

"Certainly, Captain!"

Travis handed Ellis the Kossuth hat. "Bury that with what you find."

Travis walked toward the major's quarters. Ellis watched him, then looked down at the hat. "Poor Johnny," he said. He led the horse to the corral.

Major Lester was wrapped in a blanket and seated in a chair. He looked up as Travis entered the stifling room. The fire snapped and crackled in the big fireplace, filling the room with the resinous odors of mesquite wood. "Good to see you, Walker," he said. "How did it go?"

"The woman and her companion were murdered by the Apache."

Enos Lester paled. "They left the town?"

"Yes."

"The fools!"

"They had a reason. But they paid for their foolishness."

Lester drew his blanket tightly about his shoulders and shivered a little. "The defenses of the town are all right?"

"As well as can be expected. I don't think Cuchillo

will make an open attack on Santa Theresa, but he'll probably make nuisance raids."

"I'm sure Captain Cass is doing all right there."

"He is," said Travis dryly. There was no use in complaining about Charles Cass. There was no one else to replace him. Travis hoped his treatment of the drunken fool would straighten him out, but he had little faith in the thought.

"Let us hope our two remaining couriers will get through. It is a terrible responsibility for a sick man here, Captain Walker."

Travis nodded. "I know, sir. I'll give you all the support I am able to. But you must know that Trooper Nolan is dead."

Lester swallowed quickly. "That leaves Duryea to carry the dispatches."

"Yes."

"What happened to Nolan?"

There was no use in telling the gruesome details to the shaken man in front of him, thought Travis. "I found his body half a mile from the fort, sir."

Enos Lester plucked at his lower lip. "I had no faith in sending those men, sir! You practically overruled me on that, Captain! *You* sent those men to a sure death!"

Travis did not answer. He knew Lester wasn't through castigating him.

"In forty years of service, sir, I have developed a foresight into such matters. All you have done is to weaken the garrison still further. It was your idea to garrison Santa Theresa and weaken us still beyond that point. Now we have other troubles. Someone on this post is trying to incite some of the enlisted men to desert and join the Confederacy. I assure you, sir, that man will be shot as a traitor if I can find him."

"You're sure about this, sir?"

"Certainly!" snapped the major. "I have not manufactured the rumor out of whole cloth! My orderly, Private Kelligan, reported it to me."

"Where did he hear such a tale?"

"It is being talked about in the enlisted men's mess, but no one has mentioned the culprit's name. I want you to investigate, sir! If you identify the man, he must be court-martialed."

"Yes, sir."

Lester waved a pudgy hand. "I am surrounded by fools and traitors. Beset by the Apache. Sick in body but not sick in the heart. I am a soldier, sir!"

"I know, Major."

Lester leaned forward. "I suppose you think we should abandon the fort and strike for the Rio Grande?"

"I mentioned that once before, sir."

"Do you think it could be done?"

"It's possible yet, Major."

"Tell me how?"

"But your orders say that you must remain here until ordered otherwise."

The major looked away. "Well, it might be left to my discretion. If it was, and, mind, I'm not saying it is so, how would you perform the evacuation?"

Travis eyed the old man. He was in a hell of a nervous condition for sure. "I'd strip the command down to fighting gear, carrying nothing but rations and all the ammunition we have on hand. I'd take just enough wagons to transport rations, ammunition, women, and children. The infantry could march with the wagon train while the cavalry, under my command, could fend off Apache attacks. The Apache don't like to attack steady infantry. In some cases, the Indians are more afraid of infantry fire than they are of a cavalry attack. We could strike for the road to the Rio Grande and fight our way through."

"And supposing we met a strong force of Confederates if we got past the Apache?"

"Why, sir, we'd have to surrender and take the fortunes of war."

Lester flushed. "That would end my career of forty years of loyal service. I would be put on half pay if I was to be paroled."

The old man was a downright fool, thought Travis.

Enos Lester pounded the arm of his chair. "Was ever commanding officer put into such straits?"

"I imagine similar circumstances have beset commanding officers before, sir."

Lester shook his head. "Forty loyal years. Did the Commanding officer of the Department of New Mexico think of that? Did he care about me? Not at all, sir. Not at all. I will not go home on half pay, discarded like a condemned mule, to face my people and make excuses for the remainder of my life. I will not have it!"

Travis eyed the frightened old man. He was more concerned about his damned reputation *if* he had any at all, than he was about the lives of the people who depended on him for protection.

"Let me alone," said Lester quietly. "Find the man who is a traitor. Oh, I'll crucify him!"

Travis left the stifling room. He remembered the talk he had had with Martin Newkirk. There had been something in Newkirk's tone when he had suggested that Lester's orders could not include Travis. Travis meant to pry specific information out of Newkirk.

Travis walked toward his quarters. Lester wanted him to locate the traitor who was supposedly inciting the enlisted men into deserting the army to join the Confederacy. There were mostly Northerners among the enlisted men, with a leavening of Border States' and Southern States' men. One of the latter two types might be responsible, but it wouldn't be easy singling out the culprit.

The door of the infantrymen's quarters hung open. The thin music of a fife drifted out into the night, backed by the soft beating of a drum. Travis stopped to listen. It was a moment before he recognized the tune. It was *The White Cockade*. Travis slowly walked to the door and looked inside. A grizzled corporal sat on a stool near the door, tootling his fife, while a young infantryman rattled away on the drum. The fifer stopped as he saw Travis and slowly lowered his instrument while the drummer played on and then stopped in the middle of a roll.

The corporal stood up. "Attention!" he roared.

The men tumbled from their cots and stood at attention.

"As you were," said Travis.

"Maybe we were making too much noise, sir?" said the corporal.

"No," said Travis. "Was that *The White Cockade*?"

The fifer grinned. "It was, sir. A fine tune, is it not?"

"It's been a long time since I've heard it. I always liked fife and drum music."

"I'm Corporal Stewart, sir. B. Company."

"How many years' service?"

The man drew himself up. "Twenty years, sir."

"You were in the Mexican War?"

"I was, sir. Fourth Infantry."

"Come outside a moment."

Stewart followed Travis outside. "Yes, sir?"

"What part of the country are you from, Stewart?"

"New Jersey, sir. But I was born and raised in Massachusetts."

"A real Yankee, eh?"

"I'm proud of it, sir."

"I'm sure you are." Travis walked away from the barracks. He turned. "You know the men of your company pretty well?"

"I've been with most of them over two years, Captain."

"Have you heard any talk about deserting and joining the Confederacy?"

Stewart flushed a little. "Well…"

"Speak up!"

"Well, sir, there has been some talk about it"

"Who started it?"

"I don't know, sir."

Travis nodded. "You don't know, or you won't say?"

"Let's put it this way, Captain Walker, if I had heard any such talk, I would have lambasted the man who said it. All I've heard are rumors."

Travis rubbed his jaw. "I haven't any doubt about your loyalty, Stewart. Keep your ears open and let me know if you can find out who the man is because as sure as I'm standing here, there has been such talk."

"It hasn't come from my squad, sir, nor from my company. In fact, I don't know of any enlisted man who has been talking such tripe."

"Thanks."

Stewart hesitated. "I don't know for sure about the officers, though, sir."

"What do you mean?"

The old soldier fingered his battered fife. "If you're looking for such a man, sir, you'd better look twice at some of your officers."

"Who?"

"I'd rather not say, Captain, because I ain't sure."

"Thanks. Go back to your quarters."

"You want us to stop playing, sir?"

"Stop at *Tattoo*."

"Right, sir." The noncom saluted and returned to his barracks. A moment later, Travis heard him speak. "All right, Billy, let's try *Hell on the Wabash*."

"What did the captain want to talk to you about?"

"My fifing. He wants to hear *Hell on the Wabash*. Let's go! One! Two! Three!"

The reedy music started in again, with the soft beat of the drum underlying the tune. Travis shrugged.

Someone moved from behind a wagon. It was Maggie Gillis. "You've been away, Captain. We've missed you."

Travis smiled. "Who has? Ben Joad?"

She laughed. "Ben ain't been feeling too chipper since you marked his ugly face."

"I was sorry for that."

"I'm not. I hate him."

"Now, Maggie!"

She came close to him. "Watch him, Captain. He don't never forget things like that."

"I'll watch him," promised Travis.

She looked at the barracks. "I heard what you asked Sam Stewart."

"So?"

"He was right. It ain't no enlisted man who's been talking about treason."

"Go on."

"It's an officer."

"Who?"

"You won't say it was me who talked?"

"I'll keep your secret."

"It was Mr. Carlie."

"You're sure?"

"As sure as I'm Maggie Gillis."

"I see. Tell me about it."

She looked about and then came closer. "I was sleeping in the wagon, one night, where it was cooler. Mr. Carlie was officer of the guard. He came by the wagon, and some of the enlisted men was sitting outside the barracks chewing the fat. They was talking about the war, and one of them said he was from Tennessee and didn't want to go back East. He said he'd rather fight Apache than Confederates.

"Another one agreed with the first one who talked. Then Mr. Carlie began to talk about it, saying he wasn't so sure the Federal government had any right to fight against the South because they was only sticking up for States' Rights, which he believed in.

"They got into quite a palaver about the whole thing.

Mr. Carlie said a man had a right to forget his oath of allegiance to the Federal government, for anyone who gave his oath gave it to the whole country, not just to the North."

Travis nodded. "Thanks, Maggie."

"You said you wouldn't say who told you."

"I won't."

Corporal Stewart was now playing *Peas Upon a Trencher.* Maggie turned her head. "Pretty, ain't it? I like music. Do you?"

"Yes."

"Will we leave here soon, Captain?"

"I don't know. I wish we would."

"You'll make sure I go with you?"

"Yes. Good night, Maggie."

"Good night, Captain."

Travis turned to go. She pulled his arm. "Sometime, Captain, will you come and talk with me?"

He turned and looked down at her piquant face, half that of a woman and half that of a girl. He raised her chin and kissed her. "Maybe, Maggie. We'll see."

She looked after him as he walked. "A real gentleman," she said softly. There was a suspicious glinting in her big eyes.

Corporal Stewart raised his voice. "Damn it, Billy! You're off half a beat most of the time! Let's try *The Wrecker's Daughter*, and mind you get the time!"

Travis walked to his quarters and went in. Clint Vaughn was seated at his desk. He looked up as Travis entered. "Welcome home," he said.

"Thanks."

"You've got an odd look on your *cara*."

Travis dropped on his bunk. "What do you know about Ken Carlie?"

"He's a better officer than any of them here, you excepted."

"Gracias."

"Why do you ask?"

Travis rolled over and looked at Clint. "Where's his home?"

"Maryland, I think."

"Has he ever given you any cause to think he isn't loyal?"

"No. Well...maybe no. I've heard him talk about States' Rights a few times. He was in Texas for some time. Some disloyal talk made an impression on him. At least that's my opinion."

"Someone is inciting the men to desert. I'm sure it's Carlie."

Clint whistled softly. "I'm penned up in that damned warehouse so much I've lost track of post gossip. What do you intend to do about it?"

"The major wants whoever is doing the talking to be brought up for court-martial."

"Now? With Cuchillo sitting out there watching us twenty-four hours a day?"

"Yes."

Clint stood up and filled two glasses with brandy. He handed one to Travis. "Be careful, Travis. It's a terrible thing to accuse an officer of."

Travis did not answer. Clint raised his head to look into Travis' eyes, then almost flinched at what he saw. "For God's sake, Travis," he said quickly, "before you do anything rash, you'd better make sure you're right."

Travis downed his drink and placed the glass on the table. "Where is he now?"

"Probably in his quarters. He's not on guard tonight."

Travis walked to the door.

"Do you want me to go with you, Travis?" asked Clint. "Ken has a hell of a temper. I've seen the killing rage in him. You might arouse it if you accuse him of treason."

Travis turned. "I can stand almost any kind of officer, Clint. God knows this post has one of the oddest assort-ments I've ever experienced. If I had the authority, I'd cashier some of them right now. Some of them I like, and some of them I dislike. I know for sure I hate one. Personally, I like Ken Carlie, but if he's inciting treason on this post, I'd just as soon kill him as look at him." Travis closed the door behind him.

Clint emptied his glass. He shook his head, remembering the cold look he had just seen in Travis Walker's eyes. Clint pulled on his shirt and then buckled his gun belt about his waist. When two men like Travis Walker and Kenneth Carlie got together with a bone of contention between them, someone was going to get hurt.

CHAPTER TEN

Travis rapped on the door to Carlie's quarters. The officer bunked alone in the last room of Officer's Row.

"Come in!" called Carlie.

Travis opened the door. Ken Carlie lay on his bunk, a book lying open on his chest. His left hand held a cigar, and in his right hand was his service pistol, cocked and pointed at Travis' belly. For one tense moment, Travis thought the man suspected why he had come. A lump of ice seemed to form in his gut, and the instinct to go for his Colt was hard to bridle.

Carlie smiled. He lowered the Colt, then let down the big hammer to half cock. "Good evening, Captain." He sat up and dropped his long legs over the side of the cot. "Sorry about your reception. I've spent too much time on outpost duty to take chances on accepting without question anyone who knocked on my door."

Travis nodded. He looked about the little room. It was hung with the usual pieces of clothing and equipment. A stout Indian bow hung on the rear wall over the washstand.

"Drink?" asked Carlie.

"No thanks. Just had one. I got back a little while ago

from Santa Theresa."

"How was it?"

Travis dropped into a chair, out of line with Carlie's shooting hand. "Not bad. Things are beginning to get done."

"With Charlie Cass in charge? Times have changed."

"You don't have much of an opinion of him, Carlie."

"No...and neither do you."

Their eyes met. Under other circumstances, Travis would have accepted the young officer as a kindred soul, for there was much in Carlie that matched Travis' thoughts and ways. "I'll take a cigar if you have one, Carlie," said Travis.

The box of cigars was on the little table at the foot of the cot. Carlie leaned toward it, reaching out with his right hand to get the box, moving himself out of position to get hold of his pistol in a hurry. As he did so, Travis stood up and walked toward the bed. He stopped just beside the Colt. "I think the major and myself have some questions to ask you, Carlie," he said quietly.

Carlie's hand stopped just over the cigar box. He turned his head to look up into Travis' eyes. Then he dropped his eyes to see Travis' hand resting on the butt of his revolving pistol. He knew right away he had been deliberately feinted out of position. "Concerning what, Captain Walker?" he asked.

"You'll find out when you get there, mister."

Carlie sat up straight. He knew better than to make a try for the pistol he wanted so badly. Travis would either draw and shoot or grapple with him, and Carlie wasn't so sure he could take the tall man in front of him.

"Get up and get ready," said Travis coldly.

Carlie stood up and reached for his shirt. He pulled it over his head, tied his scarf about his throat, and reached for his gun belt, half expecting Travis to tell him to leave it hang, but Travis said nothing against his putting it on. He placed his hat on his head.

Travis picked up Carlie's Colt and let the hammer down easily. He passed it to Carlie butt foremost, and his eyes never left Carlie's. He wants me to try him, thought Carlie.

For a few seconds, they stood there, and then Carlie raised the flap of his holster with his left hand and let the heavy six-shooter slip down inside the sheath. "I'd still like to know what this is all about," said Carlie.

"I think you do, mister."

How much did he know? Ken Carlie reached for the lamp to put it out.

"Leave it on, mister," said Travis. "Walk to the door."

Carlie walked to the door. The light went out behind him. Carlie had wanted to make a try for Travis in the darkness, but now he knew his broad back was silhouetted in the doorway. He walked out on the parade ground and waited for Travis.

Travis shut the door behind him. "Go on," he said. "You know where the major's quarters are."

Carlie turned his head and then smiled. "Senior officers first," he said.

Travis couldn't help but admire the man. "We'll walk together," he said.

Carlie turned to face Travis. "I know why you want me to go to the major. It's about the talking I've been doing."

"You don't have to talk to me, mister. It's up to Major Lester what to decide to do with you."

"You think he's got the guts to order me shot?"

"I have."

Carlie wet his lips. "Look," he said quickly, "you're in a hell of a spot here, Walker. You're the real commander of this fort. You'd be a hell of a lot better off if the old man wasn't here at all. Use your head."

"Keep talking. I'll give you another minute."

Carlie lowered his voice. "The moral here is bad enough as it is. Supposing you do accuse me of seditious talk and possibly of treason? Most of the men like me. Some of the officers do, too. If you bring me up to trial and have me shot, the morale will plummet to the bottom, and you might lower it enough to hurt the defense of the fort if it is attacked."

"You sound like a damned guardhouse lawyer. Get moving."

"I haven't yet made my point."

"Go on, then."

"I've been planning for some time to resign and join the Confederacy. Let me leave here tonight, Walker, with my written resignation in your hands. You'll get no more trouble from me."

"It's a good thought, Carlie, except for one thing."

"So?"

"How far do you think you'd get from Fort Joslyn?" Carlie rubbed a hand over his lean face. "By God, you'll not have me shot, Walker!"

"Get moving."

Carlie came a little closer to Travis. "What difference does it make to you?"

Travis raised a big hand and gripped the officer by the slack of his shirtfront. He drew Carlie closer. "You made the mistake of not resigning months ago, as other United States Army officers who sympathized with the South had the honor to do. No, you stayed around for a last stab in the back. Well, sonny, you stayed around a little too long!"

Travis shoved the officer back. For a moment, Carlie stood there; then, suddenly, he sprinted for the corrals. Let him go, something seemed to say in the back of Travis' mind, but something else made him drop his hand to his Colt. He ran forward. Carlie turned and drew. Travis jumped sideways as Carlie fired. Then the Colt seemed to leap into Travis' hand. The big hammer was thumbed back, and the bullet sped into the powder smoke that wreathed Carlie. Ken Carlie staggered forward. He tried to raise his smoking Colt, but the strength was draining from him. He dropped the heavy pistol and then reeled closer to Travis.

Men shouted in the background, and boots thudded against the hard caliche. Ken Carlie raised his head and looked at Travis. "Damn you," he said. "I had a feeling you'd get me one way or another." He pitched forward on his face and lay still. A slow stain of blood spread across the hard earth beside him.

———

TRAVIS STOOD under the ramada in front of his quarters, watching four enlisted men carrying off Ken Carlie's body. Clinton Vaughn stood beside Travis. "I had a feeling that was going to happen," he said quietly.

"That son of a bitch Walker killed Carlie without giving him a chance," a man said from near the civilian wagons.

"Ben Joad," said Clint.

"That's not true!" said Maggie Gillis.

A woman laughed. "You got a feeling under your dress for him, Maggie. Well, you won't get nowhere with his type. I oughta know."

There was the sound of flesh striking flesh. "Break it up, Maggie!" yelled Joad. "She's right. Besides, it ain't you nor any other civilian woman he's interested in. I think Carlie knew about him, and Travis Walker shut his mouth the only way he could. With a bullet in the belly!"

Clint Vaughn gripped Travis' arm. "Keep away from him," he said. "He's been doing some talking about you. Hinting at this and that."

Travis turned. "Such as?"

"Jesus! You don't want me to get involved, do you?"

Travis gripped the wrist of the hand which held his left arm. "Damn it! Talk? What does Joad mean?"

Clint winced as the steely fingers tightened. "All

right," he said. "Come into the quarters."

Travis followed the quartermaster into the dark room. Clint lit the lamp. He walked back to the washstand and opened a drawer. He took something from it and handed it to Travis. Travis looked down at a filmy handkerchief. The faint aroma of jasmine rose to his nostrils. He looked up at Clint. "Well?" he asked.

Clint walked to the door and kicked it shut. "I found it on the floor the night you sent out those couriers. I don't know who left it here, Travis, but I can damn well guess."

Clint poured two drinks. "She's a lusty bitch," he said over his shoulder. "This is a lonely place. I can't say that I blame you."

Travis balled the handkerchief and threw it into the fireplace. "She was in here when I got here," he said. "The lamp was out. I damned near shot her."

"Maybe you should have. You shoot fast and well, Travis."

"Meaning?"

Clint shrugged. He turned and handed a glass to Travis, "Here," he said. "Drink this. You'll need it when you talk to Enos Lester...God help you."

Travis downed the drink and felt it hit his belly like a dose of canister.

Clint leaned against the wall. "Someone must have seen her come in here or else leave. You know how gossip is on a post like this. Since then, I've heard latrine rumors about something going on. It didn't surprise me about hearing her name. It *did* surprise me about hearing yours. God, but Charlie Cass can build this thing up into a dandy mess, and he's just the man to do it.

"There's nothing so outraged as a philandering husband or wife when they find out the tables have been turned."

"And what's your opinion, my philosophic friend?"

Clint waved his glass. "Look," he said quietly. "Until

you showed up out here in the furthermost suburbs of hell, I almost had *cafard*, as the French call the desert madness.

"Lester was slowly driving me mad. Cass made me sick. I could stand Carlie and Newkirk, but DeSantis irritated me to such an extent I nearly challenged him once. That might surprise you, looking at me, but I damned well meant to do it.

"Then there were other things. Evelyn Cass swishing her butt at every male on the post. Those civilians with their slatternly women. At first, I thought they were just poor refugees. I should have known better."

"How so?"

Clint spat into the fireplace. "Have you seen any children among the lot of them? They represented themselves as honest frontier folk to old Enos, and he swallowed it hook, line and sinker. Some of them are as bad as the Apache. At that, I'd almost trust Cuchillo more than I would Joad."

Travis nodded.

Clint straightened up. "So you see, Travis, you saved me from myself. I don't quite know how, but I'm grateful to you. Whatever you've done and whatever you do, I'm with you, and don't ever forget it."

"Thanks, Clint."

Clint reached into the fireplace and spread out the tight ball of the handkerchief. He struck a block match and set fire to the filmy cloth. The two of them watched it burn.

Someone rapped at the door, and Travis opened it. A trooper saluted. "Captain Walker, sir, Major Lester wishes to see you in his quarters at once."

Travis returned the salute and nodded.

"Shall I go with you?" asked Clint.

"No sense in you listening to him on a hot night like this. Besides, he'd probably order you to leave anyway."

Clint shrugged. "Marty Newkirk invited me over for a

game. I'll be over there if you need me."

Major Lester was pacing back and forth in his heated room, swathed in a flannel robe. His loose slippers made a dry husking noise on the earthen floor. He whirled as Travis entered. "My God, Captain Walker!" he cried. "What have you done now?"

"The man was a traitor. The major himself said he'd court-martial and shoot any such man he found. I happened to find him. I was bringing him here. He made a break for freedom. I was almost willing to let him go, thinking the Apache would deal with him soon enough. Mr. Carlie turned and fired at me. I killed him."

"Just like that?"

Travis nodded. "Just like that."

Lester mopped his dripping face. "How can I report this thing? I'll be brought up for investigation with you. It is only your word against perhaps a dozen others that Kenneth Carlie was a traitor."

"I'll take my chances on a court of investigation. Yes, and at a court-martial, too."

Lester's eyes seemed to bulge out. "Yes...*you* will! But what about me? Within months of a promotion. Within a few years of a pension and honorable retirement. Did you think of my gray hairs and my forty years of service when you shot that man down?"

"No, sir."

"Well then, sir, just what *were* you thinking of?"

Travis couldn't help letting the ghost of a smile travel across his face. "Of a bullet in my belly, Major."

For a fraction of a second, a change seemed to come over Enos Lester, as though he *had* been a real field soldier in years gone past and some of the power of command over a subordinate had mysteriously returned, but then the pudgy face sagged into the usual petulant expression of a man beset on all sides by tribulations over which he had no control.

"I'm sorry, Major," said Travis. "My sense of humor

sometimes gets the best of me."

Lester dropped into his chair and rested his right elbow on the arm of the chair, cupping his sweating forehead in his hand. "A man comes in here with blood upon his soul. He puts his commanding officer in a terrible position. He jokes about killing a man. Just what and who are you, Mr. Walker?"

Travis did not answer. He felt no need for speaking, for Enos Lester did not expect an answer. It was like trying to make intelligent conversation with a petulant child or a semi senile old woman.

Lester looked up. "You may leave, sir. I will not sleep a wink this night while trying to figure a way out of this latest dilemma."

"Good night, sir."

Travis softly closed the door behind him, then gratefully breathed in the fresh night air. Somewhere out in the night, a coyote howled. Travis walked slowly toward his quarters. In the excitement of the night, he had almost forgotten the principal peril to all the lives at Fort Joslyn and Santa Theresa, the Apache, but *they* had not forgotten. With spidery patience, they were weaving their almost invisible net about their quarry.

Travis paused for a moment, removing his hat to let the breeze dry the sweat on his forehead. A curtain was pulled aside in one of the windows of Captain Cass's quarters, and Evelyn Cass looked out at Travis with brooding eyes.

Travis walked on. Theresa crept easily into his thoughts and settled down in a corner of his mind like a contented kitten. She drove out the Apache, Ken Carlie, Enos Lester, and everything else.

Travis reached his quarters. Fort Joslyn and its intrigues sickened him as though it had a graveyard smell. He'd soft-talk the major into letting him return to Santa Theresa the next day. Somehow he seemed to know his future lay in the town rather than in the fort.

CHAPTER ELEVEN

The steady drumming of hoofs sounded like the rhythmic shaking of pebbles in a gourd rattle. Yellow dust swept ahead of the lone rider and shrouded him from the view of the men standing alertly at the gate of Fort Joslyn with cocked musketoons.

"'Tis a Mex!" said Trooper Doherty. "I can see his hat!" Travis Walker nodded. "Stand easy," he said.

The early afternoon sun beat down upon the fort, and there wasn't a breath of air on the desert. The hills were seen dimly behind a plum-colored haze. The horseman stood up in his stirrups and waved his hat at Travis. It was Jorge Valadez, the man who had helped Travis find the bodies of Maria Diaz and Teodoro Vaca. *"Hola, Capitan,"* he yelled in a dust-hoarse voice.

"Hola, Jorge! Come on, man!"

Jorge drew in his big dun. He slid from the saddle and wiped the sweat from his broad face. "How goes it with you, *Capitan?"*

"Forget the formalities. Why are you here?"

Jorge spat dryly. "There is trouble in Santa Theresa."

"So?"

"Cuchillo struck at dawn, driving off many of our horses and mules. A house was burned down. A child was wounded, and two men and a woman died in the fight near the corrals."

"And the soldiers?"

Jorge looked up with hate in his eyes. "*Them?* I urinate on them!"

Travis gripped the Mexican by his arm. "What the hell do you mean by that?"

Jorge raised his head. "They run wild in the town when you are not there. Captain Cass, I spit upon his name, does nothing to stop them from lolling in the *cantinas* and chasing the women of Santa Theresa. Our *alcalde* is much upset. He has sent me to see if you will come to Santa Theresa and take charge."

Travis nodded. "I'll talk to the major. Get some water. Tell Sergeant Ellis to have my horses saddled."

"*Si, mi Capitan.*"

Travis hurried to the major's office. The commanding officer was working on a pile of papers. "Yes, Walker?" he asked.

"I'd like the major's permission to go into Santa Theresa on an inspection."

"Again?"

"I'd like to have the work well done, sir."

Lester rubbed his sweaty jaw. "Well, all right. One thing, however—take Mrs. Cass with you."

Travis jerked as though stung with a lash. "*Sir?*"

Lester did not look up. "Mrs. Cass is anxious to see her husband, poor lonely woman. I told her I'd let her go with you on your next tour of inspection."

"I haven't time to wait for her, sir."

Lester looked up. "So? Why?"

Travis bridled. He didn't want the nervous old man to know what had happened. "I'm sorry, sir," said Travis quietly. "I'll wait for her."

"Good! Be careful, Captain. I'll expect you back no later than tomorrow at noon, sir."

Travis nodded and saluted. He stamped out of the

office. Evelyn Cass was standing under the ramada of her quarters, wearing a fashionable riding habit. She pulled on her gloves as Travis approached. "I'm ready," she said.

Travis eyed her closely. "How did you know I was going into Santa Theresa?"

"Why, Captain! I knew your duty would force you to go back as quickly as possible. When I saw that Mexican courier, I dressed as quickly as possible so as not to slow you down."

Travis looked into her, but there was no hint of guile in her immense eyes. "I'll see that you get a mount," he said.

"Don't bother. Kelligan is getting my mare."

Trooper Kelligan, as though he had received some sort of mental message from Evelyn Cass, was trotting her mare toward them.

Evelyn adjusted a scarf over her hat and across her face. "Poor Charlie misses me," she said.

Travis nodded. "I'm sure he does. Can hardly bear to be away from you." He walked toward his quarters. Jorge had Travis' horse ready.

"The woman goes along?" asked Jorge.

"Yes."

"This is madness!"

"It's the major's order."

"Then he is mad!"

Travis shrugged. He went into his quarters, took a stiff hooker, then got his weapons and gear. He walked outside. "Get Baconora, Jorge," he said. "We might need him."

"*Sí!*"

Travis led his horse and Jorge's back to Evelyn. She had mounted her mare and sat sidesaddle, with the long skirt of her riding habit carefully draped over her long shapely legs.

She smiled archly at Travis. "I knew I'd have my way," she said.

"I hope you're satisfied."

"I had to be with you one way or another."

"You will be until we get into Santa Theresa."

She adjusted her riding habit. "Oh, I don't know. Charlie won't bother much about me. I have a good idea about what he's doing there. I'll enjoy seeing you and Charlie have a nice friendly talk as officers and gentlemen."

"You won't."

She laughed at him. "I have a feeling I've dumped over your pretty little apple cart, Travis." She laughed again. "What's the great attraction in Santa Theresa?"

Travis did not answer. He saw Jorge and Baconora coming toward them. Then Travis turned. "I hope to God you can ride that mare, as well as being able to sit her there posing like a picture from Godey's Ladies Book."

She looked closely at him. "Why, Travis?"

He swung up onto his sorrel. "Because, Mrs. Cass, if we're jumped by Mimbrenos between here and Santa Theresa, you might have the ride of your life. To win that ride is to win your life; to lose it is to die."

She paled. For a moment, she glanced uncertainly back at her quarters, then out toward the silent and sun-beaten desert. "You're trying to frighten me!" she said.

Travis shrugged. "Have it your own way, Ewie." He grinned crookedly. "I'll save the last shot for you."

She bit her lip. Maybe she hadn't been so clever after all. "Perhaps you had better get an escort?" she suggested.

"From *here*? No, ma'am! There's hardly enough men here to stand guard. We go as we are, and we go fast, and the devil—or Cuchillo Rojo, as the case may be, will take the hindmost."

Sergeant Mack Ellis stood under the ramada in front of headquarters and eyed Evelyn Cass. By God, she was a real filly but absolutely forbidden for an enlisted man. Mack Ellis knew he was as good a man as any officer on the post, with the exception of Travis Walker. He knew damned well he was better than Charlie Cass but not good enough to have a woman like Evelyn Cass to bed. Now she was riding into Santa Theresa along a desert road, under the greedy eyes of the watching Mimbrenos, and she was a sight good enough to make a man's head swim. It was too much for Mack Ellis. He wanted to be with her that long, anyway.

Mack Ellis walked forward and saluted Travis. "The captain is going into Santa Theresa?"

"Yes, Ellis."

"I'd like to go along, sir."

Travis eyed the big noncom. He wasn't the only one. Evelyn Cass never missed a chance to study any man who looked as though he had more than his share of masculinity.

"Well, sir?" asked Ellis.

"All right. Get moving."

Baconora swung up on his horse and hooked a leg about the big Mexican pie-plate pommel. "Quite a party this is getting to be," he said. "I'm looking forward to going into Santa Theresa. I hear Ben Joad pulled out before dawn and went there." The scout eyed Evelyn. "Old Ben sure has a big mouth."

"What do you mean?" asked Travis.

"Nothing, Captain...nothing at all."

Ellis appeared, booted, and spurred, leading his horse. The little cavalcade rode out past the guardhouse.

"Damned fools," said a trooper on guard to a lounging civilian.

"Oh, I don't know. With the exception of that Cass woman, I think that little party can damned well take care of itself."

The trooper grinned. "I know where she can beat all of them when it comes to taking care of herself."

The civilian spat. "That's for sure, Milligan. I'd like to try her myself."

—

THERE WAS no sign of Apache as the five rode the dusty road toward Santa Theresa, raising a plume of saffron dust behind them. Not even a hawk sailed through the skies.

Halfway through the place where the low ridges crowded the rutted road, Evelyn Cass laughed. The four men turned to look at her with varying emotions on their faces. "What is it, *senora?*" asked Jorge.

She pulled her filmy scarf from her face. "The four of you have been riding like boys past a graveyard at midnight, whistling to keep up your courage."

"So, *senora?*"

She thrust a gloved hand toward the deserted ridges. "What are you afraid of? There isn't even a jackrabbit on those ridges."

"Before God, *senora,* do not say such things! They may be watching us even now."

"Who, Jorge?"

"*Los Indios.* The Apache."

She burst into laughter again. Mack Ellis smiled. He loved to hear her full-throated laughter.

Baconora spat juicily. The amber hit the dust with the sound of a dropped pack of playing cards. "Yuh keep laughing like that," he said quietly, "and yuh might draw them outta those ridges."

"I'm not afraid."

"Yuh ever seen a bloodthirsty buck up close, Mrs. Cass? Yuh ever smell the grease on 'em? Yuh ever see what they do to white women?"

"Shut your gab!" said Ellis.

Baconora turned in his saddle. "I'm only trying to get some sense into her head."

"You're trying to frighten her."

Jorge looked at Travis and shrugged. Evelyn Cass studied Mack Ellis with new interest.

"Yuh saw that Maria Diaz out in the desert," said Baconora slowly. "Maybe this woman should have seen what was left of Maria."

Ellis drew rein and then leaned toward Baconora. "I told you to shut up, scout."

Baconora rested his hand on the butt of his Colt. "Yuh aimin' to make me, soldier?"

"Damn it!" Travis spurred his sorrel in between them. "While we're standing here like sitting ducks, the Mimbrenos could ambush us. Baconora! You ride ahead. Ellis! You take the rear. Move! *Vamonos!*"

The two men did as they were bid, but a last look of hate passed between them like clashing blades.

Evelyn spurred her mare and rode ahead of Travis and Jorge. Jorge crossed himself. "The woman is a fool," he said.

Travis nodded. "In a way," he said dryly.

"The big *Sargento* has his eyes on her all the time."

"So? I hadn't noticed."

Jorge smiled. "The *Capitán* has eyes for many things. But some of the things right beneath his nose he does not see. I do not mean to offend, *Capitán*."

Travis looked back at Sergeant Ellis. The man dared not look at an officer's wife with interest. Then Travis recalled how Ellis had looked at her as he volunteered to accompany the party into Santa Theresa. His defense of her against Baconora seemed to be more proof that the veteran had more than a passing interest in Evelyn Cass. One woman could raise more hell among woman-starved troopers of an outpost garrison than the whole Mimbreno tribe on the warpath.

Baconora was fifty yards ahead of them now. Suddenly he turned his horse into tight little circles, pointing with the carbine in his hands toward the sand ridge to the west. It was the Indian sign for enemy in sight.

Travis looked toward the ridge. Three Apache sat their horses in full view, looking down at the little party below them. They did not move, and their weapons were not raised. Ellis closed up at a canter. "Sir!" he called out. "Look!"

Travis turned. Three more Apache sat their mounts in the road behind them, just inside the mouth of the shallow pass.

"Madre de Dios," breathed Jorge. "Look! To the east!"

Three Apache had appeared on the ridge-top as though they were ghostly puppets manipulated by unseen hands. Travis looked to the north. The road was open.

"What shall we do?" asked Evelyn. There was a shaky huskiness in her voice.

Travis moved his horse to her right side. "We'll go on as we are," he said. "Jorge, stay on the left side of the *senora*. Let's move out."

Baconora waited a little until he was fifty feet ahead of the others, then rode steadily on toward Santa Theresa. Travis glanced sideways at Evelyn. There was panic riding her shapely shoulders, and panic could easily shift its load to the others. One scream would trigger the action and cause a stampede that would result in the deaths of all of them. But these men were veterans, used to the dangers of the open road in Apacheria, and they each knew that a wild break for freedom would have but one result.

"Do something!" pleaded Evelyn. She raised her head, and her neck muscles stood out sharply as the strain of her tension took control.

Travis looked away from her. Panic is an ugly sight, not to be looked upon by any man unless his control is exceptionally strong.

"Do something," she repeated.

The green smell of her fear seemed to overcome the feminine smell of her, usually carefully concealed by the artful use of jasmine. She was all woman now, stripped of any subterfuge, deathly afraid of those silent figures watching the small group on the dusty road.

Travis rode easily, reins in his left hand, right hand swinging freely by his side, looking straight ahead as though on parade. "Talk to me," he said out of the side of his mouth.

She shot him a look of intense fear. "Talk?"

"Yes, damn it."

"But those are Apache, Travis."

"They won't attack us."

"How do you know? Do something, I tell you!"

Travis glanced at her. There was nothing attractive about Evelyn Cass now. "Talk," he said coldly. "If they had meant to attack, they would have remained concealed until time to strike. They are guerrilla fighters, Evelyn. Their specialty is the quick raid and the ambush, never the hand-to-hand, last-ditch fighting of the white man."

"Then why are they just sitting there watching us?"

"To put the fear of God into us."

Jorge looked ahead. "There is the town in the distance," he said.

"Let's make a run for it," said Evelyn. She raised her quirt, but Travis leaned over toward her and gripped her wrist so hard she winced in pain.

"If we make a run for it, they'll lance in on us and cut us off one by one. So long as they are just sitting there, we'll ride as though we were just out for a canter. Now talk pleasantly. Laugh. Above all—ignore them."

Baconora had dropped back toward them. He spoke over his shoulder. "There's Cuchillo Rojo," he said. "The one with the yellow-stained cow horns on his headdress riding that splotched appaloosa."

Travis slowly turned his head. The Mimbreno sat his gaudy horse on the highest point of the western sand ridge, He was too far away from Travis to distinguish any of his features, but it wasn't really necessary because an aura of hate and evil seemed to flow down the slope toward the party of white people. The cow horns thrust themselves out from a thick mat of some kind of fur, lending a grotesque and diabolical appearance to the war chief.

Jorge crossed himself and then thrust out his left hand toward the distant chieftain, first, and little fingers extended as though warding off the spell of a *brujo* wizard.

Ellis closed up behind Travis. "We can hold that crew off," he said.

"Yeah," said Baconora, "but they may have a whole damned war party hidden behind them hills."

The hoofs thudded steadily on the road, and the dust rose to wreath about the riders. The Mimbrenos did not move. Cuchillo Rojo still sat there, watching them as they rode past.

Suddenly Travis hated Cuchillo Rojo with all his soul. It was all part of the game he was playing with them. The eternal menace, with just enough harassment to keep the whites on a constant vigil, while the Mimbrenos came and went at will. Cuchillo Rojo, who could neither read nor write, was a master at psychological warfare and far more skilled at it than the educated professional soldiers he faced.

Travis could see the first buildings of the town, vague and ill-defined because of the shimmering heat waves which rose from the baking earth. Then they rode out into the clear. Suddenly a demoniacal cry tore through the quiet like the slashing of a saber. The bloodcurdling wail came again. Evelyn Cass swayed in her saddle. Travis gripped her and held her up. He looked back into the shallow pass. There was no sign of the Apache in there now, nor on the low sand ridges. There was just a wraith of dust spiraling up in the faint wind.

Baconora spat. "That was Cuchillo," he said laconically.

"*Demonio!*" said Jorge.

Mack Ellis shoved back his hat and let the sweat sting his overheated face. "I'm glad that's over."

"It is—for a while," said Travis.

They rode on into the town, watched by silent towns-people. Travis drew rein in front of the *alcalde's* house, then helped Evelyn to the ground. Her fingers dug into his arms as he did so, and he looked into her eyes. She was no longer the frightened woman of the pass but the wanton again, seeking Travis' attention.

Baconora had vanished, but his horse stood outside Jonas Simpson's *cantina.* Jorge slapped the dust from his clothing. "Baconora has the right idea," he said. "My legs are like water."

"Go with the sergeant and get a drink, then," said Travis.

Travis walked up onto the porch and hammered at the door until it was opened by Angelique. The woman smiled. "The brave *Capitán!*" she said with a toothy smile.

"Good afternoon, Angelique. Captain Cass is here?"

"No. He is in the town somewhere."

"This is his wife. Can she stay here until he returns?"

Angelique's expression did not change, but there was something in her eyes as she surveyed Evelyn. It was as though she knew the seamy side of Captain Charles Cass and wondered what kind of woman would put up with him. "I am sure the *alcalde* will want her to stay. He is having his *siesta.*"

"And the *senorita?*"

Angelique smiled as though she shared a great secret with Travis. "She is in her room," she said. "I will tell her that the brave *Capitan* is here."

"I'll take Mrs. Cass to her husband's room."

Angelique bobbed up and down, then vanished into a corridor. Travis took Evelyn down the long central corridor and out into the patio. Evelyn pulled the scarf from about her face and looked around the patio. "Beautiful," she said. "Charles always does well for himself. I hope the *alcalde* keeps a sharp eye on his young serving girls."

Travis looked away from her. There was a sour bitterness in her voice, and he wondered which of the two of them had failed the other. He guided her across the shady patio and opened the door of Charlie's room. She walked in and quickly raised her scarf across her nose. "Good God," she said thickly.

The low-ceilinged room stank of liquor slops, sweat-soaked clothing, and the musty smell of a room which hasn't been aired in some time.

Evelyn Cass looked at Travis. "I almost expected to see half-gnawed beef bones on the floor among the rushes. Charlie would have made a fine medieval baron. You may be sure he doesn't leave our quarters at Fort Joslyn in *this* condition."

Travis nodded. He walked to the edge of the open patio. Theresa Morris had appeared at the far side. There was a catch in his throat, and his heart seemed to dash against his ribs. It was a feeling Travis had never experienced before, and he liked it, but mingled with it was a feeling of half melancholy.

Evelyn walked up to Travis. "The mistress of the house?"

"Senorita Theresa Morris, the *alcalde's* granddaughter."

Evelyn nodded. "I've heard of her. A rose blooming in the desert. I can see now why Charlie likes it here."

Travis turned a little. "Be quiet," he said.

She studied him for a moment, glanced at the girl, then back at Travis. "So that's it," she said softly.

Theresa was almost upon them now. She held out a slim hand to Travis, and the touch of it was like a key to another world, a world of promise and love. *"Senorita Morris,"* said Travis, "this is the wife of Captain Cass, Evelyn Cass."

Theresa bowed her head a little. "It is a pleasure to meet you, *senora*."

"Thank you, *senorita*. I have heard a great deal about you."

Their eyes met, and to Travis, it seemed as though invisible blades had been thrust out, had made contact as though to test their opponent's mettle, then had been withdrawn for another, later trial.

"I am sorry the captain is not here, Mrs. Cass," said Theresa.

"It is quite all right. The captain probably has many duties which require his absolute attention." There was the faint mingling of scorn and bitterness in the older woman's voice.

"Yes," said Theresa quietly.

"I'll wait in his room," said Evelyn.

"You will stay the night?"

Evelyn shrugged. "I'll see."

Travis eyed her. "I'll not be leaving here much before late tomorrow morning, Evelyn."

"In that case, I'll accept your invitation," said Evelyn to Theresa.

Theresa smiled. "I'll have Angelique straighten up the captain's room."

She shook her head. "No," she said, as though reluctant to have even a serving woman see the mare's nest in the room. "I'll do it myself."

"But..."

Evelyn raised her head. "It's quite all right," she said coolly. "I must have something to do until he gets back." She walked into the room and closed the door behind her.

Travis drew the girl close and kissed her. For a moment, her lips blended with his, and then she drew back. "Someone might be looking," she said.

"I'm worried."

She laughed. "You sound like it. Anyway, we have all day and tonight to see each other."

"Not today, Theresa. I came into town to see about that raid."

"And not to see me?" she pouted.

He grinned. "I'll admit I was planning to think of an excuse to come in. But I'm here now, and we have this evening to be together."

She leaned back against a post. "Cuchillo has been seen in the hills. It is said he led the raid himself. I have never seen him, Travis. What is he like?"

"I saw him for the first time today. That is, I saw him at a distance. I don't really know what he looks like."

She looked up at him. "You have a great deal of respect for him, don't you?"

"In a way. He's diabolically clever."

"He has said that he will rule this country from the Piloncillo's to the Rio Grande and from the Gilas far down into Chihuahua."

"We'll see about that."

"How can you stop him? He has many warriors and many fine guns. He knows the country. The soldiers are penned up at Fort Joslyn, and we, people of Santa Theresa, dare not travel the roads as we did for so many years. Who is there to stop him, Travis?"

"I don't know. Sometimes I feel as though we whites will never know this country as the Apache do. Perhaps it was never meant for us to rule over it."

She placed a hand on his arm. "You're worried. I can feel it. What has been happening at the fort?"

"Nothing but routine."

Her dark eyes held his. "That is not true. Something has happened there which has scarred you deeply. I *know*, Travis. It seems as though you are never very far away from me. It seems as though I know everything of which you think."

He thrust out his right hand, first and little fingers extended. "*Bruja* witch," he said teasingly.

She shrank back a little, and her face paled. "Travis! Please don't joke about it."

He drew her close and kissed her. "I'm sorry. Come with me to the door."

They walked across the patio with their arms about each other's waists. The door of Charles Cass's room swung open, and Evelyn Cass stood there and watched them walk across the shade-dappled patio. Her mouth drew down tightly, and she gripped her throat with her right hand. Then she turned to look at the mess her husband had left behind. She spat into the fireplace.

Travis stood at the door and looked down at Theresa. "Tonight then?"

"Tonight," she promised.

He kissed her then left the house. The sun was beating down on the dusty plaza. He turned and looked back at the house. He felt a raging impulse to go back for Theresa and take her away from there, at night, to strike for the Rio Grande. But he knew it was hopeless. It would end up with him penned down in some arroyo, shooting it out to the last, saving the last bullet for the woman he loved. No, there was nothing for him to do but stay on duty, hoping and praying for some guidance which would help him defeat Cuchillo Rojo. The prospect was pretty damned gloomy.

CHAPTER TWELVE

Travis walked across the plaza toward the town corrals. There was the usual coterie of gamblers playing monte under a sagging brush ramada. One of them looked up from beneath a huge steeple hat. "It's the *bravo*," he said. "Hey, Captain!"

Travis turned to look at the little man called Vince. Vince grinned. "Looks like old Cuchillo ain't much afraid of you soldier boys here," he said loudly.

The gamblers laughed. Vince stood up and leaned against a post. "Some garrison we got," he jeered. "The commanding officer spends most of his time drinking and chasin' women and the rest of the time sleepin' off a drunk."

Jorge crossed the plaza toward Travis. "Let me handle him," he said to Travis.

"Let him talk. He's just looking for trouble."

Vince spat. "You soldiers oughta let *real* men take over here. Whyn't you scuttle off to the Rio Grande like the rest of the garrisons? Yuh ain't doin' a damned bit of good here."

"Hear him!" screamed a woman. "My husband was killed at the corrals, and my baby son was wounded by those cursed Apache while the soldiers played in the *cantinas*!"

"She is right," said a pock-faced man.

A crowd had begun to gather near Travis. They eyed him hotly. Jorge whispered to Travis. "I do not like the looks of this."

Hands rested on knives. Vince swaggered out from beneath the ramada. Then two men appeared from Simpson's *cantina* and walked toward Travis and Jorge. It was Mack Ellis and Baconora. They walked right through the center of the milling crowd, shoving the small Mexicans aside. Ellis grounded his musketoon as he reached Travis' side, and Baconora hefted his rifle. The crowd drew back a little. It was a rugged quartet they faced.

Vince came forward. "Well, Captain," he sneered. "What have you to say for the United States Army?"

"Keep quiet," said Baconora. "You always did talk too much, Vince."

"Let me get at him, sir," pleaded Ellis.

Travis looked at the crowd. They were angry, and they probably had a right to be. Travis had not seen a soldier of the town garrison since he had arrived in Santa Theresa; more of the townspeople began to drift toward the threatening crowd.

"We oughta run all these damned soldier boys outta *our* town," said Vince.

Baconora laughed. "Listen to him," he jeered. "Been run out of every town in New Mexico, and now he calls Santa Theresa *his* town."

"I wonder what his angle is," said Mack Ellis quietly to Travis.

"I don't know, Sergeant, but he's got these people eating out of his dirty hands."

Hoofs thudded on the hard caliche of the plaza, and a dusty horseman, followed by half a dozen others, appeared near the corrals. The leader was Captain

Charles Cass. His face was reddened by the sun and sweat streaked through the dust coating it.

"Where's he been?" called out Vince. "Chasing 'Pache squaws through the brush?"

Cass swung a thick leg over his saddle and dropped to the ground. He walked toward Travis with the stiff-legged walk of a weary man. He saluted casually. "I didn't expect to see you here, Walker," he said.

"I learned there had been a raid here."

Cass nodded. "I pursued some of the Apache."

Travis looked beyond the big officer. "With *six* men?"

Cass waved his arm. "It was all I needed to teach those filthy beggars a lesson."

"What lesson?" called out Vince.

Cass turned. "Armstrong!" he yelled. "On the double!"

A lanky trooper came forward carrying a heavy sack.

"Open it," said Cass.

Armstrong cut the drawstring. Two rounded objects thudded to the ground like heavy melons.

"Jesus," said Ellis. "Apache heads."

"Yeah," said Baconora dryly. "And wimmen's heads to boot."

"Squaws!" said Jorge.

Travis looked down at the bloody, dusty heads dotted with buzzing flies. "Get them out of sight," he said thickly.

Armstrong casually picked them up by the hair and dropped them into the sack. The crowd was terribly quiet. Cass took off his Kossuth hat and slapped the dust from his clothing. "We caught them near the big dry wash three miles from here. Dropped them as neat as you please at no less than one hundred and fifty yards, offhand."

"Were there any warriors with them?" asked Travis.

"No. Why do you ask?"

"You would have never made it back here if there had been. What did you do with the bodies?"

Cass grinned. "Left them for the ants and the *zopilotes;* what else?"

Travis looked over the heads of the crowd toward the heat-hazy hills. "Cuchillo and his warriors will never rest until they find the man who killed those two squaws. God help him when they do."

Cass paled beneath the dust on his face. "They didn't see us close up, I'll warrant."

"They know you were soldiers. At least they know you were wearing uniforms."

"Just what do you mean by that, sir?"

Travis eyed the big officer. "You figure it out, Cass. *You figure it out...*"

The crowd had begun to break up, drifting toward the *cantinas* and the shade of their homes. Vince had returned to his game of monte, but Travis could feel the little man's eyes studying him as he walked toward the Morris house.

Travis spoke over his shoulder. "Sergeant Ellis, rout out every man jack of this garrison. Have them line up at the *torreon.* Baconora, you take a ride toward the hills to see what Cuchillo is up to. Jorge, warn the people that they must stay close to their homes and have their weapons ready at all times."

"I thought I was in command here," protested Cass.

"You are—under me, Cass."

"I punished those raiders, didn't I?"

"You're lucky you got back at all. Thank God Cuchillo and his warriors were watching us come into town. If he had found those women and cut you off in the desert, you would have died a hellish death, Cass."

"I'm not afraid of Apache."

Travis turned as he reached the porch of the mayor's house. "I believe you, Cass. You're brave, but you're ten kinds of a damned fool."

"Take care how you talk!" blustered Cass.

Travis smiled thinly. "I haven't even begun to talk. I'd have you up for court-martial if we didn't need you."

"Well, thanks, damn you!"

Travis felt for a cigar and lit it. "You're damned lucky Cuchillo didn't decide to take the whole *placita* while he was running off those horses and mules."

"We were on duty."

"Where?" Travis eyed Cass through the smoke. "In the *cantinas* or the *casas de putas?*"

Cass raised a big freckled fist. "You go too far, Walker!"

Travis took the cigar from his mouth. "Go on into the house and cool off. Your wife is waiting for you."

The remark took Cass as though a six-pounder shot had hit him in the belly. "Evelyn? *Here?*"

Travis nodded. "I came in to see about that raid. Major Lester said she was to go along to see you."

Cass's pale eyes studied Travis. "Very touching," he said.

"It was her idea, Cass. I'm not so sure she thought it was a good idea when Cuchillo and some of his warriors sat their horses on the sand ridges and watched us go by."

There was no flicker of emotion in the big officer's eyes. It was almost as though he had said he had wished Cuchillo *had* gotten Evelyn.

Travis settled his hat on his head and took a drag at his cigar. "See you," he said briefly.

Cass watched Travis walk toward the *torreon*. Then he closed his big fists and spat deliberately on the ground where Travis had just walked.

———

THE LONG AFTERNOON had dragged by with nothing to break the monotony. Travis had inspected the little garrison. Some of the men were obviously suffering from hangovers. Travis had decided to assign First Sergeant Mack Ellis to the garrison. Ellis would keep the men in line if anyone could, and it was a cinch that Charlie Cass was so absorbed in his own pleasures he'd probably welcome the big noncom to take some of the responsibilities from his shoulders.

Baconora came in at dusk and reported to Travis. "Ain't much doing around here, Captain," he said. "Tracks seem all to head to the southwest, probably to those hills west of Fort Joslyn. It's my guess that Cuchillo might be aimin' to give the post some trouble."

Travis nodded. "Hit Santa Theresa, then hit Fort Joslyn. I wanted the major to either garrison the town *or* the fort, but not both."

Baconora whittled a fresh chew. "I found them bodies in the desert. Dumped them into a gully and covered them with rocks and brush. I hope to God the coyotes don't drag 'em out again. If Cuchillo saw what Cass had done, I wouldn't give a used chew of this tobacco for his chances of leaving New Mexico alive."

Baconora stuffed the chew into his mouth and worked it into pliability. He grinned. "Jesus, what a ball they'd have with that big bastard once they got at him with their knives and their little torture fires."

Travis looked out toward the dim hills. "Keep an eye open tonight, Baconora. Get some food, and then keep on patrol. Maybe Jorge Valadez will spell you."

"You don't think Cuchillo will hit 'em here again, do you?"

"I don't know anything except that Santa Theresa is one big target for Cuchillo any time he feels like hitting it. There isn't too much he can do at Fort Joslyn except make nuisance raids and cut off anyone who leaves the post. But here, he can strike whenever he pleases, and the raid he just made was just a token of what he can do."

"Yeah. Where can I find you if I need you?"

"At the Morris *casa*."

Baconora's reddish eyes studied Travis. "Yeah," he said

quietly. "I figured as much." He walked silently off into the darkness.

Travis walked about the wide plaza. Sentries were on duty here and there. A cool finger of breeze felt Travis wet forehead as he stood near the corrals. A mule bawled noisily. Somewhere behind Travis in the *cantina*, a guitarist softly strummed away. It seemed so peaceful, but the night was like a great sleeping tiger, soft of fur, with rounded pads on all four feet. But that tiger could easily awaken and bare fangs and sharp claws from the softness to rend and tear.

Travis walked toward the Morris *casa*. He had been invited to stay the night at the mayor's house and to have dinner there. He hadn't seen Charlie Cass all afternoon, nor had he seen Evelyn. He wondered how those two lovable people, man, and wife, had been getting along. He grinned to himself.

Travis looked toward the old *torreon*. He could see a steeple-hatted Mexican on guard atop the structure. Two men stood outside Jonas Simpson's *cantina*. One of them was Charles Cass, but it took a moment for Travis to recognize the other one until the man lit a lucifer to ignite his pipe. It was then he recognized the saturnine face of Ben load, badly marked by the healing scars of the burns he had suffered when Travis had knocked him into the fire at Fort Joslyn.

Travis stepped behind a building buttress and watched the two men. Joad was talking swiftly, and as he did so, Cass nodded again and again. Then Cass clapped Joad on the back and walked toward the Morris *casa*. Joad lounged into the *cantina*.

Travis rubbed his jaw. It seemed that everywhere he looked, he saw enemies. He cursed himself for stopping at Fort Joslyn and then realized his foolishness. If the fort had not been there, he might have been killed by the Mimbrenos and even now be drying out in the desert. Then, too, he might not have met Theresa, and she alone was worth all the troubles he was exposed to. Again he had the impulse to get her and take her away from Santa Theresa, but he knew the futility of it. Sink or swim, live or die, their lives were immutably bound with the course of events that would take place at Santa Theresa.

———

THE CANDLELIGHT GLISTENED SOFTLY on the polished furniture in the dining room of the Morris *casa*. It also glistened as softly but with infinitely more warmth on the bared shoulders of Theresa Morris and Evelyn Cass. Charlie Cass was feeling his liquor again, but his eyes were constantly on Theresa rather than on his wife. It was a good thing that James Morris could not see what was going on at his table.

Travis leaned back in his chair. Now and then, the level gaze of Evelyn Cass's great eyes met his. She had been drinking wine steadily all through the course of the meal, and her clear skin was flushed and delicately dewed with sweat. In contrast, Theresa looked as cool as the night wind sweeping across the desert. She studiously avoided Charles' gaze, but Travis knew she disliked his scrutiny of her. Charlie Cass had a way of undressing a woman with his eyes, and most women could feel the sensation.

James Morris sipped at his wine. "It is a pleasure to have two such gallant soldiers at my table," he said. "Santa Theresa is fortunate indeed to have such defenders."

"Thank you," said Travis.

Charlie Cass emptied his wineglass and quickly refilled it. "Don't worry about Santa Theresa, or *Theresa* for that matter, while I'm here, Morris."

Evelyn slowly turned her head to look at Theresa, then at her husband, then at Theresa again. "I'm sure Charles would defend *any* woman to the death," she said.

Charlie turned to look at her, and there was pure hate in his pale eyes. "Including *you,* my dear?"

Evelyn Cass looked away from him. "I should hope so, Charles dear."

Angelique bustled in to clear the table. Travis leaned toward Theresa. "It is quite warm in here. Would you like to walk on the patio?"

She smiled. "If it is all right with Grandfather."

The old man seemed lost in a world of his own. "Yes," he said. "I am retiring soon. It has been a long day."

Travis stood up and drew back Theresa's chair, damnably conscious of Evelyn's hot eyes on him. Charlie Cass was refilling his wine glass. "Nice place you have here, Morris. Quite an inheritance for someone." He looked at Theresa.

Theresa flushed. She adjusted her mantilla over her comb and hair. James Morris brushed back his white hair. "Yes. It all goes to Theresa. The house and money. Mining properties here and in Mexico. Then, too, there is the large house in Santa Fe, which I own, as well as other properties there and in Albuquerque. She will want for nothing when I am gone."

"A fine dowry for the lucky man," said Cass.

Morris seemed a little annoyed. "Help me to my room, Angelique," he said. "You must excuse me, my guests."

Angelique helped the old man from the room. Evelyn Cass looked at Theresa. "You're very fortunate," she said. "Some lucky man will live comfortably for the rest of his days with you." Her eyes seemed to drift toward Travis.

Charles hiccupped. "Yes," he said thickly. "And Travis Walker might make it yet."

Travis turned, but he felt the gentle pressure of Theresa's hand on his arm. "Please," she whispered.

Travis guided her to the door and into the hall. He shut the door behind him, hearing Cass's loud laughter.

Theresa looked up at Travis. "That man frightens me," she said.

"Don't worry about him. I taught him one lesson."

"Do you think it was a permanent one?"

Travis opened the door at the end of the hall and felt the cool night breeze blow in from the patio. "I can always do it again."

"You're worried, aren't you?"

"A little."

"Don't avoid the question, Travis. Tell me."

He closed the door behind him and took her by the arm. "Yes, I am. I don't like conditions at the fort, and I like them a lot less here in Santa Theresa. I'd like to get you out of here, Theresa, but it is impossible until we meet and defeat Cuchillo."

"If you *do* defeat him. What if you don't?"

He closed her soft mouth with a kiss. "You know what will happen. One way or another, we must defeat him."

She looked up at the stars. "I would not leave here anyway," she said quietly. "I will not leave my grandfather nor the people I have known most of my life."

They paced to the west end of the patio. A night bird chirped from the clinging vines. It seemed so quiet and peaceful there.

"Why did she come here?" asked Theresa.

"Mrs. Cass? Why to see her husband."

The girl looked up at Travis. "I don't think so. There is no love between those two. They are bound together by a marriage which certainly was never formed in the eyes of God."

He passed a hand across her smooth cheek. "Little wise one," he said softly. "Let's talk about us."

"What is she to you, Travis?"

"Nothing."

"The way she *looks* at you!"

"She looks that way at many men."

"She does not look at her husband like that."

Travis shrugged. "I'm sorry for the two of them."

There was a faint silvery touch of moonlight in the eastern sky. The night wind whispered through the vines and the leaves of the shade trees. Travis drew her close and kissed her. A door opened, and yellow lamplight flooded into the patio, revealing Travis and Theresa to Evelyn Cass. Evelyn walked toward the room she shared with her husband. She turned to look squarely at them. "Good night," she said. The door closed behind her.

"It's getting late," said Travis. "Look—there is Angelique."

The serving woman had opened the hall door and stood there, looking at them. "It is late, *senorita*!" she called.

"My *duenna*," said Theresa. She laughed softly. "As though I weren't safe with you, Travis."

"Don't be so sure. I only have so much resistance."

She touched his face. "There will be a day when I will not expect to meet such resistance." She walked swiftly toward her room on the north side of the patio.

"Wait!" called Travis.

She shook her head. She nodded to Angelique, and the serving woman followed Theresa into her room. The door clicked shut behind them.

Travis lit a cigar and walked toward the main body of the house. He could see yellow lamplight in Cass's room. Evelyn had brought a gown with her, and she had worn it for one purpose, to excite Travis that night. But she had not reckoned on Theresa. Travis was almost willing to admit he was glad that Theresa had been between him and Evelyn, for the older woman was certainly more than just attractive.

Travis opened the hall door and paced down the cool hall. The dining-room door was ajar, and he heard the smash of glass. He looked in. Charlie Cass lay with his arms and head on the white tablecloth amid a litter of broken wine glasses and scattered bits of food. The wine had stained the cloth blood red, as though Cass had bled his life away as he lay there.

Travis shook his head in disgust. He shut the door and walked to the great outer door of the *casa*. He took his hat from a hook and walked outside. The moon was silvering the western slopes of the mountains to the east. It was as quiet as the grave—a rather gruesome simile, thought Travis, as he walked about the plaza.

The sentries were still on duty. Here and there, a seraped Mexican stood at his post. There were few lights on in the town other than those of the *cantinas,* which never seemed to shut their doors.

Sergeant Ellis appeared out of the dimness like a great genie. "Good evening, sir," he said.

"How does it go, Sergeant?"

"Quiet, sir—too damned quiet, begging your pardon, Captain."

"Where's Baconora?"

"Prowling about somewhere. He gives me the creeps the way he moves about. One minute you see him, the next minute he's gone. I'll swear to God, sir, that man moves quieter than an Apache."

Travis leaned back against the warm wall behind him. "You don't have much use for him, do you, Ellis?"

"I didn't say that, sir!"

"You didn't have to."

The big noncom studied Travis. "I didn't like the way he spoke to Mrs. Cass, is all, sir."

"He spoke the truth."

"The lady was frightened enough as it was."

"I won't argue about that."

"Will she stay here, sir? That is, I mean, she won't go back to the fort with you tomorrow?"

Travis relit his cigar. "I hope not," he said.

"It's dangerous enough for men out there, sir."

Travis puffed his cigar into life. "Yes," he said quietly.

Evelyn Cass could make it damned dangerous for any man in Fort Joslyn or Santa Theresa. He remembered what Clint Vaughn had said about her: *Evelyn Cass is quite a woman. In fact, she's all woman, with most of the faults and few of the virtues, but she can still turn the eye of every man on this post except two.* One of those men had been her husband and the other Major Lester.

Travis looked at the first sergeant. The man was carrying a bitch of a crush on Evelyn Cass. Maybe Mack Ellis was the type of man she should have married instead of her drinking, skirt-chasing husband.

"Well, good night, Sergeant," said Travis.

"Good night, sir."

Travis walked back to the Morris *casa*. He rapped on the door until old Esteban opened it. Travis walked to the dining room. Charlie Cass still lay there, his face pasted to the cloth by liquor slops. The candles guttered and flared in the draft from the open door. A vigil light also shone before the carved wooden *Santo* in the wall-niche. The impassive Indian-looking face of the crude carving seemed to be studying the drunken man who lay across the table.

Travis shook his head and walked to the patio. There were no lights. He walked across to the room which had been allotted to him on the west side of the patio. He walked into it and lit a candle. It was a big room and clean as a barracks just before Saturday inspection. The tiled floor had been waxed and polished, and the walls had been freshly whitewashed, while coarse *gerga* cloth had been hung along the lower parts of the walls to protect the clothing against contact with the whitewash.

Travis stripped to his drawers and washed himself. He combed back his thick hair and walked to the window which opened to the west. He unlatched the thick shutters and let them swing open so he could see the distant moon-washed hills. There was no sign of life on the desert west of the town.

Travis was about to get into bed when he thought of something. Cuchillo might raid again, and the next time he raided, he might go full out. Travis pulled on his trousers, placed his boots close by the side of the bed and put his gun belt, and holstered Colt on the chair beside the bed. He blew out the candle and lay down on the bed, lacing his fingers behind his neck, staring at the ceiling, thinking of Theresa.

CHAPTER THIRTEEN

Maybe it was the cool breeze flowing through the open window that awakened Travis; maybe it was the distant wailing of a coyote; maybe it was a subtle warning deep in the subconscious. He opened his eyes and looked up at the dim ceiling. He shivered a little in the cold and reached for the thick blanket which was folded at the foot of the big bed. Then he raised his head. There was nothing but the usual night sounds, but he still felt as though something was warning him.

He swung his legs over the side of the bed, wincing as his bare feet struck the cold tiles. He pulled on his socks and boots and took his Colt from its holster. He padded to the window and looked out upon the desert. The moon was gone, but there seemed to be an unnatural and eerie light on the wastelands. Travis pulled the shutters to and placed the bar across the rests.

He walked to the door and opened it, stepping out onto the patio. The breeze rustled the shade trees and vines, and he could hear the wash of water against the sides of the fountain bowl. The odors of flowers were mingled with those of sage and mesquite from the desert, wafted across the walls by the ceaseless wind.

There were no lights visible. Travis shrugged and turned to go back to bed, but something again arrested him. He walked softly toward the south side of the patio where the Cass room was. There was no light or sound from it, and the door was closed. He walked to the eastern side of the patio. All the doors were closed.

Travis rubbed his jaw. He felt like a damned fool, prowling about in the dimness. He walked up the northern side of the patio. Then he saw that Theresa's door was ajar. He was about to pass toward his own room when he heard what he thought was harsh breathing and, a moment later, the ripping of cloth. Travis pushed the door open. "Theresa!" he called out.

There was a muffled sound and then a grunt. "Theresa!" he called again. He pushed the door wide open. Then, intermingled with the perfumed feminine odor of the room, he caught an odor he recognized at once, the sour, clinging, and acrid sweat odor of a man. He knew damned well who it was, Charles Cass. There was a muffled curse from the darkness, and then Theresa screamed.

Travis lit a match, and, in the flickering light, he saw the girl standing in a corner of the room, holding the shreds of her nightdress about her body. Her eyes were wide, and her dark, unbound hair hung across her face.

Charles Cass stood in the center of the room, staring at Travis. He was dressed only in his trousers. His broad face was dewed with sweat, mingled with trickling blood from a number of deep scratches. His eyes were glazed, and his mouth hung open, a trickle of spittle coming from it. The match seared Travis' fingers at the same time Charlie Cass charged.

Cass butted into Travis with all his weight, driving him back against the door, which smashed shut behind him. The Colt flew from Travis' hand as his head hit the door. Cass stood there, legs wide apart, hammering home vicious blows that held Travis against the door. He planted both hands on the sweaty, bloody face of the big officer, pushing up on his palms, clawing at Cass's nose and eyes with his fingertips. Cass gasped and fell back in time to receive a left to the mouth that drove him back against the end of the big wooden bed.

Cass cursed as he charged again. Travis moved back, covering his belly against the triphammer blows of the heavier man. He fell over a stool and staggered sideways, just as Cass threw a sledgehammer right which skinned past Travis' head and glanced from the wall. Cass emitted a hoarse animal-like scream. Travis swung his left arm in a backhander, the edge of his hand striking hard at the base of Cass's neck, driving the big man against the wall.

Cass slid to the floor and instantly grappled for Travis' legs, dumping him sideways. The sweat-stinking officer rolled atop Travis and clawed at his face. His breath was sour with liquor, and he fought in a frantic way, utilizing every dirty trick he knew, but he was beginning to tire. The alcohol which had sparked him was now turning against him.

Travis brought a knee up into Cass's groin. The man grunted in pain. He raised himself, and Travis drove in short, chopping blows to his face until he rolled free from Travis and into a patch of dim light on the floor. He saw the Colt close at hand and grabbed for it, but Travis was too fast. He planted a boot heel on Cass's wrist and ground down as hard as he could. The big man cursed.

Travis stepped back and, as Cass sat up, drove a boot heel home to his jaw, smashing him back against the foot of the bed. Cass lay still. Travis reached for the Colt.

"No, Travis!" screamed Theresa.

The killing urge suddenly left him. He thrust the Colt beneath the waistband of his trousers, then handed Theresa a blanket from the bed. She wrapped herself in it. Travis lit a lamp. He picked up a pitcher from the washstand and dumped the contents over the battered mess of a man on the floor. Cass gasped and spluttered. He got to his feet and raised his big fists.

"Cass," said Travis thinly. "I should have killed you. If you make one move, I *will* kill you."

Theresa moved close to Travis. "I was asleep. I felt his hands on me and awoke to look up into his face. He is mad with liquor."

"It's more than that," said Travis.

Cass wiped the blood from his face. "Who are you to talk?" he asked thickly.

"What do you mean?"

Cass laughed. He looked at Theresa. "The whole damned post knows about him. Travis Walker, the *bravo*! Yeah, the lover!"

"I don't understand," said Theresa quietly.

The reddened eyes turned to look at Travis. "Took advantage of me being gone on duty to dally with my wife. Don't deny it, Walker! She was seen leaving your quarters. Ben load's woman told him, and he told me."

Travis flushed as Theresa looked at him.

Cass walked unsteadily to the door. He turned. "If you don't think there is something going on between him and my wife, Theresa, maybe you can remember how she kept looking at him during dinner tonight." He closed the door behind him.

Theresa walked away from Travis. "Well?"

"The woman came into my quarters, Theresa."

"Then you don't deny it?"

"She came to my quarters, and I sent her away."

Theresa turned away and rested a hand against the wall. "Thank you for saving me from him."

"Is that all you have to say?"

She turned to face him. "Yes. Please leave."

He walked toward her and held out his arms. She turned away again. "Please let me alone," she said.

"Let me explain."

"It isn't necessary."

Travis picked up his Colt. "Good night, then," he said. She nodded.

Travis walked outside and shut the door behind him.

Theresa Morris threw herself on the bed, and sobs racked her body as she beat on the covers with her small fists...

Charles Cass knelt by the fountain, splashing water over his face and upper body. Travis stopped behind him. "Get out of here the first thing in the morning," he said. "If I so much as see you around this house, I'll kill you."

Travis walked to his room and closed the door behind him. He took a cigar and lit it, dropping into a big armchair. There was hell to pay now. He felt sick inside. He closed his eyes and rested his head back against the chair. Damn Charlie Cass and his wife. They had been nothing but trouble for him ever since he had arrived at Fort Joslyn.

———

A COLD EARLY morning wind swept across Santa Theresa. Travis left his room with his gear and walked across the patio, hoping to get out of the house without seeing anyone, but he was doomed to disappointment. The door of the Cass room swung open, and Evelyn Cass appeared, wearing her riding habit. "Travis!" she called out.

He stopped and turned to face her. She came up to him. "Are we going back today?"

"Evelyn, I don't give a damn what you do."

She studied him. "I think I know what happened last night. Charlie got a terrible beating. He left at dawn."

"Where did he go?"

"I don't know, and I don't really care."

"Nice," said Travis dryly.

"Take me back with you."

"You've got me in enough trouble now."

"What do you mean?"

He eyed her coldly. "You know damned well what I mean."

"Charlie said something about it when he came in last night. He says he won't have anything more to do with me."

"What can you expect?"

She flushed. "Do you think it has been easy living with that animal?"

"You haven't done so badly yourself, Evelyn."

She stepped back. "Damn you! I'm glad I came to your quarters. I'm glad I started a scandal about you. Most of all, I'm glad I've wrecked your chances with that young bitch."

Travis's right hand caught her full across the cheek. She staggered back with the blow and quickly raised her hand to the reddening flesh. There were tears in her big eyes. Travis walked away from her and did not look back.

Jorge Valadez met Travis near the *torreon*. "There is a message from Cuchillo," he said quietly.

"What?"

Jorge turned and whistled. A peon, dressed in ragged and dirty white, shuffled forward, taking off his battered hat. "This is Timoteo Castro," said Jorge. "A muleteer. He does not speak the *Ingles*."

"What does he have to say?"

"He says he was in the sand hills trying to find one of his mules when he was surrounded by Apache. Cuchillo Rojo prevented them from killing him. Cuchillo, who speaks Spanish well, told Timoteo the message he wanted to be taken to *Alcalde Morris*."

"Keep talking."

Timoteo began to speak in a trembling voice. "Cuchillo says he is not afraid of the soldiers. That he is the greatest of war chiefs, that men tremble when he rides the earth."

"Go on!" snapped Travis.

Timoteo swallowed. "He says there are certain conditions which must be met if he is to leave Santa Theresa alone. He wants twenty horses and ten mules. He wants arms and ammunition, food and blankets." The little muleteer's voice trailed off.

"Go on," prompted Jorge.

The big brown eyes lifted to look at Travis. "There is one other thing, *mi Capitan.*"

"Go on, damn it!"

"Cuchillo has two squaws, he says, but he wants another. The granddaughter of our esteemed mayor."

Travis gripped Timoteo by the shoulder. "You're sure?"

There were tears in the big brown eyes as Travis gripped harder. "*Si! Si!* I would not lie. I was glad to escape with my life."

Travis looked at Jorge. "Cuchillo has seen Theresa?"

"Yes. In times of peace, the Apache came here to trade and barter. Cuchillo has seen her many times."

Timoteo nodded. "He knows her well."

Travis rubbed his jaw. "The message was for the mayor. I may as well tell him."

Travis went to the big house with Jorge while Timoteo squatted ON the porch. The old man was seated in his big chair when Travis and Jorge entered. Travis told him of what had happened.

James Morris fingered his ornate cane. "Jorge, tell Tomaso Quintana, Guillermo Castillo, Carlos Martinez and Jethro Arnold to come here at once."

"Yes, my mayor." Jorge hurried from the room.

"They are the leading men of the town," said James Morris. "We will decide what to do."

"There is only one thing to do—tell Cuchillo to go to hell!"

The old man raised his head. "I am the mayor," he said. "I cannot make decisions of my own without consulting the representatives of the people."

"Jesus," said Travis softly. He walked to a window and looked out into the sunlit patio. Theresa was cutting flowers and placing them in a basket. The sun shone on her glossy dark hair.

The four men came breathlessly into the huge room. Quintana, Castillo, and Martinez were typical New Mexicans, while Jethro Arnold was a tall, gangling Anglo whose bones seemed to protrude through his flesh. His Adam's apple slid continuously up and down his long turkey-like throat.

James Morris explained the situation to the four men and then patiently awaited their decision. Arnold was the first to speak. "Tell him to go to hell," he said in a nasal Yankee twang. "We've got guns and men who know how to use them. We've got soldiers here, too. The *torre* is now strong again. No Apache in his right mind will buck up against determined men shooting from behind thick walls. What do you say, Captain?"

Travis nodded. "Cuchillo is bluffing."

Tomaso Quintana wet his lips. "No, he is not," he said quietly. "He has already killed some of our people. He has many warriors in the hills, well-armed and well-mounted. He has been but playing with us up until now. He means business, my mayor."

"So?" asked Travis.

"Let him have what he wants."

"Including Theresa?"

Tomaso flushed. "I did not say that."

"Guillermo Castillo," said Morris quietly.

Castillo was a plump man with darting eyes. "I agree with Tomaso Quintana," he said. "The soldiers will be of little help. Cuchillo can raid us at will. The girl is but a girl."

"Would you send your own granddaughter, Guillermo?" asked Jethro harshly.

Guillermo smiled. "Cuchillo does not want *her*," he said.

"Carlos Martinez?" asked Morris.

Martinez was a big man, lean and strong-looking, with a mahogany face with the look of a hawk upon it. "Fight!" he said loudly. "To the last wall! To the last cartridge! To the last man! Are we to pay tribute to that half-naked savage? We are men of men! Fight, I say!"

Morris bowed his head. "We can give him horses, mules, ammunition, guns, and supplies. I cannot give up my granddaughter."

"It is for the common good," said Tomaso Quintana.

"After all," said Guillermo Castillo, spreading out his hands, "she *is* part Opata, is she not, my mayor?"

"That is true," said Tomaso.

"Be quiet!" snapped Jorge.

Morris looked toward Travis. "I am an old man. There is no use in deluding myself otherwise. I can no longer make decisions. It is time for a younger man to take over. Captain Travis, will you meet and talk with Cuchillo under a flag of truce?"

"Him?" sneered Guillermo Castillo. "What has he to do with us?"

"He may be the means of saving your miserable bodies, if not your misbegotten souls," said Carlos Martinez. He raised a big hand over the head of Castillo. Castillo shrank away from the angry man.

Tomaso Quintana wet his thick lips. "There is no harm in the captain talking with Cuchillo, of course, providing Cuchillo will meet him."

Jorge held out a hand. "Timoteo Castro told me Cuchillo would come into the town to see our mayor."

Tomaso rubbed his throat. "Perhaps we could ambush him."

Martinez laughed. "*We?* You'll be under your bed when Cuchillo comes into our *placita*. Have you the courage, you squeaking mouse, to face Cuchillo, much less plunge a blade into his back?"

"It was but a suggestion," muttered Quintana.

Jethro Arnold paced back and forth like an ungainly stork. "Let Captain Walker meet and talk with Cuchillo. But the Apache must have a safe conduct."

"Pah!" said Guillermo Castillo.

James Morris thudded the tip of his cane against the floor. "So be it. You will do this for us, Captain?"

"I will be glad to. But suppose he will not negotiate? Suppose he insists upon having Theresa?"

"Theresa shall not go," said Martinez.

They all looked at each other, then at the blind mayor. Travis beckoned to Jorge Valadez. "Send Timoteo back to Cuchillo. Tell him to tell the chief that I will meet him at the edge of town on the road to the north when the sun is at its highest. I will bear no arms, and neither must he. Will I need an interpreter?"

"Baconora could interpret Apache, but it will not be necessary, for Cuchillo speaks Spanish well."

"That's more than I can do. You will come along to help out, perhaps?"

"I would go, but Baconora is your man."

"Yes, I think so. Besides, he knows the ways of those people better than any of us. He would be of great help."

"I will tell Timoteo and then go to find Baconora."

"It will do no good," said Tomaso Quintana in a doleful voice. "We are under the thumbs of the Apache."

"Shut up, you vermin!" roared Carlos Martinez.

Travis walked to the window again and looked out at the beautiful young woman he loved. There was a cold feeling in the pit of his belly as he looked at her and thought of the demand of Cuchillo Rojo.

————

BACONORA LOOKED up at the cloud-dotted sky. "It's about time," he said.

Travis nodded. He unbuckled his gun belt and handed it to Jorge, then unsnapped his carbine from its sling and gave it also to the Mexican. Baconora had already removed his weapons.

"Can he be trusted?" asked Travis.

"I wouldn't be going out there without weapons if he couldn't be," said the scout dryly.

"Seems strange a savage like him can be trusted in such matters."

Baconora filled his pipe and lit it. "They have their points of honor. Besides, it's to his advantage to talk with you to try and get his way. He doesn't want to lose any of his warriors if he can grease his way into what he wants."

Some of the townspeople watched Travis curiously as he mounted his sorrel. Others of them stood on rooftops or atop the *torreon*. "There is dust on the road, Captain!" called one of the men on the *torreon*.

Travis uncased his field glasses and focused them on two approaching horsemen. They were Apache, and one of them was Cuchillo Rojo. There was no mistaking the matted headdress and the two yellow-stained horns protruding from it. "Let's go," said Travis to Baconora.

They rode slowly out upon the rutted road. Two hundred yards from the last building, Travis drew rein and waited for the two Mimbrenos to approach. There was no sign of weapons about them, but Travis knew they usually carried a short curved *besh*, or reserve knife, in their breechcloths.

The two warriors drew in their horses fifty yards from Travis and Baconora. Baconora held up a hand, palm toward the two warriors. Cuchillo responded the same way. The two Mimbrenos rode forward and sat their horses fifteen feet from the two white men. Travis studied the chief with interest. He was of medium height but had the chest and shoulders of a wrestler. His mouth was thin, with the corners drawn down, while his hooked nose gave him the look of a predatory animal. His eyes were large, with a basilisk look about them. A four-stranded medicine cord hung about his neck, strung with turquoise, petrified wood, rock crystal, eagle down, hawk, and bear claws. Travis knew four-stranded medicine cords were rare among the Apache and held great power for the wearer.

"How are you, my brother?" asked Baconora.

Cuchillo did not answer. His hard eyes studied Travis from head to foot.

Travis was annoyed. "Tell him we did not come out here to sweat under the sun."

Baconora spoke swiftly in slurring, guttural Apache.

The hard eyes held Travis' eyes. "I speak Spanish," said the chief. "Does this white eagle speak it also?"

Travis nodded. "Well enough, Cuchillo Rojo."

"It is well. You have heard my demands. Why have you come out here to talk?"

"Because we do not intend to meet your demands."

"So? What is there to stop me from taking the town and everything in it?"

"The soldiers at Fort Joslyn."

The bluff did not work. There was a trace of amusement in the chief's voice as he spoke again. "So? They do not dare leave their walls and come out into the open to fight Cuchillo Rojo. I would sweep them to the Rio Grande like the flash floods of the high mountains."

"The chief talks big," said Travis quietly.

Cuchillo slapped a hand against his bare chest. "I own this country and everything in it. Fort Joslyn and Santa Theresa are mine. Go back into the town, white eagle, and have my supplies and the woman brought out here. I will give you until sundown."

"No," said Travis.

Cuchillo raised his big head. "There is nothing you can do to stop me. I have killed your messengers. I have run off your horses and mules. I have stopped you from using the roads. There are no more soldiers coming here. There are no soldiers between here and the Colorado. This I know. You cannot stay here, and you cannot escape. It is up to Cuchillo Rojo to decide what to do with you."

"You talk like the night wind in the mountains."

The mahogany-hued face tightened. The Mimbreno thrust out a clenched hand. "You have until sundown!"

Baconora puffed at his pipe. "Supposing we give you the supplies only?"

The proud head came up, and the eyes seemed to spark. "I want the supplies and the woman, all! *All*!"

Travis yawned. "There is a cannon at Fort Joslyn," he said. "If you attack us, Cuchillo Rojo, you will all die."

The chief spat into the road. "The white eagle has not been to his fort for some hours," he said harshly. "Perhaps he had better find out what has happened there before he threatens Cuchillo Rojo."

A cold feeling surged through Travis as he eyed the Mimbreno.

Baconora spoke out of the corner of his mouth. "He isn't pulling our legs, Captain. He's been up to some deviltry in the past few hours."

Cuchillo looked at the hills. "My warriors are ready for battle," he said. "Usen is on our side. Stenatliha, the mother of warriors, will be with us in the battle. You have until sundown, white eagle. Remember. *Yadalanh!*" He turned his appaloosa and rode off, followed by his companion.

Baconora tamped down the tobacco in his pipe. "Well?"

"He knows what he can do."

"Yeah. But he's got aces and kings, Captain."

"What the hell did you expect me to do? Give him the girl?"

"No, but how are you going to stop him from coming in and taking her?"

Travis turned his mount. As he did so, he saw a pillar of smoke rising to the south, about where Fort Joslyn was situated. Baconora took his pipe from his mouth. He whistled softly. "By Jesus," he said, "maybe Cuchillo wasn't bluffing after all."

There was a dusty courier in the plaza when Travis and Baconora returned. He saluted Travis. "Sir, there's hell to pay at the fort. Some Apache got close into the walls and set fire to the forage stacked behind the corrals and the quartermaster warehouse. Corporal Cole and five men were killed when they ran off the warriors and were ambushed. The major orders you back at once."

Travis nodded. "Can we get through?"

The trooper shrugged. "I didn't see a damned Apache on the way here, sir."

Travis rubbed his jaw. He looked up at the sun. Cuchillo wanted his answer by sundown, or there would be hell to pay in Santa Theresa as well as Fort Joslyn.

Baconora looked at Travis. "We can make it to the fort and be back here in plenty of time, Captain."

"Let's go!" snapped Travis. He hated the thought of leaving now, but he was sure Cuchillo wouldn't attack the town until he was positive his demands would not be met. Travis hailed a trooper. "Tell Captain Cass he is in charge. Have him tell the mayor that I will be back here before sundown."

No one is to leave town, and the guards are to be doubled. No man is to go about unless he is armed." "Yes, sir!"

The courier led the way out of the town. Travis looked back at the mayor's house. He wanted desperately to see Theresa before he left, but he knew his duty was first to Fort Joslyn and second to the people of Santa Theresa.

The smoke was drifting off when the three riders debouched from the sandy pass to look toward the post. "Looks like the fire is out," said the courier. "Yeh," said Baconora, "but look to the west." Dust was drifting up from a flat area a mile west of the fort, and sunlight glistened from bright metal.

"'Paches," said Baconora, "a whole Gawdammit mess of 'em, and they ain't out gathering cactus apples to make *hoosh*."

"There's dust at the post too, sir," said the courier. Dust spiraled up from near the gateway of the fort. A dozen troopers spurred their horses toward the Apache. An officer led them on a fine black.

"DeSantis!" said Travis. "Come on! Shake the dung!" They rode swiftly toward the post, but DeSantis and his men had too good a lead. Two hundred yards from the milling Apache, DeSantis drew his saber and yelled a command. The yelling troopers drew their pistols and sabers and shot forward into the dust, led by Nerval DeSantis seeking the glory trail.

The Apache parted before the onslaught of the troopers, letting them pass beyond the war party, and then the warriors closed in behind the troopers, cutting them off from the fort. "They've had it now," said Baconora. Dust coiled up from the beating of many hoofs. The sun glanced from deadly bright metal. Guns popped in the melee, and sabers rose and fell. The circling combatants moved farther and farther away from the fort until a deep swell in the desert hid them from view but did not hide the dust. Hoarse yells and shrill whooping were punctuated by the rattle of gunfire.

Travis drew rein a hundred yards from the fort. Troopers and infantrymen stood between the buildings with ready rifles and musketoons. The howitzer was manned and pointed toward the distant conflict. Major Lester stood to one side of it, bared sword in hand and Kossuth hat drawn tightly down to just above his eyes.

"Look!" said the courier.

A knot of hard-riding Apache appeared above the rise of the dip in the desert, racing toward the post like brown centaurs. Travis drew his carbine around to rest it on his pommel as he cocked and capped it. Baconora raised his head. "Best get inside," he said.

They rode toward the gateway. The Apache shot past the northern side of the fort. One of them hurtled something toward Travis and his two companions. Baconora jumped to one side as the rounded object thudded against the wall beside him.

"Jesus," said the trooper. He turned and retched violently.

Travis looked down at the dusty, bloody head of Norval DeSantis. The eyes were wide in the head as though not comprehending what had happened to him.

"He got his Gawdammit cavalry charge," said Baconora.

The Apache circled the post, yelling like furies. They raced across the knoll south of the fort and headed west toward the main body of warriors. Travis looked up to see Enos Lester flourish his sword. "Fire!" yelled the major.

A trooper jerked the lanyard. The friction tube sparked, and the brass howitzer belched flame and smoke. Then there was a grating, cracking sound and the roof of the warehouse collapsed. The major disappeared from sight inside the warehouse.

"Jesus God!" said Travis. "I knew that would happen."

The shot from the howitzer struck the desert floor a good fifty yards behind the yelling warriors, then bounded from sight amid the thick brush.

Baconora picked up the head which lay at his feet. He carried it into the quadrangle and snatched up a sack that lay over a railing. He covered the head and looked at Travis. "What the hell do I do with this now?"

Travis did not answer. He sprinted toward the warehouse. Clinton Vaughn and two men were trying to open the front door, which had been jammed by the collapse of the thick dirt roof. Vaughn looked back at Travis. Sweat dripped from his face. "Thank God a sane man has arrived," he said.

They pried the door open and walked into the dust-choked interior. A trooper lay beneath a beam, his sightless eyes staring at them. Another trooper sat back against the wall, nursing a shattered leg. Major Enos Lester lay across the broken trail of the howitzer, coated with thick dust. His sword had snapped at the hilt, but he still held the handle in a shaking hand. He turned to look at Travis. "Mr. Travis," he choked. "Take command, sir. I have been mortally injured in the service of my country, sir."

"Get him out of here," said Travis in disgust.

They carried the sagging form of the major to his quarters. Medical orderlies took care of the injured trooper while four men carried out the dead man. Clinton Vaughn leaned against the wall. "My God," he said. "You would never have believed it, Travis."

"Let's get a drink."

They walked across the sunlit quadrangle. Men still stood with ready weapons, but there was no sign of the Apache other than a dust wraith that drifted off before the wind.

Clint poured two big hookers. They downed them. "Tell me the details," said Travis quietly.

Clint wiped the sweat and dust from his face. "They fired the warehouse. I think they must have gotten close to the walls last night and hid themselves under blankets and sand until they had a chance to fire it. Corporal Cole and five men went after them and were cut down within sight of all of us. DeSantis bulled the major into letting him go after the Apache."

"I saw what happened," said Travis quietly.

Clint refilled his glass and downed the potent liquor. "What do we do now?"

"Cuchillo Rojo has demanded supplies, guns, and ammunition from the people of Santa Theresa. In return, he'll let the town alone."

"Why don't they let him have them?"

"There's more to it than that, Clint. He also wants Theresa Morris as his squaw."

Clint paled. "You're fooling me, Travis!"

"No."

"My God. How long has he given them?"

"Until sundown."

"You'll have to tell the major."

"I've got more than that to tell him. We should abandon this fort and garrison at Santa Theresa, instead."

"He has his orders."

"Yes, but he'd better damned well start making decisions to get himself out of this mess."

There was a rap at the door. "Come in," said Clint.

Kelligan, Major Lester's orderly, opened the door. His face was pale and drawn. "Sir," he said thickly to Travis, "you'd better come at once to the major's quarters."

"What's happened?"

"The major just blew out his brains, sir."

CHAPTER FOURTEEN

Martin Newkirk was standing in the major's quarters, holding a sheaf of papers in his hands, as Travis and Clint entered. His face was pale as he nodded toward the door that opened into the duplicate set of quarters on the far side of the hallway. "He's in there," he said quietly.

Travis opened the door. Major Lester lay across a roped trunk. His service pistol lay on the dusty floor below his hanging right hand. Blood had wormed its way around the corner of the trunk and made a rivulet on the floor. The major's head was hanging on the far side of the trunk. Travis looked about. The walls were hung with family pictures and pictures of the major in uniform at various stages of his forty years of service, from a fresh-faced cadet at the Academy to a picture which could not have been taken more than several years before.

Travis shut the door and walked into the major's quarters. Newkirk raised his head. "I came in here to see if he was all right. The old man seemed stunned and broken, as though he had suffered a terrible blow. His very face sagged. He looked at me as though he had never seen me before and asked me what I wanted. I brought his attention to these orders I have in my hands. Then he said a very curious thing..."

"Go on," prompted Travis.

"He said he knew I had found out about him and that there was no use in his carrying on the masquerade. He asked me to wait here, and then he walked into these quarters across the hall. A moment later, I heard the report of his pistol. I looked in and saw that he was dead and sent Kelligan to tell you, Captain."

"What are those orders?"

Newkirk wet his dry lips. "They had been sent to Major Lester by Colonel Canby, dated June sixteenth of this year, ordering him to abandon Fort Joslyn, to remove his command and all government property to Fort Craig. In addition, he was to afford military protection for the inhabitants of Santa Theresa who wished to evacuate the town and travel to the Rio Grande. The orders contain an appendix to the effect that the major must declare martial law and order the evacuation of Santa Theresa, or the government would not be responsible for the safety of the inhabitants."

Travis stared at the adjutant. "Did you know about this before?"

"No. The orders were kept in the major's private file. It always seemed peculiar to me that we at Fort Joslyn were left out here on the edge of nowhere when all the other posts were abandoned. The major seemed to be holding something back from me."

"He sure was," said Clint dryly. "Maybe he held it back just *too* long."

Martin Newkirk took off his spectacles. "Captain Travis, do you remember me remarking about the major's order for you to remain here?"

"Yes."

"He had no right to do so. Included in this sheaf of orders was one which was sent to Major Lester a week or so before you got here. He had specific orders to speed you on your way to Fort Craig and thence to Santa Fe. There was also a peremptory order for him to follow his instructions as laid down in the preceding order of June sixteenth and a request for an immediate reply as to why he had not complied with those orders."

"Jesus," breathed Clint. "Why did he conceal those orders?"

Martin Newkirk wiped his glasses and replaced them on his nose. "I think I can guess why," he said quietly. "Major Lester knew how he stood in the department. He knew there was little chance of his ever receiving any type of field command again. He would be relegated to paperwork again, as he had always been. Perhaps he thought he would establish a reputation as a field soldier and eventually get his regiment or brigade."

"But the man was incapable of commanding in the field," said Clint. "Why would he deliberately seek such duty?"

"I don't really know," said the adjutant. "The major probably felt that he had been a failure all during his forty years of service and perhaps thought he might redeem himself, although he probably knew it was a hopeless task. Still, he was like a dog in the manger, fighting to save what rank he had."

Travis nodded. "You've hit it there, Newkirk."

"What are your orders, sir?" asked Newkirk.

Clint nodded. "Your whole staff is here, Captain."

Clint's words were like a dash of icy water on Travis. He had forgotten that the three of them were all that was left of the original complement of officers at Fort Joslyn. Major Lester had died by his own hand in disgrace; Ken Carlie had been shot to death by Travis as a traitor; Norval DeSantis had died in a mad charge against the Mimbrenos; Charles Cass was on detached duty in Santa Theresa and was up to God knew what deviltry.

"Well, Travis?" asked Clint.

Travis walked to the window and looked out upon the

sunny quadrangle. His duty was clear. Fort Joslyn should have been abandoned weeks ago. Perhaps now it was too late, but there was nothing he could do about that except to try his best to get his new command and the people of Santa Theresa back to the safety of Fort Craig. Then there was the matter of Cuchillo Rojo, who within the next five or six hours would close in on Santa Theresa, safe in the belief that he could override and despoil it with little or no opposition.

"We're waiting, sir," said Martin Newkirk.

Travis turned and eyed the two serious officers. He needed more shoulder straps, but these two would have to do. "Clint," he said, "you'll have to remove enough supplies from the warehouse to feed and clothe the command for at least two weeks. I don't have to go into detail. You're quartermaster and a damned practical man to boot. You'll know what to do.

"Martin, I want you to destroy all papers which are not important. Vital papers will be transported with us. When you have taken care of that, you will prepare the command for movement to Santa Theresa. Each man is to carry forty rounds, a full canteen, and nothing else beyond his rifle or musketoon. The civilians will strip down to essentials. Every civilian man on the post will march with the wagon guard. Do you think you can handle it? You're really a paperwork soldier, I'm afraid."

Clint grinned. "Don't worry about Marty, Travis. Beneath that scholarly exterior, there beats the heart of a real field soldier who hates paperwork and likes to hear the whistle of rifle balls and smell the stink of burned powder."

Travis bent his head. "Hop to it then. Shake the dung. I want to be in Santa Theresa no later than an hour before sundown."

Clint whistled softly. Newkirk wiped his brow. Travis took the orders from the adjutant's hand. "I'll take charge of these," he said.

The two officers saluted and left Travis alone. Travis scanned through the orders and mentally cursed the dead man in the next room. The egotistical little failure had almost doomed scores of people to death.

———

THE SUN WAS SLANTING low in the western sky when the convoy was made up in the post quadrangle. Sweating, cursing men finished up the last details. A great pile of furniture, blankets, tents, cases of supplies, and food-stuffs lay in the center of the quadrangle. A powder train had been laid just outside the quartermaster warehouse, and it led to several kegs of powder in the center of the heaped supplies buried under the collapsed roof.

The cavalry stood to horse, booted, and spurred. Minutes before, they had done the most painful duty a mounted soldier can perform—killing the horses and mules that were too weak for the forthcoming trip across the country to the Rio Grande.

Noncoms went from building to building, making sure nothing was left in them which could be used by the Apache. Axes rang as they cut through the spokes of extra wagons that could not be taken along. Like most men, the troopers seemed to have taken a perverse delight in the work of destruction after they had been told what material was to be taken along and what was to be destroyed to prevent its being used by the enemy. Now and then, the crashing of glass punctured the sharp strokes of the axes.

Travis walked along the line of barracks, taking the reports of the noncoms. "All clear, sir."

Travis reached the head of the column. He looked about the fort. Already it had a curiously lonely look about it. "Prepare to mount!" commanded Travis. "Mount!"

Troopers rose and smashed down into the leather of their saddles. Teamsters mounted to their wagon boxes.

"Forward ho!" called out Travis.

The advance detail of eight cavalrymen under a corporal moved out smartly. The lead wagons pulled out with a line of plodding infantrymen on each side. Dust roiled up from the big wheels as the whole line of wagons got into motion. Then followed the rear guard of a squad of infantrymen followed by a squad of cavalrymen. The rear guard cleared the gate. Clinton Vaughn looked at Travis. "Now?"

Travis nodded.

Clint pulled down the United States flag, folded it, and placed it in one of his saddlebags. He looked again at Travis.

"Fire the train," said Travis.

Clint knelt and broke off a match from a block he held in his hand. He touched off the powder train. It fizzed and sputtered, making swift speed along the heaped black line of powder. Travis took the block of matches and broke off a match. He lit the whole block and tossed it onto the oil-soaked pile of torn blankets and uniforms at one side of the big pile on the parade ground. It caught at once and began to chew into the pile of abandoned goods.

Travis and Clint mounted and rode past the two gate buildings. "How long?" asked Clint.

"Ten or fifteen minutes. The powder train is long enough."

"You don't think the Apache will attack the wagon train?"

"With the post abandoned before their eyes? They'll be in for loot before too long."

The bitter dust of the wagons' passage swirled about them. There was no sign of life out on the desert, but both men knew the Apache were out there, watching the curious actions of the white-eyes.

The two officers reached the rear guard and rode silently along with it. Travis looked back. A pall of smoke was rising against the late afternoon sky, dotted with fat sparks that winked in and out of the streamers of smoke.

There was a movement out in the mesquite, and a group of Apache rode slowly toward the fort. The wind shifted, and the smoke blew toward them. They increased their pace and, in a few minutes, were within fifty yards of the post.

"The powder train must have burned out," said Clint.

Travis shrugged. As he did so, there was a hollow booming noise, and a cloud of smoke and flame shot up into the air, dotted with fragments of supplies and adobe. A wash of gas and flame met the oncoming Apache and shut them from view. The explosion echoed faintly from the distant hills.

Clint Vaughn grinned. "Well," he said, "they got their damned loot, right in their greasy faces."

———

THE WAGONS GROUND into the plaza of Santa Theresa and came to a halt in swirling dust as the sun seemed to rest motionless atop the western hills. Clint Vaughn saluted Travis. "What are the captain's orders?"

"Find Captain Cass and notify him that I have taken command. Find quarters for the civilians we have brought with us. Incorporate the temporary garrison here into the troops who came with us. The wagons will be placed in a defensive square here in the center of the plaza. All horses and mules are to be placed in the town corral and a double guard placed over them."

A burst of drunken laughter came from a nearby *cantina*. Travis looked toward it. "Have Mr. Newkirk post a notice to the effect that Santa Theresa is now under martial law. As of sunset tonight, all *cantinas* will be closed to business until I order otherwise."

"Yes, sir."

Travis dismounted. "I'll go to see the mayor."

Clint looked up at the dying sun. "It's almost time, Travis."

Travis crossed the dusty plaza and rapped on the outer door of the Morris *casa.* Angelique opened the door. Her face was red and swollen. "Thank the good God you are here," she said brokenly.

"What is wrong, Angelique?"

"Theresa...Theresa...my God, I cannot say it, *Capitan.*"

"Speak!"

"She is gone."

Travis gripped the woman by her shoulders. "Gone? Where?"

"We do not know. Captain Cass came here and spoke to her. She left the house with that swine. Esteban told me later she had been wearing her riding habit."

Travis pushed passed the sobbing woman. He hurried into the great room where James Morris usually sat. The old man looked up at him. "Where has Theresa gone?" asked Travis.

"I do not know. I do not understand how or why she would leave with that man. She did not say anything to me, her own grandfather."

"I brought back the troops to defend the town against Cuchillo. We had until sundown to meet his demands."

The old man bowed his head. "She was gone so quickly we had no time to talk with her. It is said they were seen riding south from the town, but it was Timoteo Castro who saw them, and Timoteo is known as a great liar who likes attention and will tell wild tales to gain it."

Travis hurried from the room and looked about the deserted patio. He went to her room and opened the door. Her waist and flowing skirt lay on the floor beside the little beaded moccasins she usually wore.

A shadow darkened the floor beside Travis. He turned to look into the eyes of Evelyn Cass. "Do you know anything about this?" he asked, pointing to the clothing on the floor.

She shrugged. "She left town with Charlie, although how he talked her into it is beyond me."

There was a cold feeling within Travis. "But why?"

She leaned against the side of the doorway. "You don't know Charlie very well, Travis. You shamed him more than once. He knew you loved Theresa, and, although he could do nothing about that, he wanted revenge."

"But where did he take her?"

She looked away. Travis gripped her by the shoulders and shook her. "You'll tell me," he said harshly, "or I'll break your pretty neck."

Her eyes held his, and there seemed to be a glint of malice in them. "I think he's taken her to Cuchillo Rojo," she said.

He dropped his hands. "I don't believe it."

"No? I'm sure he has. Charlie knew you'd turn in a report against him. He knew his army career would end if you did so. Perhaps he thought he'd gain favor with Cuchillo by bringing Theresa to him. I don't know. There was always a touch of madness in Charlie. Only I knew it. This is just the type of revenge he'd seek against you, Travis."

Travis pushed past her.

"Where are you going?"

"After her."

She gripped his right arm. "No, Travis! Let them go! Why risk your life for her?"

Travis turned. "I don't think you'd understand why I would risk my life for Theresa. It's beyond your comprehension."

She came closer to him. "Travis, forget about her. She

can't give you anything. Charlie is gone. He'll never come back. Am I so unattractive to you?"

He walked away. "You pick the damnedest times to get romantic," he said over his shoulder.

The sun was gone when Travis found Clint Vaughn. "Cass has taken Theresa away," said Travis. "Evelyn says he has taken Theresa to Cuchillo Rojo."

Clint paled. "She's lying!"

"I don't think so."

"What can we do?"

Travis looked at the darkening hills to the west. "I'm going after her."

"I'll get the men ready."

"No. A detachment would never make it, Clint. There's a slim chance I might get through alone. If I don't get back, the command is yours. It's a big responsibility, but if you get through to Fort Craig, there will be a promotion in it for you."

"Damn the promotion!"

Baconora came through the darkness to them. "You're going after Theresa, Captain?" he asked quietly.

"Yes."

"I'll go with you. I know where Cuchillo's camp is."

"You realize the odds against us?"

Baconora grinned crookedly. "I've had odds against me before. Besides, I'd rather take my chances out there than sit around here and wait for the 'Paches to gobble us up. A man would have a chance to get away out there. If Cuchillo hits Santa Theresa, there might not be a man left to tell the tale."

"Cheerful beggar," said Clint dryly.

"I call them the way I figure them," said the scout.

Travis sent a trooper for his horse. He looked again at the dark hills. He might be able to save the girl. Perhaps if he killed Cuchillo, the strength of the Apache force would be lost. It had happened before when a good leader was killed. But the odds of Travis getting out alive were stacked high against him.

———

FIRST SERGEANT MACK ELLIS knocked on the outer door of the Morris *casa*. The door swung open under the blows of his big fist. There were no lights in the house. Ellis walked down the long corridor which led to the patio. The house seemed deserted until he reached the patio and saw a light in one of the bedrooms. He crossed to it and rapped on the door.

"Who it is?" called out Evelyn Cass.

Ellis felt a surge of heat go through his big body as he heard her voice. "It's Sergeant Ellis, Mrs. Cass," he said. "I'm looking for the captain."

She opened the door. "I think he has left town," she said.

"Left town, ma'am? I don't understand."

She eyed the big noncom. Maybe this was her chance. She had noticed the way Ellis looked at her. "I think the captain has pulled out on the rest of us," she said.

"I don't believe that!"

"No?" She tilted her shapely head to one side. "Captain Walker knows that Santa Theresa is doomed. Theresa Morris has been taken by my husband to the camp of Cuchillo. At least, I think that is what he has done."

Ellis was bewildered. "But why?"

"My husband hates Captain Walker. It is a form of revenge for my husband. Captain Walker said he was going to find Theresa Morris, but I don't believe him at all. I think he has deserted us to make for the Rio Grande, don't you?"

"He mentioned a couple of times that he wished he had gone on to the river alone."

She nodded. "I don't want to stay here, Sergeant, and

die under some greasy warrior's hand, nor do I want to save the last bullet for myself. Do you understand?"

Ellis shook his head. She placed a hand on his arm. "Listen," she said quietly. "Cuchillo will attack Santa Theresa. We have no chance here if he does. I want to get out of here. You know the country. Take me away from here, Sergeant."

He looked down at her. She was a real filly, all right. He had thought of her many times at Fort Joslyn. She pressed close to him. "You will, won't you?"

"It would be desertion," he said.

"Look, Sergeant—no one will know. In time Santa Theresa will be wiped out. You know that as well as I do. Think of what a feather it would be in your cap if you saved an officer's wife from the Apache."

Ellis swallowed thickly. She raised her face to his. He drew her close within his big arms and kissed her. Her arms crept about his neck, and he felt her press close to him. She withdrew her lips. Ellis looked at the bed and lifted her from her feet, but she pressed her hands against his flushed face. "No," she whispered. "Not now. We haven't time. You'll get everything you want when we reach the Rio Grande."

"But you're an officer's wife," he said anxiously.

She smiled. "A man like you won't always be an enlisted man," she said. "I'll talk to your superior officers. After saving my life, surely they'll consider you for a commission."

"Yeah," he said. He looked up. "Yeah. By God, you've hit it."

"Get horses and food. Hurry now." She kissed him again.

Ellis hurried off. She leaned against the side of the door, watching him, wrinkling her nose at the sour sweat odor of him, which still clung about her. "My God," she said. She laughed. "The poor damned fool."

———

THE DESERT WAS SHROUDED in darkness, and the wind swept across it, rustling sage and mesquite. Now and then, Baconora stopped to listen. Travis looked ahead toward the dim, brooding bulk of the hills. The scout had said he knew where Cuchillo's camp was situated.

Baconora turned to Travis. "We'd best ride north toward the end of the hills, then turn in behind them toward Cuchillo's camp. They won't expect anyone coming that way."

"How long will it take?"

"What difference does that make? We sure as hell won't be able to get close to his camp coming this way."

"Lead on, then."

They rode to the north. After twenty minutes, Baconora halted. "Listen," he said.

Above the rushing of the night wind, they heard the muffled beating of hoofs. They slid from their mounts and led them down into an arroyo. Travis stayed with the horses while Baconora dropped at the edge of the arroyo. In a few minutes, he came to Travis. "Big war party," he whispered. "Heading toward Santa Theresa."

"Did you see Cuchillo?"

"No. Leastways, I didn't see any buck wearing a horned headdress, and I know damned well Cuchillo won't go anywhere without that headdress. It's big medicine for him. It's my thought that Cuchillo has sent his warriors ahead to lay siege to the town."

Travis nodded. "I wonder if he's still in those hills?"

"There's only one way to find out, Captain."

"Let's go, then."

They rode on to the north.

———

Sergeant Mack Ellis already had his misgivings. The woman rode silently behind him, her face muffled in a silk scarf. The dark hills were to their left as they rode for the old stage road north of Santa Theresa. Ellis had thought he might catch up with Travis Walker and Baconora, but now he knew he had been mistaken. It was too dark for him to see much of anything. It would be daylight before they found a place of shelter. There were many miles between them and the Rio Grande. He glanced back at her. She had played him for the fool, leading him on into desertion, with payment of a few kisses and a vague promise of other favors.

"Do you know where you are?" she asked sharply.

"Yes."

"You're lying."

He turned to look at her. "Maybe you'd rather go back?"

"No!"

"All right then." He spurred his horse and rode on.

The eastern sky was alight with the false dawn as Travis and Baconora rode through malpais country, torn and tumbled masses of rock mingled with ocotillo, catclaw, and mesquite. The wind had shifted and now came from the east. Travis looked up at the rough hills. "I thought we'd be closer than this by now," he said. "Damn it, man, I thought you knew this country!"

"I do," said Baconora quietly, from behind Travis. "That's why I came this way."

"We can't ride up those slopes now. They'd see us before we even got within carbine range."

"Exactly."

Travis turned quickly. Baconora's rifle rested across his left forearm, pointing at Travis' chest. Baconora cocked the heavy weapon with his right thumb, then curled "his forefinger about the trigger. "I'll trouble you to get off that horse, Walker," he said.

"What does this mean?"

Baconora grinned. "Now you didn't really think I was loco enough to come out here with you on a wild goose chase after that girl, knowing damned well neither of us would ever leave here alive?"

Travis looked into the scout's hard reddish eyes. "What's your game, Baconora?"

Baconora looked up toward the hills. "The Army hasn't got a chance out here anymore. There are no troops between here and the Colorado, and precious little chance of them ever being out there in the next few years. The Apache are lords of Arizona and western New Mexico now, yeah, and clear down to Durango, too.

"A wise man will play along with the Apache. I know Cuchillo. He'll reward me for my help. Silver, gold, women, anything I ask."

"He'll kill you at sight."

Baconora shook his shaggy head. "No. He can use me."

"What happens to me?"

Baconora spat. "Part of the deal with him was to bring you to him. He knew as long as you were around, there'd be resistance. I've kept my word."

Travis studied the lean scout. "You've been in contact with him all along, then?"

Baconora nodded. "Just about. Get off that horse. Gather some mesquite. It's almost dawn. I want a signal fire started."

Travis dismounted and began to gather mesquite branches. He had his Colt in his holster, but he knew he'd never get a chance to free it before he was shot down. The sky was lighter as he set fire to the heap of branches. The mesquite crackled steadily.

'Throw some brush on it," ordered Baconora. "I want smoke."

Soon a streamer of smoke arose from the fire. Baconora sat down on a rock, always keeping his rifle pointing at Travis. "Unbuckle your gun belt," he said. "Throw it over here."

Travis did as he was told. There was no sign of life in the hills, but as he looked to the east, he saw dust rising. His heart seemed to skip a beat.

Baconora suddenly laughed. "I'm thinking of that damned fool Cass," he said. "He was stupid enough to think Cuchillo would make the same kind of a deal with him that he made with me. Now Cuchillo probably has the girl. I wonder if she saw how Cass died."

"You think he's dead then?"

"Yeah. But if he ain't, he might as well be after Cuchillo gets through carving him up. Hawww!"

The sky was much lighter now. The wind shifted a little. The smoke drifted toward the quiet hills. Travis eyed the scout, hoping for a break, but Baconora was too wary.

Baconora stood up. "Look," he said. "We got company."

Travis turned. Two riders were approaching them. One was a soldier, the other a woman. Baconora grinned. "It's that Cass filly and that damned fool of a first sergeant, Mack Ellis."

Travis turned as though warned by some subtle sense. He started a little. A group of Apache had materialized up the slope from them. Even as Travis watched, he saw most of the warriors lash their horses down the slope and start off at a long swinging pace toward the two riders east of the fire.

Baconora spat. "Damned fools," he said.

Travis could see the horned headdress on one of the Apache who had not ridden after Mack Ellis and Evelyn Cass. There were two other Apache with him and another rider, slight of figure, who rode just behind the chief. He knew it was Theresa.

"This oughta be good," said Baconora. "That stiff-backed sergeant is goin' to get his comeuppance."

Travis turned. The Apache had spread out into a crescent and were closing in on the two riders. Mack Ellis
swung down from his horse and shot it with his pistol.
He turned to Evelyn Cass, but the woman sat bolt
upright on her horse, staring at the painted death which
was swooping down at her. Then she screamed and
turned her horse to urge it back to the east. Mack Ellis
yelled at her above the thudding of the hoofs. He raised
his musketoon and fired at a leading Apache. The warrior
went down. Carbines and rifles flatted off, and the big
sergeant went down on one knee.

The Apache ringed the sergeant. Slugs rapped into
him. Evelyn Cass was racing through the brush, followed
by half a dozen screaming Apache. Mack Ellis dropped
another Apache with his pistol. He fired again and
dropped a warrior's horse. He turned to look for the
woman who had led him into a death trap.

Somehow Evelyn Cass had broken away from her
pursuers. She lashed at her horse as she tried to reach
Mack Ellis. Her long hair had broken free and streamed
behind her as she rode.

Baconora spat. "She led that poor bastard to his
death," he said. "At that, he's better off than she is. Wait
until they get their hands on her."

Travis looked up the slope. Cuchillo sat his appaloosa,
watching the fight on the flats below him. He was not
looking toward the fire. Travis glanced at Baconora. The
scout was watching the fight with avid interest. "Damn!"
he said. "Ellis got another one of 'em!"

Travis' right hand closed on a rock. Two swift
strides took him close to Baconora. The scout whirled
in time to get hit full in the face with the rock. He
gasped as blood streamed from his nose and mouth.
Travis jerked the rifle from the scout's hands and
clubbed Baconora over the head. Baconora went down,
spraying blood on the sand and rocks. Travis raised the
rifle once more and drove the steel-shod butt down in a

smashing blow to the base of Baconora's neck, breaking his spine.

Travis snatched up his gun belt and buckled it hastily about his waist. He looked up the slope. Cuchillo was still watching the hopeless fight. Guns popped like grease in a big skillet. Travis got his Sharps and capped it. He took Baconora's rifle and placed it atop a flat rock. He got the scout's Colt and thrust it through his belt. As an afterthought, he took off the scout's blood-spattered hat and put it on his own head.

Mack Ellis was almost through. Evelyn Cass was trying to reach him. A warrior shot in close beside her and gripped her streaming hair. Mack Ellis turned. He raised his Col and fired at her. She jerked and slid from her horse, and the hoofs of the warrior's horse thudded against her body

Travis looked away as the Apache closed in on the big sergeant. There was nothing he could do to help Mack Ellis

Cuchillo was riding down the slope, followed by his two warriors and Theresa. The smoke drifted in between Travis and the little party. He stepped behind a big rock and gripped his carbine tightly in his hands. Three to one. The odds were high, and what he had to do, he must do before the Apache on the flats below rejoined their chief. But they'll worry the bodies of the two dead people in childish fury. That would give him a slim margin of time—a last desperate throw of the dice for life or death.

CHAPTER FIFTEEN

C uchillo guided his gaudy appaloosa down the rough slope. It was then that Travis Walker saw the rope held in his right hand, the other end of which was tied to Theresa's horse. Theresa was very pale and wan in the gray light of dawn.

The three Apache were fifty yards from the arroyo when Travis fired his Sharps, dropping the right-hand warrior instantly with a bullet through the heart. The other warrior's horse reared, and a slug from Baconora's rifle took the horse in the chest. The horse pitched as he came down, throwing his rider to the ground, pinning him helplessly against sharp-edged rocks.

Cuchillo jerked at the rope he held and tried to turn his appaloosa, but Travis Walker was clearing rocks as he raced toward the chief. The smoke drifted between them. Cuchillo dropped the rope and reached for his rifle, but Travis fired his Colt. He missed, but the slug sang thinly past Cuchillo's ear and startled him. Theresa took her cue. She dug her heels into the sides of the pony she rode, and the mount carried her into thick brush.

Travis stumbled and went down on one knee. He fired up at the chest of the appaloosa as Cuchillo drove the horse at him. Travis darted to one side, gripped the chief's right leg, and upended him out of the Mexican saddle he rode. Cuchillo went down heavily on the far side of the horse. The appaloosa streaked for the flats, leaving Travis and Cuchillo face to face.

Cuchillo fired his pistol, but Travis was under it, gripping the gun wrist with his left hand, forcing the gun higher and higher. Travis grunted in pain as Cuchillo's knee drove up into his groin. Travis fell backward, dragging the chief down on top of him. Cuchillo lost his pistol and swiftly drew out his knife. Travis jerked his head, striking it against a rock. He weakened as the knife came toward him. There was a muffled explosion behind Cuchillo, and his body jerked spasmodically. His mouth opened, and blood flooded from it, splattering Travis. Cuchillo fell sideways as powder smoke blew toward Travis. Travis looked up into Theresa's pale face. She held a heavy pistol in her slim hands.

Travis rolled the dead chief aside. He stood up and drew her close. He heard a whooping cry out on the flats. He looked over her head and saw the Apache closing in on the arroyo. Travis pushed the girl behind a rock and swiftly reloaded the rifle and carbine. He took the pistols and jumped behind a rock ledge.

There were five bucks closing in on the arroyo. Travis grinned. This was his meat. The rifle spoke and took one of the bucks through the head. Travis fired the carbine and downed another warrior. The other three quirted their horses off through the brush just as the sun showed itself over the eastern heights.

Travis slid an arm about Theresa's waist. "Let's go home," he said quietly.

CHAPTER SIXTEEN

Travis Walker stood up in his stirrups and waved his hat toward the east. "Move out! Forward ho!" he commanded.

The advance party of cavalry moved out at a smart trot, followed by the wagons and carts of the civilians. Behind the civilian wagons were the army vehicles. The wagon train was followed by a rear guard of cavalry, while lines of infantry and armed civilians plodded along each side of the column

Travis looked about the quiet plaza after the rear guard had moved out. The dust was settling on the deserted buildings. There was a somber, lonely look about the old town. Beyond the town, a tall wind devil rose on the sand flats, then moved toward Santa Theresa to sweep across the empty plaza and past the sagging *torreon*.

Clint Vaughn reined in his horse beside Travis. "I wonder how long the Apache will let this place alone?"

"*Quién sabe?* They don't like ghost towns, Clint. This might be considered bad medicine for them. Maybe they'll stay away from it."

"Someday, the Army will come back here. Until then,

this is Apacheria, and God help the traveler who tries to cross it."

Travis nodded. He looked at the heat-hazy hills. "I wonder how Ben Joad is making out up there," he said.

"He's in good company...for *him*."

Travis touched his horse with his spurs. They did not look back as they followed the column out onto the dusty road.

———

THE PEOPLE TALKED in low voices as they moved about inside the circle of wagons. The firelight glinted dully from gun barrels as sentries paced along the outer rim of the wagons, and a scarf of smoke hung low over the camp. In the distance, Massacre Peak loomed up against the dark sky.

Travis Walker stood with his back to a wagon, looking out into the darkness. Clint Vaughn came to him. "How far are we from the river?" he asked.

"About twenty-five miles."

Clint looked to the west. "Odd that we haven't seen an Apache since we left Santa Theresa."

"There may be some ahead of us."

A sentry suddenly raised his rifle. "Halt!" he called. "Who goes there?"

"Friend!" the cracked voice sounded from the darkness.

"Advance to be recognized."

A man came out of the thick brush, weaving a little as he walked, leading a blown horse.

"Who are you?" called the sentry.

"Benson Duryea, a courier from Fort Craig."

Travis ran toward the tired man and gripped him by the shoulders. "Thank God you made it, Duryea!"

The Kentuckian looked up. "I reached the river all right," he said. "They wanted to send another man back, but I insisted on coming back myself. My horse is almost gone. I ain't feeling too spry myself. I ain't sure I would have made it to Fort Joslyn, sir. Thank God I met you."

"What's the news, Duryea?" asked Clint.

"A strong reconnaissance party is following me. They should be bivouacked near Sunday Cone. They had orders to try and contact Fort Joslyn, sir. According to the commanding officer of Fort Craig, Fort Joslyn and Santa Theresa should have been abandoned weeks ago."

Travis nodded. Clint helped Duryea toward the wagons. Duryea turned. "Another thing, sir. I was told you were promoted to major and assigned to Canby's staff."

"Thanks, Duryea."

Travis walked into the center of the wagon circle. "We're safe now," he said. "We'll meet fresh troops sometime tomorrow. The road is open to the Rio Grande and Fort Craig." He walked toward Theresa's wagon.

Theresa stood beside the wagon with her shawl over her dark hair. Travis took her in his arms. "We'll make Fort Craig now," he said. "How is your grandfather?"

She glanced at the wagon. "He has hardly said a word since we left Santa Theresa."

"He'll be back there someday."

She looked up at him and shook her head. "No," she said softly. "He'll never see it again, Travis. He spoke of it a little while ago, saying he'd never see Santa Theresa again, but that he was happy for me, knowing that we loved each other."

Travis looked to the east. "This will be a long war," he said.

She rested her head on his chest. "It will pass more quickly than you think, Travis, and then we'll have a long, happy life ahead of us."

He raised her head and kissed her. The wind blew across the camp, fluttering the wagon tilts and driving the smoke of the campfires ahead of it. Far to the west,

the wind swept across Santa Theresa, raising whorls of
dust on the empty plaza and moaning through the empty
buildings. A coyote crept furtively across the plaza. A
stone fell from the old *torreon*. Santa Theresa seemed to
be waiting, patiently waiting for its people to come back
and bring it to life again. There was plenty of time. Santa
Theresa dreamed on under the dark sky.

THE BRAVE RIFLES

For the Third United States Cavalry
"The Brave Rifles"

CHAPTER ONE

L ieutenant Douglas Boyd drew rein on the low ridge overlooking the Laramie River and looked down on the lights of Fort Laramie as his company came to a dusty halt behind him. The August night was hot and sultry, and a warm wind was sweeping down from the north. First Sergeant Adam Morrisey cantered forward and kneed his mount close to that of his commanding officer. "It's good to be back again," he said as he shoved back his forage cap and wiped the sweat from his broad face.

Doug nodded. He drew a lucifer across his belt buckle and relighted his cigar. Morrisey eyed the strong planes of Doug's tanned face. "The company will miss you when you are on leave," he said quietly.

The light gray eyes studied the first soldier. "It's been a long time since I've been in the States," said Doug. There was a faint touch of the rich Irish tongue in his voice.

Morrisey glanced back at the little column of dusty troopers. "Let's hope they don't break up the company now that you've at last whipped them into shape."

"They're good now," admitted Doug. "Hard in the saddle and mean of eye."

Morrisey nodded. "Real Mounted Rifles."

Doug grinned. "Third Cavalry to anyone else but us, Adam."

Morrisey spat. "We'll always be the Mounted Rifles, sir, Washington or no—and be damned to them all!"

Doug leaned forward to look down at the river, flowing like liquid lead through its channel. "My promotion is long overdue. I don't seem to be able to get it out here. My best bet is Washington, although I dislike going over the department commander's head."

"You've more than earned it. It is not your fault that you didn't serve in Virginia or Tennessee during the war."

Doug drew in on his cigar and then worked it over to the other side of his mouth. His overdue promotion was a saddle gall with him. He had served on the frontier since 1859, rising from a trooper up through the grades—corporal, sergeant, first sergeant, and regimental sergeant major—winning his commission at Valverde under Ben Roberts while serving with McCrae's Battery as an artilleryman. He had earned his silver bar against the Navajos and had been commissioned Regular Army after the war.

Promotions didn't come easy in '67. The war had burdened the army with a maximum of career officers, and no effort had been made as yet to weed the misfits and incompetents from the service. The trouble was that a good many of them had applied for and had been ordered to duty on the frontier to gain further rank, and if a man hadn't fought the rebels in the East, he was considered somewhat of a poor and unwanted relation.

Doug thrust up an arm and pumped it up and down. "Move out!" he commanded.

Morrisey kept pace with Doug. They had served together since the end of the war and understood each other. "If you leave, we will have no officer," he said, "now that Mr. Byers is dead."

Doug did not look at Morrisey. A man took command

of a company or battery, and it reflected his personality in time. Doug's company had been his since April, juniper troopers, Johnny Raws, and snowbirds, with a leavening of veterans and ex-rebels, and he had made it into the best company guarding the Oregon Trail.

"Maybe if they give us a letter, we'd be kept together for your return," said Morrisey.

That was another sore point with Doug. The Third Cavalry was scattered throughout the Southwest, from Texas to Utah. His company was part and parcel of the Third, the old Mounted Rifles, but somehow in the wide reshuffling of regulars after the war, it had been designated temporarily as a provisional company, and the designation had stuck with it like a burr on a saddle blanket. The company guidon bore the letters U.S. in white on its red upper half, but there was no company designation in red on the white lower half. This caused no end of biting sarcasm from the other units at Fort Laramie.

They clattered over the plank bridge, dust squirting from between the loose floorboards. Doug turned in his saddle. "Kelly!" he called out.

Dandy Kelly, the company trumpeter, rode forward. "Yes, sir?"

"Trumpeter, we'll go in on the horn. Sound the Trot!"

Kelly grinned as he swung his trumpet on its yellow worsted cord. He raised it to his lips and blew softly into it to warm it up. That was Mr. Boyd's way—provisional company or no, he wanted the walk-a-heaps at Laramie to know *his* company was coming in from patrol with credit for sending Cheyenne and Sioux bucks across the Shadow Waters.

———

THE INFANTRY GUARD at the post entrance between the sutler's store and the sutler's residence raised their heads as Dandy Kelly lipped full into the Trot, awakening the sleeping echoes from the dark hills.

The corporal of the guard spat. "'Tis Ali Baba and the Forty Thieves coming in," he said dryly.

"How do you know?" asked a pale-faced Johnny Raw.

"That's Dandy Kelly on the C-horn, recruitie. Stay long enough at Laramie, and ye'll know his triple tonguing soon enough."

Doug returned the salute of the corporal as the company jingled past and turned toward the parade ground trailing a scarf of thin dust.

The recruit leaned on his Springfield. He grinned. "Ali Baba and the Forty Thieves," he said musingly. "Why, corporal?"

The Irishman looked after the company. "When they show up at Laramie after thirty days patrol, 'tis best to lock up your liquor, hide your playing cards and look to your wife."

The corporal eyed the four empty saddles at the rear of the little column. "They've had losses. Do ye see the empty saddles? One of thim is an officer's mount."

———

DOUG REINED in his bay and turned to Morrisey. "Take over, Sergeant."

Morrisey saluted. He watched Doug ride toward headquarters. There would be hell to pay when Doug reported in to Colonel Connolly.

Doug dismounted and tethered his bay. He slapped the dust from his trail uniform with his cracked straw hat and entered the headquarters. The sergeant major stood up. "Major Custis has been expecting you, sir," he said.

Doug looked quickly at him. "I'm a day early, Bennett."

The non-com nodded. "He heard the horn, sir, and came in right off."

Doug rapped on the inner door.

"Come in," a dry voice said.

Doug opened the door and walked in. Major Custis was seated at the colonel's desk, toying with a letter opener. He jerked his head at a chair, ignoring Doug's salute. He looked with distaste at the faded blue trousers Doug wore. Custis was a picture of a regular in full dress.

Doug dropped wearily into the chair and dropped his battered hat onto the floor. He looked at Custis, and all his old dislike for the man returned.

Custis leaned back in his chair. "Well?"

"We caught up with the raiders at Lost Spring. They killed both women and the child before we could save them. We killed seven bucks—three Cheyenne, four Sioux. Members of Sinta Gleska's band."

Custis flushed. "Who, may I ask, is Sinta Gleska?"

"Spotted Tail of the Brules. Big bad medicine, major."

"Any casualties?"

Doug hesitated. "Mr. Byers. Three troopers."

Custis went white. "Mr. Byers was wounded?"

"No. Killed."

"Jesus God, Boyd!"

Doug shrugged. "The damned fool was on point. He was told to wait for the rest of us. He saw three bucks and charged them. It was a trap. He was cut off."

"You made no attempt to save him?"

Tight lines formed along Doug's lean jaws. "I had my company to think of."

"Yes...*your company*."

Their eyes met like grating sabers. Custis was infantry, born and bred, and a cavalryman to him was a courier or escort, not a real fighting man.

"I might add that my three enlisted men died trying to save Byers."

Custis looked up at the wall. There was a picture of a bearded officer hanging beside the pictures of Sherman and Grant. "The general will crucify you for this, Boyd. His only son. The fat is in the fire."

Doug crossed a leg. "He wanted Gerald to get some experience. Gerald wanted a brevet on his first patrol. He got the wooden cross."

"Did you bring back his body?"

"No. General's sons stink just as bad as anyone else in this heat."

White spots showed at the corners of Custis' thin mouth. To him, Douglas Boyd was an irregular, a mustang officer with the manners of an enlisted man, with a way of saying things he felt without regard for anyone's feelings. "Is your company in good shape?" he asked at last.

"Tired but healthy. No cholera, if that's what you mean."

"Good. I have an assignment for you and them."

Doug stared at the major. "What do you mean?"

Custis leaned forward. "There is a small supply train ready to leave for Fort Purcell on the Crazy Woman. They need a mounted escort. That escort will be your company."

"Dammit, Custis! We've had our share of patrols these past three months! You can't send those men out again along the Bozeman Trail!"

"I *can* and I *will,* mister."

In the silence that followed, Doug heard Call To Quarters sound on a deep-toned infantry G-bugle. He suddenly realized how tired he was—not from the patrol itself but from the years he had spent on the frontier without leave. "What about my leave?" he asked quietly.

Custis opened a drawer and took out a paper. He placed it on the desk and neatly flattened it with a well-groomed hand. "Here it is, Boyd, but before I give it to you, there is something else I must tell you..."

"Make it good."

"General Byers is due here in a few days to inspect this post. He's looking forward to seeing his son."

"That doesn't bother me as far as my leave is concerned. I'm sorry for his loss."

"I'm sure you are."

Doug leaned forward. "What is it you're holding back, Major?"

"You know what a stickler the general is. His purpose in coming here is to designate certain units which will be disbanded and absorbed into other units. When he finds out that your company has no letter designation and is, in fact, merely a provisional company separated from duty with its parent regiment, I am sure he will order it to be deactivated."

The shaft struck home. Doug wanted that leave worse than he wanted a woman, but his company had become part of him and he of it. He felt a deep loyalty toward the tough troopers he had forged into a first class fighting detachment, bar none in the whole damned department.

Custis wasn't through with his calculated attack. "In any case, you will file your report. It might help you in your career, Mr. Boyd if you mentioned in that same report that Mr. Byers was killed in action while performing a deed of valor. It might ease the blow to the general."

"The man was killed by his own foolishness and caused the death of three of my men. I will not make a posthumous hero of him, sir!"

"Do as you will."

"I'd like your permission to speak with Colonel Connelly."

Custis politely covered his mouth as he yawned. "The colonel has gone on leave. I am acting commandant of Fort Laramie."

The brassbound sonofabitch thought Doug. *He's playing with me again.*

Custis stood up. He handed Doug his leave orders.

"File your report. Your company will leave with the supply train."

"There are four other cavalry companies here, Major."

"Yes." Custis smoothed his fine broadcloth dress blouse. "You must admit, although your company has no equal in the field, they are not the best-drilled troops stationed here at Laramie. There is no time to put them through an intensive refresher course in drill before General Byers gets here. You know the general. Every infantryman, quartermaster, medical corpsman, teamster, *and* cavalryman will be seen by him on dress parade. I'd rather have your company out on the Bozeman than here at that time."

There was no use in arguing with Leonard Custis. Doug stood up. "What are the orders?"

"Your company and a platoon of replacements for the Forty-ninth Infantry now garrisoning Fort Purcell will act as escort for twelve supply wagons. Mr. Locke Holmes will command the infantry."

"Jesus God!" blurted Doug.

Custis examined his nails. "I know that you and Mr. Holmes are not the best of friends, but he has requested duty with the Forty-ninth, and we were glad to write out his orders."

Doug was about to say he knew why, but he had learned through long experience with superior officers to keep his mouth shut regarding such matters. "How many men are in his platoon?"

"Twenty."

"I have forty men. Sixty men are certainly not enough to escort a wagon train up the Bozeman, Major."

The cold blue eyes held his. "There are no other troops available."

"With a regiment of infantry here and four companies of cavalry?"

"You seem to have forgotten that General Byers is due here for his inspection."

"Mustn't forget that," said Doug dryly. He ripped his leave orders in half and threw them into the wastebasket. "Gone but not forgotten," he said ruefully.

Custis walked to the door. "You will leave the day after tomorrow."

"My men are tired, sir. Our horses need rest and grazing."

"Perhaps you'd rather have me assign another company?"

Doug felt like smashing the man's smooth face.

"You can get fresh horses, Boyd."

"Yes, sir."

Custis opened the door. "One other thing, an ambulance will be issued to you for the women to ride in."

Doug whirled. "Women? *What* women?"

"The two Misses Rochelle, Louise and Diane, daughters of Colonel Manning Rochelle, commanding officer of Fort Purcell."

It was as though Custis had been playing a game with Doug and holding an ace up his broadcloth sleeve.

"This is madness," said Doug.

"So?"

"I won't take the responsibility."

"You will."

"Whose brainstorm was this?"

Custis turned with his back to the door. "Those girls have been here for over a month waiting for a chance to get to Purcell. A courier came in from there asking why they had not arrived. Connelly didn't want to let them go, but you know Manning Rochelle. He has influence and isn't afraid to use it."

Byers initialed their request for transportation as quickly as possible to join their father. There you have it."

"I sure do," said Doug dryly. "One hundred and thirty-five miles to Fort Reno and fifty more to Fort Purcell, with sixty men guarding twelve supply wagons and an ambulance carrying two beautiful young women. My God, but the hostiles will laugh at us for being the damned lost fools we are."

Custis opened the door. "You can get reinforcements at Fort Reno, in all probability."

"In all probability," echoed Doug.

They walked out onto the parade ground. Custis looked at the well-lit junior officer's quarters, Old Bedlam. "I'm due over there for charades. See me in the morning for anything you need."

"Yes, sir." Doug saluted.

Custis returned the salute and walked off. He turned. "One more thing, Boyd!"

Doug turned. "Yes?"

"For God's sake, get out of that non-regulation rig you're wearing! Remember you're in the Regular Army of the United States, not in the Royal Inniskilling Dragoons!"

"Yes, sir." Doug watched the ramrod back of the officer as he walked toward Old Bedlam. "Charades," he said. "For the love of God!" He shook his head as he walked toward Officer's Row.

CHAPTER TWO

Doug rapped on the door of Colonel Connelly's quarters. Louise Rochelle opened the door and stared at him. "Doug! I didn't know you were back from patrol."

He eyed her in appreciation. The gown she wore, of pale blue in the latest New York fashion, set off her full figure and her wide eyes. The faint scent of jasmine came to him, and he was suddenly conscious of the sour sweat aura about him from his trail uniform. "I just got in," he said quietly. "I had to see you at once."

She raised her eyebrows. "I didn't know you cared *that* much, Doug."

He waved a hand. "May I come in?"

She nodded as she stepped back, eying him curiously. Louise Rochelle was taller than the average woman but made no effort to compensate for it, carrying herself with shoulders back and head held high—for she was an army brat, born and bred into the service. Doug had met her the year before when she had visited Fort Laramie with her half-sister Diane. There was a great deal of difference between the two girls, as every junior officer stationed at Laramie well knew.

She turned toward the living room. "How was the patrol?"

"Gerry Byers was killed."

She looked at him in shocked surprise. "But he was so young, Doug! And on his first patrol!"

Doug shrugged. "I didn't want to take him into the company, but he was eager to go. He should have been kept here to stand Stables and do guard duty until he learned something about soldiering other than what rubbed off on him at the Academy." He shook his head. "Carrying a Castellani saber and a pair of matched and engraved Colts. The whole thing seemed a gay excursion to him."

She looked away. "What will his father think?"

"His father is a soldier," said Doug quietly.

"I know you well enough to know you would have saved him if you could."

"Thanks. As it was, he cost me three of my best men."

Her eyes held his. "Your men mean a great deal to you, don't they?"

"Yes." He looked about. "Where is Diane?"

"At Old Bedlam with Locke Holmes."

"Doing charades," said Doug dryly.

"What is bothering you, Doug?"

"This madness of you and Diane traveling to Fort Purcell."

"How did you know about that?"

"Major Custis told me. My company has been detailed as escort."

"But you were due to go on leave."

"Canceled."

"Through Leonard Custis?"

"In a way."

"He doesn't like you, does he, Doug?"

He smiled. "He's in good company. I've never been too popular among the Academy boys."

"That isn't fair!"

"I should have known better than to say that. I forgot about your father and your brother being Academy men."

"It isn't that at all!"

Doug rested an arm on the mantel and surveyed her. He could never make up his mind whether he liked the touch of anger she was capable of at times or if he preferred her normal calm self. Maybe it was the Irish blood in him that made him like a spunky woman.

"*Benny Havens, Oh!* Cozzens Hotel. Moonlight on the Hudson," he said with a cutting edge to his voice.

She tilted her head to one side. "You always give your-self away, *Mr.* Boyd. Acting the part of the tough mustang officer, scornful of Academy men. You think they despise you because of what you are, and yet it is you who despises them because of what *they* are. You made it the *hard* way, Mr. Boyd. More time in the mess line and in the sanitary sinks than they have in the service as a whole. Is that it, Mr. Boyd?"

There was a dark rush of blood beneath his tanned skin. He opened his mouth and shut it. She was right, damn her! She could cut to the bone with that tongue of hers. He turned on his heel and walked toward the door.

"Doug," she called.

He turned.

"Did you know that brogue of yours becomes very pronounced when you're angry?"

For a moment, he stared at her, and then he smiled.

"That's better. Now, what was it you wanted to say to me about our traveling to Fort Purcell?"

"It's damned foolishness for you to do so; more than that, it's criminally insane!"

"You have such a nice way of putting things," she said.

"Congress made me an officer; they didn't bother much about the gentleman part of the deal in those days."

"Tell me why you don't want us to go."

He thrust out an arm toward the northwest. "The Sioux and Cheyenne's are determined to close the Bozeman Trail. Red Cloud said he would stand in the way, and by God, Louise, he'll keep his word, which is more than the government has done for him with their scraps of paper!"

She sat down and looked up at him. "But surely Major Custis will send enough troops along with us to make the journey safe?"

"Sixty men," he said quietly. "Boyd's Provisional Company of the Third Cavalry, and a platoon of mud crushers on their way to join the Forty-ninth, under the command of Mister Locke Holmes."

Her eyes widened. "Good Heavens! You and Locke in the same escort detail? Leonard Custis is crazy!"

"Maybe it's his way of getting rid of the two of us," Doug said soberly. "We've been under his white skin ever since he came here." He looked quickly at her as a thought struck him like a Sioux pipe axe. "Now I get it!"

She shook her head. "Pray tell, just what it is you *got?*"

He smashed a fist into his other palm. "Locke Holmes requested duty with the Forty-ninth!"

"I knew that."

Their eyes met. "It's Diane, isn't it?" he asked.

"Yes." She studied him. "Go on with the rest of it."

"What do you mean?"

"You're wondering if it was her idea or his."

He flushed a little.

"Isn't that it, Doug?"

"Yes."

She stood up and walked to the mantel. There was a full-length picture of Diane Rochelle there. She was shorter by far than her half-sister and dark of hair and eyes. The look in those eyes set bachelors a little wild and made married men wonder a little about what the chances were.

"Well?" Doug asked quietly.

She spoke over her shoulder. "Personally, I don't think either one of them is in love with the other. Locke is ambitious—too ambitious to suit me. What he lacks in ability he'll make up by any means he can use to further his career."

"And Diane?"

She turned quickly. "She's my sister. She's been babied and petted all her life. Even when she was a child, the troopers and officers used to make fools of themselves over her, and when she reached the age of puberty, she was already entangled in an affair." There was a harsh bitterness in her voice, something Doug had never noticed before. "My father was always too busy with his career," she continued. "My mother died at Fort Jessup, Louisiana, while my father was fighting in Mexico. I was four years old before I ever saw him.

"My stepmother, Diane's real mother, never realized my father had married her for his convenience—to have a mother for me—until Diane was six years old. My father was always away somewhere. Fighting Indians, surveying, making inspections, and every other duty he could serve at to further his career. When he returned, at last, my stepmother knew she meant little to him."

Doug turned away. "Please stop," he said. "These things are not for me to hear."

She walked to him and gripped him by the arm with surprising strength. She looked up into his face. "You wanted to know why I want to go to Fort Purcell. Well, Mr. Boyd, I was leading up to that. Now have the goodness to hear me out!"

"Go on then."

"My stepmother was a good woman but not overly gifted mentally. She was a pretty woman and loyal to the one man she thought she loved. When she was treated coldly by my father, she did the only thing she could do—she killed herself.

"When I was ten years old, I was looking out for

Diane. There was a whole succession of nurses,, colored mammies, tutors, but never a mother, nor a father. We saw little of my father during the war. We were passed from relative to relative like little lost sheep. I was a grown woman when the war ended and hardly knew my father at all—but I did know my sister, and that was enough for me to determine to take her to my father before it was too late. Do you understand?"

He studied her thoughtfully. "And what about you? Risking your life to cross Indian country, with the odds high against your ever making it. No matter what she is, it is you I'm thinking of now, Louise."

"I must go," she said quietly.

He drew her close and raised her chin with his hand to look into her unfathomable eyes.

Feet grated on the front porch, and before Doug could kiss Louise, he heard the door handle turn. He stepped back from her and turned to see Locke Holmes holding the door open for Diane Rochelle. The two men's eyes met over her dark head, and anyone could see there was no friendship between them.

Diane smiled archly up at Doug. No matter what man she was with, she always had eyes for other men. It infuriated the man she was with, but she would look the same way at him if she happened to be with another man. It was all part of the game. Anything with trousers on— and particularly officer's trousers—was fair game for Diane, and more than one rumor from the sanitary sinks suggested that a man didn't really need a commission to make time with Diane Rochelle.

Holmes closed the door behind him. "Boyd," he said. "Is it true you are taking your company as escort to Fort Purcell?"

Doug nodded.

Locke Holmes was a little taller than Doug, but his shoulders were not as wide. His hair and skin were fair, and his eyes were such a startling light blue they seemed to spoil his handsomeness.

Holmes took off his forage cap. "That makes you commander," he said bitterly.

"Naturally," Doug said dryly.

"It isn't fair!"

Doug leaned against the mantel. "Perhaps, with your vast experience in Indian-fighting, you'd rather command?"

The barbed words struck home. Tiny, tight lines radiated from the corners of Holmes' mouth. Holmes had served in the Trans-Mississippi during the war, earning a first lieutenant's brevet at some obscure crossroads skirmish in Missouri or Arkansas. What rankled Holmes was that his brevet rank of first lieutenant pre-dated Doug's actual promotion to first lieutenant.

Holmes cut a hand sharply through the air. *"Indian fighters,"* he said curtly. "I've popped more caps in an affair of outposts than most of you. Indian fighters have in a year's service out here."

"Ever hit anything?"

A film of ice spread over the pale blue eyes, and Doug thought that the tall officer would start after him.

Louise Rochelle stepped in between them. "It's getting late," she said quickly. She smiled at Locke. "Both of you should be fined for talking shop."

The bitterness between the two men seemed to excite Diane. Her full lips parted a little, and her breasts rose and fell steadily.

Doug walked to the door. He turned. "Speaking of shop talk, Holmes. We have one day to get ready for the Bozeman. My company is bunked in Sibley's, near the hay yard. I'm staying with them. I'll expect you there at the crack of dawn to get ready for the journey."

Holmes nodded.

Louise walked to Doug. "We'll be packed and ready

by noon," she said. She touched his face. "Good night, Doug."

Diane laughed. "It's all so exciting! Have you been up the Bozeman, Doug?"

"Yes, Diane. I was with General Connor's so-called Powder River invasion in the summer of '65."

"Will it be exciting?"

He looked into her dark eyes. "You'll have your share of excitement," he promised soberly.

Locke Holmes followed Doug outside and kept pace with him as he walked to headquarters to get his bay. "We'll need a scout or two," he said.

Doug nodded. "I'm asking for Tobe Burgess."

Holmes stopped in his tracks. *"Him? The squawman?"*

Doug stopped and turned. "You'd better not call him that while he's around."

The officer laughed. "He won't be around! He's in the guardhouse now. Corporal Killigan of my platoon called him a Cheyenne lover. Burgess had a knife at his throat before Killigan knew what had happened. It took three men to get them apart. By God's grace alone, Burgess hasn't got a murder charge against him."

"Damn! Was Burgess drinking?"

"Naturally."

"He never drinks on duty."

"The man is unstable. I don't trust him. Let him get near the hostiles, and he'll betray us."

"He'll go with us if I can get him out of the brig."

"You're a God-damned fool!"

Doug's big left hand shot out to grip Holmes by the front of his blouse. He drew the big man close and looked into his eyes. "Listen, soldier, I take that from no man," he said softly.

Holmes raised a hand and gripped Doug by the left wrist. He tried to break the hold, but it was impossible for him. Doug shoved him back. "Get out of my sight," he said thinly. "'Tis bad enough I have to ride with you to Purcell."

"You commissioned bastard!"

Doug's right hand slapped Holmes hard across the mouth.

Holmes did not move. He did not want to try the big Irishman. It wasn't the time nor the place. He touched his bruised lips with the fingers of his right hand. "I'll remember this," he promised quietly.

"See that you do!"

Holmes watched Doug stride toward his bay. "I'll make you pay for that, Boyd," he said softly.

———

THE CORPORAL of the guard let Doug into the row of cells. "It's against the regulations, sir," he said.

"I'll be but a minute, Corporal."

Doug walked to the end cell. A man lay on the cot with his hands locked behind his head. His long dark hair flowed over the gray issue blanket he had rolled into a pillow.

"Tobe," said Doug.

Tobe Burgess turned to look at him. "Doug," he said quietly. His eyes were bloodshot, and dried blood crusted his lean face. The scout stood up. He thrust a hard hand between the bars to grip Doug's.

"I can never leave you alone without you getting into a hell's playground."

Tobe nodded. "It was Killigan," he said. "I could never figure out how you and him could both be Irish and him such a sonofabitch."

Doug took out his cigar case and gave one to the scout, lighting it. "I'm leaving for the Bozeman day after tomorrow."

The dark eyes lit up.

Doug leaned against the end wall. A vagrant breeze

blew in from across the Laramie and dried the sweat on his neck. "I need a scout," he said.

"Take me."

"What about the charges against you?"

"Killigan is back on duty with a scarred face."

"Yes, and his platoon goes with me up the Bozeman."

"Chihuahua! Well, it can't be helped."

The mingled odors of sweat, tobacco smoke, and greasy buckskins clung about the man. Tobias Burgess had a deeper knowledge of the Cheyenne's, Arapahoe's, and Sioux than any man Doug had met in Wyoming. Men said he might have been born a Cheyenne for his vast knowledge of them. Doug wondered if Tobe might agree to scout for him with the thought of breaking away and returning to the old free life. It was said that once a man tasted their way of life, he never lost the desire to return to it.

Doug looked out of the barred window. The Laramie was a dull pewter trace below the bluff. The wind blew through the warm corridor.

"There is blood on that wind," said Tobe quietly.

Doug turned.

"Makh-pia-sha stands in the way."

Makh-pia-sha was Red Cloud of the Bad Faces band of the Oglala. He had more coups or strike-the-enemy feats than any other warrior of the Oglala. Some of the Sioux chiefs had signed a treaty to let the white men build a road through the Powder River and Big Horn country of Wyoming, thence on west across Montana as a shortcut to the goldfields. "I shall stand in the trail," Red Cloud had promised. Pontiac had used the same words to Major Rogers one hundred years before in the East.

"I'll ask Major Custis to have you released."

"He'll be glad to get rid of me."

Doug gave the rest of his cigars to the scout. "Get some sleep—you'll need it. Until tomorrow then."

Tobe nodded. He watched Doug leave the corridor, then dropped onto his bunk and drew in on his cigar. The wind whispered to him of the Big Horn Mountains, of Medicine Lodge Creek and Piney Creek. He nodded in quiet contentment.

CHAPTER THREE

They were nine days' journey out from Fort Laramie and one day out from Fort Reno on the Bozeman Trail, but not one Sioux nor Cheyenne had yet been seen. Doug Boyd looked back along the small column. The afternoon sun shone on the white tilts of the supply wagons, headed by the light ambulance which transported the Rochelle sisters. A hundred yards behind the column was the dust-eating rear guard of eight troopers under Corporal MacKenzie.

Doug had been pushing the little command all day, trying to reach Crazy Woman Crossing. It was somewhere ahead of them beyond the ridge, which seemed to swim in a plum-colored haze. He shoved back his faded campaign hat as he saw a lone horseman top the ridge as though it had materialized out of the haze. Doug thrust up an arm to halt the column. *Enemies in sight.*

First Sergeant Morrisey cantered up to Doug and drew rein. "I've been waiting for this, sir," he said.

Doug nodded. "Pull the wagons up tight. Have the doughboys form about them. Have the troopers dismount and stand to horse. Stay put until further orders." Doug spurred his bay and rode toward Tobe.

He glanced back as he reached the base of the ridge.

Morrisey had acted quickly. The infantrymen stood about the wagons leaning on their long Springfield muzzleloaders. The troopers had formed ahead of the wagons with their Sharps breech-loading carbines in their hands. Doug saw the flutter of a skirt as one of the women got down from the ambulance. That would be Diane. He grinned as he saw Adam Morrisey talk to her. She got back into the vehicle. She had been nothing but trouble since they had left Fort Laramie.

Tobe had dismounted and was squatting in the scant shade of his shaggy roan. "Stay off the skyline," he said laconically. He shifted his chew and spat an amber stream down the far side of the ridge.

Doug swung down and ground-reined the bay. He walked to Tobe and then squatted beside him. The wide bottoms along the Crazy Woman seemed devoid of life.

Tobe scratched his head. They're in the willows along the crick, Doug."

"How many?"

Tobe shrugged. *"Quién sabe?* I saw three of them. No telling how many of them are down there—or in the hills to either side of the Trail."

Doug felt for a cigar and lighted it. "Right in the way, Tobe."

Tobe nodded. He was never in a hurry. One Sioux or five hundred, it was all the same to him.

The sun glinted on the sluggish shallow waters of the creek.

Tobe spat again. "Red Cloud stands in the trail," he said. "We can always head back to Fort Reno."

"I have my orders," said Doug quietly.

"Jesus God!"

Doug eyed the creek. It might only be a scouting party. He had had a feeling they were being watched all the way from Pumpkin Buttes to the very gates of Reno. No Indians had been seen, of course, but Doug knew they were there.

Tobe cut a fresh chew and spat out the old cud. He worked the fresh one into pliability. "We're only 'bout thirty miles from Purcell. I can make a try to get there for reinforcements."

Doug eased off his left boot and inspected a hole in his sock. "No real help there, Tobe. Just the Forty-ninth Infantry, mostly Johnny Raws with a leavening of old timers."

"So, what do we do?"

Doug pulled on his boot. "Cross this ridge and follow the creek until we find a place to hold them off if they attack."

"Some decision," the scout said sarcastically.

"You have a better idea?"

"Happens, I don't."

Doug stood up and looked down at his little command. He raised an arm and waved it in a circle. Morrisey got the command into motion almost at once. He threw out a line of flankers on each side of the wagons. They rolled up the slope with a thick scarf of dust rising in the windless air.

Tobe stood up and eased his crotch. "How come they picked you for this crap detail? I never did ask you."

Doug shrugged. "It was go along or lose the company. Maybe Colonel Rochelle will give me a good report if I ever get there safely."

"Granny Pussyfoot? Hawww! Old Rochelle thinks a hoss soldier is good for only one thing—shoveling manure!"

"So I've heard. God bless the infantry and to hell with the horse soldiers."

Morrisey rode up and dismounted. He shoved back his forage cap and wiped the sweat from his red face. "What now, Mr. Boyd?"

Doug waved an arm toward the creek. It looked so peaceful and quiet down there, just as though painted and feathered death was far from the Crazy Woman.

Morrisey studied the willows. "Want me to flush them, sir?"

"No. We'll see them soon enough. They're probably waiting for us to try and cross the creek, thinking we're heading for Fort Phil Kearney."

Locke Holmes was riding beside the ambulance. Tobe eyed him. "One thing you got to give *him* credit for," he said dryly. "He'll sure reassure them wimmen. That boy has the most beautiful set of manners to match his polished teeth, whatever else is wrong with him."

Morrisey grinned. "He'll be all right, Tobe."

"Yeah—if he don't get killed first. Told me the other day he could ride plumb through the Sioux Nation with a platoon. Right now, he's as useful as a broken wagon wheel."

Morrisey took out his tobacco pouch and began to fill his pipe. "Look there!" he said suddenly.

Three warriors had appeared out of the willows. The sun shone on the brass trim of their rifles. They did not look up the ridge.

"Shields covered," said Tobe. "No paint. Bait, I calls it. Now, Adam, my boy, you just ride down there and ask if they'll help you pick up that tobaccy you're spilling all over the Bozeman Trail."

Morrisey shut his pouch. He thrust his pipe into his pocket.

Doug uncased his German field glasses and focused them on the three bucks. Their broad faces swam into view. They were riding north along the edge of the creek away from the willows.

Tobe patted his long-barreled Sharps rifle. "I make it three hundred yards, Adam. Pity, a man can't shoot right now."

Doug scanned the willows with his glasses. There was no sign of other warriors there. "We'll move out," he said.

Locke Holmes cantered up behind them. His handsome face was alight. "Look at them! Let me take a squad after them, Boyd! I'll round them up!"

"Why?" asked Tobe.

Holmes flushed. He hated Tobe damned near as much as he hated Doug.

Doug cased his glasses. "They're just bait, Holmes. Last December near Fort Phil Kearney, Bui Fetterman, with about eight men, made the mistake of chasing Red Cloud across Lodge Trail Ridge. Seems as though there were about two thousand Sioux and Cheyenne's waiting for him. Captains Fetterman and Brown saved their last cartridges for themselves..."

Holmes shot a look of disgust at Doug, then he turned his horse away and rode toward the wagons. Tobe grinned. "You should have let him go, Doug," he said suggestively.

The three bucks were riding slowly along the bank of the Crazy Woman, never looking back.

The little column reached the bottom of the ridge, and instead of heading for the crossing, they turned to follow the creek. Half a mile beyond the three warriors, there was a place where a horseshoe-shaped mound of earth extended from the higher ground east of the creek. It was the only possible place for a defense if the Sioux moved in on them.

The troopers rode with their carbines across their thighs, forage caps pulled low over their eyes, watching the willows for the first sign of the hostiles.

"Look," said Tobe out of the side of his mouth.

Doug turned in his saddle. A file of mounted warriors had emerged from the willows, and the leaders were now splashing through the shallow waters. The hoofs threw up sheets of spray tinted redly by the sinking sun—an ominous sign to Doug, for there was much Celtic superstition in his blood.

"Up ahead," said Tobe.

Doug turned quickly. More warriors were fording the

creek north of the mound of earth.

Doug stood up in his stirrups and pumped his right arm up and down. The horsemen broke into a trot, and the teamsters plied their whips on the dusty backs of their mules. Dust rose and swirled toward the creek, and the jangling progress of the command echoed back from the low heights.

Doug sank the steel into his bay and turned the big stallion to race down the side of the column. "First squad to me!" he commanded.

Corporal MacKenzie led out his men. They raced after Doug, who had turned again and was leading the way toward the mound. The Sioux behind the column quirted their ponies.

Doug and the squad reached the mound before the Sioux, who were north of it. "Dismount! As skirmishers, Forward!" yelled Doug.

The squad dismounted. The two-horse holders took charge of the mounts while the rest of the squad doubled forward with carbines at the ready. They spread out along the Up of the hollow. "Take charge, MacKenzie!" called out Doug. "No shooting unless they charge!"

Doug swung the sweating bay and started back toward the jangling, dust-shrouded column. The Sioux had closed up behind them, and Locke Holmes had drawn his saber. The sun flashed on it. The wagons were grinding up the slope, swaying crazily from side to side. Doug's eyes picked out the girls in their ambulance as they shot past him, and then he was among the rear guard. "Fall back!" he commanded.

Holmes turned a flushed face. "We can drive them!"

"Damn it! Fall back!"

The sweating troopers looked at Doug and then at Holmes. They glanced at the oncoming warriors. Discipline took hold. The troopers rode after the wagons, now and then throwing an anxious look over their shoulders, for no matter how many times a man has seen the Plains

Indians moving in for the attack, he never quite gets accustomed to it.

The wagons had reached the hollow, and Doug could see Adam Morrisey through the dust, cursing and shouting commands as he forced his horse against the lead mules of the first wagon to make them circle within the lip of the hollow to form the defensive circle. Troopers had dismounted while the infantrymen had dropped from their precarious perches on the wagons and had trotted forward to ring the hollow with their ready rifles.

The pursuing warriors had halted. A broad-chested warrior rode out ahead of them, almost within good rifle range. Tobe reined in beside Doug. "It's Sinta Gleska," he said.

Doug nodded. He had met the tough warrior before, and the odds were about even up on who would win the next hand. Doug wiped the sweat from his face. "We've had our share of luck this day, Tobe," he said.

They retired to the hollow. Morrisey was busy setting up the defense. The two Rochelle girls had gotten down from their ambulance and now sat beneath it. Diane was laughing with excitement, but there was no smile on Louise's calm face. Locke Holmes was clearing the ground for them, holding a blanket in his hand.

"Big help Mr. Holmes is," said Tobe dryly.

Spotted Tail sat his gaudy Appaloosa and watched the troopers. He was a first-rank fighter among the Sioux and a wary battle chief. The white eyes were in a fine defensive position. His decoys had failed. He had expected the command to cross the Crazy Woman on their way to Fort Phil Kearney.

Spotted Tail turned to his warriors and motioned them to cross the creek. There was plenty of time to take the soldiers. There were no other troops within thirty or forty miles. He could afford to wait to make his victory sure.

CHAPTER FOUR

A coyote's shrieking laugh carried through the night from the dark hills along the Crazy Woman. There was a faint trace of the rising moon in the eastern sky. In the silence about the bivouac, the faint rushing noise of the creek could be heard, mingled with the sighing of the wind through the trees. The wind stirred the ashes of one of the bivouac fires and carried a wraith of smoke toward the hills.

Doug Boyd padded through the darkness. The hollow already stank of manure and the nitrogen smell of the horses and mules. If the hostiles kept his command penned up in there a few days, the place would become a pesthole. They had enough water, on short rations, for several days, but the horses and mules would have to do without any.

A ring of troopers and infantrymen was fanned about the lip of the depression. It wasn't likely that the Sioux would attack before dawn, for an Indian killed at night would wander forever in the cold darkness, but some young buck, eager to gain coups, might make a try for a soldier.

Beyond the ring of troopers, there would be another concentric ring; that of the Sioux and Cheyenne's, belly flat to the ground and knives in hands, watching the bivouac like cats, waiting for someone to make a break. Doug could almost smell them above the stench of the camp.

The white tilts of the wagons shone dimly in the darkness. Doug walked past the ambulance. Its curtains were drawn, but the rear ones were pulled aside as he passed. "Doug?" called Louise.

"Yes."

"Wait."

He helped her down to the ground. "Have the Sioux gone?" she asked.

"No."

"How can you tell?"

He smiled. "I can smell them."

She leaned back against the wheel. "How serious is the situation, Doug?"

She was a soldier's daughter. There was no use lying to her. "Very serious, Louise." Diane was young and flighty, the type who would possibly crack up and scream her lungs out when the chips were down, but Doug had a feeling he'd rather have Louise to back him up in danger than some men he knew.

"There is no chance of getting help from Fort Purcell?" she asked.

"None. There are no cavalry troops there. I'd ask for a volunteer to get through, but it wouldn't matter. By the time your father's men got here, it would be over for all of us."

The coyote shrieked through the darkness like a soul in torment. Louise raised her head. "Why do they do that?"

"They are signaling to each other."

"The *coyotes?*"

He laughed. "No. The hostiles." The smile faded from his lean face as he looked toward the creek. "Tobe is out there somewhere."

"He is a strange man."

"Yes, and a first-rate scout. He only came along because I got him released from the guardhouse. He said he had a feeling that something would happen. As usual, he was right. He has an uncanny way of forecasting the future. He speaks Sioux and Cheyenne even better."

"Aren't the two languages alike?"

"No. The Cheyenne call themselves *Tsi-tsi-tsas,* or Our People. The Sioux call them *Sha-hi-'ye-na* or People of Alien Speech. Yet they are allies, and good ones, too, and the Cheyenne are the equals of the Sioux in battle. Some say they are even better, and that's about as high a compliment as you can give them."

"Do you speak any of the Indian tongues?"

He shrugged. "After a fashion. A little Sioux, a little Cheyenne, some Pawnee. I can make myself understood in Apache."

"You've been out here a long time, Doug."

He smiled wryly. "Too long, some say."

She looked toward the dark hills. "Is it right to take this land from the Sioux? Red Cloud did not want this road through his people's hunting grounds."

"The weak go down before the strong," he said thoughtfully. "The Chippewas drove the Sioux from Wisconsin and Minnesota. The Sioux, in turn, drove the Crows from this country. Now the white men are trying to drive the Sioux from it. It's all relative."

"They told us at Fort Laramie that it was perfectly safe to travel the Bozeman."

He nodded. "By people who do not *have* to travel the Bozeman. I'm still surprised that your father permitted you to come."

She looked up at him. "He has the same opinion as that of many other officers. He wrote to me and told me the Sioux and Cheyenne's would soon be reservation Indians begging for meat and flour on issue days. He said that the army has put the fear of God into them and will hold them easily in check."

God help us, thought Doug. He had met Rochelle's type before. In some ways, because of their low opinion of the mighty Teton Sioux, they were more dangerous to the army than the Sioux themselves.

A shadow seemed to detach itself from the night and drift toward them. Doug's hand shot down to the butt of his Starr revolver. "Evenin,' Miss Rochelle," the shadow said. It was Tobe Burgess. He tapped Doug on the shoulder. "I got something to tell you, Doug."

"You'll excuse us, Miss Rochelle?" asked Doug.

She nodded. Doug gave her a hand up into the ambulance. "Good night," he said. "If shooting starts, you must get beneath the wagon. There are boxes lined up there to hide behind."

"Yes."

"If anything happens—shooting, I mean—you must stay low." He hesitated. "One other thing..."

She looked down at him with steady gray eyes. "I have a revolving pistol, Mister Boyd. I assure you that I know how to use it and *will* use it if it is necessary." She pulled the canvas curtain closed.

Tobe and Doug walked away from the wagon and then stopped. Tobe spat juicily. "She's all right," he said in a low voice. "No lollygagger like that other little filly. When she wiggles them little hips of hers, I'll swear every man in this outfit forgets about home, mother, and next payday."

"Take it easy, Tobe!" Doug glanced at the ambulance.

Tobe waved a hand. "Oh, *she* ain't in there. She's waiting for the moon to come up, along with Mr. Holmes."

Doug flushed. He had ordered Holmes to see that the two women were comfortable and then to make the rounds of the defense line. It should have taken him at least an hour, and he had set out only twenty minutes ago.

Tobe looked toward the creek. "There ain't too many bucks out beyond our lines. Most of them is across the Crazy Woman. They're making big medicine in the hills over there. The horses is herded between the creek and their camp."

Doug looked closely at Tobe. The scout's lower clothing was dark with water. "You crossed the Crazy Woman?"

"Yep."

"You're loco!"

"Mebbe...mebbe not. Wasn't no use in crawling around here waiting for a Sioux to see how deep the meat is on me with a Green River knife."

"How many bucks does Spotted Tail have?"

"Between a hundred and a hundred and fifty."

"Not enough to attack troops in a defensive position, yet enough to hold us here until we're out of water."

"Yep—unless he's sent for more warriors."

Doug rubbed his bristly jaw. "Yes," he said quietly.

Tobe cut a fresh chew. "Now, if one or two of us was to get across that crick and try to stampede them horses, it would take the wind out of Spotted Tail's sails, wouldn't it?"

Doug looked at the taciturn scout. Tobe could do it if any man could, but Doug doubted if there was another man in the command who could back Tobe's play, with one exception—Doug himself.

"Understand," said Tobe, "it ain't going to be any shadbake over there."

"Yes."

"If you don't get back, Locke Holmes will have to take command."

"How did you know I was thinking of going?"

Tobe grinned like a hungry wolf. "You think I'd trust anyone else out there, you Irish polecat?"

Doug looked down the alley. Fort Purcell was about thirty miles downstream, a hard forced march, and God alone knew how many hostiles were in the hills. Locke Holmes was no Indian fighter and was glory-hungry to boot. If anything happened to Doug and Holmes took over command of the column, he'd still have those thirty dangerous miles to travel. There was no alternative. Morrisey was a veteran of frontier duty who was capable enough, but he had always had a tendency to lean a little too heavily on his commanding officer.

"Well?" asked Tobe.

"We'll go."

Tobe scratched his head. "The moon will be full up within an hour. Just time for us to get across the crick. We might be able to stampede the head before the bucks get ready for a dawn rush."

"Happy days," said Doug wryly.

"Now ain't it a fact?"

Doug walked toward the wagon where he kept his gear. Two shadowy figures moved quickly apart, and Doug found himself face to face with Diane Rochelle and Locke Holmes. Diane hastily fumbled with the collar of her dress. Holmes touched the brim of his forage cap. "Sir?"

There was no use in rawhiding him in front of the girl. Holmes' place was with the men, keeping the veterans to then-work and keeping up the rookies' spirits. But he might end up as column commander, and the more respect the men had for him, the easier his task would be.

Diane Rochelle shivered a little as the coyote gave tongue again from the hills overlooking the bivouac.

"If you will excuse us, Miss Rochelle," said Doug, "there is something I must tell Mr. Holmes."

She tilted her head to one side. "This is all so thrilling. Can't I stay and hear what is going on?" She laughed. "Locke tells me there is little danger. That we can easily drive off the hostiles if we meet them in the open field. It will be something to talk about in the Officer's Club at Fort Purcell."

He was about to tell her she might never see the Officer's Club at Purcell if indeed there was such a luxury at a rude frontier post. "Your sister is expecting you," he said.

She looked quickly toward the ambulance. "Louise is *always* expecting me." She placed a hand on Locke's arm. "Until the morning," she said and walked off into the darkness.

Locke Holmes expanded his chest. "Christ, what a woman."

Doug nodded. "Holmes," he said, "you might as well know the odds. The Sioux will sit out there until we run out of water. First, we'll have to get rid of the horses, which will pin us down on foot. Then we'll run out of rations. In time Spotted Tail will get reinforcements, and when we're too weak to resist, he'll sweep over us like a flash flood."

Holmes smoothed down his fine broadcloth shell jacket. "Come now, Boyd," he said lightly, "we can take care of ourselves. Aren't you doing a little crying in the wilderness?"

Doug almost lost his temper, a luxury he rarely afforded himself on field duty. "Mister Holmes, forget the idea that we're in a good position here. In fact, we're in one hell of a spot, with no troops to relieve us. There is only one way we might get out of this trap. Possibly the *only* way."

"Yes?"

Sergeant Morrisey came through the darkness. "Mr. Boyd, sir," he said, "In case we can make a break for it, I've taken the liberty of lightening some of the wagons."

"Good! Stay here, Morrisey. I want you to hear this, too."

"Yes, sir."

"The main body of the hostiles is across the creek.

There are just enough of them on this side of the Crazy Woman to contain this command. I propose to cross the creek with Tobe here and make an attempt to stampede the hostiles' horse herd."

"*Jesus*," said Morrisey.

"If we succeed, it will give this command the superiority of being mounted. A slim chance, but better than none."

"But why you, sir?" asked Morrisey. "We can't spare you."

Doug looked toward the creek. He looked to the east and saw that the sky was lighting with the faint glow of the rising moon. "I've done enough scouting to make it possible. I know of no other man in this command who might succeed with Tobe."

Holmes traced the course of his dry lips with a forefinger. "That leaves me in command then."

"Yes."

Holmes was grateful for the darkness which shielded the look in his eyes. "And if you don't make it back, sir? God forbid, of course!"

"You will take the command on to Fort Purcell."

"Yes, sir."

"Understand that it will not be all beer and skittles. We *might* stampede the herd. We *might* be able to break away. The odds are high, and the deck might be stacked. It is more than just a calculated risk."

"You're a courageous man, Boyd."

Doug spat dryly. "Right now, I'm plain scared. Tobe and I must cross the creek before the moon lights it up. We'll have to play cat and mouse with the hostiles until the waning of the moon. Once we stampede the herd, it is up to you and Morrisey to get this command into motion as though Satan himself was jabbing you in the rump with a pitchfork."

Holmes and Morrisey nodded.

"One more thing—I don't want any of the men to know I have left here."

"Why not?" asked Locke Holmes.

"They rely on me. If I get the job done and get back, they'll know I was out there, but I don't want them to be concerned about it now. They have enough on their minds as it is. You understand?"

"Of course."

"Good! Morrisey, arrange it so there will be some kind of a commotion to attract the attention of the Sioux on this side of the creek to keep them from hearing us."

"Yes, sir."

Doug walked to his wagon and got out his gear. He stripped to his drawers and pulled on his old, trail-worn Mounted Rifle trousers. He pulled a gray flannel shirt over his head and then drew on the thigh-length, thick-soled, button-toed Apache moccasins he used for scouting. He bound a black silk scarf about his hair.

He buckled on his gun belt, complete with cap pouch, ammunition pouch, and sheathed Green River knife. He drew out the heavy Starr double-action .44, which he carried in preference to the issue Colt. He checked it and slid it into its holster. He placed several blocks of phosphorus "strike-anywhere" matches in his shirt pockets.

He padded toward the head of the wagon line. Tobe was leaning against one of the wagons. "Ready?" he asked.

"As much as I'll ever be."

"Good." Tobe turned and walked toward the hill behind the hollow. He glanced back at the camp and then slid into the brush as silently as a cat. Doug followed him. They worked their way through the brush until they were a good fifty yards from the command. Tobe slid down into a shallow draw and lay flat on his lean belly. Doug dropped beside him.

Tobe gripped Doug by the nape of the neck and placed his mouth close to Doug's ear. "This leads to the crick," he whispered. "Snake it, amigo. We get found out, we split. Me north. You south. Meet you two miles or so down the crick if we make it." Tobe crawled away into the darkness.

Doug raised his head. The night was quiet except for the occasional stamping of a horse or mule and the sighing of the cool wind. He crawled on after Tobe.

They were a few feet from the creek when the wind shifted and carried a noise to them. A man shouted from the south side of the bivouac. Doug grinned. Morrisey had timed it just right.

CHAPTER FIVE

The water was almost waist deep and surprisingly chilly. Doug Boyd stopped in midstream, crouching low to see the dim figure of Tobe Burgess. The night was playing tricks with his eyes, moving the willows to form grotesque and menacing shapes. He looked toward the eastern bank, seeing the dim white tilts of the wagons above the rim of the hollow. He raised his gun belt higher in his hands as he went on, feeling the gravelly bottom with his feet. The water was deeper and faster near the bank where the stream had scoured a channel.

Tobe rose from the brush and waved Doug on. Doug crawled out on the bank and lay still, feeling the water draining from his trousers and moccasins. He got up on his knees and buckled on his gun belt, probing the darkness with his eyes while he listened to and analyzed the night sounds.

Tobe waved him on. They ascended a coulee which cut into the bank. Tobe vanished into the brush, and Doug followed him cautiously. The scout had senses like an animal.

Tobe was out of the coulee and lying on the flat ground looking to the west. The faint, pungent odor of horses came to Doug, along with the feeling of movement in the darkness ahead and below them. Tobe pointed down the slope. It took Doug a while to see anything, but then he saw the dark mass of the quiet herd.

The bitter odor of burning wood drifted about them as the wind rose and shifted. Tobe drew Doug close. "The camp is around that saddleback ridge over there."

"How many guards on the herd?"

"Three, four—not many—they feel pretty secure, I guess. In Crow or Blackfoot country, they'd have a dozen horse guards. Shows you what they think of us. The guards here are young bucks, untried warriors."

The moon was higher. The first of its rays shone down into the valley of the Crazy Woman and made a pewter-colored trace of the creek center. A coyote howled mournfully from the far bank. A faint sound of drumming, mingled with the shrill tones of a bone whistle, came from the Sioux camp.

Tobe moved on to get downwind of the herd. The valley was flooded with silvery light when at last, they stopped atop a brushy knoll where they could see both the herd and the camp across the creek. It took Doug some time to pick out the horse herders. There were four of them. One of them stood on a ridge, looking toward the creek. Two of them were mounted and riding slowly up and down on opposite sides of the herd. The fourth guard squatted on a rock overlooking the herd, with his rifle across his naked thighs.

The night had been playing tricks with Doug's eyes, but now he seemed to see much better than before. He looked back the way they had come. The moon had already illuminated it. If they had been twenty minutes later, they would never have been able to come that way.

The sky to the west was tinged with a pinkish glow that faded and then rose in intensity. It was the corona from the Sioux fires. The drumming never stopped. The wind carried the smoke across the saddleback ridge where it hung in a rifted layer over the grazing herd.

Tobe lay flat on his belly, exploring his hair with his fingers, while his jaws moved steadily at chewing the tobacco wad. "There's a mess of dry grass upwind," he said at last.

Doug nodded. The grass was tinder dry and would burn like fury.

Tobe leaned back against a rock. "Seems to me if a fire was started upwind, them horses would stampede right down this little valley. Then they'd have to turn toward the Sioux camp. Jesus God! They could sure raise hell stampeding through there, Douglas, my boy."

"It's a good picture, Tobe. I wonder where we'll fit in it."

"There you go—thinkin' again! I thought you was a soldier! A soldier on active duty ain't got time to wonder about such things." Tobe slid a hand inside his shirt and drew out a flask. He handed it to Doug. Doug took a stiff jolt and gave the flask back to Tobe. He could feel the liquor work down into his vitals.

"Get some sleep," said Tobe. "We've got plenty of time." Doug lay down and closed his eyes. Tobe was right. There was no time to think of what might happen.

———

TOBE'S HAND was cold on Doug's forehead. Doug opened his eyes. The moon was a faint trace in the western sky, and a cold wind was sweeping over them. Tobe handed the flask to Doug again. Doug drank, and so did Tobe. Then the scout stoppered the flask with an act of finality. "Come on," he said.

They set off upwind, keeping away from the herd. The going was rough and slow. They stopped fifty yards beyond the herd, keeping well back so that the herd would not scent them.

Doug probed the darkness with his eyes. They had lost sight of the guards. Tobe finally turned to Doug. "We better not move about too much. I figure we can work along behind that ridge. I'll cross over the ridge on the far side of the herd. Give me about half an hour, then watch for the flame. Then get your fire started and dust out of here."

Doug nodded. "Head north along the creek. Maybe we can get across to meet the column in time."

Doug could not see the expression on Tobe's face, but he knew it was an odd one. He gripped Tobe's hard hand. Tobe vanished into the darkness.

Doug worked his way along until he could look down on the herd. He could sense them rather than see them. The grass was thick about him. He lay flat, waiting for time to pass.

There was a movement behind Doug. He turned. Why in hell's name had Tobe come back? The dawn was almost upon them.

Doug stood up and instantly realized his mistake. The figure in the dimness was almost as tall as Doug and wider through the shoulders. Doug closed in swiftly, feeling for the warrior's throat to stifle any outcry. The warrior grunted as Doug brought a knee up into his crotch. Doug's hands closed about the muscular throat of his opponent, and then he got the surprise of his life. The buck fell backward and raised his knees up into Doug's gut. Doug fell heavily, and the two of them slid down the slippery grass slope.

The warrior was on top of Doug, but Doug's hands still held their death grip. Fingers probed for Doug's eyes. The rank odor of the warrior almost stifled him. His fingers slipped on the greasy throat. He threw the Sioux to one side and smashed a left to the mouth, and followed through with a right to the gut.

The Sioux rolled free and got up on his knees. Doug launched a kick, catching the buck on the jaw. The man grunted. Then he was up on his feet like an uncoiling spring, and the two of them closed together. Sweat dripped from their faces, and suddenly Doug realized he could see the Sioux's broad countenance. It was the false dawn.

The Sioux broke free and whipped out his knife. Doug jumped back, clawing for his own knife. He fell heavily, and the buck darted in, raising his knife. Doug hooked his left foot behind the right ankle of the warrior and then drove his right foot against the inside of the Sioux's knee with all the strength of his strong leg muscles. The buck was hurled back, and Doug was up on his feet with his knife out. He kicked at the broad face, then drove his knife in deep below the warrior's left ribs.

The Sioux's body rose into an arc and then sagged down. He coughed, and blood flooded down on his bare chest. Then he lay still, staring up at Doug with eyes that did not see.

The wind shifted, and Doug heard a crackling noise. He ran up the slope and saw a patch of flame at the far side of the herd. A warrior yelled. Doug sheathed his bloody blade and took out a block of matches. He crouched out of the wind and broke one of the matches from the block. He scratched it on his belt buckle, shielded the flame, and then lit the block. He tossed it down into the grass, and it caught instantly.

The fires flared up as the wind caught them, and long runnels of flame licked hungrily through the yellow grasses. Horses whinnied and neighed in terror. There was a slow movement toward the mouth of the valley. Doug drew his Starr and raised it. He pulled the trigger five times, and the crashing shots echoed and re-echoed through the valley. The herd broke into a frenzied run for the mouth of the valley, raising a cloud of dust that swirled to meet the thickening smoke.

There was no sign of Tobe—the scout had raised dust getting out of there. Doug sprinted toward the ridge.

Two mounted warriors saw him and quirted their ponies toward him. He whirled and saw that his only hope of escape was toward the creek. He ran toward it and saw another warrior top a rise in the ground, shaking a lance.

Doug turned again, cursing himself for leaving himself only one shot in the Starr. The pair of bucks were closing in. One of them raised a rifle while the other swung a pipe axe. Doug fired at the rifleman, and the warrior slid from his mount and was smashed by the hoofs of the second horse.

A wall of flame danced in front of Doug. There was only one way to go. He raced toward the flames, hearing the high-pitched yells of the braves. The flames seemed to leap to meet him, and the smoke and heat caught at his lungs. He coughed, then looked back. The two horses were rearing and plunging. The lancer hurled his weapon as Doug turned again. It seemed as though a tongue of flame hit his left shoulder up high. The shock of the lance hitting him drove him forward through the flames into the clear.

The lance dragged behind him as he plunged into a smoke-filled coulee and staggered toward the ridge. The dawn was filled with smoke and flames, a crackling hell of conflagration, while behind him, he could hear the low thunder of unshod hoofs and the frenzied whinnying of the horses as they streamed toward the Sioux camp.

He reached behind himself and gripped the lance. He jerked at it, and a shaft of pain shot through him. He almost fainted, but some inner strength kept him on his feet. He steeled himself and jerked at the weapon again, but it had caught somehow in the thick muscles of his back. Sweat streamed down his face as he stood there in the wreathing smoke, feeling the blood flow stickily down his back all the way down into his moccasins.

He leaned forward and slogged up the ridge with the weight of the lance dragging at his tortured muscles. Doug reached the top of the ridge and looked across the valley to see the column in swift motion, with the wagons swaying and bouncing in the middle of the yelling troopers. There was a spate of carbine and rifle fire, and then the column had broken through the thin fringe of Sioux and was in the clear, leaving a pall of dust and gunsmoke drifting behind it like a protecting shield.

He slid down the slope and into the thick willows. His throat raw with burning thirst, Doug crawled to the creek and plunged his face into the water. The pain engulfed him again as he lay there, half-conscious, with the shaft protruding from his bloody back like some horrible and alien growth that would kill him in time.

He drew out his Starr with shaking hands and propped himself up on an elbow to reload the weapon. There were a few warriors across the creek looking after the retreating column. Doug crawled back into the thick willows and downstream until he could see no more of the hostiles.

He pulled himself to his feet by holding onto a willow. The lance had sagged down and dragged at his back, and his senses swam as he clung to the tree. Once more, he tried to free the shaft, but it was no use. He looked downstream with tortured eyes. There was no sign of the column now other than the settling dust. The eastern sky was alight with the coming dawn. He walked toward a thick motte of cottonwoods and through it before he stopped again to feel the wound in his shoulder, cutting' his fingers on the edge of the lance blade.

He stood there looking at his bloody hand. There was no time to halt. He had to keep going, for the Sioux would round up their ponies quickly enough—and then they would strike down the valley after the column.

His strength ebbed as he plodded on with the end of the lance dragging a little furrow behind him. It would be thirty miles of hell to Fort Purcell.

The sun was up when he stopped and leaned against a tree. The valley seemed to lift and waver in front of him, and he knew he could go on no longer with that blade digging into his back. There was a place where a tree had split sometime in years past, leaving a V-shaped crotch. He lifted the lance and slid it through the crotch, then with shaking hands, he lashed the lance haft to the tree with his headscarf. He stood there for a long time, trying to build up his courage for the severe test he planned for himself.

He looked up at the clear sky and breathed a short prayer, then lunged forward to rid himself of the blade. There was a ripping, tearing sensation and a spate of hot blood down his back. Then his face smashed against the hard ground, and mercifully he knew no more.

CHAPTER SIX

The metallic rays of the sun beat down into the valley of the Crazy Woman. The waters of the creek danced and sparkled in the sunlight. Doug Boyd opened his eyes. His shirt was pasted to his back with blood and sweat. He eased his left hand behind him, feeling for the lance, and he was relieved when he could not feel the shaft. But there was still something in the wound. He probed cautiously, and then his fingers touched the hot steel of the blade. He had rid himself of the shaft but was still burdened with the lance's head. Perhaps his blood had loosened the rawhide lashings which had bound the blade to the tough ash shaft.

He lay quietly. There was no sign of life along the valley other than a splattering of crows drifting high overhead like black rags against the blue sky. They would be as bad as buzzards if he was too weak to move. First, the eyes, then the softer parts of exposed flesh would be eaten until the buzzards arrived and drove off the crows so they could finish the gruesome feast.

He knew he had to stay away from the creek to avoid the hostiles, but his thirst was a deep-seated agony within him. It was now a thirst of the bones which would increase until he went out of his mind.

There was a thread of distant smoke to the north, like a coarse hair placed across pale blue linen. It rose straight up into the windless air. The smoke could mean that the Sioux had struck the column and set fire to the wagons. Or, since it was too close to be smoke from Fort Purcell, it might be a signal of the hostiles.

He crawled toward a brushy draw and into it after he had drunk his fill. It was best to wait for the cool of the evening. He had had no food since his last evening meal of hardtack and issue bacon.

———

THE MOON WAS up when he awoke. He could remember fitful awakenings, but the whole past day had been a dim thing. He moved suddenly and instantly regretted it, as fire seemed to blaze through his shoulder. The wound throbbed like an Arapahoe thunder drum. He crawled to the creek and rolled into it, feeling the water flow about the hot wound. It would become infected. Gangrene would set in. The hostiles had ways of poisoning weapons. A fresh deer liver would be thrown on an ant heap to let the ants fill the meat with their venom. Then the meat would be allowed to rot and then dry. The dry meat would be pounded to a powder and mixed with grease to tip arrows and lances. Fear seemed to rise from the willows and settle about Doug Boyd.

He got to his feet and forced himself to walk unsteadily to the lance shaft. He loosed it, bound the scarf about his head, and then took the shaft for a walking staff. Doug set off downstream, plodding on, driving his unwilling legs forward.

He had had more than his share of luck in escaping. He feared delirium and hoped to God he would have enough strength and sense to put a bullet into his brain if he were trapped.

Pictures formed themselves in his wandering mind.

The shapeless trunk of what had once been an emigrant near Sage Hen Creek who had been exposed to the little torture fires of the Sioux. The gruesome remains of an eight man-patrol on the Poison Spider—eyes had been gouged out, and noses, ears, and tongues had been severed and piled neatly atop a rock. The men had been gutted, and their greasy entrails had been drawn from them like rags. Arrows had bristled from the corpses like the spines of a porcupine.

He forced the thoughts from his mind and hitched his heavy Starr forward, closer to hand.

The moon was on the wane when he waded across the shallow creek and turned north again. Then he saw the ash beds of fires. A broken hardtack box was lying to one side, and there was a spur beneath a bush. The column had made it that far, in any case. Locke Holmes might get through to Fort Purcell.

He found a half-eaten hardtack biscuit and gobbled it hungrily. There were some berry bushes up the slope, and he filled himself with fruit. As he turned to start his trek again, he caught the flutter of a filmy bit of cloth out of the corner of his eye. He took it from the bush, smelling the faint odor of jasmine. Louise Rochelle had been wearing such a scarf the last time he had seen her. He thrust it inside his clammy shirt and plodded along the bank of the stream.

The dawn wind flowed along the valley of the Crazy Woman and swayed the brush and trees. Doug opened his eyes, his head throbbing. He had walked most of the night and then had dropped with exhaustion. He had no idea how close he was to Fort Purcell. He looked down the slope toward the creek and saw a stand of timber, noticing the many stumps there. He got to his feet and walked down to the creek to drink.

He looked about the timber. Some of the stumps showed where they had been freshly cut. Wagon wheel ruts and hoof marks showed that troops had been there cutting the timber. Hope surged through him. He could not be far from Fort Purcell.

He sat off at a slow pace, following the ruts. His stomach ached for lack of food, and he was lightheaded, but he had enough sense to plod on. If he fell and was not able to get up, it would be the end of him.

The sun tipped the hills. The creek had been trending to the northeast for some time, and he saw a low line of hills far ahead of him. He stopped and stared. Smoke hazed the sky to the northeast. It had to be from Fort Purcell.

———

IT WAS late afternoon when he heard the bugle faintly from the northeast. He increased his pace, staggering a little in his weakness until he climbed a rise of ground. The creek had curved again, more to the east. He made his way up a slope and into a thicket. Then he saw the fort.

The buildings seemed to be scattered like blocks left there by a child. The sun shone on the white flagpole, and even as he watched, he saw the flag being hauled down. Then he saw a puff of smoke and, shortly thereafter, the dull boom of the sunset gun.

The fort was only partly palisaded. Smoke drifted from some of the log buildings. The sun glinted from shiny metal. He could just make out moving figures on the parade ground.

Doug sat down on a rock and held his head in his hands. Now that he had slogged his way this far, he did not seem to have the strength to go on. Shadows fell in the valley. Then it was dark, and he could see the yellow lights of the frontier post winking through the velvety darkness.

He stood up and gripped his lance staff. He hobbled down the hill, heading for those blessed lights. One foot ahead of the other, with each step a torment. He kept his head down so that he could not see the lights, for they did not seem to be any closer. One foot ahead of the other. The tune of *Benny Havens, Oh!*, seemed to run incessantly through his tired brain. He laughed several times at the senselessness of it—why should *he* be thinking of an Academy song?

THE SENTRY WALKED across the gateway. The huge gates had not been hung as yet, although both halves lay on the ground, bolted and trimmed, ready for their hardware. The wind swept down the valley and slapped the halyards against the flagpole. A door banged shut across the parade ground.

The sentry stopped and stared out into the darkness. Slowly he raised his Springfield and cocked it. There was something out there, moving steadily toward the gate.

"Halt! Who goes there? Halt, or I fire!"

The figure stopped and leaned on a staff.

"Who goes there?" yelled the sentry.

There was no movement from the figure.

"Corporal of the guard! Post Number One!" called out the sentry. He swung his rifle to high port and backed away a little.

The corporal of the guard came from the partially constructed guardhouse, buttoning his blouse. "What is it, Barker?" he asked.

The sentry spoke out of the side of his mouth. "A man. Just standing there."

"Challenge again."

"Who goes there? Advance one to be recognized!"

"Jesus," said the corporal. "There's only *one* man *there*, you jawbone recruit!"

Doug walked forward.

"A white man," said the corporal. "In damned bad shape."

Doug raised his head. He took three more steps and fell headlong on the hard ground.

———

WHEN HE OPENED HIS EYES, his face was close to a rough issue blanket. Someone was working on his shoulder. He winced as the crusted flannel was cut loose. "Lay still," said an unmistakably Irish voice above Doug.

Doug closed his eyes again. He ached from head to foot, and his face was bruised where he had fallen on it.

"Knife wound?" asked the man.

"Lance," said Doug weakly.

"A few more inches, me lad, and ye'd be among the blessed."

The smell of carbolic floated about Doug. He glanced at the basin placed on a stool. The water was pinkish in hue. Then he felt a tearing sensation in his shoulder. "Jesus God!" he said.

"'Tis out, mister. Now lie ye still. I must exude the pus. It will hurt ye."

"Thanks," said Doug dryly.

"Ye want a bit of wood to bite on?"

Doug shook his head. "A thick steak will do."

The man laughed. "Ye hear the man, Kennedy? 'Tis a sense of humor he has."

"Aye, sir."

Doug could feel the fingers against his puffy skin. He felt the beginning pressure and then a stab of fiery pain. Then he seemed to be caught up in a swirling mist, and he plummeted down into darkness...

Cool water touched his face, and something was thrust under his nose. The smelling salts brought him around. He lay on his back, looking up into a round Irish face graced with ginger-colored burnsides. "'Tis all over.

The pus is out," said the surgeon. "Swabbed and cleansed ye are. How do ye feel?"

Doug grimaced. "Hungry."

"Good! A healthy sign, Mr. Boyd."

"You know me?"

"One of the troopers from yer company recognized ye as ye were brought in here. I'm Surgeon Michael Beirne, Forty-ninth United States Infantry, at yer service."

"Thanks for your ministrations, surgeon."

"'Tis me duty." The Irishman turned. "Kennedy, ye faithless son of Erin! Will ye not bring in that broth?"

"Coming, sir."

Beirne grinned. "Kennedy spent so many weeks in the guardhouse he thought it was home. There was no company commander would have him, so the good colonel suggested, as an Irishman, that I take in me countryman."

Doug smiled. "Is my company all right?"

"Aye. Mr. Holmes did a fine job of bringing them in."

"I'll be glad to get back on duty with them."

A shadow seemed to cross Beirne's ruddy face. "It will be some time before ye can get up and about. I caught the wound just in time. It was in a bad place for gangrene."

"Are the ladies all right?"

"Just fine."

Kennedy brought in the broth, and Doug spooned it up greedily. The orderly looked at Beirne. "Shall I tell the colonel that Mr. Boyd can see him now?"

"Let the man finish his broth!"

Doug emptied the bowl and placed it on the table. "How long before I can take command of my company again?"

Beirne took out a cigar case and offered a cigar to Doug, who shook his head. Beirne selected a cigar and lit it from the lamp. "Ye can be about in a week or so. But I do not know when ye can take command of yer company, mister."

Doug looked quickly at him. There was a curious undertone to the man's voice. "What do you mean?"

Beirne inspected his cigar. "Until the colonel hears yer story, there will be no decision made about ye."

"I don't follow you."

"The fact is, me boy, ye're in a bit of a pickle, so to speak."

"Dammit, man! Tell me what is wrong."

"Attention!" snapped Kennedy.

Doug looked toward the doorway. A tall, spare man, in dress uniform with silver eagles on his shoulder straps, was standing there. He wore a Kossuth hat on his head with the wide brim turned down all the way, similar to the way General Meade had worn his during the war. Strangely enough, the officer resembled Meade a great deal.

"Colonel Manning Rochelle, commanding officer of the Forty-ninth United States Infantry and commander of Fort Purcell," said Beirne. "This gentleman is First Lieutenant Douglas Boyd, Colonel."

Rochelle advanced into the room. "I will see Mr. Boyd alone," he said quietly.

The two Irishmen left, closing the door behind them.

Rochelle's gray eyes studied Doug. "You are feeling better, mister?"

"Yes, sir."

"That is good. Have you any explanation for your conduct, sir?"

Doug looked curiously at the colonel. "I don't understand the colonel."

Rochelle looked thoughtfully at Doug. "You deserted your command in time of war, sir."

Doug leaned forward. "What is *that,* sir?"

"Lieutenant Locke Holmes took command of your

company and brought it here to Fort Purcell with my daughters."

"I know that, colonel. It was done at my orders."

"That is not what Mr. Holmes reported."

"So? Just what *did* he report, Colonel Rochelle?"

The tall officer walked to the window and looked out on the parade ground. "He reported that you, and a civilian scout by the name of Tobias Burgess, did on the night of the 17th of August desert the command bivouacked at a site near the Bozeman Trail, on the Crazy Woman."

Doug stared at the officer. "For the love of God, sir! Surely you are joking?"

Rochelle turned slowly. There was a cold look in his gray eyes. "I *never* joke, mister."

"Mr. Holmes is lying, sir. Sergeant Morrisey knows why Burgess and myself left the command."

Rochelle smoothed down the front of his blouse. "Sergeant Morrisey was shot and killed by a Sioux warrior while scouting ahead of the column in company with Mr. Holmes."

Doug passed a hand across his forehead. The past few days, his mind had been in a turmoil, confused and shaken, but surely he had heard the colonel's last words correctly. There was no one else in the column who had known the two of them had taken a desperate chance to stampede the Sioux ponies.

"Is there anything you have to say in your defense? I must warn you that anything you say might be used against you."

"Used against me?"

"At the inquiry and possibly your court-martial, Mr. Boyd."

Doug rested his head back on his pillow. Suddenly the little room seemed stifling hot, and the smell of carbolic sickened him. He couldn't think. All he had thought of in the past few days was to make Fort Purcell and be back with the command he had saved from massacre. This charge of the colonel's had taken him by surprise.

Rochelle walked to the door. "You'll need your rest," he said coldly. "You will remain here, under arrest in quarters, until such time as an investigation may be made of your conduct. These are serious charges, Mr. Boyd...very serious indeed." The colonel left the room.

Beirne came in and thrust a chair between his legs. He rested his hands on the back of the chair and his chin on his hands. "Ye're in a hell of a mess, me boy."

"How much do you know?"

Beirne grinned. "The walls are thin. Besides, there is little going on about Fort Purcell that the inestimable Kennedy does not hear."

"Do you believe those trumped-up charges?"

Beirne shrugged. "I do not know ye, my boy. Nor do I know Mr. Holmes very well. But, betwixt the two of ye, I'd lay me bets on ye. There is something about that one which does not ring true. He came onto the post like a conquering hero with his wee bit command as though he had ridden berserk through the whole Sioux Nation."

Beirne drew out his cigar case and placed a cigar in Doug's mouth. He lighted it and then one for himself. He half closed one eye and studied Doug carefully. "Ye'll tell me the true story?"

"After a drink."

Beirne stood up. "Boyd is the name, and Irish, too."

"Scotch-Irish. My mother was a MacMillan."

"A Ulsterman! Well, ye cannot help that." He took a bottle from a shelf. It was labeled POISON. He filled two-issue cups. "If I did not mark me liquor so, that sponge Kennedy would swill it all."

Doug sipped the strong liquor. It brought new strength to him. He told his story to the sympathetic surgeon.

Beirne refilled the cups. "Of course," he said, "it is only yer word against his."

"True."

Beirne tugged at his sideburns. "I have been in the army for a long time," he said, "since the Mexican War. If this Mr. Holmes has plotted against ye, he has covered his tracks well, very well indeed."

"I have no witnesses except Tobe Burgess, and God alone knows where he is now."

"Aye." Beirne hitched his chair closer. "But I have never been on a post or with a regiment where the enlisted men did not know more about what was going on than the officers did."

"So?"

"So there is me orderly—a scrimshanker, a drunk, a woman chaser—but loyal to me, Doug Kennedy can eavesdrop about the enlisted men. Perhaps there is something he can find out. Something which will help ye."

Doug looked out of the window. Call To Quarters blew across the post and echoed from the hills. "It doesn't seem as though even God can help me now, surgeon."

CHAPTER SEVEN

D oug Boyd stood at the window of his room and looked out across the parade ground. Colonel Rochelle had chosen his post site well. There was abundant water, timber, and grazing. He had built quarters, barracks, a hospital, stables, shops, storehouses, and a laundry. Doug couldn't help smiling as he watched two enlisted men in the process of constructing an octagonal bandstand.

A timber cutting detail rolled by with their wagons and an escort of infantrymen riding in ambulances. The fort, not completely palisaded as yet, had a great gap on the side toward the creek. There were piles of logs lying there, being trimmed by adze men. A partially completed trench ran along the place where the palisades would be set into the ground.

Rochelle had built his magazine well on a rise of ground, constructing it of fieldstone, with loopholed walls. The door was of hewn planks, but layers of the wood were on each side of an iron sheet, and the door was thickly studded with bolts. With all the work going on, Manning Rochelle had made sure that none of his command forgot they were soldiers. A platoon was practicing movements and timings with their heavy Springfield muzzleloaders. Recruits were learning the school of the squad under the command of a leather-lunged sergeant.

Doug leaned on the sill and lit one of the cigars Beirne had given him. He wondered just how effective the Forty-ninth U.S. Infantry would be against the Sioux. There was little the infantrymen could do other than hold the fort against an attack. An attack, however, wouldn't be likely, for the Sioux chiefs were too wily to throw their men against palisades-protected riflemen. That wasn't the red man's way of fighting. They never made almost suicidal assaults against fortifications and into the hell of artillery fire at point-blank range. The Plains Indians liked the subtle decoy and then the hard-hitting ambush. They liked the maneuverability of their swift horses and the quick attack and quicker retreat.

There was one thing the Plains Indians feared as much as artillery fire—well-timed volleying of veteran infantry—but the opportunities of luring the warriors in for such tactics were few and far between. Infantrymen fought where they stood, and in most instances, when attacked, there was little they could do but peer through the dust and powder smoke at the irritating horsemen who were as hard to hit with a musket as a bird on the wing.

Doug snatched the cigar from his mouth. A familiar figure was walking toward the stables where a detail of cavalrymen were lining up their mounts. It was Locke Holmes. The sun sparkled from his brilliant buttons and the hilt of his imported and engraved saber. His leather and brass were immaculate.

Holmes took the report of the non-com who had formed the men, and then he led his detail from the post.

"He's looking for the Sioux," said a dry voice behind Doug.

Doug turned to see Surgeon Beirne. "He's liable to find more than he bargains for," said Doug.

"Which might not displease ye, I take it?"

"It would displease me. I want to take care of him myself, Mike."

"Aye."

"Did Kennedy learn anything?"

Beirne sat down on the cot. "'Tis plain yer Mister Holmes is not too popular with the company, Doug."

"He never was."

Beirne tugged at his whiskers. "Already, he has broken Corporal MacKenzie and promoted a Private Holleschied in his place."

"Good God! MacKenzie was up for his third stripe! Holleschied is nothing but an opportunist and a bootlicker."

Beirne smiled. "That figures out. Two of a kind, him and Holmes."

"Anything else?"

"It seems as though Mr. Holmes had dinner with Rochelle's last evening. Mr. Holmes is pressing his suit with Miss Diane. The lass is the apple of the colonel's eye."

"She'll lead any man a merry chase," said Doug dryly.

"The two of them might do well. They are both ambitious—and perhaps a little ruthless. It occurs to me that Mr. Holmes, if he plays his cards well, will keep command of yer company and earn a promotion soon. In time he will get his first lieutenancy. By marrying Miss Diane, whose father is not a poor man, the spalpeen can set himself for life."

Doug threw his cigar into the fireplace. "I'd like to set his damned neck."

Beirne waved a hand. "Give that type enough rope, and they will hang themselves. It might interest ye to know that Mr. Holmes, far from being a dyed-in-the-wool yellow leg, has agreed with Colonel Rochelle's theories on the use of the mounted arm."

"How so?"

Beirne relit his cigar. "Rochelle thinks cavalry are of little use except as escort troops, orderlies, couriers, and such like. He has already posted an order to the effect that one of yer platoons be dismounted, the horses to be turned over to the Forty-ninth for the use of the officers."

Doug paled. "He can't do that!"

"He *can*, and he *did*. Colonel Rochelle ranks next to God out here at the end of nowhere."

"Not to the Third Cavalry, Mike!"

Beirne smiled. "I gave ye credit for being a sensible man, Doug. It doesn't make a damned bit of difference to the man *what* cavalry regiment he is dealing with. In his opinion, the Third is nothing but a group of mounted orderlies to supplement his beloved mud crushers. The Brave Rifles indeed!"

Doug looked down at the green welt along his trouser leg. The Mounted Rifles had been authorized by an act of Congress in May of 1846 for service along the Oregon Trail. That early duty had been waived for a time, and they had joined Zachary Taylor's army in October. Later they had served with Winfield Scott on the advance to Mexico City. At Cerro Gordo, they had fought on foot and had suffered eighty-four casualties. They had fought well at Contreras and Churubusco, capturing horses in the latter fight and charging into battle as they were supposed to, as cavalry.

They had charged at Chapultepec Castle on foot in company with some Marines who had lost their commanding officer. When the army had marched into Mexico City, the flag of the Mounted Rifles had been raised over the National Palace, and General Scott had doffed his hat, bowed low, and given them the nickname which had become their regimental motto. *"Brave Rifles!"* he had said. "Veterans! You have been baptized in fire and blood and have come out steel."

In 1849 the Mounted Rifles had ridden out on the

Oregon Trail for duty. They had served at many outpost forts with distinction, even as far as Idaho and Oregon. In later years they had served in Utah and in Texas. The war had found them in New Mexico, where they had fought at Valverde and Glorieta. In August of 1861, they had been redesignated as the Third Cavalry.

Doug had never served with any other regiment but the Third. There had been times when he had served on detached duty, but his assignment had always been with his original regiment.

Beirne stood up. "Another thing, Miss Louise Rochelle requested permission to see ye."

Doug turned quickly. "Yes?"

"Her father refused to let her do so."

Doug shrugged. He might have expected that. "Any news on Tobe Burgess?"

"None. I might add that Mr. Holmes suggested to the colonel that Burgess might have returned to his old life with the Cheyenne's. Squawman, he called him."

"Tobe is worth a dozen of him, squawman or no."

"Let me look at that wound."

Doug stripped off his shirt, and the surgeon removed the bandage. "There is no proud flesh," he said. "Ye'll be all right."

"Can't I get out of here?"

"No. Rochelle was going to place a guard over ye, but I talked him out of it. Ye will share my quarters, and I will be responsible for ye."

Their eyes met. Doug had found a real comrade in the genial Irishman.

Beirne grinned. "It is not so bad. I have books, cigars, and whiskey in plenty. Kennedy will take yer gear there."

Doug looked down at his trail filthy clothing. "This is all I have here. My uniforms and equipment were in one of the wagons."

"He'll get them for ye."

They left the little hospital and walked toward Officer's Row. An infantry officer looked curiously at them, nodded shortly to Beirne, and ignored Doug. The story of his supposed defection would be common post gossip by now.

A woman was walking in front of the quarters. It was Louise Rochelle. She stopped as she saw Doug, scanning his drawn face and haggard eyes. "I am sorry about your troubles," she said quietly.

"They will be cleared up, Louise."

She studied him. "I hope so."

"You believe the charges?"

"I don't want to, but I really don't know what to believe."

Doug felt sick inside, but he knew she was a soldier's daughter, and the iron bands of discipline and duty bound her as tightly as they did any soldier.

She looked away. "It has been said that you were not the best type of officer, Doug. That you had little discipline, I don't believe that is so."

"Then you'll talk to your father?"

Her eyes held his. "My sister has confirmed Mr. Holmes' accusations against you. She said that he was right. That you left without a word to him, that Mr. Holmes had taken on your responsibilities."

"She's lying, Louise."

She nodded. "My father listens to everything she says. It has always been so. Even when we were children." She looked at him, and there was deep sorrow in her eyes. "I will do what I can, Mr. Boyd." She walked away.

Beirne watched her. "A nice girl," he said.

"Yes."

They walked into his quarters. An extra cot had been set up in the small room. Doug looked about. The walls were lined with books, and a few etchings had been hung about. The place was comfortable enough.

Beirne waved a hand. "It isn't much, but I call it home. Army quarters have been my home since '46."

Doug dropped into a chair. "Is there any chance of getting a message out to Fort Laramie?"

Beirne held out his hands, palms upwards. "How? The hills are thick with Sioux. Besides, ye cannot go over the colonel's head in such a matter. We are isolated here, Doug. Almost as though we were on the moon. There is nothing ye can do but hope for the best. Ye know I am with ye. Besides, the lass may do ye some good. It is all ye have to depend on."

Doug nodded. He watched Beirne fill two glasses from a decanter. He accepted the whiskey and sipped at it. The company he had whipped into shape, his pride and joy, had been taken from him and was in danger of losing its identity under the command of the colonel. Locke Holmes had framed him as neatly as one of Beirne's etchings of the Irish countryside.

━━━━

DARKNESS HAD enveloped Fort Purcell when Locke Holmes returned with his detail. Doug stood at the window and watched the tired troopers as they led their mounts to the stables. He saw Holmes swagger a little as he walked toward the headquarters building.

"Hendricks!" called out Doug as one of the troopers passed the quarters.

Hendricks halted and walked toward the window. "It's you, sir! How are you, Mr. Boyd?"

"Well enough. How was the patrol?"

Hendricks looked behind him. The rest of the patrol were already at the stables. "I was scared all the way, sir," he said. "Mr. Holmes was not only looking for Sioux—he was looking for a fight."

"Any sign of Sioux?"

Hendricks hesitated. "In a manner of speaking, sir. We ran into three of them—an old man, a boy, and a squaw near Clear Creek. They rode away, but they were on poor mounts. We chased them. They separated. The boy escaped, and the old man dropped behind to let the squaw escape. All the old buck had was a flintlock trade rifle and a bow and arrows."

"Go on."

"The old man was brave. He fired at Mr. Holmes and missed him. Corporal Holleschied wounded the old buck. The Sioux shot three of his arrows. One of them ripped a hole in Mr. Holmes' blouse. Mr. Holmes could have captured him easily enough."

Doug leaned forward. "Well?"

Hendricks looked away. "I don't like Indians, Mr. Boyd. God knows I've killed a few of them, but it was always in battle. Holmes draws his saber and charges the old man. I know a little Sioux. The old man yells out that it is a good day to die, sings a few lines of his death song, and bares his chest to the saber. It went clean through his belly. He only lived a little while."

"Good God!"

Hendricks nodded. "It made us sick. Holmes fired a shot into the old man's head at point-blank range. His hair was afire when we rode off. Holmes gathered up his weapons and brought them along for souvenirs."

Doug handed him a drink through the window. "Where is Mr. Holmes quartered?"

"The end room of Officer's Row. He's there alone. Mr. Steptoe, who bunks with him, is in the hospital."

"Thanks."

Hendricks downed the drink. "I needed that. Thanks, sir."

We hope to have you back soon, Mr. Boyd. Good night, sir." Doug turned away. He stripped off his clothing and put on his fatigue uniform. Mr. Holmes would have an unannounced caller that very night.

CHAPTER EIGHT

The soft tones of *Taps* died away in the hills. Here and there, about the post lights died away. The wind swept across the parade ground, rattled the halyards of the flagpole, and blew into the warm rooms, dispelling the heat of the day.

Doug turned down the lamp. Surgeon Beirne was attending a big poker game in the quartermaster's room. Doug walked outside and stood there for a time under the porch roof. There was no one in sight except a sentry pacing back and forth near the gate.

Doug walked softly toward the far end of Officer's Row. He stepped into a doorway as two troopers walked past.

There were lights in the colonel's quarters. As Doug watched, he saw a man leave the quarters and walk toward Officer's Row. The man was an officer, and he went into the quarters at the end of the row. The light came on in the room.

Doug walked to the end of the row and glanced in at the window. Locke Holmes was standing with his back toward Doug, pouring himself a drink. His saber and pistols hung on the wall above his cot.

Doug turned around and looked back at the colonel's

quarters. The lights in the living room there were extinguished even as he looked. He walked to the door of Holmes' quarters and opened it quickly.

Locke quickly turned as Doug stepped into the room and closed the door. The officer's face paled. *"You!"* he said.

Doug looked about the room. A bow and some arrows lay on a table. A battered flintlock trade musket leaned against the wall, its stock studded with brass tacks. A pair of Sioux moccasins lay on the floor.

"What do you want, Boyd?"

Doug eyed Holmes. The man was extraordinarily handsome, and his uniform fitted him as though he had been poured into it.

Holmes glanced quickly toward the window. Doug walked over and closed it, pulling the curtains across it.

"You're supposed to be under arrest in quarters," said Holmes.

Doug nodded. "I wanted to have a little talk with you, Holmes."

Holmes waved a hand. "Now?"

"This is as good a time as any."

"I have nothing to say to you."

"I have something to say to *you,"* said Doug.

The young officer downed his drink and placed the glass on the table. "Get out," he said.

Doug leaned against the wall. "What's your game, Locke? Do you really think you can get away with it?"

"I don't know what you're talking about."

"No?"

"You pulled out and left me with the company and the care of those two girls. Thank God I managed to get them here safely."

Doug studied the man. "You'd better talk to the colonel in the morning," said Doug. "Make a clean breast of the whole thing."

Holmes laughed. "You're out of your head. You have no witnesses. Burgess is gone. Morrisey is gone."

"I meant to ask you about Morrisey."

The blue eyes became veiled. "He got in the way of a Sioux bullet."

"So? Who was with him?"

"I was!"

"That figures."

"*What do you mean?*"

"Morrisey knew where I had gone."

Holmes refilled his glass. His hands were steady enough. The man had nerve. "Supposing I did tell Rochelle that you had gone to stampede the herd? Supposing I told him I had fabricated the whole thing? What do you think would happen to me?"

"That's your concern. You've tried to ruin my career. Did you really think you'd get away with it?"

The man moved fast. He ripped one of his Colts from its holster and cocked it, holding it at belly level. His cold eyes held Doug's. "Yes," he said thinly. "I'm gambling for big stakes, Boyd. You were in the way. I have nothing personal against you, but I had to get rid of you."

The gun muzzle did not waver. Doug would get a bullet in the belly before he could move a finger.

"The war ended before I could really get into it. I was sick of hearing about the exploits of those officers who *had* served in the war. I knew I'd be just another brow-beaten shavetail out here. Slogging through dust and mud. Eating rotten food. Taking orders from veterans—men like you. I'd go maybe ten years before I had any promotion and perhaps end my career as a captain. That's not for me, Boyd."

"A man can get glory out here. Glory brings publicity. Publicity brings promotion. Rochelle has promised me a promotion. I have your company now, and by God, I'll harry the Sioux with them!"

"Like you did today?"

Holmes flushed. "Don't move," he said. "I've already killed a man today."

Doug looked at the pitiful trophies of the hero in front of him. "Holmes," he said softly. "You stink of rottenness." He walked toward the door. "Stay where you are!" snapped Holmes.

Doug turned.

Holmes smiled. "You didn't think I was going to let you get out of here alive, did you?"

Doug moved like a cat. He jumped to one side and clamped a big hand down on the barrel of the Colt while his right fist drove up under Holmes' jaw. Holmes released his grip on the gun butt. Doug smiled, then tossed the pistol into a corner and walked toward Holmes with cocked fists.

Locke raised his hands, but the cold fury of Doug's attack was more than he had expected. Doug hit him five times, belly and jaw, dumping him into the corner so hard that pictures fell from the walls.

Doug stepped back, wiped his bleeding knuckles on his trousers, and waited for the man to get up.

Holmes stood up slowly. "I've had enough," he said. But even as he spoke, he snatched up a chair and swung it at Doug with all his strength. Doug turned and caught the chair against his back. The full swing had upset Holmes' balance, and Doug's fists began to batter savagely at his opponent's red face.

Holmes went down hard. He shook his head, and a dribble of blood and saliva came from his slack mouth.

Doug kicked the chair aside. "Get up," he said.

"No."

"Get up, damn you!"

"Go to hell!"

Doug gripped Locke by the collar of his shell jacket, twisting his hand to tighten the collar about the man's throat. He hauled the man to his feet and cut savagely at the handsome face with his open right hand. They staggered back against the table, and the decanter crashed to the floor, flooding the air with the ripe odor of whiskey. Doug shoved Holmes against the wall. He shoved a fist up under Holmes' nose. "I'm going to drag you to the colonel," he said.

Holmes brought up a knee into Doug's groin. Doug winced in pain as he let go of the battered officer. Holmes snorted in triumph. He rushed Doug, battering at him viciously, trying for the eyes. Doug hit the far wall, braced a foot, and swung blindly. Luck was with him, for his fist caught Holmes flush on the jaw, almost lifting him off his feet. He hit the table, scattering his trophies, and fell heavily to the floor.

Doug wiped the blood from his split lips. His breath came harsh and heavy from deep in his chest. He walked unsteadily toward the door. His wounded shoulder throbbed in pain. The door opened as he reached for the knob, and he found himself looking into the gray eyes of Louise Rochelle. She wore a dark shawl over her beautiful hair.

She stared at him and then at Holmes. "Doug," she said, "what have you done?"

He stepped to one side. "Cornered a rat," he said. "I'm sorry I spoiled your rendezvous. You might be able to clean him up a little, Miss Rochelle."

He looked into her wide eyes for a moment and then pulled the door shut between them. He walked to his quarters. Beirne was sitting on his cot in his drawers. He stared at Doug's battered face. "Mother of God," he said. "Where the hell have ye been?"

Doug poured a drink. "Visiting Mr. Holmes."

Beirne stood up quickly. "Did anyone see ye?"

"No." He did not want to mention Louise Rochelle.

Beirne took out his medical kit and wiped the blood from Doug's face. He bathed it in a solution. Doug could feel warm blood trickling down his back. He peeled off his fatigue blouse. Beirne whistled. "Ye busted it wide open." He packed and bandaged the wound.

"The fat is in the fire now," said the surgeon.

"I don't give a damn!"

"Ye're a blasted fool!"

"Shut up, Mike!"

Beirne shook his head. "How does he look?"

"Worse than I do."

"I like that well enough, but not what will happen when he tells the colonel."

"He won't get a chance."

"What do ye mean by that?"

"I'm pulling out of here."

"In God's name, why? Rochelle will be sure then that ye are guilty!"

Doug looked up. "I'm going to find Tobe Burgess."

"Ye're mad! The hills are thick with Sioux!"

"I'll need a horse, a rifle and cartridges, food, my revolver."

Beirne paced back and forth. "Kennedy can get them for ye." He pulled on his uniform. "The lad left Ireland two jumps ahead of the Royal Irish Constabulary for stealing a thoroughbred pacer."

Doug poured himself another drink after Mike left. He had to work fast before Holmes recovered in time to stop him. He changed into his trail uniform and pulled on his moccasins. He was ready to leave when Beirne returned.

Beirne closed the door and lowered the lamp. He handed Doug the gun belt, complete with holstered Starr and sheathed bowie knife. "Kennedy has the horse. He got it through a gap in the palisade. There is a Spencer carbine and plenty of cartridges with it. Blankets, a canteen, and other necessary gear. Ye won't change your mind?"

"No."

Beirne shrugged. He took a flask from a drawer and

handed it to Doug. "This might be of more help than a Bible," he said. "I'll go along with ye. I'll cover for ye if ye are seen."

Doug buckled on his gun belt and slid the flask inside his shirt. Beirne put out the lamp. They left the quarters and walked quietly behind the row of buildings. Beirne led the way to the west end of the fort. They passed behind Holmes' quarters. Beirne laughed softly. "I'll enjoy seeing his face tomorrow."

"Maybe your face won't be so happy when the colonel finds out you let me get away."

"Pish! The luck of the Irish is with me. I kissed the Blarney Stone—not once, but three times."

They followed the palisade until they saw a gap. Beirne looked about. "Get through with ye!"

Doug stepped into the gap and held out a hand. Beirne gripped it. There was nothing to say. Doug padded off into the darkness. He heard a soft whistle, and Kennedy came toward him. "The bay is in that draw a hundred yards off, sir," he said.

"Thanks, Kennedy."

"'Tis nothing, sir. I'd do anything for a friend of the surgeon's."

"I'll see that you get a promotion, Kennedy. Maybe in the Royal Irish Constabulary."

The man stared at him. "Ah, 'tis a wit ye are, sir! Good luck to ye!"

Doug started for the draw. There was a hoarse challenge behind him from the top of the palisade. He turned to see the head and shoulders of a man standing there. "Halt! Halt or I fire!" the sentry yelled.

Doug sprinted forward. The musket roared behind him, and the slug hummed over his head. He crouched and darted toward the draw.

"'Tis the Sioux!" yelled Beirne. "Alarm! Alarm!"

A musket exploded sharply. Doors banged open. Men yelled.

Doug slid down into the draw and saw his bay. He gripped the reins and led the mount up the draw toward the lower hills, thick with brush and scrub timber.

All hell had broken loose behind him as a result of Beirne's strategy. Boots pounded on the hard parade ground. He heard Kennedy yell out, "They are near the creek!"

Doug swung up on the bay and spurted him through the brush. He looked back toward the fort. Lights flashed here and there, and then the bugle sounded the alarm. It echoed brassily from the sleeping hills.

Doug let the bay have its head. It trotted steadily to the west, and when they were a good mile from the fort, Doug rode down toward the creek where the going was better and let the bay full out.

The noise from the fort died away behind him. He looked to the west. Somewhere ahead of him, he might find Tobe Burgess. If he did not, and the Sioux did not find Doug, he might just as well keep going west, for there would be no returning to Fort Purcell.

CHAPTER NINE

There was an uneasy restlessness in the night wind on the plains. Doug Boyd drew rein and looked back along the valley of the Crazy Woman. He was miles from the fort by now, but he felt that he was being followed. There was a great weariness within him. He had lost more strength from being wounded than he had realized, and his hard fight with Locke Holmes had drained more of it from him.

He turned the bay toward the stream and rode into the shallow waters. The bay made noisy progress through the shallows, and the cold sweat of fear ran down Doug's sides until, at last, he forded the creek and rode through the willows and brush up the side of a ridge.

———

THE MOON WAS UP HIGH when he made his camp somewhere between the Crazy Woman and the Clear. He dropped his carbine, blankets, food, and water in a hollow that was ringed with brush and then led the bay a quarter of a mile away, picketing him in a shallow valley. He walked wearily back to his camp and unrolled his blankets. He ate without relish and washed down the food with water, followed by a stiff jolt of whiskey.

Tired as he was, he found it impossible to sleep. He examined the Spencer repeater which he had found on the horse. The initials M.X.B. were carved into the stock, and he realized that the weapon must be Mike Beirne's own. It was a seven-shot repeater and had a magazine cut off. None of the other Spencer's Doug had fired or been equipped with a cutoff. There was a leather-covered wooden box with the Spencer. He opened it and found that it contained seven tin tubes which held seven .56/50 cartridges.

A good shot could make a good accounting of himself with the chunky repeater, for he could churn out seven rounds and reload in a matter of seconds.

Doug lay back on his blankets and looked at the sky. He felt lonely as a hawk. Maybe Tobe Burgess was dead, and his thatch of iron-gray hair was already drying on a hoop in a Cheyenne or Sioux lodge. Maybe the taciturn scout who knew so much and said so little was already across the Shadow Waters. Doug began to realize how much of a friend Tobe had been. They had never talked too much together when they were alone on some mission, but there had been a silent companionship between them. They knew each other and allowed for each other's faults. They had bunked together and fought side by side.

It was Louise Rochelle who had thrown him completely. Coming to Locke Holmes for a rendezvous while her sister's kisses were still wet on the man's lips. Doug had known many women, and he had loved some of them and lost them. That was all in the past now. His duty with the Third had become more important to him. But somehow, Louise Rochelle's gray eyes had begun to bother him during the last days on the journey to the Crazy Woman. He closed his big hands and looked at them. He should have beaten Holmes to a pulp, but he knew now he had played fully into the man's hands. He might have escaped a court-martial; Tobe or Louise might have cleared him. Now he was truly on the run, absent without leave no matter what his reason for so doing.

He picked up the carbine and began to climb the slope above his camp. The moon was bathing the landscape in silver light when he reached the top and squatted down to study the terrain. Tobe might have escaped and then avoided the valley of the Crazy Woman because of the strong possibility of running into hostiles there. If he had been cut off from the route to Fort Purcell, he might have struck out for Fort Phil Kearney, which was built on a plateau between two branches of Big Piney Creek, a tributary of the Powder.

Doug half closed his eyes to make a mental map of the country. Fort Kearney was about thirty-five miles from the Crazy Woman in a northwesterly direction. Fort Reno was about twenty-five miles away in a southeasterly direction. Fort Purcell was about thirty miles away in a northeasterly direction. The scout might have tried for any one of the three posts. They stood in a rough triangle with a perimeter of about one hundred and twenty miles.

Something moved in the moon-bathed valley below him, and he slid from the skyline, dropping belly flat to watch the valley. His field glasses were with his gear, but the moonlight was bright enough for him to discern a party of mounted men, and he knew well enough they weren't white men.

They were moving steadily toward the south, and even as he watched, they turned to the west toward the broken country. He slid down the slope and forced his way through the thick brush until he was on a level about fifty feet above the valley floor, with the wind blowing toward him. Then he saw the white man riding among the warriors. His hands were bound behind his back, and a reata was looped about his neck with the other end held by a buck.

Tobe! The name raced through Doug's mind. It was him, all right!

Doug worked his way around the foot of the ridge until he reached his camp. He gathered up his gear and hurried to the bay. It took minutes to saddle the horse, load, and then mount him. He rode to the north until he saw the valley.

There was no sign of the riders, but he cut their trail in a few minutes. He looked toward the silent brooding hills. Then he checked the magazine of the Spencer and placed the repeater across his thighs. He rode steadily up the long draw into the darkness, for the moon had not risen high enough to drive away the shadows. He felt as though he were riding into the pit itself, but his chances of ever finding Tobe again were one in a million.

He led the bay down toward Clear Creek and watered him. There was a place where the marks of unshod ponies had pocked the soft bank. Doug forded the Clear and picked up the hoof marks on the far side.

The moon was on the wane when he caught the bitter odor of wood smoke drifting toward him. He led the bay into a thicket and tethered him there. Then he walked through the dimness until the smell of the wood smoke came thick and heavy to him.

They were camped beside a small stream. Some of them Were about the fire, squatting on their haunches roasting meat. Others lay about on the ground wrapped in their blankets. The horses were beyond the stream.

The white man lay on the ground below a bush, and he did not move. Doug tried his glasses, but it was no use. The man lay with his back toward Doug. He wore nothing but filthy trousers, and the firelight picked out the dried blood on his naked back.

There were ten warriors near the fire. There must be several with the horses. Doug wet his lips. They were pretty damned careless about their camp security, but then they were in their own country, knowing full well the white-eye soldiers were hard put to stay within their log walls without bothering the Sioux and Cheyenne's in the open country.

Doug watched them until they let the fire die down. They rolled themselves in their blankets and lay down to sleep. There was no chance for Doug to snake his way into the camp, cut Tobe loose, and get away with him. Even an Apache would have had a helluva time getting within range of the captive, and they could move as silently and as unseen as stalking cats.

Doug went back to his bay and got a blanket. He led the horse deeper into the thicket and picketed him there. He took his canteen and walked back to a place where he could see the dying fire winking through the dimness. He wrapped himself in the blanket and sat down to wait. There wasn't a damned thing he could do now but wait.

———

THE FALSE DAWN was pewtering the eastern sky when Doug opened his eyes. He started. He must have slept for hours. His back ached, and his muscles were stiff. The Sioux were still there, lying in their blankets. The white man had been left uncovered during the cool night.

Doug arose stiffly and found a place where rocks and tumbled logs gave him a small natural rifle pit. He dug away the loose dirt from beneath a log and found that he had a fine rifle and observation post.

Now the Sioux were up and about. Doug focused his glasses on them. They were all big men, obviously veteran warriors. Some of them had their Sun Dance scars outlined with paint on their deep chests. Their rifles and carbines lay close at hand, and Doug saw several Sharps, two Henry repeating rifles, and some issue Springfields. They were unusually well equipped with long guns.

They roasted meat again at the fire, now and then looking speculatively at their prisoner. Doug could not get a good sight of the captive. The bush partially concealed him, and he was still turned away with his face hidden.

The sun rose higher, and still, the warriors lay about their fires, now and then lazily roasting a bit of meat. They seemed to be in no hurry. When the sun was at its zenith, several of them rode up the valley.

The sun beat down into Doug's position. He ate and drank a little. When he was finished, he looked out to see three of the Sioux arranging a wooden framework of peeled saplings near one of the fires. They worked slowly, with much talk between them and the other bucks. When they had finished, they tested the structure for strength. They pulled the white man to his feet and lashed him to the framework. One of them ripped the tattered trousers from the prisoner, leaving him stark naked. Some of the warriors eyed the man and talked among themselves.

Doug wet his lips. He could not see the white man's face. They hadn't spent all that time erecting that structure to keep the man from escaping; there was only one reason for it—*torture*.

———

DOUG TOOK his hands from his ears. It was no use. He could hear the piercing shrieks of the white man even through his hands. The screaming had been going on for over two hours. The Sioux were experts, and they were not pressed for time. Knife and fire were the tools they used, and they used them well. It was really only the beginning of the horrible ordeal for the unfortunate white man. They could keep him alive for hours until the last flickering spark of life, at last, died out of the hardly recognizable body of the tortured.

Doug rested his Spencer on the lower log of his barricade. The carbine was sighted for nine hundred yards, but the effective range was about one hundred and fifty to two hundred yards. Doug estimated the range from his position to that of the suffering white man as a little over two hundred yards. A piercing shriek carried to him on the wind. He closed his eyes and gripped the sweat-greasy stock of the carbine. It would be so easy, just one shot. But the man would be put out of his misery only to place Doug in jeopardy. He might get a few of the warriors before they got him, but even if he made a break away from them, they would hunt him down like human bloodhounds.

———

THE SUN WAS low over the hills. The man was still alive, but there was no sound from him now. His body was a mass of blood and tatters of skin, and when the wind increased, Doug could smell the sweetish odor of burning flesh.

Hoofs thudded on the dry ground. Doug looked up the valley. The Sioux who had left the camp earlier that day were returning, and they were moving fast, with their quirts rising and falling like pistons. They shouted as they neared the camp, but there was no way of learning what they said.

The warriors snatched up their rifles and possessions. They plunged into the stream and crossed it to get their horses. In a few minutes, they were racing up the valley, raising a cloud of thin dust behind them. The dust mingled with the smoke of the dying fire. The man still hung from the framework.

Doug stood up slowly. He hooked his canteen to his belt and picked up his Spencer. He walked through the woods until he found the bay. The horse softly whinnied as it saw Doug.

Doug loaded his gear onto the horse and then rode it down toward the valley. The sun was beyond the hills now, but there was still enough light for him to see that the Sioux had not returned. The smoke drifted from the fire, and there was no movement from the man.

The captive did not move as Doug approached the framework. "Tobe!" called Doug.

There was no sound but the wind in the trees and the soft chuckling of the little stream.

"Tobe!"

The man did not move.

Doug kneed the horse around the framework and looked down at the man. Even in the dimness, he could see the human wreck who hung from the tight rawhide thongs. A sour taste rose in the back of his throat, and he could not look at the man.

There was a strange sound from the captive.

Doug slid from the bay and walked toward the man. Somehow he could not touch him. The face was hardly recognizable as a face, but the eyes had been untouched. They looked at Doug as though watching him from the gates of hell.

"Tobe?" said Doug, but even as he said the name, he knew it wasn't the scout. It was some poor loner who had underestimated the Sioux. He drew out his knife to cut the man loose. The man had enough strength left to shake his head. He looked at the carbine and then at Doug. A croak that sent a cold wave up Doug's spine was the only sound the man could emit.

Doug swung up on the bay. "Can you understand me?"

The man did not move.

Doug wiped the cold sweat from his face. There was only one thing to do. He couldn't cut the man down and leave a gun for him because he did not think the man had the strength to use it, and some of the fingers were missing from both hands.

Doug turned the bay away and rode off fifty feet, then

turned again. The wind moaned through the trees. Doug brought the carbine hammer to full cock, raised, and sighted the weapon. "God forgive me," he husked. He punctuated the sentence with the flat report of the gun. The man jerked as the slug tore into his head. Doug swung the bay and slapped him with the butt of the carbine, urging him across the stream and into the woods.

The report of the carbine slammed back and forth in the little valley and then died away. There was no sound now but the steady thudding of the bay's hoofs and the sighing of the night wind, and soon enough, the thudding of the hoofs grew fainter and then died away altogether.

CHAPTER TEN

The bay placidly cropped the grass in the swale behind Doug Boyd as he lay on a hill looking down on Fort Phil Kearney. Colonel Carrington had built his new post well.

Kearney was a much bigger post than Purcell and was much better situated. The post was garrisoned by men of the Eighteenth Infantry and a few troopers of the Second Cavalry.

Doug rubbed his bristly jaws. He had no way of knowing whether Tobe Burgess was down there. He might take a chance and go down to try to locate the scout, but there was always the risk that some officer or enlisted man would recognize him or that a courier had come from Purcell with news of Doug's defection. Tobe Burgess himself might be penned up in the post prison on the same charge.

Doug studied the fine fort. In the time since he had left Fort Purcell, he had had little sleep. He had seen no hostiles, but the feeling was always with him that they were not too far away. He had heard stories of how the Sioux, Arapahoe's, and Cheyenne's kept watch on Fort Kearney. Only last December, they had wiped out Bill Fetterman and his command.

Wagons appeared over a ridge and rolled down toward the fort. They were heavily laden with timber. Infantrymen rode in two of the wagons with their rifles between their knees while a detail of troopers jangled along behind the column.

Doug rested his chin on his hands. If he could talk to one of the garrison, he might learn if Tobe was there. He didn't want to enter the post. The best thing to do was to watch for the next timber-cutting party and follow them, hoping to talk to one of the men.

He led the bay down the slope and watered him in the Big Piney. There was an ominous look about the surrounding hills as the sun went down, staining the western sky with a reddish hue, almost like blood. It was an omen Doug did not like.

He made his way into the hills, picketed his bay far from his simple camp, and rolled into his blankets for a night's sleep with his Spencer and Starr at his side.

———

THE SUN AWOKE HIM. The smell of the pines filled the morning air. He gathered his gear together and walked toward the bay. Below him, beyond the Big Piney, he could see the wagon tracks of the timber-cutting parties. He loaded his gear on the bay and then sat down on a log to wait patiently.

A squirrel came down a tree and eyed him brightly. He frisked about and then scampered across a clearing. Suddenly, as though startled, he leaped for a tree and instantly vanished around it.

Doug dropped behind the log and eyed the valley with slitted eyes. A hawk floated toward him, then suddenly veered off and sailed downwind.

Minutes ticked past as the sun rose higher. There was a movement in the brush across the valley. Doug took out his glasses and rested them on the log. The broad face of a warrior swam into view. He was watching the road.

Doug looked back. The bay was well hidden.

A noise came to him on the wind. The popping of whips and the creaking of dry axles. Then the wagons appeared with their escort of soldiers. They drove along the rutted road right under the eyes of the watching warrior.

Doug scanned the valley slopes, but there was no other sign of warriors.

The warrior vanished. Doug went to his horse and led him along the slopes toward where the wagons had gone. He heard the ringing of axes in the thick woods and came out on a low bluff where he could see the timber camp. The wagons stood in a circle with sentries inside of it. Beyond the wagons, high on a slope, the sun glinted on axes. Soldiers stood guard over the contract timber cutters. The horses grazed near the wagons, watched by a mounted detail.

Doug worked his way down the slope through the trees and brush until he was within fifty yards of a trooper who sat his horse in the shade of a tree. The rest of the detail were on the far side of the little herd of horses.

Doug stood up and walked toward the trooper, who suddenly straightened up and swung his carbine toward Doug. "Halt!" he called out.

Doug halted. He smiled. "Nervous? Can't you see I'm a white man?"

The trooper lowered his carbine. "Sure. Who are you? What are you doing out here?"

Doug took a chance. "Government contract hunter for Fort Kearney."

"That so? Never seen you around the post."

"I've been working out of Fort Reno. Looking for one of my friends. I headed this way when I heard he was a scout and hunter here at Fort Kearney. Name of Tobe Burgess. Know him?"

The trooper nodded. "I knew him at Fort Laramie. He was up here last year when Colonel Carrington brought in the Eighteenth to build Kearney. Tobe ain't here now, though. I don't know where he is."

"Thanks anyway."

"Don't mention it. Say, you sure look like you been out beating the brush."

Doug grinned. "I'm not dressed for company if that's what you mean."

"No offense."

"Any trouble with the Sioux around here?"

The trooper spat. "Was. They got a comeuppance here the second day of this month, and they ain't got over it yet. They was almighty cocky about massacring Fetterman and his men last year. This time they wasn't so lucky."

Doug looked toward the other men. They were talking among themselves. Now and then, one of them looked toward him. He wanted to dust out of there away from the gabby trooper now that he was sure Tobe Burgess wasn't at Fort Kearney, but he didn't want to break away too fast. Frontier troopers were quick on the trigger when their suspicions were aroused.

Doug could see the other troopers riding around the herd toward them. One of them wore sergeant's chevrons.

"Wilhelm!" yelled the sergeant. "Who is that man?"

"Says he's a contract hunter from Kearney."

"This time of year? Hold him there, Wilhelm!"

"He ain't going anywhere."

Doug backed off a little. "Thanks," he said. "I'll be off."

"Why? The sergeant wants to see you."

"I've got to get to work."

"Stand where you are!" yelled the non-com.

Doug jumped behind a tree and started up the slope.

"That's that officer from Purcell who deserted!" bellowed the sergeant. "It's Lieutenant Boyd sure enough!"

Doug darted up the slope.

"Halt! Halt or we fire!"

Doug's breath was harsh in his throat as he climbed. A carbine cracked flatly behind him. The slug smacked into a tree. Another carbine fired. Then there was a steady rattling of gunfire as carbines and Colts tried to bring him down.

He swung up on the bay and spurred him along the ridge. He looked back. Smoke was drifting across the meadow. The horses were milling about. The troopers spurred along the edge of the woods, firing as they rode, but Doug was safe enough.

He guided the bay behind a shoulder of the ridge. He felt like a damned outcast. "The son of man has no place to lay his head," he said aloud.

———

HE MADE his simple camp on a branch of the Big Piney. He was almost out of food. All he had left was a can of embalmed beef and some hardtack. He needed time to think. Where in hell's name was Tobe? Perhaps he was dead. Perhaps he was at Fort Reno, and there was even a remote possibility he might have gone on to Fort C. F. Smith.

He ate his frugal meal and lighted one of the cigars Beirne had given him. If the commanding officer at Fort Kearney had been warned about him, it was probable that the commanding officer of Fort Reno had also been warned. If Tobe Burgess was dead, then Doug might as well be dead himself as far as his military career was concerned.

The bay whinnied a little. Doug looked up quickly.

The wind was swaying the brush. He reached for his carbine and levered a round into the chamber. He scouted through the trees but saw nothing.

The thought occurred to him that he might ride to Fort Laramie and take his chances on an investigation of the case there. General Byers was certainly no friend of Doug's. He'd take the long view of the case.

He walked to the bay and moved him so that he'd have better grazing. The big horse was nervous. He whinnied now and again. Doug turned to scan the woods—they were as quiet as the grave. The simile made him feel a little uneasy. He remembered vividly the bloody wreckage of the man he had put out of misery near the Clear.

The powerful Dakotas—the Nation of the Lakota—owned that country. The Tetons were the strongest of the Dakotas and formed half the Nation. They had been warring with the whites steadily since 1855 over the killing of a crippled cow by a *Min-i-con-jou* at Fort Laramie.

Allied with the Tetons were the mighty Northern Cheyenne's and the Arapahoe's, a slim warlike people with the look of eagles.

The red allies far outnumbered the white troops in that country, and they knew the country like the palms of their greasy hands. Doug felt that Wyoming might be another China where the people absorbed their conquerors.

The bay whinnied and snorted. Doug turned quickly and raised his carbine. The sun was almost gone, and the forest lanes were shrouded in shadows. He padded forward and looked down a slope. There was nothing there. He shook his head. His nerves were beginning to get the best of him.

Doug walked back to the horse, debating whether or not he should pull out of there and get higher into the hills. It was getting too dark for safe travel. On the plains, he would have stayed hidden by day and ridden at night, but this country was too treacherous for that.

Something seemed to warn him. He got his gear together and placed it on the horse. He made a last look about his camp to see if he had left anything.

The bay shied suddenly. Doug whirled, his hands tightening about the stock of his carbine. Three warriors stood between him and the bay, and they held rifles in their hands. Their impassive faces seemed dead except for their swiftly moving eyes.

There was no chance for Doug. A green wave of fear swept over him. The very thing he had dreaded had happened. He started to raise his carbine and heard the double click of a rifle hammer as it came back. He dropped the Spencer and slowly raised his hands. The warriors came toward him.

CHAPTER ELEVEN

The dawn wind was sweeping through the trees. The valley of Piney Creek was far below. All Doug knew was that they were somewhere in the Big Horns and close to the timberline. He looked at the back of the Cheyenne ahead of him. The warrior had not turned toward him for hours, but Doug knew the other two were close behind him and that one of them carried Doug's Spencer across his thighs with the hammer at full cock.

They had not spoken a word to him since they had captured him, but he had heard them speak in low voices to each other in the Cheyenne tongue. His wrists were lashed together, and his ankles had been bound by a rawhide rope that ran under the belly of the bay. His thighs were tired from gripping the barrel of the horse.

He heard the rushing of water, and then the leading buck forded a little stream and turned north. The faint odor of wood smoke drifted through the pines, and then Doug saw the winking red eye of a fire in a clearing. There were half a dozen lodges pitched in the clearing.

A horse whinnied from somewhere beyond the camp, breaking the stillness, and then a warrior padded toward them with a trade rifle in his hands. His eyes narrowed as he saw Doug.

The warriors swung down from their mounts. One of them drew out a knife and approached Doug. He cut the rawhide rope which bound Doug's ankles together and then pulled him roughly from the tired bay. Doug staggered a little and then leaned against a tree. There was no feeling in his hands. The buck cut the thong which bound Doug's wrists and then stepped back. A gun muzzle nudged his back, silent warning that he must not move. He rubbed his swollen wrists and began to feel the prickling as the blood began to flow.

One of the bucks placed wood on the fire, and it flared up. A woman waddled from a lodge, glancing curiously at Doug, and then she filled a brass pot at the stream and suspended it from a tripod over the fire.

The warriors who had brought him divested themselves of their weapons and dropped on the ground. They looked at a small lodge set apart from the others, and Doug heard the shrill whistling of a bone pipe and the muted thudding of a drum. It stopped, and a warrior emerged from the lodge. He stood up straight and looked at Doug. A cold chill crept down Doug's spine. The man looked hardly human.

He wore a thick mat of buffalo fur on his head, and from it protruded two big buffalo horns. The mat was in the form of a cape that hung over his shoulders, concealing his upper body. He wore trousers of red trade cloth, and his lower legs were covered with buffalo fur. His arms were bound with wide brass bracelets, and copper wire had been bound about his powerful wrists. In his left hand, he held a bone whistle, while in his right hand was an eagle wing.

But it was his face that drew and held Doug's attention. His eyelids had been painted white, and a band of white ran across the fleshy tip of his huge nose and turned upward to circle about his dark eyes. Eagle-down waved from his shoulders and from the bottom of the shaggy fur cape. He was a sure-enough medicine man. He looked like something from an ancient Druid ceremony waiting to begin the awesome ceremony of the Beltane fires.

A superstitious crawling of fear came over Doug. The medicine man stepped aside and waved with his feathered wing. Doug was shoved forward. Another man had come from the lodge, and he eyed Doug closely. This man was old, with a face wrinkled like a dried apple, but he held himself proudly erect.

Doug was pushed toward the lodge. He bent and walked into it. A fire smoldered in the pit, and smoke rifted through the dwelling. Backrests stood to one side. Blankets and hides had been piled atop something at the rear of the lodge. Then Doug made out a face. He walked forward and recognized Tobe Burgess. The scout's face was drawn and white with a pallor almost deathlike on it. Doug knelt by his friend and placed a hand on his forehead. It was dry. He looked behind him. The old man stood there watching him.

Doug squatted on his heels. "What is it you want?" he asked the old man in shaky Cheyenne.

"You speak the tongue of the *Tsi-tsi-tsas*?"

"A little."

The old man squatted beside him and looked at Tobe. "He is very sick. Maheo wants to take him to the Shadow Land."

Doug was puzzled. Then he looked at the old man. "How are you named?"

The old man looked at the medicine man who had entered the lodge. The medicine man spoke in a low voice. "Two Bears."

Doug wiped the sweat from his face. Two Bears was a sub-chief of the Northern Cheyenne's. A brave warrior with many strike-the-enemy feats to his credit, he was noted as a chivalrous brave who welcomed single combat and was a famous member of the warrior society of Crazy Dogs. But what made Doug breathe easier was the fact that Two Bears had spoken in counsel against fighting the white men, and although he was known to be not too friendly with the whites, at least he was not hostile.

Doug squatted there in the dim tent, wondering how all this had happened to him. The smoke swirled about his head, and he could smell the sweetish rank odor of the two Indians who stood close behind him. He felt nauseated but fought to keep control.

The old chief knelt beside him and drew back the covers to reveal Tobe's naked upper body. The black chest hair was in startling contrast to the white skin. But it was the area of the lower left ribs which caused Doug to stare in horror. The area was swollen and discolored, and there was a puckered hole in the center of the inflammation. It was undoubtedly a bullet wound and a bad one. Bad enough, if a surgeon had been there at the time of the wounding, he would have had his hands full.

Doug wiped the sweat from his face again. "How did he get here?" he asked.

Two Bears waved a hand. "Some of my warriors found him near the Crazy Woman."

"But why did you save him?"

The old man looked at the unconscious scout. "He was the husband of my daughter and the father of my grandson."

"But why was I brought here?"

The old man looked up at the medicine man. "Good medicine," he said quietly.

Doug glanced at the hideously painted and dressed medicine man. There was no expression on his ferocious-looking face.

"What is it you want me to do, father?" asked Doug.

The old chief looked at Doug with steady eyes. "Heal him."

Doug held out his hand's palm upward. "I am not one of those who heals, father."

Two Bears spoke swiftly to the medicine man, who then left the tepee. Doug placed a hand on Tobe's forehead again for lack of anything else to do. He placed his hand over the area of the wound. "*Nohetto*—a real bad thing, father," he said.

The medicine man re-entered the tent carrying a doctor's instrument case in one hand and a wickerwork basket in the other. Doug looked at them—spoils from some forgotten frontier fight, saved for some obscure reason a white man would never understand. Then the thought came to him that the old man had canceled out the mystic treatments of the medicine man to put his trust into the white man's magic of razor-sharp scalpel and pungent carbolic. But it took more than instruments and drugs to make a surgeon. Doug had had his share of experiences in extracting bullets and setting of broken limbs in past years with the frontier troops, but this was something even a skilled surgeon might hesitate to attempt.

He looked at Tobe's drawn face. The badly wounded man was the only witness Doug had to save him from disgrace in his chosen profession, but it was more than that fact that made Doug want to save his life.

Doug suddenly glanced up at the medicine man to find himself looking right into those fierce eyes. The Cheyenne had not been able to do anything for the wounded man, and Doug knew damned well he wouldn't cotton kindly to Doug if he saved Tobe. On the other hand, if he failed...

Sweat greased his hands as he took the instrument case and the basket. Had it been mere coincidence that the three warriors had found him, or had they *known* he was Tobe's friend? It was beyond understanding. There was one thing he did know—if he was to try and save Tobe's life at all, he must do it soon. Some powerful force had brought him there, either God or Maheo, and it was possible that they were one and the same.

"*Nonotov*! Hurry now!" said the old man.

Doug opened the instrument case and looked at the shining contents how he could use Surgeon Michael Beirne right now. "Hear me now, father," he said quietly. "I am a soldier. A Long Knife. I will do this thing, although it is not my work. He may live, or he may die."

"He *must* live!" said Two Bears fiercely.

Doug studied the wrinkled face, old except for the ebony eyes, and he knew what would happen to him if Tobe died. "Let me alone with him," he said quietly.

The two Cheyenne's left the lodge. Doug laid out the instruments and materials from the basket. He picked up a brass pot and walked outside. The warriors were watching him. One of them sat on the ground with his back against a log, polishing his rifle with deer fat. He sat in such a way that he could see the rear of the lodge. They were taking no chances on Doug slipping away.

He filled the pot at the stream and carried it back to the lodge, hanging it from the tripod over the fire. Then he checked the instruments, trying desperately to figure out which of them he would use. For want of anything better to do, he bathed the surface of the wound with a strong carbolic solution. The wounded man moved a little as he did so, but he did not open his eyes. It was then that Doug noticed the scars on Tobe's chest, and a cold feeling came over him. He had seen such scars before. Two Bears also had them on his chest. The scars of the mystical Sun Dance of the Plains Indians.

Tobe had been more than a squawman among these people. The Sun Dance was the master expression of the Plains Indian religion. It was the culminating discipline, drawing in power and joy from the tribe and the universe to the individual breast.

Cuts were made on the breast of the Sun Dancer and wooden skewers thrust through them to which was attached a rawhide rope. The dancer would lean back against the rope which held him to the Sundance pole until he had pulled the skewers through his bleeding flesh while he constantly blew on an eagle bone whistle. The dance lasted four days and four nights and was rich in symbolism. Besides the sun, other powers of the earth and sky—the stars, mother earth, the thunder, and the four cardinal directions—were represented in dance, painting, and song, and the symbolism of the buffalo and of war were prominent throughout.

It was as though some unseen being had come into the lodge to stand beside Doug. Perhaps the Maiyun, the spirits which floated like smoke from the earth, or Heammawihio, the sky dweller. He knew now that Tobe Burgess had been as much of a Cheyenne as he could have been without having their blood in his veins.

The water was boiling. *A witch's cauldron* thought Doug wryly. He forced his superstitious thoughts from his mind, praying to God that he would save the life of Tobe Burgess, white man or squawman, Christian or pagan. He placed the instruments into the water and then peeled off Tobe's shirt and undershirt. He washed his upper body after he had taken the instruments from the pot.

As he uncovered his friend's body, a ray of light seemed to touch the wound, and he turned quickly to see the sun flooding the tepee entrance and thrusting golden rays through holes in the hides. It was a good omen.

———

THE SWEAT DRIPPED from his face and greased his bloody hands as he turned away from Tobe Burgess and looked at the mutilated slug he had taken from the wound. His hands shook a little, but he wiped them clean and poured antiseptic into the bullet hole. In a few minutes, he had the wound covered with a wad and bandaged. He squatted on his heels and looked at Tobe's white face. The scout was breathing harshly and erratically.

Minutes ticked past—minutes which seemed like hours spent in the fiery suburbs of hell—for Tobe's breathing became weaker, and the red stain on the clean white bandage was getting bigger and bigger.

The sun was now beating down on the lodge, and all the old trapped smells of stale grease and body sweat rose about Doug.

There was no sound from the camp. Nothing but the faint chattering of squirrels and the chirping of birds broke the heavy and oppressive silence as Doug watched Tobe Burgess. Fear coursed through Doug—fear that he had failed. There was also curiosity about the man he had thought he had known so well.

A shadow fell across the unconscious man. Doug looked up into the wrinkled face of Two Bears. The Cheyenne's eyes were fixed on the bloody bandage, and then they shifted to look at the blood-stained instruments beside Tobe. The sun's rays touched the blade of a scalpel, and it was as though the steel was bathed in liquid fire. Doug felt the skin on his face tighten.

"*Nohetto,*" said Two Bears.

"Man dies...the mighty buffalo dies. Only the earth and the mountains live forever, father," said Doug, and the measured, fatalistic Cheyenne words seemed unutterably stupid in his dry mouth as he did so.

"*Eahata!* Listen to this!" said the chief in a strong voice. "The choice is up to you, white man! If this man is taken to the Big Shadow Land, you will follow him, but slowly, dying for many hours. If he lives, and may Maheo make it so, you will be given back your weapons and horse and allowed to go where you will. I, Two Bears, have spoken!"

Doug watched the old man stalk from the lodge. It was as though Two Bears had spoken in such a voice as he might have used in the old days when he had addressed the Ho-ta-min-tanio, the Cheyenne Crazy Dogs, before charging into the battle they loved so well.

Doug sat beside Tobe Burgess till sundown. Then he heard the measured treading of feet on the hard-packed earth outside of the lodge. He stood up and faced the doorway.

It was Two Bears who entered first, followed by the medicine man—and behind the medicine man were the three warriors who had captured him and brought him there.

Two Bears looked at Tobe. The scout's breathing was softer, but it was still irregular.

Then Two Bears looked at Doug. He opened his mouth to speak, but suddenly Tobe moved. They all looked down at him. His eyes opened, and he looked up at Doug. "Hello, cousin," he said quietly.

Two Bears opened his clenched hands. He touched his fingers to his forehead as he looked at Doug. "*Enitoeme*—I honor him!" he said in a ringing voice.

The five Cheyenne's left the darkening lodge. Doug placed some wood on the fire for light. He glanced at Tobe. "You bastard," he said softly. "You sure took your time in coming around."

"So?"

Doug ran a finger across his throat. "This would have been too leaky to hold water right now if you hadn't taken just that moment to wake up."

The scout looked at the flickering fire. "I don't know how you got here, cousin, but I ain't asking any questions."

"I've got some questions I'd like to ask you."

"*Later*, cousin...*later*."

Doug wiped the cold sweat from his face. "I'm not even sure the old bastard will keep his word and let me go," he said almost to himself.

Tobe moved a little, grimacing in pain, to look up at

Doug. "*Oxahos!* Dry pony dung! You stand aces-high with the old man from what I just seen. Besides, with me here and alive, he won't get a chance to bother you. Now get to hell out of here and let me sleep."

Doug pulled on his shirt and walked from the lodge. A cool breeze dried the sweat on him. He walked to the stream and washed himself, ignoring the watching Cheyenne's. His life was safe enough now, but he had to get Tobe Burgess back to Fort Purcell, and he wasn't sure that Two Bears would let him do that.

A cool wind swept along the timberline. A squaw waddled from a lodge to a fire. She stirred the contents of a steaming pot and placed a wooden bowl beside the fire. She looked at Doug, motioned to the pot, and then returned to her lodge. Doug suddenly realized he was ravenous. Whatever it was she had in the pot, venison, or tender puppy meat; he didn't really care.

CHAPTER TWELVE

He had been in the Cheyenne camp for a week now. Tobe Burgess had recovered enough to sit up and feed himself. The scout was all rawhide and steel, and he had been wounded several times before. Doug was treated courteously by the Cheyenne's. Two Bears talked to him quite a bit, and even the ferocious-looking medicine man—whose name was Bad Juice, Bad Soup, or Bad something-or-other—had been friendly enough although he never relinquished his professional-looking scowl.

The Cheyenne hospitality was good for however long Doug wanted to accept it. There was an itch in him to get moving, but whenever he mentioned it to Tobe, the scout became more distant. It was a life Tobe had known and liked in the old days. His squaw had died several years before, and although Doug knew Tobe had a son, his name was never mentioned. All Doug knew about the boy was that he was in his late teens and was somewhere with another sub-band of the Cheyenne's. Beyond that, nothing else was said about him, and Doug suspected that the boy had either disgraced himself or was in some sort of trouble...

The sun had gone down one evening when Doug walked to Tobe's lodge. The scout was seated with his back against a rest, smoking his pipe and looking into the embers of the lodge fire. He motioned Doug to an adjoining backrest and handed him a pipe and a pouch of Indian tobacco. Doug filled the pipe and lit up.

Tobe leaned back and watched the smoke drift toward the hole at the top of the lodge. The camp was quiet. Now and then, a horse whinnied from the meadow up the creek.

"You can leave when you like," said Tobe after a time.

"Thanks."

"Your gear will be returned to you and the horse as well. Two Bears wanted the big bay and was willing to give you two ponies for it."

"No."

"That's what I told him."

"How's the side?"

"Sore but healing. I'll be all right."

Doug studied him. "You're coming back with me?"

"No."

"Jesus, Tobe, you know the situation I'm in."

"Yes. It isn't my idea not to help you. It's just that Two Bears wants me to stay."

"Tell him you'll be back."

Tobe sucked at his pipe. "It isn't as easy as that. It involves something you don't know about, Doug."

"Tell me then!"

Tobe half closed his eyes. "The Cheyenne people have a pretty stiff religion. I never told you this before, but my father had a pretty good education. A helluva lot better than I ever got, but I never blamed him for that. I was wild. He was out here after the Mexican War trying to make Cut-Hairs out of the Cheyenne and the Sioux."

"Cut-Hairs?"

"Christian Indians. He never got very far with them.

Came home and told me about these people. He came back with me in tow and then died of Asiatic cholera along with quite a few members of Two Bears' band. I was damned sick myself. My father died trying to save Two Bears' second wife. These people didn't become Cut-Hairs, but they *did* honor the old man.

"I stayed on with them and recovered. I was considered good medicine. I left for a time and then came back and married Pretty Hands, one of Two Bears' daughters."

In the silence that followed, Doug glanced at the scout. Tobe seemed far away.

Tobe shifted a little and felt his side. "Sore as a bitch," he said.

"Go on!"

"We had a son. Two Bears took him to the Medicine Lodge, the midsummer medicine meeting, where all the Cheyenne villages gather in a great camp on the plain. They have four days of dances and ceremonies. On the third evening, after the day's dancing was done and the ceremony of the pipe-cleaning was over, Pretty Hands took my son to the central meeting place where the children-in-arms are cried out for by the old crier to ask someone of importance to have their ears pierced.

"I wasn't there. I was trading for Lancaster rifles for my band. Old Bad Juice, the medicine man here, was asked to pierce my son's ears, as is the custom. It was a big thing to do, but he did it. The boy was a breed. Pretty Hands thought that him having his ears pierced by Bad Juice might help him through his life. It didn't help..."

The lodge was dark now except for the glow of the embers and the two pipe bowls.

Tobe looked at Doug. "The boy was never right for some reason or the other. He brought bad medicine. The hunting was poor that fall, and it was a harsh winter. The Crows struck us and stole many horses, killing one of Two Bears' sons. When the boy was eleven years old, he was wild and vicious. He wounded another boy, blinding him in one eye. His mother died shortly after that; some say because her heart was broken. All I know was that it damned near broke mine. I got restless and left the band. The war came on. I was in it, as you know.

"I saw Two Bears at Fort Laramie in June of last year. He was there, of course, for Colonel Maynardier had specially asked that he be there. In those days, his words were strong in council. He signed the treaty and has kept his word. But others were stronger. They talked against the treaty and the Bozeman Trail. Many of the Northern Cheyenne's joined the Teton Sioux in the war against the whites.

"While at Fort Laramie, Two Bears told me that my son, who was now called Iron Shield, had left the band to join the hostiles. He was seventeen years old but already known for several strike-the-enemy feats. Bad Juice said that he must return to the band to bring back good medicine.

"When you and me stampeded the Sioux herd on the Crazy Woman, I broke away, looked for you, and couldn't find you. I made my way north toward the Clear and ran plumb into a passel of Sioux. One of them was a young warrior who wounded me. Two Bears' band was near the Clear. They found me and brought me here. To them, it was mighty good medicine. Now they want me to find my son and bring him back."

"So?"

Tobe knocked out his pipe and looked directly at Doug. "Do you know who the young warrior was who tried to kill me?" Tobe swallowed and looked away quickly. *"It was my son."*

Doug took the pipe from his mouth and looked at his friend's dim white face. "You're sure?"

Tobe nodded. "Bad Juice told me."

"Good God! Did your son know it was you?"

Tobe held out his hands in a helpless gesture. "I don't know—that's the hell of it, Doug."

The complications of the whole thing stunned Doug. There was no understanding of the involved religion or medicine practices of the Cheyenne's.

Tobe looked at Doug. "Do you see now why I can't go with you?"

"How did they find me?"

"Who knows? I told them the bullet must come out. It was beyond their skill. I told them to look for a white man and bring him here...*any* white man. I told them to look for you, too. They found you, brought you here. You saved my life."

"Yes." Doug stood up. "I've never asked you for much of anything, Tobe. I got you out of the guardhouse at Laramie. I saved your life. Don't you think you owe it to me to come with me to Purcell and clear me?"

Tobe did not move for a moment, and then suddenly, the pipestem snapped in his hands. "Yes."

"Then come with me."

"I can't get away from them."

"Then I'll help you get away."

"Too dangerous. They won't hurt me. They've allowed you your freedom, but if you try to get me away, they'll kill you like they would a sidewinder!"

"I'll take that chance."

"You would."

"You'll come with me then?"

Tobe looked up. "Yes."

Doug awoke at dawn and rolled over on his side to look across the lodge toward Tobe. The scout was still asleep. Doug pulled on his freshly washed clothing and walked outside. There wasn't a warrior in sight, but he knew well enough he was being watched as he bathed at the stream.

He ate just as the sun came up and then saw Two

Bears approaching him. Doug touched his right fingers to his brow in respect for the old warrior. "Good morning, father," he said.

"Good morning," said Two Bears. "Is it in your thoughts to leave us today?"

"Yes."

"Your weapons and horse are ready."

"You knew I was going, father?"

The wise old eyes studied Doug. "Yes. You are restless like all white men. You will return to the Long Knives?"

"It is my duty."

It was a word the old chieftain knew well. He nodded. "*Eahata!*" he said. "Listen to this! My young men have been in the hills. It is the time of war. Some of the *Tsi-tsi-tsas,* Our people, fight with the *O'ho-omo-io,* those you call the Sioux. It is a bad time, my son. Your trail will be dangerous. There is a way, south of here, high in the hills, whereby you will be safe. Do not follow the streams as white men prefer to do but stay high in the hills."

A squaw brought Doug food. A warrior brought his bay horse and his weapons. The Cheyenne's stood around and watched him. Doug felt in one of his saddlebags and gave the old squaw a mirror. He wanted to give the old chief something. Then he remembered the silver-mounted knife he had bought in Santa Fe at the end of the war. He took it out and gave it to the old man. There was no expression on the chief's face, but he nodded. "*Ha ho,* my son. Thank you."

Doug swung up on the bay and urged him toward the stream. The faces of the people held no expression, with but one exception. Bad Juice stood beside Tobe's lodge, watching Doug suspiciously.

Doug turned and waved as he reached the far side of the stream. There had been no need to say anything to Tobe. They had made their plans.

———

As the sun was dying over the wolf-fanged mountains and long shadows crept down the eastern slopes, Doug watched a hawk from his hideout. The hawk swung high overhead, intent on something on the valley floor. If there had been Cheyenne's or Sioux on Doug's trail, the hawk would have alerted him by flying off.

Doug gnawed on some tough jerky. He ground the meat between his teeth as he looked down the slopes. It would take him two hours to reach the vicinity of Two Bears' hidden camp. If Tobe failed to meet him, he'd have to take off like a striped-assed bird for fear the Cheyenne's would spot him, and this time they wouldn't call him friend.

———

The timber was pitch-dark when he left the big bay and made his way on foot through the pines with his Spencer at half-cock and his breath quick in his body. The night was filled with the usual sounds. The sighing of the wind, the rubbing of branches against each other, the scuttling of nocturnal animals, and the faint rushing of the stream.

He worked his way toward the direction of the cool wind, straining every sense to evaluate each sound. Tension grew in him as he neared the camp.

Then he caught the faint odor of bitter wood smoke and the smell of horses. He stopped and faded into the deeper shadow of a massive pine.

There was a thickening of the darkness twenty feet from him, and an almost imperceptible movement felt rather than seen or heard.

Doug slowly lowered his upper body to get the unseen object between him and the skyline.

"*Niva tato!*" the voice challenged crisply.

Doug leaned his carbine against the tree and then eased his knife from its sheath.

The shadow moved quickly toward Doug, and he came unwound, darting forward with his knife held under the thumb, blade edge upward for the swift disemboweling stroke, while his left hand felt out for his victim's throat.

"Doug!"

The familiar voice stopped Doug inches from Tobe even as he began the upward sweep of the knife.

"Jesus Christ, Tobe!"

The scout spat. "You moved like a Strongheart. Let's vamoose. If we don't, the Cheyenne's will turn this night into a hell's delight."

"How so?"

Tobe looked back over his shoulder. "I think Bad Juice is wise to me."

"You're sure?"

"Pretty sure. Let's go!"

Doug snatched up his carbine and led the way through the whispering woods with the cold sweat of fear trickling down his sides. Good God! If Bad Juice knew Tobe had left, he would alert Two Bears. The warriors would cover the woods like a red blanket, and when they found Tobe and Doug, there would be a hell's delight, as Tobe had said.

"Come on!" urged Tobe in a hoarse voice.

Doug spoke over his shoulder. "If I go faster, I'll lose you."

"Chihuahua! Wound or no wound, Mrs. Burgess' favorite son Tobias can keep up with *you*, soldier! Shake the dung, or our scalps will be drying on willow hoops by tomorrow afternoon!"

They hurried through the dark woods. There would be a faint moon later on, which would help them find their way—but it would also help the Cheyenne.

Somewhere high above them, a wolf howled, and the sound echoed faintly from the heights.

Doug looked at Tobe. "Wolf?"

"Cheyenne."

Doug drew his Starr and handed it to the scout. Then he plunged down the slope, heedless of the clinging brush which lashed at his face and body.

CHAPTER THIRTEEN

The scout's labored breathing began to bother Doug. He looked back and saw Tobe's face tightly drawn. There was something dark around Tobe's gasping mouth, and Doug knew it was blood. Without a word, he turned, took the Starr from Tobe's hand, and holstered it. He handed the Spencer to Tobe and then picked him up.

"Jesus!" snapped Tobe.

"Don't try to be a hero now, you dumb bastard!"

"You'll never make it. Leave me and the carbine. I'll give you running time."

"Shut up!"

Doug settled the scout on his broad shoulders and worked his way through the thinning trees. There was a faint trace of moonlight in the sky, and he could distinguish things a little better in the open spaces. The moonlight accentuated the darkness and shadows in the timber, and Doug's fertile imagination peopled those shadows with Crazy Dogs.

He heard the faint rushing of the stream and could smell the water above the winy odor of the pines. Then he heard the faint whickering of the big bay. He grinned in triumph and hefted Tobe to a better position. He was close to where he thought the bay was when something rose from behind a fallen log.

Doug stopped as he saw Bad Juice's hatchet face. Then he tilted his body to one side and dumped Tobe. The scout hit the ground with an agonized grunt. Doug ripped out his knife as Bad Juice hurdled the rotting log and closed in, swinging a murderous axe made of a long knife bound to a wooden handle.

The axe swept over Doug's head, and he drove in with the knife, missing by an inch. The medicine man recovered in time to avoid the return thrust of the knife. He leaped back and parried another thrust.

They circled on the slippery pine needles. Tobe coughed harshly in the background.

Bad Juice was at least fifty, but there wasn't an ounce of fat on his wiry body. His eyes never left Doug's face as he protected his body with a slow weaving of the deadly knife-axe.

Doug could have freed his Starr and killed the Cheyenne instantly, but the crashing shot would alert every buck within a mile.

Bad Juice closed in. He knew Doug was winded from carrying Tobe. He slashed with the axe, recovered, and brought it back with a whistling stroke, reversing the cutting edge of the knife by a deft wrist movement. The blade seemed to skid through Doug's hair.

The moon was up higher now, and the Cheyenne's eyes glittered malevolently.

Doug circled, watching the Indian's eyes. Doug had learned knife-fighting from Jesus Diaz, a scout with the Third Cavalry in Navajo land. Diaz had no peer in the art, but he came from a fighting people who had been born with a knife as an extension of the hand. He had once admitted that Doug was good for a gringo, but nothing Doug could ever do had given him the edge with Jesus Diaz.

Bad Juice stamped his feet and grunted deep in his

throat. He darted in, weaving a pattern of cuts and slashes which drove Doug back. Doug glanced at Tobe. The scout was lying down, with his hands clawing into the pine needles and soft earth while the Spencer lay behind him.

Kill or be killed! The inexorable old rule of the bayonet fighter shot through Doug's mind like the summer lightning over the Big Horns.

Doug moved in and struck, but the Cheyenne was too wary. Bad Juice leaped to one side and slashed in a counter-stroke. Doug crouched and felt the knife-axe rip into his right shoulder as swiftly as a striking rattler. He staggered back and saw the triumphant look in Bad Juice's ebony eyes.

The blood flowed down his back in an increasing flood. Bad Juice threw out his chest. He waggled his head, and the buffalo horns made him look like something straight from the deepest pit of hell.

Doug circled again. Bad Juice drove in hard, and Doug's knife ripped a shallow furrow along the Cheyenne's muscular belly.

Bad Juice swung his weapon over his head and then from side to side in a whistling pattern of cuts and slashes, forcing Doug back down the slope. There was no chance to get above the medicine man. Doug slipped and went down on one knee—and the accident saved his life. The axe bit through the air at a level where Doug's throat had been but an instant before.

Doug's powerful legs drove him forward, toes digging into the soft earth. He thrust with the knife and felt it sink into yielding flesh. His right wrist jerked toward him and back, marking the deadly figure 7 into Bad Juice's yielding bowels.

The medicine man stood there staring at Doug with unbelieving eyes. The knife-axe dropped from his nerveless hand. Then he pitched forward down the slope and slid until a tree stopped his progress.

Doug wiped the sweat from his face. His right forearm was sheeted with Cheyenne blood.

Tobe raised himself. *"Ho hecheta!"* he said weakly. *"That* was a fight!"

Doug leaned against a tree. Suddenly his stomach rebelled, and he spewed vomit on the pine needles. He dropped the knife.

Tobe picked up the reddened blade and handed it to Doug. He jerked a thumb at Bad Juice. "Scalp him," he said.

"You're loco!"

"Scalp him and leave him here. It will stop the Cheyenne's."

"No!"

"Don't be a damned fool!"

There was no way out. Doug walked down the slope to Bad Juice's lifeless body. He looked up at Tobe. Tobe described a circle about his head.

The medicine man's face looked even more hideous in death than in life. Doug looked down at him.

"Nonotov!" snapped Tobe.

Doug went down on one knee and tore off the Cheyenne's buffalo horn headdress. He gripped the greasy hair, drawn back by pine gum. Then he did what he had to do.

CHAPTER FOURTEEN

The Forty-ninth had just held Dress Parade and Retreat, and the dust from their tramping feet still hovered over Fort Purcell in a faint yellow cloud.

Tobe Burgess shifted his chew and spat at a grasshopper. The drenched insect hopped away. "Dress Parade," said Tobe scornfully. "Out *here. Chihuahua!* Old Granny Pussyfoot don't forget much, does he?"

Doug lay flat on his belly in the high grass, wondering what to do next. It had taken them four days to cover the fifty miles to Fort Purcell, with Tobe riding most of the time while Doug slogged it on foot, traveling by night and hiding by day. Now that he was back at Fort Purcell, he didn't really know what he would do.

Tobe nudged Doug. "You asleep?"

"No."

Tobe scratched in his beard. "What do we do now?"

"Beats me."

"Well, the way I look at it, Colonel Rochelle ain't got nothing on me. Supposing I was to go down there and tell him you didn't desert your command like Holmes said?"

"Holmes may have painted you with the same tar brush he used on me."

"Bull crap! I ain't no soldier! Besides, I've been in the guardhouse before."

Doug rolled over on his back and looked at the cloudless sky. "You might as well go down. If Rochelle has you arrested, ask for Surgeon Mike Beirne and tell him what happened to us. If anyone can help us, it will be him."

"What about Miss Louise?"

Doug looked away from the scout. "Forget about her!"

Tobe sat up and felt his wounded side. "Beats me how you steer away from talking about her."

Doug could remember only too well how he had last seen her, more beautiful than he could remember, coming to meet Locke Holmes for her rendezvous.

"Well?"

"Shut up, dammit!"

Tobe shrugged. "You sure get a high boiling point when I mention her." He stood up and stretched. "I'll walk down there. You might need your cayuse."

Doug nodded.

Tobe looked down at him. "One way or another, I'll clear you. I'd like to test the edge of a Barlow knife against that bastard Holmes' lying throat."

"Don't look for trouble."

Tobe looked shocked. "Me?"

"Yes...*you*."

Tobe waved a hand. "I'll be seeing you." He walked slowly down the ridge. Fifty feet from Doug, he turned. "If anything happens, if they come looking for you, take off like a greased pig and head for Caballo Crick."

"What about you?"

Tobe grinned crookedly. "I'll be along. There ain't no corporal's guard can hold Tobe Burgess when he gets a hankering to move on. Caballo Crick! You hear?"

Doug nodded.

Tobe kept on down the ridge. He was in no condition to get to Caballo Creek even if he did escape, but somehow Doug knew he'd meet the scout there if anything went wrong.

He saw Tobe approach the gate, speak to the sentry, and then enter the fort. Tobe was escorted across the parade ground by a soldier and then disappeared into headquarters.

The sun was low now, and in a short time, it would be dark. Doug looked up the creek, and his eyes caught a movement in the willows on the far side of the Crazy Woman. He stared at it; then he walked to his picketed bay to get his field glasses. As he did so, he looked up the ridge that rose high behind the one upon which he stood. A cold feeling came over him as he saw a file of mounted warriors debouch from a motte of timber and vanish from sight in the shallow valley between Doug and the far ridge.

He pulled out the picket pin and led the bay to the north, wondering what the hell had happened to Tobe.

He checked his Spencer, and as he replaced it in its sheath, he saw another group of warriors sitting their horses on the ridge a quarter of a mile to the east.

Doug looked behind him, and just as he did so, the first of the warriors appeared from the valley.

There was no time to lose. There was no other place to go to but Fort Purcell, and he wasn't so damned sure he was going to make it with a lamed and tired horse.

He swung up on the bay and hammered at it with his heels. The bay's hoofs drummed on the hard earth like the devil beating tanbark.

The yelling of the hostiles was almost drowned out in the thunder of hard-hitting hoofs.

The bay was tiring. A splatter of foam hit Doug's face like a clammy hand. The bay's head began to sag, and the power in his loins was gone.

Doug freed his Spencer and turned in the saddle. The

bile rose in his throat as he saw the nearest warrior—a young buck, not thirty feet behind Doug—racing on with an extended coup stick in his left hand and a massive horse pistol in the other. Doug fired, and the slug smashed into the buck's chest, driving him back on the haunches of the horse. Then he fell beneath the hammering hoofs of the other horses while his riderless pinto veered off and headed for the creek bottoms.

The echoing of the shot slammed back and forth from the heights. Doug fired two more times, and the acrid powder smoke blew back against his face, half-blinding him.

What the hell was wrong with them at the fort?

Suddenly a musket cracked from the gateless fort. A moment later, a brass howitzer, mounted on an uncompleted tower beside the gate, roared loudly.

Doug was a hundred yards from the gate when the bay went down. Doug kicked his feet free from the stirrups and hit the ground running, half expecting a lance or a bullet in his back. He sprinted for the gate through the drifting smoke from the howitzer. Soldiers were yelling. Some of them were on the catwalk behind the wall, and they opened fire with their Springfields.

A slug sang over Doug's head. Another spurted dust inches from his right foot. He turned and fired once and then forgot about shooting any more. He dropped the Spencer and sprinted for the gate with painted death fifteen feet behind him, reaching for his life with a bent bow and a broadhead arrow.

There was a hell's delight of crashing firearms, screaming warriors, yelling troopers, and thundering hoofs, all wrapped up in a rifted pall of stinking gun smoke.

Doug was five feet from the gate. He looked back as the buck loosed his shaft. Something ripped through his right sleeve, and the next thing he knew, he was pinned to one of the thick logs of the palisade like a butterfly in a collection.

Some of the Sioux hammered past not fifty feet from the palisade, shrieking like souls in torment as they loosed arrows and bullets.

Doug reached across to free himself from the arrow, and as he did so, he looked up. A man was staring down at him through the smoke, and his face seemed distorted and unreal as he hung his right arm over the top of the wall and cocked a Colt revolver. He was heedless of the attacking warriors as he aimed carefully at Doug, and all Doug could see was that black pistol bore. He ripped himself free from the shaft and jumped to one side as the Colt flashed fire. The slug struck the ground right where Doug had been.

Doug ran to the gateway and darted through it as a Sioux fired a shotgun at him. He heard the charge strike the logs beside him.

"Jesus God!" a soldier yelled. "Ye have the devil's own luck this day, sir!"

Doug leaned weakly against the wall. He heard the retreating of the ponies and the last defiant yells of the Sioux.

Doug looked up at the wall. The man who had fired at him was standing there looking down at him. It was Locke Holmes.

CHAPTER FIFTEEN

Colonel Manning Rochelle looked up at Doug Boyd with intense disgust on his face. "So, Mr. Boyd," he said coldly, "you have returned to Fort Purcell. Why, may I ask?"

Doug couldn't help but smile a little. "My return was a little *hurried*, sir, as you well know."

The lamplight shone on Manning Rochelle's neat desk and on his spotless brass and linen. Doug, in' vivid contrast, could only be described as a fair stand in for a brigand. The two of them were alone in the office, for Manning Rochelle had wanted to hear Doug's story alone. Doug gave him grudging credit for that.

The colonel steepled his fingers and leaned back in his chair. "Do sit down, Mr. Boyd. You look as though you have had more than your share of hardships."

"Thank you, sir." Doug sat down and became acutely conscious of the trail stench of his body and uniform.

Rochelle looked up at the ceiling. "What shall I do with you, sir? The record of your offense is increasing, and now you provoked an attack by the hostiles against us."

Doug's jaw dropped. "*Me*, sir?"

"*You*, sir!"

"I had sent Tobe Burgess ahead to clear the way for me, so to speak, when I noticed the hills were thick with Sioux. I couldn't stay where I was. I couldn't break through them. There was only one thing to do, that was make a break for the fort."

The cold eyes held Doug's. "And precipitate an attack."

"What, may I ask, would the colonel have done in my place?" Doug knew what the answer would be even before the colonel opened his mouth.

"I would have stood my ground, sir, and *fought* them— or better still, would have led them away from the fort, sacrificing my life if necessary to save the post."

Doug nodded. He wanted to get the colonel off the subject, and there was only one way to do it. Fight fire with fire. Provide a counterirritant. "Maybe the colonel is right," he said quietly. "The Forty-ninth was lucky to have staved off that attack."

"Just what do you mean by that, Mister Boyd?"

Doug waved a hand. "The fort isn't complete, and the Forty-ninth hasn't exactly got the reputation of being veteran Indian fighters."

"Where did you hear that, sir?"

Doug couldn't resist the last shaft. "At Laramie. The long-term men there have a way of classifying a regiment in Indian country."

The office was stuffy, but even so, Doug seemed to feel the chill of ice in the colonel's voice. "So? And how did they classify *my* regiment?"

"I'd rather not say, sir."

"Tell me!"

Doug swallowed. "The Halt, the Lame and the Blind."

In the silence that followed Doug's searing words, there came the heavy tramp of feet as a patrol made its rounds.

"Let me tell you, Mr. Boyd, that the Forty-ninth United States Infantry can hold this fort until hell freezes over—and that when the time comes, it shall carry the fight to the Sioux and drive them from the Powder River country!"

Doug leaned forward. "I'm sorry, sir. My tongue gets away from me at times. But the Sioux are massing, sir. The Northern Cheyenne's are with them, and the Arapahoe's. Fort Kearney is under constant surveillance from them. The Bozeman Trail will soon become closed. You are in a dangerous spot here, sir. Even if you finish the construction of Fort Purcell, you will not be able to stir from behind these walls if Red Cloud so wills it."

Rochelle smashed a hand down on his desk. "No Indian can pen the Forty-ninth Infantry behind walls, Mr. Boyd. My scouts have reported that there are only straggling bands of the hostiles in the hills."

"May I ask who is scouting for the colonel?"

"Mister Locke Holmes has taken over those duties."

"You'd listen to *him*?"

The cold eyes held Doug's. "There is no reason not to believe him. Mr. Holmes has proved himself to be a brave and efficient officer. I am recommending him for a brevet for his skill and courage in bringing in the wagon train and your command, Mr. Boyd, when you so shamefully deserted them."

"I brought back Tobe Burgess to bear witness to the fact that I did not desert the command that day on the Crazy Woman, Colonel Rochelle."

Manning Rochelle cut his right hand sideways. "The man's word is valueless! He has a record of drunkenness and trouble-making! He has been a squawman! May I ask where you found him, Mr. Boyd?"

"In the camp of Two Bears."

The officer leaned forward. "Two Bears?"

"A Northern Cheyenne."

"A prisoner?"

"Not exactly."

"Then explain yourself, sir."

Doug quickly told the story of his finding Tobe—or rather Tobe's finding of Doug—and the subsequent events which had taken place in Two Bears' camp. He brought the story up to date and then leaned back in his chair.

Rochelle toyed with a letter opener on his desk. "A rather fanciful tale."

"It's true, sir!"

"You'll swear to that?"

"Yes."

"Do so."

Doug looked curiously at the commanding officer of Fort Purcell. He stood up and said, "I swear that everything I have told you is true, upon my word as an officer and a gentleman."

Rochelle nodded. He looked at a partly open door. "You may come in now, Sergeant Major, and you, too, gentlemen."

The door swung open, and two officers came in, followed by the sergeant major.

"Mr. Boyd, these gentlemen are First Lieutenant Barclay Innes, my adjutant, and Captain Homer Talbot, commanding officer of Company A, Forty-ninth United States Infantry. Sergeant Major Webster, do you have your notes?"

The non-com handed a sheaf of paper to the colonel. Rochelle wrote his signature at the bottom of the last sheet and handed the pen to Talbot, who signed, followed by Innes and the sergeant major.

Rochelle clipped the papers together. "Would you like to read this report, Mr. Boyd?"

"What is it, sir?"

"Every word of our conversation was taken down by the sergeant major. Every word was heard by these two officers."

A cold feeling came over Doug. "What does this mean, Colonel Rochelle?" he asked quietly.

The officer stood up. "These will be used to draft additional charges against you."

"Then the witness I have brought back is of no value to me?"

"He'll be listened to, but with his record, his statements will be of little value."

"What are the charges, sir?"

"Desertion of your command in the face of the enemy. Absence without leave. Desertion from this post while under confinement to quarters. Assault and battery upon the person of Lieutenant Locke Holmes. Consorting with the enemy. Giving aid and comfort to the enemy. Precipitating an enemy attack upon this post."

"Anything else, sir?" asked Doug dryly.

"Nothing."

Doug looked at the two officers and at the expressionless face of the sergeant major. "There *is*. Insubordination, Colonel Rochelle. This was a cheap, underhanded trick, sir."

"Enough!"

Doug walked to the desk and placed his dirty hands flat upon it while he looked Manning Rochelle in the eye. "You haven't given me a fair chance. You've listened to a pack of lies from that sonofabitch Holmes. Well, perhaps you're protecting him. I hope not. Because if I can ever get myself to a place where I'll have a fair hearing, I'll crucify that lying bastard if it's the last thing I do!"

Rochelle whitened. His mouth twitched, and he looked at Captain Talbot. "Captain, you will place this officer under arrest in the guardhouse in a private cell. He will be kept under constant surveillance by a noncommissioned officer of sergeant grade or above. He will be served his food from the officer's mess at my expense."

"Thanks," said Doug.

Talbot walked forward. Doug turned to the door.

"One more thing, Captain Talbot—Mister Boyd shall be held incommunicado until further orders."

Talbot escorted Doug through the outer office and out onto the porch. He looked at Doug. "I'm sorry about all this," he said quietly.

"Thanks."

They walked toward the guardhouse.

Talbot led the way past the curious eyes of the guards and down the hall to the end cell. He opened the door and then locked it behind Doug. "Anything I can do for you?" he asked.

"Clean clothing. Shaving tackle. You know what I need. Surgeon Beirne has them in his quarters."

"I'll have them sent right over and also arrange for a tub of water." Talbot took out a cigar case and handed Doug a cigar. He lighted it. "You must not misjudge Colonel Rochelle, Boyd. He is a brave and loyal man with a great deal of responsibility here. I don't know how Locke Holmes has become his favorite, for the two of them are as far apart in character as the poles."

"I'll tell the whole story someday—*if* I have a fair chance."

"You will."

Talbot left, and a moment later, a burly sergeant took up his post outside the cell, with a Colt holstered at his side.

"Where is Tobe Burgess?" asked Doug.

"I'm not to speak with you, sir."

"I see."

"Sorry, sir."

"Forget it."

Doug pulled off his moccasins and socks. He stripped off his soggy, filthy shirt and swabbed his upper body with it. He threw it into a corner and dropped onto the harsh army blankets which covered his cot. He watched the smoke drift through the small barred window.

First Call for Mess sounded from the parade ground

and echoed from the dark hills. A moment later, a wolf howled from across the Crazy Woman to be followed by another howl from the heights south of the post. The Sioux and Cheyenne's were sitting out there, biding their time.

CHAPTER SIXTEEN

Tattoo had just been blown when the sergeant on guard outside Doug's cell looked up and then stood at attention. Doug glanced up from his bunk and then got to his feet as he saw Michael Beirne's red-whiskered face. The surgeon grinned. "Faith, the Irish blood in ye will not let ye live the quiet life, me boy."

The sergeant moved forward. "Mr. Boyd is not to speak with anyone, sir."

"Pish! Am I not the post surgeon?"

The sergeant was puzzled. "Yes, sir."

"This officer was in me care when he left here some time ago. That was an order of the colonel's, which to me knowledge was never rescinded. The man was wounded then and was not well. I cannot be responsible for his health in this drafty hole of a place."

The sergeant shoved back his cap. "What am I to do, sir?"

"Walk down to the end of the hall and wait there. Do ye think I'd let him overpower me and escape?"

"No, sir."

"Then get ye gone."

Beirne waited until the non-com was at the end of the

hall, and then he looked at Doug. "Burgess is locked up in a cell in the powder magazine."

"Why?"

He reported in and was immediately arrested. He put up one devil of a fight, but of course, weak as he was, there was little enough chance he had. The man seemed out of his mind, so the colonel had him placed in the cell. 'Tis not the place for him, though. I looked at his wounds. Those he received while fighting the guards and the one he says ye took care of for him.

"By Saint Patrick, Douglas, ye should have been a surgeon! Beautiful work!"

"Maheo was with me."

"Maheo? One of the lesser saints, no doubt."

"No doubt."

Beirne tugged at his whiskers. "I have been in to see Mr. Innes, the adjutant, and told him I would not rest until ye were out of here."

"You've done more than enough for me."

The Irishman grinned. "They never did get wise to the fact that Kennedy and meself started that Sioux scare to cover yer retreat. By God, I never thought to see ye again. The Sioux would get ye, I thought, or perhaps ye would be wise enough to follow the Oregon Trail and never come back. But ye did, and now it is up to me to get ye straightened out."

"Forget it, Mike."

"No! I did not care much for Mr. Holmes, little as I knew him when ye left here. With closer association, I have developed a definite disgust toward him."

"The sensitivity of the Irish."

"No, for I am not the only one who hates his guts, as I well know. There has been trouble in yer company. Fights, insubordination, attempted desertion, and many other charges. Did ye get a look in the other cells here?"

"No."

"Well, ye'd see twenty percent of your company languishing in them."

Doug's big hands gripped the bars. "It was a good company once, Mike."

"Aye, Ali Baba and the Forty Thieves."

"It's a hell of a mess," said Doug. "Tobe is the only witness I have, and the colonel discredits him. Holmes is in the saddle and riding hell for leather."

"Perhaps to a bad fall."

"I can't wait for that to happen. What shall I do, Mike?"

"First ye must get out of here."

"You know the orders."

"Mr. Innes agreed with me that perhaps if ye were held in my quarters with a guard at the door, the colonel might consent to release ye to my custody again."

"If he does that, he's slipping," said Doug dryly.

"No. Ye will not attempt to escape."

"No?" Doug looked into the Irishman's steady eyes. "You're right, Mike."

"Once ye are there, we will have time to see what can be done. Perhaps Miss Louise can get the colonel's ear and do ye some good."

"I want nothing from her, man," said Doug bitterly.

"Are ye mad? She may be the only one who can help ye."

"I want no help from her!"

Beirne shrugged. He turned away. "Wait to hear from me."

Doug shook the bars. "What else can I do?"

Beirne turned slowly. "Ye might try a bit of a prayer."

———

BEIRNE HAD WORKED one of his tricks of legerdemain. By the time Taps blew across the post, Doug was back in his old place of confinement, the surgeon's quarters, but this time there was a difference a sergeant of infantry stood guard outside the door.

Orderly Kennedy bustled about the quarters. "'Tis a shame the way ye have been treated, sir," he said as he turned down the covers on Doug's bunk. "It took a man —an Irishman I'm proud to say—to leave here and ride through the whole damned Sioux Nation to get Tobe Burgess and bring him back here."

Doug stood at the window, looking toward Colonel Rochelle's quarters.

Kennedy patted down the covers, raising a cloud of dust. "The enlisted men of yer old company have been hoping and praying ye'd come back and take command of the company. There is not much love there for Mr. Holmes. It is said someone shot at him the last time he was on patrol, and it wasn't a Sioux, ye understand."

Doug turned slowly. "If any man in my company kills him, I'll kill *that* man myself."

Kennedy looked up quickly. "The lieutenant is in enough trouble as it is, without adding murder to it."

Doug looked down at his big hands. He closed them slowly.

Kennedy looked about as though someone might be listening. "Now, sir, there are men and I'm not saying I know them personally—right here on this post, who might, if the price was right, go so far as to take care of Mr. Holmes."

"You heard what I said!"

"Yes, sir!" Kennedy straightened up and saluted. "Will there be anything else, sir?"

"No."

"Any message for the young lady, sir?"

The look in Doug's eyes sent the orderly scurrying from the room.

Beirne came in shortly after Kennedy left. He pulled off his blouse and shirt and then his shoes. He sat down in a chair and filled two glasses. "Burgess will be moved to a regular cell in a few days, Doug."

"Thanks, Mike."

The surgeon handed a glass to Doug. "The colonel has his faults, but he is not a cruel man. Faith, I honestly believe he feels sorry for ye."

"He can keep that. All I want from him is a little faith and a chance to clear myself."

"The man has much on his mind. Things are not going well. He requested a battery of artillery and reinforcements to bring the Forty-ninth up to full strength. Ye know what he got?"

"No."

"Not a damned thing! Besides that, he has orders to build a strong point, or outpost, or some such a thing across the Crazy Woman, in order to protect the timber cutters. I suppose the Wagon Box Fight is still fresh in the minds of the department commander."

Beirne sipped at his liquor and then lighted a cigar. "So one company of infantry has been detailed to build this outpost on that bluff across the creek. This garrison is weak enough as it is."

"Infantry behind cover can hold off the Sioux easily enough at odds of ten to one."

"Aye! To that, I agree! I have seen it done. But the colonel has it in his mind to take a strong force from this very post and march toward Wildhorse Creek within a week or so because of a scouting report brought in by yer Mr. Holmes."

"A strong force? Infantry and a handful of cavalry?" Doug shook his head. "What was this report?"

"Holmes claims the main forces of Red Cloud are encamped on the Wildhorse."

"What does Rochelle plan to do? Surround ten Sioux with one soldier?"

Beirne leaned forward. "Do not doubt but that Rochelle is a fine soldier. His war record is second to none, and the only reason he did not rise higher in grade during the war is because of his personality, which ye must admit is rather cold. It is said that no command under Manning Rochelle was ever defeated by the Johnny Rebs, and Rochelle saw more combat than most officers and against some of the best troops of the Confederacy."

"So, what does he plan to do?"

"March at night. Find the camp of the Sioux. Move in close and make a dawn attack."

"Jesus God!"

Beirne crossed himself and looked upward. "Aye."

"The man is mad."

"Perhaps. It is said by good authority that the occupational disease of the army is insanity. Something has stung deep into Colonel Rochelle's subconscious. Something which has been said or done to him within the past few hours. Something which makes him want to prove that the Forty-ninth can whip the Sioux."

Doug slowly lowered his glass. "Good God," he said.

Beirne looked at him curiously.

Doug took one of Beirne's cigars and lighted it. "He was riding me for drawing that attack onto the fort. I made some careless remark about the Forty-ninth being lucky to have staved off that attack. I also said something about the Forty-ninth not being Indian fighters.

"Rochelle insisted I tell him the nickname by which the Forty-ninth is known in the department."

"Ye *told* him?"

"Yes—the Halt, the Lame, and the Blind. I didn't tell him the name by which he is known to other units— Granny Pussyfoot."

Beirne downed his drink and quickly refilled his glass. "Faith, but ye are a damned fool! Is there no diplomacy in ye, man? Colonel Rochelle is in his office now, poring over his maps, issuing orders on supplies, munitions, transportation, and the increased training of the Forty-ninth so that they may meet the Sioux."

"He can't leave this post unprotected."

"He can and he will! Never forget that Rochelle served with Sherman. Cut loose from yer base, says Sherman, and march through the enemy's country like an avenging host, living off the country and leaving not one stone atop another."

"That was in Georgia, Mike! Sherman wasn't fighting the finest light cavalry in the world! He outnumbered the rebels and had veteran infantry to fight his battles. Rochelle is outnumbered. His men are green. He has no cavalry. Certainly, the department commander won't allow such madness."

Beirne shrugged. "Rochelle has blanket orders. First to build Fort Purcell, secondly to hold this country against the Sioux by whatever method he sees fit. That covers a multitude of choices. His choice is to look for the Sioux and strike them, and he'll do it with the force at his command—the Forty-ninth United States Infantry."

Doug stood up and paced back and forth. "The only way you can hurt the Sioux is to strike them during the wintertime when they stay near their lodges. Then you must destroy their winter stores of meat and furs. Infantry can do that, but in the summertime, when the Sioux are as free as eagles, infantry hasn't got one damned chance to defeat them on an offensive fight."

"Ye tell him that," said Beirne dryly.

Doug stopped at the window and looked toward Rochelle's office. The lights were still on. He looked toward Rochelle's quarters. Two people stood on the porch, silhouetted by the light from a window. Locke Holmes and Diane Rochelle. Even as Doug looked, he saw his enemy take the girl in his arms and kiss her. Doug bitterly wondered if Louise would have her rendezvous with her sister's lover later on.

CHAPTER SEVENTEEN

The Forty-ninth United States Infantry was preparing to take to the field, at the time of the year when the ponies of the Sioux and Cheyenne's were at their best, and when the red man's foraging was a simple matter. The Forty-ninth wheeled and maneuvered in platoons, companies, and battalions on the wide dusty parade ground of Fort Purcell. From the rifle butts west of the fort came the steady thudding of the .58 caliber muzzle loading Springfields, the rifles which had won the Civil War but were now as outdated as the flintlock.

Farriers and blacksmiths worked long hours, readying the supply wagons, horses, and mules. Quartermasters issued extra shoes and socks. Ordnance repaired rifles and pistols, while from the blacksmith shop came the steady whine of the grindstone as swords and knives were ground to an edge.

A company had marched from the fort that morning to cross the Crazy Woman and ascend Lone Butte, a mile from the fort. The afternoon sun shone on the scoured picks and spades as they rose and fell, throwing up dust and dirt. The company was readying a base for the new outpost, which theoretically would not only command the ford of the Crazy Woman but which would also protect timber-cutting parties on the nearby hills. The trouble was that the Crazy Woman, at most times of the year, was fordable all the way from the Big Horns to the Powder. And if Manning Rochelle persisted in his theory that he could destroy Red Cloud's warriors with infantry, there would be no need for further timber cutting to complete Fort Purcell. It was a confusing situation.

But there was a lively air about Fort Purcell. Veteran officers thought of whipping the elusive Sioux and then going home for a well-earned leave. Untried junior officers practiced cuts and right and left moulinets in the privacy of their quarters, slashing grimly about with their swords and thinking of the glory which could so easily be won just over the next hill. Johnny Raws thought nervously of the nasty habits of the Sioux among their enemies' wounded, while the few veterans which leavened the regiment aided their thoughts with minute descriptions of the hostiles' torture methods.

Only the small handful of women at the fort seemed to show the fear they felt. They had heard about the fate of Captain Fetterman and the command of two officers and seventy-nine men who had died swiftly on the snow-covered Lodge Trail Ridge. They looked, too, at the unfinished palisade of Fort Purcell, knowing that even if it had been completed, there would not be enough men left to garrison Fort Purcell. It would take at least a battalion to man the catwalks and loopholes, and it was rumored throughout the post that Colonel Rochelle had no intention of leaving a garrison that large.

The heights along the Crazy Woman had been bare of watching Sioux for some days now, ever since Lieutenant Boyd had made his race for life to the gate of Fort Purcell. Manning Rochelle took it as a good sign, but the few in his command who were familiar with the Indians knew that the time to look for them was when they couldn't be seen.

There were no smoke signals in the hills, no mirror flashes from the heights, and the only howling heard near the post at night was from coyotes and a stray wolf or two. There was an uneasiness in the handful of veterans at the post and especially in prisoners Douglas Boyd and Tobias Burgess.

Colonel Manning Rochelle was holding a meeting of his officers. The sergeant major had pinned a large but incomplete map of the area to the wall of the officer's mess. The mess was packed with the officers of the Forty-ninth and those who were attached to it and Fort Purcell. Surgeon Michael Beirne, as a non-combatant, had been relegated to a position as far back as possible, near the door. He was grateful for this because he meant to slip out when the colonel wasn't looking his way.

The colonel took a pointer from a table and rapped it against the map. "Gentlemen, your attention, please!"

Feet shuffled on the floor, and the coughing died away.

Rochelle traced the course of the Crazy Woman to the Powder and then north along the course of the Powder to its meeting with Wildhorse Creek. He tapped the line which marked Wildhorse Creek. "This is where Red Cloud has bivouacked, gentlemen. No doubt many of you junior officers have been wondering just what the Forty-ninth will do about that red gentleman who is sitting right under our very noses, so to speak.

"You senior officers know of my plan. To you junior officers, I say this, Red Cloud does not expect an attack by infantry against his band. He knows there is not enough cavalry available in this department to force him into a showdown. So there he sits in his glory, defying the whole United States Army.

"I have carte blanche from the department to hold

this country against the Sioux by any means I may see fit."

The colonel lowered his pointer and turned to fully face the assemblage. "My means are to find the Sioux and strike him with the Forty-ninth United States!"

"Hurrah!" yelled a delighted shavetail.

Rochelle smiled benignly. He could forgive such an outburst. It was indicative of the spirit of the regiment.

Rochelle traced a line across the country from Fort Purcell to the Wildhorse. "We will leave here after dusk and march steadily at night until we can go into conceal-ment between Fortification Creek and Wildhorse Creek. The Sioux must not discover us. We will travel as lightly as possible with each man to carry three days' rations, with an additional six days' rations in the wagons. Are there any questions?"

A white-headed captain looked up. "Sir, what about Fort Purcell?"

"It shall be garrisoned, never fear, Captain Ledbetter."

"May I ask by how *large* a force?"

Rochelle paced back and forth. "We have a company of cavalry here, of course. We shall take one platoon of that company for scouting purposes."

Ledbetter stared at Rochelle. "*One* platoon? Sir, we need a squadron at least. You must realize that the Sioux are horsemen, not infantry."

Rochelle's eyes became fixed as he looked at the offi-cer. "There are no horsemen in the world who can charge a regiment of steady infantry firing volleys."

Ledbetter's face became red.

"You question that, Captain? I think you do. Remember that we will also have a battery of artillery."

"Manned by a scraped-up crew of infantrymen."

Rochelle waved a hand. "I hardly think they need fire accurately. The hostiles are notoriously afraid of the so-called wagon guns. The noise and smoke will be enough to put the fear of God into them."

Ledbetter opened his mouth and then closed it. He had been a captain since '63, and most of his Academy mates had achieved far more rank than he had. There was little daring in Samuel Ledbetter. He was known more for obeying orders to the letter and never using his imagination, but this time his imagination persisted in running riot.

The colonel walked to the window and looked out on the parade ground. "The garrison here will consist of the remainder of the provisional company of the Third Cavalry—and a platoon of infantry, men who are not fit for such an arduous expedition as I plan on. Odds and ends of the garrison, about fifty or sixty men."

Locke Holmes shifted a little. "Who will remain in command, sir?"

"Captain Samuel Ledbetter," said Rochelle over his shoulder.

Rochelle turned to face them again. "Mr. Holmes, you will turn over your first platoon to Mr. Gretzar. You will remain here at Fort Purcell as second in command to Captain Ledbetter."

Locke Holmes' face showed no expression. He doubted the success of the expedition. If the Sioux attacked Purcell, it would be a chance for him to make a hero of himself. There was no doubt in his mind that he could take over from Ledbetter. The man would go to pieces in an independent command.

"Captain Ledbetter, you will detail a squad or more to hold the new outpost across the Crazy Woman. They will have the howitzer there. Should the enemy attack here, which isn't likely, the fire from the howitzer can drive them off."

"Jesus God," said Michael Beirne in a soft voice.

"You gentlemen will go through your commands with a fine-tooth comb and eliminate all the misfits. Those men will be assigned to Captain Ledbetter's command. That is all, gentlemen. Officer's Call will blow in four hours. At that time, I expect you to report that your commands are in readiness to take the field. Dismissed!"

The officers rose to leave. Rochelle looked at Michael Beirne. "Surgeon, remain here. I wish to speak with you."

Beirne came forward. When the officers had left, Rochelle motioned to a seat, and Beirne sat down. "Surgeon," said Rochelle, "How is Mr. Boyd?"

"Well enough."

"He will remain here under confinement until my return. At that time, we will set up the court-martial board."

Beirne nodded. "He is a good man, sir. Ye have few skilled Indian-fighters in yer command. Nothing has been proved against Mister Boyd. Would it not be wise to take him along?"

Rochelle straightened up. "Mr. Boyd is under serious charges. If he were the only man in this territory, sir, who could help me in my expedition, I would refuse to have his services."

"This is no time to be picking and choosing, sir. Ye need the man. Can't ye see that?"

"Surgeon Beirne! You have charge of the medical detail here and have nothing to do with administration!"

"That I well know, sir," said the Irishman.

"You are ready to take the field?"

"Yes, sir. Four ambulances. One supply wagon. Eight men."

"Good! You are dismissed, surgeon."

Beirne saluted and walked to the door.

"Surgeon Beirne!"

Beirne turned.

"Rest assured that Mr. Boyd will have the fairest of trials. He is a brave man, although headstrong and undisciplined. I hope in my heart that he will be proven innocent. You may tell him that."

"I will, sir. And thank you."

Manning Rochelle walked to the window and looked out at his post. He had done well. He had driven his men hard, it was true, but they were shaping up. This was his chance to further his career, and nothing would stop him. Nothing.

CHAPTER EIGHTEEN

The Forty-ninth United States Infantry, with attached troops and a battery of six-pounder brass Napoleons, had been gone from Fort Purcell for two days, moving out at night and vanishing through a faint mist which had overhung the Crazy Woman.

The hills overlooking the post had been burned brown and yellow by the hot August suns, and the creek itself was hardly more than a trickle.

Beyond the Crazy Woman, on Lone Butte, a detail of cursing infantrymen had completed the thick rock walls of the outpost and were insetting the thick timber rafters which would hold up the roof. A little brass howitzer squatted on a timber platform, staring down at the crossing of the creek as though wondering just *what* it could do if the hostiles took it into their minds to attack Fort Purcell.

It did seem as though Colonel Manning Rochelle's strategy had a good chance of being successful. There hadn't been a sign of a single warrior since the day the Sioux had chased Doug Boyd to the very gates of Fort Purcell.

But to the few veteran Indian fighters behind the

incomplete walls of Fort Purcell, there came the insidious feeling that the fort was being watched. Manning Rochelle was trying to pin down the hostiles with his column of foot-sloggers, was like a madman weaving a net to snare moonbeams. What the colonel should have done was to stay at Purcell until the fort was complete and ready to stave off enemy attacks.

Douglas Boyd stood at the rear window of Mike Beirne's quarters, stripped to the waist, studying the sere hills with his field glasses. He lowered the glasses and wiped the sweat from the eyepieces. It was no use. Not even a jackrabbit moved on the heights above the fort.

———

CAPTAIN SAMUEL LEDBETTER sat at Colonel Rochelle's desk, looking distastefully at the mass of paperwork on the surface before him. Rochelle was one of those men who could plan a fort and see that it was built while maintaining the training of his command as well as handling the spate of paperwork necessary to the proper functioning of a command, post, or station of the United States Army. Samuel Ledbetter was not such a man.

Sam Ledbetter wiped the sweat from his face and wished to God he had a drink. It had been three years since he had imbibed. His last bout with the bottle had cost him a majority and had kept him almost permanently in his present rank.

But the weight of his responsibility was wearing Sam down. He felt that he should be outside watching the slow progress of work on the uncompleted creek-side wall of the fort. Perhaps he should ride across the Crazy Woman and see what was being done at the outpost. Perhaps he should stay at his desk and try to lower the pile of papers in front of him. Perhaps, if he had a drink, he'd be able to clear his mind and decide what to do.

He walked to the office door and closed it. Then he

reached down behind a chest in the corner and felt his fingers close about the warm and reassuring neck of a bottle.

———

TOBIAS BURGESS STOOD at the window of his cell, holding the bars with his thin hands. He looked down at those hands. He hardly recognized them. The wound, the hard journey to Fort Purcell, and the subsequent confinement had made his strong hands look like the skinny talons of a buzzard. Each black hair on the back of his hands seemed to stand erect by itself.

Tobe pressed his forehead against the hot bars. Surgeon Beirne had managed to get him out of the cell in the magazine, pleading that he would not be responsible for Tobe's health if he was kept there. Beirne had made his point. Tobe had been in the hospital, under guard, just long enough for the regiment to leave. After that, Locke Holmes had damned well seen to it that Tobe had been taken back to the cell in the magazine.

Tobe closed his eyes. Only the night before, someone had been prowling about outside the window. Tobe's keen hearing had picked up the sound of a gun being cocked, and he had rolled from his pallet to the filthy floor and across it to lie flat beneath the window, his heart pounding. Then he had heard the soft grating of boot soles as the prowler had vanished.

Tobe opened his eyes and looked at the hills. There was no way for him to go back to the Cheyenne's now. In the short time he had been back with his adopted people, wound and all; he had regained some of the peace of mind he had lost years before when he had left the band of old Two Bears. There was a big jagged piece of Tobe Burgess missing now, and somehow he knew he would never fit it back into place again.

————

LOUISE ROCHELLE SAT in her room, rocking slowly back and forth, listening to the subdued voices of her sister and Locke Holmes as they sat in the living room talking, with a pause now and then as they kissed and fondled. It was typical of both of them. They did not have the sensitivity other people had to feel unseen tensions. They lived for one day and the pleasures to be gained during that day. They did not worry about the future.

Louise felt her old anger. To think that Doug Boyd believed that she had had anything to do with Locke Holmes. She had gone to see Locke, to talk to him about Boyd, promising to help Locke as much as possible when the real truth of the events at Crazy Woman Crossing came out. But Doug Boyd loved and hated hard. That was his way, and perhaps she should have realized that. Perhaps that was why she knew she loved him.

It was as hot as the doormat of hell in the guardhouse cells of Fort Purcell. Not even a breath of warm air moved through the sprawling log building.

The guardhouse was newly built, of fresh pine trees cut on the distant slopes of the hills, but even the hot pungent odor of the pine resin could not overcome the smell of the place now. It stunk like an Indian lodge after a long winter.

Ex-corporal Hector MacKenzie rubbed his skinned knuckles. There was a mouse under his left eye and a crusted scar along the side of his skull where a rifle butt had struck him into unconsciousness for his spirited resistance against the guard. Now and then, his blue eyes would glance from the barred window toward the distant skyline.

"You wouldn't get five miles from the fort, Mac," said big Darnell Stevens.

"The hell I would'na!"

Darnell grinned as he heard MacKenzie's broad Scots tongue.

Dandy Kelly, erstwhile trumpeter of Boyd's Provisional Company of the Third Cavalry, yawned. He rested his elbows on the ledge below the bars of the window. "There is one man, right enough, who could spring us from this pokey," he said.

"Aye!" snapped MacKenzie. "But he's under arrest, too!"

Trooper Walk-along Smith, so-called because he possessed the unfortunate knack of having a mount shot from under him in almost every fight his company had been in since the previous April, looked up quickly. "I've got a hoof-file cached in my left shoe," he said quietly. He glanced at the thick window bars.

Kelly eyed the short, broad-shouldered man. "Ye're a man of foresight, Walk-along."

Walk-along's tremendous laugh boomed out. "I've been in the pokey before," he said. "I mind one time at old Fort Bliss—it was a warm summer night, like tonight will be. Well, I—"

"Jesus God!" said MacKenzie. "We've no time now for recollections of the past. 'Tis the present we have to consider, me lad."

"True," said Smith gloomily.

A bleary-eyed infantryman looked up from his sweat-soaked blanket. "Shut up, you horse soldiers, and let a real soldier get some sleep."

MacKenzie spat. He rubbed his knuckles and looked at Kelly. Kelly eyed the ten sweating infantrymen in the tank with the five Mounted Rifles. "There are only two apiece for us, Mac," he said thoughtfully.

The Scot grinned lopsidedly. "They'll have to do, Dandy."

Three of the infantrymen got up slowly and blew on their knuckles.

Walk-along yawned. He stood not over five feet six inches, but he was seemingly as broad as he was tall.

Feet grated on the floor of the corridor, and a hard-faced non-com looked between the bars of the doorway. "You bastards start a fight in there, and we'll come in and clean out the bunch of you."

The fifteen prisoners turned as one to look at him. They knew him—Sergeant Holleschied, who had risen from a private to three-striper in a matter of days. He was Mr. Locke Holmes' boy, and there were some members of the garrison who hated his guts almost as much as Holmes.'

A lean infantryman glanced at MacKenzie. "Tell you what, Mac," he said, "let's hold off until Holleschied comes in here to clean us out. After that, we can take up where we left off."

"Agreed," said MacKenzie. It had been Holleschied who had taken over MacKenzie's two stripes—and the third stripe which Mr. Boyd had promised him.

Holleschied spat. "Keep quiet," he said. "Damned if a man can get any sleep in this weather without you jail-birds making it rougher." He walked away.

It was too hot to argue and too damned hot to fight. Holleschied meant exactly what he said. His guard would be in there with swinging rifle butts and no skulls spared.

An infantryman walked over to Dandy Kelly. "You boys thinking of taking a break?"

"Maybe."

"You can't make it without us."

"True."

The men eyed each other. They knew damned well they'd sweat it out in the pokey or on the fort walls until Colonel Rochelle came back to pass final judgment on them. That might be many days *if* he got back at all. The Sioux might delay him permanently.

"What's the plan?" asked the infantryman.

"We're to work on the outpost tomorrow. Might be

only a squad there to guard us and watch for the Sioux. We figure we can make the break there."

"And then?"

Kelly shrugged. "Take to the hills."

"Ain't no place to go except to Reno, Kearney, or Smith."

MacKenzie looked up. "The Bozeman goes clear up into Montana country. There's gold up there. They say it will be a grand cattle country someday. I know cattle. Strong men, with the will to make a way, might be big men up there someday."

The doughboy spat between his yellowed teeth. "Yeah. I'm Slim Gipson. Count me in, Mac."

"We need a leader," said Smith.

"Why?" asked Gipson. "We don't need anyone to show us the way."

MacKenzie lowered his voice. "There is Mr. Boyd. He knows the country like a book and the Sioux as well. If he was to agree to lead us, we'd make it all right."

Gipson laughed. "Him? That damned traitor?"

MacKenzie swung from the hip. His right caught Gipson flush on the jaw and knocked him back over a cot. He hit the wall with his head and lay still.

Feet pounded on the hard earth of the corridor, and Holleschied looked in suspiciously. "What was that?"

"Why, sergeant," said Walk-along with a beaming smile, "you're *so* nervous!"

"What's wrong with Gipson?"

"He's resting."

Holleschied turned. "Three men here!"

Three guards appeared. The non-com unlocked the door and walked to Gipson. He pulled the unconscious man to his feet and looked at the red mark on his jaw. Then he dragged Gipson from the tank and locked the door behind him.

"Poor chap," said Kelly. "The heat is too much for him."

"Aye," said MacKenzie solemnly.

The five Mounted Rifles laughed...

Outside in the guard room, Gipson came to. He drew Holleschied close. "Watch for a break," he said softly. "Kelly and MacKenzie. They have ideas of freeing Mr. Boyd to lead them to Montana."

Holleschied nodded. He wiped the sweat from his face. "Come with me to see Mr. Holmes. That wasn't a bad idea of his to plant you in there, Gipson."

Gipson felt his jaw. "No. Let's go. I want to see what happens when Holmes hears about this deal."

The night was ominously dark along the Crazy Woman. The only relief was the dim lights of Fort Purcell and the faint reflection of firelight from within the walls of the new outpost.

Doug Boyd lay on the cot in his dark room, staring up at the ceiling. The days were bad enough at Fort Purcell —but it was the nights that were mental torture. He thought of the exposed fort and its weak garrison while Manning Rochelle and his green infantry regiment slowly slogged their way through the dust to find and fight the Sioux.

If the Sioux attacked, they would have all the odds. They could drive the defenders into one spot and then fire the dry wood of the palisade and the new buildings. Then they could close in, picking off the defenders until there was nothing left to keep them from the women and the military stores.

"Fort Perilous," he said aloud.

Something moved outside the open rear window. Doug moved softly and reached for the Starr revolver which Beirne had smuggled in to him.

Minutes dragged past. Doug crept to the window and flattened himself against the wall at one side of it.

A shadow seemed to form just outside the window. Doug moved swiftly. His left hand shot out to grip the throat while he raised the Starr for a chopping blow. His left hand struck a full soft breast, and the odor of jasmine came to him.

"Doug?"

It was Louise.

He helped her into the room, wanting to draw her close—but his damnable pride would not let him do so. Her cool hands touched his face. She spoke swiftly. "I went to see Locke because of you, Doug, and *only* because of you."

"A likely story."

She moved back. "For the love of God, Doug! It's you and only you, I love. Please believe me!"

He drew her close and kissed her. She rested her head on his naked chest. "Thank God," she said softly.

He walked to the front window and closed it, then drew the curtains. "Is that why you came?" he asked.

"Partly."

"So?"

"I'm afraid, Doug."

"Who isn't?" he said.

She sat down on the cot and drew him down beside her. "Captain Ledbetter is drunk. I went to headquarters to speak with him about you. The man was incoherent."

"That's all we need," he said grimly.

"Locke is full of confidence, and he doesn't care a rap about anything else but himself and perhaps Diane, although I can't be sure of that. He's with her now."

"He'd better look to his defenses."

She leaned back against the wall. "What can we do?"

"Nothing but sweat it out."

"What about the Sioux?"

He shrugged. "When you can't see them is the time to look for them."

"Have we a chance?"

He stroked her soft hair. "Perhaps. Perhaps they can be bluffed if they show up."

"And the odds?"

"A thousand to one, Louise."

"Why did my father leave?"

"Who knows. He's on the glory trail."

"He wants his star."

Doug laughed without humor. "He'll never get it if he loses Fort Purcell—but then, on the other hand, he probably felt as though he wouldn't get it here anyway. Your father is gambling for big stakes. The fort, many lives, his career—"

"I never did know him very well. It is a strange thing to say."

A faint wind crept up and blew through the window. He looked down at her, suddenly realizing she was frightened and lonely. She had never really known her father, and she had come to him for comfort and strength. Her nearness played the very devil with his emotions. He tried to curb them until she passed a cool hand along his shoulders and traced the almost healed scar of the lance wound. "Does it still pain you?" she asked quietly.

He drew her close and felt her supple body arch to meet his. It was as though she felt there was to be no tomorrow for them and that she wanted to be with the one person she knew she really loved, perhaps to take this last memory to the grave with her.

There was no turning back now. The way was plain before them, and they were forced inexorably to follow it...

When she was gone, he paced back and forth, feeling the sweat dry on his body. Her aroma was still with him, and it would haunt him forever.

CHAPTER NINETEEN

It was Sam Ledbetter who started the whole thing. The heat of the August afternoon had been doing strange things to the mind of Fort Purcell's temporary post commander. He had been drunk the night before, and things were very vague to him now. He was in constant fear that someone would tell him that he had made a fool out of himself, but no one did—and that made Sam even more concerned.

He knew he had been a failure as an officer during the war, but no one had ever accused him of being a coward. The whole damned garrison seemed afraid of a possible Sioux attack, but Sam Ledbetter would show them how foolish they really were. He had reached his decision after three stiff shots of the hair of the dog.

Sam dressed himself in his best field uniform, making sure his brass had been polished by Marshfield, his personal attendant. He girded himself with a pistol belt and made sure the Colt was freshly loaded and capped. He snapped his sword and scabbard to his belt slings and placed his hat squarely on his head. He walked outside and looked up at the sere hills, dreaming in the molten sunlight. The sweat broke out on him as soon as he felt the sun beating down upon him, reflecting from the barren parade ground as though from a metal plate.

Captain Ledbetter had decided to make an inspection visit to the new outpost on Lone Butte.

Ledbetter turned as Locke Holmes approached him. "Take over, Mr. Holmes," he said heartily.

Locke Holmes eyed his commanding officer. The man was a fool and still drunk as a coot.

Ledbetter drew on his gauntlets, although the heat was enough to fell a Zulu. "I'll be back in less than an hour," he said.

Holmes nodded. It was in him to tell Ledbetter to think twice before he crossed the creek, but then ambition stirred deep inside Locke Holmes. If anything happened to Ledbetter, it would place Holmes in command. It was a chance he could not turn down.

Ledbetter mounted and smiled down at Locke. "Don't be worried," he said cheerfully. He touched the gray with his spurs and rode toward the gateway with his orderly behind.

A wraith of dust rose from the road as the two men rode toward the crossing. A hot wind stirred the willows and cottonwoods along the creek.

Doug Boyd came out of the officer's washhouse and looked down toward the creek. "Who is that?" he asked the non-com, his guard.

"Captain Ledbetter and orderly, sir."

Doug half closed his eyes. "Where is he going?"

There was an amused look on the sergeant's face. "Inspecting, Mr. Boyd. The outpost."

The officer had been drunk the night before. Doug had seen him that morning and knew the white worms were moiling in his guts. "The damned fool!" he said without thinking.

The sergeant nodded.

Doug walked to his quarters. "I'd like to see what happens," he said.

"It's all right with me, sir. But stay behind the quarters in case Mr. Holmes sees you."

Doug walked inside and got his glasses. He stood in the hot shade and watched Ledbetter reach the creek.

There was a movement in the thick willows, and suddenly a dozen horsemen broke from them and raced toward Ledbetter.

"Cripes—*Sioux*!" spat out the sergeant behind Doug.

Ledbetter turned in his saddle as his orderly cried out frantically. He jabbed the big gray with his spurs, and the mount reared in sudden panic. The two white men turned away and started back up the road just in time to see more warriors break from the brush and trees to their right and above them.

Locke Holmes was running toward the gate. "Sound the Alarm!" he yelled at a bugler.

The staccato notes ripped out like a brass file across the quiet of the late afternoon.

The guards tumbled from the guardhouse and clambered up the ladders to the catwalk.

A soldier stood atop the wall of the uncompleted outpost and stared down at the creek bottoms.

The orderly's horse bolted and carried the screaming man full into the warriors' surging ranks. Pipe axes and lances rose and fell. There was a spume of feathers, dust, and powder smoke along the bottoms, and then the orderly's horse broke from the press and raced along the creek.

Sam Ledbetter drew pistol and sword. He incoherently yelled as he closed with the Sioux between him and the fort. The pistol cracked two times. The sword rose and fell, shooting a shaft of reflected light from it—and then Ledbetter was almost free. A big buck swung his pinto in close to the shrieking officer. A horn bow was drawn back into a deadly arc, and the shaft flew toward Sam Ledbetter.

Ledbetter had broken through the press, but there

was something different about him now. A long arrow jutted quivering from his forehead. His legs still gripped leather, and his hands still held his weapons. The gray took the bit into his teeth and raced for the fort. Arrows flew after the horse and man. Rifles and pistols cracked. Sam Ledbetter jerked as slugs and arrows struck home. His gray reached the gate and thundered through it as the garrison opened fire, driving back the yelling warriors. Smoke drifted down toward the Crazy Woman to mingle with the yellow dust, and then the warriors were gone as swiftly as they had come.

The outpost howitzer banged futilely, and the projectile dropped into the creek.

The gray stopped in the middle of the parade ground, watched by all eyes at Fort Purcell. Sam Ledbetter fell heavily from the saddle.

"Look!" screamed a woman. She pointed toward the heights behind the fort

The people of Fort Purcell took their eyes from Sam Ledbetter and looked up at the heights. The bare hills had grown a fearsome crop. Hundreds of feather and painted warriors sat their horses there, looking down at the fort.

CHAPTER TWENTY

They had buried Captain Ledbetter on the post proper. The Post cemetery was only a quarter of a mile from the fort, but it might just as well have been a hundred miles away. In the long hours since Samuel Ledbetter's death had warned the garrison that they were almost besieged, Sioux campfires had sprung up behind the ridge south of the fort and in the low hills across the Crazy Woman.

Not a man of the garrison was allowed from his post on the walls or in the rifle pits which had been dug along the course of the uncompleted wall.

Locke Holmes knew rank fear. Suddenly he wished he had gone with the regiment. He had his own command now, just what he had wanted. A chance to make a hero out of himself again. But this assignment was more than he had ever bargained for.

He paced back and forth in the colonel's quarters with sweat streaming from his brow. He didn't have enough men to man the walls. There was a hell of a gap where the wall had never been completed. His only piece of artillery, the little brass howitzer, was cut off across the creek along with the little garrison of infantrymen who held the outpost. Those infantrymen were some of the steadiest in the small post complement of troops. Manning Rochelle—God damn him to everlasting hell—had left the sick, the lame, and the halt behind to protect the fort.

The office door opened, and Holmes whirled to see Louise Rochelle. His eyes narrowed. "Well?" he demanded testily.

Her calm gray eyes studied him. "You have what you wanted, Locke. A fine independent command."

He waved a hand. "Don't come here to laugh at me, Louise. Do you realize the situation we're in? The Sioux won't attack at night, but the dawn will be here soon enough."

She walked to the window and looked up at the distant hills. There was a faintly pulsating corona of pink light over them...the glow from the Sioux campfires. "There is one chance, Locke," she said over her shoulder.

"So?"

She turned. "There is one man here who might know how to save us."

"Boyd?" Holmes shook his head.

"This is no time to continue your feud with him, Locke."

Holmes bit his lip. By God, he needed help, advice, strength where he could get it.

"Perhaps there is nothing he can do," she said quietly, "but he has experience. He is a tried Indian fighter and a brave and resourceful man. Locke, you must free him and let him take command!"

"The man is a prisoner under serious charges."

"He would not be if you hadn't betrayed him."

"You can't prove that!"

"I can tell," she said softly.

Locke Holmes was a schemer and plotter, but like many such, he had always underestimated those he had schemed against and had always overestimated his own cleverness. Louise Rochelle was one person he had never figured out, and now he knew she was just as dangerous to him as Doug Boyd was.

She walked to the door. "Doug will take command if I ask him to," she said.

"Supposing *I* ask him? You know what he'd say!"

Their eyes met like touching foils, feeling for a weakness or an opening, and it was his eyes that looked away.

"I have written up a paper," she said coolly, "in which you exonerate Doug from the charges you made against him and Tobe when you reached Fort Purcell. You will sign that paper now and let me leave here with it. In return for signing the paper, I will see to it that Doug takes command here and saves your neck along with the rest of ours."

"You think he's God Almighty," he sneered.

"Can you do better than he can? Or perhaps I should ask whether or not you think you can do anything at all to save the people here at Purcell?"

"Give me that damned paper! You realize this will jeopardize my career?"

"That's no concern of mine," she said coldly.

"What about Diane? We were to be married."

She handed him the paper. "Her life is at stake." She looked at his thatch of beautiful blonde hair. "Your hair will look well stretched on a willow hoop drying in the smoke from a Sioux lodge fire."

He blanched as he placed the paper on the desk and read it. Then he signed it and handed it to her.

She folded it and placed it inside the bosom of her dress. "Have him released and have him report here."

"Damn you!" he said.

She smiled. "You never were a gentleman, Locke."

————

IT WAS a hushed group of men and women who listened to Doug Boyd in the officer's mess. Locke Holmes stood behind Doug, hating his guts but knowing his life might depend on what the big Irishman would do.

"The hostiles might not rush us at dawn," said Doug. "The one thing we don't know is whether or not they know the bulk of the garrison is gone on a wild goose chase. They're cautious because they don't like this type of work. But *we* know they could sweep through here like a flash flood whenever they feel like it. We can hold out for a time, but they'll win in the end. There's no use kidding ourselves about that."

"What can we do, sir?" asked a corporal. Doug paced back and forth. "If they attack at dawn, then we'll know they know the regiment is gone. If they don't, then we'll know they think the Forty-ninth is still here. Then we have until late tomorrow afternoon to hold them off to gain precious hours."

"Precious hours for what?" asked Locke Holmes sarcastically.

Doug turned to look at the man he hated. "For someone to ride to the column and turn them back."

"Now? They're miles from here."

"If you have any other suggestions, Mr. Holmes, I'd be pleased to hear them."

Holmes reddened and looked away.

Doug walked to the window. "We must try to give the hostiles the illusion that the garrison is still here. Those warriors up there have watched this post, and others like it many a time. They know the routine and post life almost as well as we do. Therefore we must bluff them into thinking we are doing our daily routine, just as though we had the full regiment here. Post calls and drills...everything we can do to create a stage play here which might save our lives."

Not a word was spoken as Doug turned toward the group. "There will be no sleep for anyone tonight. Until an hour before dawn, we'll have to work like beavers.

Then we'll have to stand to...to see if the Sioux will attack. If they *don't* attack, we go on with the play."

"And if they do?" asked a quartermaster sergeant. Doug smiled thinly. "We live or die like soldiers."

"What I don't understand sir, is why we just couldn't keep bluffing them after tomorrow afternoon, providing, of course, the bluff works in the first place."

Doug looked at the taut faces in front of him. "Because those hostiles know as well as we do that the garrison of every camp, post, and station of the United States Army stands Retreat Parade half an hour before sunset."

They all knew what that meant. Hostile eyes would watch to see how many soldiers turned out for Retreat Parade. Sunset—that was the deadline.

Doug wiped the sweat from his face. "Fires will be made in the morning to give the illusion that breakfast is being cooked. We must circulate about the post to give the illusion that we are in great strength. Move from one building to another. Change parts of your uniform and come out of another building. Carry a carbine into one building and emerge somewhere else carrying a box. Move in pairs and split up into singles and so on. The keenest eyes in the world will be watching this play, men!"

The quartermaster sergeant nodded. "We'll have to get busy on cutting doors through from one building to another."

"Yes, Richter."

"What about us women?" asked Sergeant Major Webster's wife.

"Yours may be the most difficult parts of all. You must move about as though you were safe at Fort Laramie. Do your sewing and cooking and washing, too."

Doug turned to Holmes. "Your duty is to keep the guards alert all night."

"Yes, sir."

"I'll supervise the rest of the preparations."

"What about the outpost garrison?"

Doug rubbed his jaw. "They're on their own. In a way, they're safer than we are. They are behind stone walls with a howitzer to back them up. Maybe the Sioux won't bother them."

There was an odd look in Holmes' eyes as he left the mess.

———

FEAR DROVE the little garrison of Fort Purcell with honed spurs that night.

A detail chopped holes through thick log walls to provide passage between one building and another. Another detail hauled water into the big stone magazine. But the master supply was low. The heat had caused inroads into the water stores, and there was no chance now to get any from the creek. The wells within the palisade had not been finished as yet. Doug's plan was to hole up in the magazine building for several reasons. It was the strongest building on the fort grounds and was fireproof. There was another reason—one Doug kept to himself. There were seven women on the post.

If the Sioux were about to carry the magazine by assault, Doug would have a fuse laid to the powder kegs and touch it off himself at the last minute.

Every spare rifle and carbine on the post was loaded and placed in the magazine. Every person in the fort was ordered to be armed at all times.

Doug walked to the guardhouse with Tobe Burgess. The veteran scout was weak, far weaker than Doug had imagined. It had been in Doug's mind to ask Tobe to get through to the column, but he knew Tobe would never make it. It was up to someone else, and Doug wanted a Mounted Rifle to do the job.

The prisoners were released and armed, then ordered

to report to Locke Holmes—with the exception of the five Mounted Rifles. Doug looked at them in the dimness —MacKenzie, Stevens, Hendricks, Kelly, and Smith. All good men. All Brave Rifles.

Doug briefed the five men on what had happened and what he planned to do. "I need volunteers to try and reach Colonel Rochelle."

"I'll go," said Dandy Kelly.

"No. I need you here to play post calls tomorrow."

"Jesus Christ!" said Kelly. "Beg pardon, sir."

The other four men stepped forward.

"I'm senior, sir," said Hector MacKenzie.

"I'm the biggest," said Darnell Stevens.

"I know the country, sir," said Hendricks.

"I'm the toughest of the lot, sir," said Walk-along Smith. His face reddened as the others laughed.

"Ye earned the name well," said Kelly with a wide grin. "Walk-along Smith bedad."

Smith turned to look at Kelly, and the grinning Irishman sobered his face.

Tobe rubbed his aching side. "Let them all go, Doug," he said.

They knew what he meant. The odds were almost impossible against them. One man *might* make it out of the four if the gods smiled a little.

"Sounds reasonable," said Stevens.

Doug gripped his big hands together. He didn't want to order these men to their deaths.

"We'll need horses to make it," said MacKenzie. "I do not think the Sioux would miss hearing us if we rode from here."

"The Sioux have horses," said Tobe dryly.

They looked at each other in the darkness.

"Aye," breathed MacKenzie.

Doug looked up at the starlit sky. Tobe was right. "Leave as soon as you can. Separately. There is one horse at the outpost."

MacKenzie nodded. "Walk-along can have it," he said. "He'll require a cavalry mount."

Doug took each of them by the hand. "Tobe will tell you the best way to go."

He watched them trudge off into the darkness to get their gear. His company was scattered from hell to breakfast, but man for man, they had a big edge on any man in the Forty-ninth—and for that matter damned near every man in the United States Army.

The warm breeze dried the sweat on his face. He looked to the heights. The hours until dawn would be short enough. There was nothing else he could do right now beyond driving his little garrison like Jehu. Their futures were in the laps of the gods.

CHAPTER TWENTY-ONE

The false dawn tinged the eastern sky, and a cool wind crept down the valley of the Crazy Woman, making the leaves tremble. It banged a loose shutter on one of the buildings of Fort Purcell. The flagpole halyards began a gentle, rhythmic slapping against the hundred-foot-tall shaft. The hills were dark and mysterious against the paling sky.

Doug Boyd stood in front of headquarters and watched his tiny garrison move to their posts. He was tired, and his eyes felt like two holes burned into a blanket, but he had done all he had planned to do.

The women were already inside the stone magazine. A detail was just finishing the last of the newly cut loopholes. Other men were making last minute inspections of their weapons. A few men stood at their exposed posts on the wall catwalks. If the dawn rush came, they would have to race for the magazine or die where they stood.

Across the creek, on Lone Butte, the outpost stood out against the sky, but there wasn't a sign of life about it. Doug wondered if the men up there had died during the night under Sioux knives and pipe axes.

Doug walked toward the magazine. Locke Holmes had worked hard during the night. Doug could not have asked for a better subordinate, much as he hated the man. Holmes was entering the magazine. Tobe Burgess leaned against the thick stone front wall with his jaws moving steadily. He spat as he saw Doug. "Time's come," he said laconically. He picked up the long-barreled Sharps rifle he had borrowed from a civilian teamster. "Ready, Doug?"

Tobe walked inside the magazine. The last of the defenders hurried inside. Doug walked in and closed the massive, bolt-studded door behind him. He placed the oak bar in the slots.

The water barrels were full. There was plenty of food and ammunition in quantity. Everything but enough men to hold off a major attack.

Doug looked at Trooper Downes. "If the Sioux attack and the men on the walls make a break for here, you'll be ready to open the door."

"Yes, sir." Downes wiped the sweat from his face, although the air was cool. "And if the warriors are too close behind them?"

Doug looked into Downes' dark eyes. "They die where they stand."

Downes swallowed. "Yes, sir." It was no use telling Mr. Boyd that Downes' kid brother was one of those men on the walls.

———

UP IN THE HILLS, the warriors were astir. Some of them slowly polished their rifles with greasy rags. Others made the last painstaking touches to their face paint. Covers were stripped from tough buffalo hide shields. The shrill notes of an eagle bone whistle came eerily through the dimness as a medicine man went about his professional business.

Cheyenne's, Arapahoe's, and Sioux waited patiently for the command from Sinta Gleska. Spotted Tail had the mass of Red Cloud's picked warriors ready to overwhelm Fort Purcell if the chances were good.

————

THERE HAD BEEN four white men moving about in the darkness. Four Mounted Rifles. Miles Hendricks lay in a gully a mile from the fort, his fingers dug into the soft soil. He would be dead in a few minutes—horribly dead, for a rattlesnake had struck him full in the face as he had crept toward the creek. There had been nothing he could do except to die quietly so as not to alert the surrounding hostiles...

There were two dead men lying in the shallows of the Crazy Woman a half a mile from the fort. One of them was a pockmarked Cheyenne buck who had died with Darnell Stevens' powerful fingers dug into his windpipe. He lay under the water with his right hand still gripping the knife which had ripped the life from the big trooper...

Hector MacKenzie had made it far beyond Fort Purcell and had been within a quarter of a mile of one of the Sioux horse herds when he had stepped off into space. He had hit the bottom of the coulee and had felt his left thigh snap. When he had regained consciousness, he knew he would never make it back to the fort nor anywhere else.

He dragged himself into the thick thorny brush and drew out his service revolving pistol. His carbine lay at the top of the coulee, but he had his canteen and a pocketful of hardtack.

He cocked the big handgun and looked at the muzzle. "Six shots," he said quietly. "Five for the Sioux; one for Hector MacKenzie..."

Walk-along Smith crawled from the brush on the side of the creek opposite Fort Purcell. He had made it across the creek easily enough, and then he had heard movements in the willows. He had stayed doggo until the coming of the dawn had driven him on.

Sweat dripped from his face as he forced his thick body up the slope. The others would make it, of that he was sure. They were all good men and more skilled than he in this type of work, but he had said he would try, and try he would.

He saw the outpost, but there wasn't a sound from it. He had visions of being hit by a .58 caliber slug from the Springfield of a frightened sentry. It was then he saw the big mount quietly grazing near the outpost. The horse moved, dragging its picket pin on the long rope.

Walk-along inched toward the powerful dun. It was big enough to carry Walk-along's compact two hundred pounds.

The dun wandered away from the outpost and disappeared in a motte of cottonwoods, followed by the sweating, cursing Mounted Rifle.

The light was much clearer when he reached the dun and spoke softly to it. He sang a little as he patted the horse. He led the dun down the slope toward a coulee and down the coulee until he was half a mile beyond the butte with the icy sweat of fear dripping down his body.

He could hold out no longer. He swung up on the dun and urged it toward the northeast. Walk-along Smith was on his way.

———

IT WAS GETTING LATE for one of the favorite tactics of the Plains Indians—the swift, murderous dawn rush. The birds had awakened in the trees, and the eastern sky was alight, beginning to filter down into the valley of the Crazy Woman.

The warriors looked down on the fort. They could see the sentries pacing the catwalks with ready rifles.

Dandy Kelly stood beside the door of the magazine

with his polished trumpet slung from his shoulder by its yellow worsted cord. He looked at Doug Boyd, who stood at a loophole studying the heights behind the fort through his field glasses. "Now, sir?" he asked.

"Not yet, Dandy."

"It's almost time, sir."

"Not yet!"

The people in the magazine looked at each other and then at Doug Boyd's sweat-stained back. There was an aura of fear in the stone building.

Doug crossed to the eastern side of the magazine. He could see the light through the loopholes. The sun was just under the mountains, miles to the east. It was now or never.

"All right, Dandy," said Doug. He shoved back his cap and wiped the sweat from his face.

Downes withdrew the door bar and let the door swing open. Dandy wet his lips and grinned, then stepped outside. Those who could, crowded to the loopholes while the less fortunate stood behind them, waiting to hear what happened and hoping to God it wouldn't be an outburst of gunfire.

Kelly strode across the lightning parade ground, looking neither to the right nor the left. He stopped beside the flagpole and swung his trumpet forward. He nourished it and placed it to his lips. A moment's hesitation—and then the sharp brazen notes of Bugler's Call rang out to echo back and forth from the heights on either side of the creek.

Doug saw no movements on the heights. He turned to look at the taut white faces. "Places, everyone," he said quietly. "Act One, Scene One."

They moved quickly. It wouldn't do for those keen eyes above them to see them coming out of the magazine rather than their usual places of habitation.

Dandy Kelly had skipped Assembly at Doug's suggestion. It wouldn't do for the little garrison to line up in

plain sight and reveal how pitifully small in numbers it
was. He blew Reveille, and then in a little while, he blew
Stable Call. That would be easy to comply with. There
weren't more than fifteen or twenty horses in the big
corral. Troopers hurried toward the stables in their white
stable frocks.

The long morning dragged past. The play had been
going well. A trooper or infantryman would enter one
building wearing a campaign hat and shirt, only to reappear from another building in blouse and forage cap. A
man would leave the hospital alone and enter the
barracks to reappear moments later with several other
men to walk slowly to the stables.

A horse squad drilled near the corrals under the
command of a loudmouthed non-com. A man sat outside
of the cookhouse, methodically peeling potatoes. Mrs.
Webster, the sergeant major's wife, sat on the porch of
her quarters steadily knitting as she swung back and
forth in the only rocking chair at Fort Purcell.

Doug walked into headquarters and got his glasses.
He moved about the fort, taking care that the sun would
not reflect on the glasses while he scanned the shimmering heights. Now and then, he could make out a
watching warrior or could see a thread of dust rising from
behind a ridge. They were still there—waiting,
waiting...*waiting*.

———

WALK-ALONG SMITH HAD DRIVEN the big dun hard, and
he could hear the snuffling of its breath loose in its
throat. Now and then, a fleck of foam blew back and
touched his heated face like a little damp finger.

The hills swam in a purple haze, and the sun was like
the touch of a heated saber blade against his neck.

He crossed the shallow, sluggish Powder and then
swung down to lead the weary dun on. Walk-along

wanted to stop for a rest, but he kept on, slogging through the dust and feeling it coat the insides of his nostrils and his mouth. He kept looking about for a tell-tale dust streamer. He hoped he might meet one of the other couriers. He should have seen signs of at least one of them. The thought came to him that he was damned alone out there in the middle of Sioux country. The gods had shortchanged him.

The sun was nearing its zenith. He was no more than eight miles from Fort Purcell due to his roundabout route. *How many miles to the column?*

SMOKE ROSE from the blacksmith's shop at Fort Purcell, and the steady ringing of sledge on iron carried to the hills.

Sweating men went about their business, not daring to look up at those ominous hills. A detail worked slowly, erecting freshly peeled pine logs to advance the unfinished palisade. The odorous resin of the pines hung heavy in the air. Dust rose as the earth was shoveled in at the base of the palisades and tamped down hard.

A drummer and a fifer practiced together in the hot shade of the bandstand. The tunes of *Sergeant O'Leary, The Belle Of The Mohawk Vale, The White Cockade,* and *Hell On The Wabash* were bravely played.

Doug Boyd stopped at the Rochelle quarters. Louise sat on the porch fanning herself. Her eyes met his, and an unspoken message went between them.

"You're playing a fine part," he said.

"I wanted to be an actress once. Never again. Do you think they know what is going on?"

"I don't know. They are probably suspicious."

"Surely, if we have bluffed them this long, we can keep it up?"

He looked away. They could make a showing of

Stables at four o'clock, but Retreat Parade would expose the whole illusion. They could not fool the hostiles then.

"Do you think your messengers got through?" she asked.

"Yes."

She stood up and placed a hand on his shoulder, and the touch thrilled him. To think that she was his, but for how long, dear God? *How long?*

CHAPTER TWENTY-TWO

Walk-along Smith saw the dust rising to the north and east right in his path. He led the bay into a motte of scrub timber and picketed it while he found a hollow in which to lie down. He checked his weapons, wiped the sweat from his face, and slanted his forage cap low over his eyes. It didn't take long for the hostiles to get within sight. There were three of them riding hard as though eager to reach Fort Purcell before the attack began.

Walk-along closed his eyes and breathed a short prayer. They were heading straight for the motte. He opened his eyes and flipped up the rear sight of his Sharps. He would let them get within a hundred yards—or closer if he dared—before opening fire.

They were about to bypass the motte when the big dun whinnied shrilly. As one man, the three warriors turned directly toward the motte.

Walk-along rested his carbine on the lip of the hollow, aimed at the belly of the leading warrior, and squeezed off. The carbine thrust back against his shoulder, and a puff of stinking smoke blew back across his face. The lead buck slid from his horse, threw out his arms, and hit the ground like a sack of wheat.

The remaining warriors parted and then turned in, driving hard for the hollow. There was no time to reload the Sharps. Walk-along drew his Colt and cocked it. He squeezed off, and the Colt misfired. The two warriors were fifty feet from him as he fired again. The right-hand warrior's horse went down, pitching the buck ahead of him. Before he could regain his feet, a slug hit him in the top of the head to hold him where he was.

The third warrior fired and missed. He cast aside his rifle and jerked up a pipe axe. Walk-along jumped clumsily to one side as the axe whistled over his head. The horse struck him and drove him back against a tree. He fell and lost his pistol. The warrior hit the ground and closed in swiftly.

Once again, the axe swept close over Walk-along's head, taking his cap with it. Walk-along closed in, gripping the buck about the chest with his short, thick arms. The warrior grunted. This was *his* kind of fighting!

They strained against each other, the Sioux having a six-inch height advantage. Sweat sprayed from their faces as they dug in their feet. The warrior tried to hunch his shoulders up to get his arms into action, but the stocky trooper had a grip like a grizzly bear.

The Sioux spat into Walk-along's eyes, half-blinding him, but the inexorable pressure of the trooper's arms grew stronger as they swung back and forth in the death struggle.

The buck brought up a knee into Walk-along's crotch, but the trooper turned a little and then lifted the panting buck from the ground. He swung the heavy warrior around like a stuffed doll and drove him back against a tree. A stub hit the warrior in the kidney area and Walk-along could feel him weaken. Again and again, he battered the slippery body against the tree. Fingers clawed at his face and then settled about his corded throat, but he drew down his chin, pinning the hands against his chest.

He tightened his grip. The warrior jerked. Something cracked within his chest, and he opened his mouth. Blood dripped from his mouth and nose, splattering the trooper's sweating face. Then the buck sagged inside the powerful arms.

Walk-along dropped the buck. He picked up the pipe axe and sank it again and again at the base of the warrior's skull. Then he cast it aside and retched violently.

Walk-along picked up his weapons and reloaded them. He turned to look for the dun. "Jesus!" he said. The dun was galloping swiftly away from the motte with the two Indian horses.

Smith spat. His water was with the horse. "Walk-along Smith!" he said in disgust.

He looked to the northeast. There was no sign of life along the distant course of Wildhorse Creek. He looked to the east and saw nothing but heat-shimmering plain. To the south was Fortification Creek. Something glinted in the sunlight. He stared at it with tired eyes—maybe it was the regiment. The three horses were galloping to the south. There was nothing to do but follow them and hope the regiment was somewhere in the same direction.

———

It was an hour to sunset. Douglas Boyd walked about the sprawling post. Stables in half an hour. Warriors had been seen on the ridges and along the creek bottoms. Many warriors.

Dandy Kelly approached Doug and saluted. "Stable Call in half an hour," he said.

Doug nodded.

Kelly looked up at the ridge behind the fort. "What's the odds, sir?"

"You know as well as I do."

"Aye."

"Tell Mr. Holmes I want several horses led into the magazine."

"Sir?"

"If they attack, we might break a man or two free."

Kelly said, "Yes sir!" and walked off. Doug walked to the gate. Sergeant Holleschied stood there looking toward the outpost. The man was badly frightened. "Any signs of life up there, Sergeant?" asked Doug.

"I thought I saw someone up there."

"Soldier or warrior?"

"Soldier, I think, sir."

Doug nodded. He could use those men. "Tell Corporal Olsen of my company to come here and bring his signal flag."

Olsen came up on the double, carrying his long-staffed signaling flag. He saluted Doug. "You wanted me, sir?"

"See if you can rouse those men at the outpost."

Olsen climbed to the tower beside the gate and began signaling. Doug watched the outpost with his glasses. Olsen finished, and then something white was waved from the outpost.

"I think they are signaling to proceed, sir," called down the non-com.

"Good! Signal that we expect an attack within the hour or possibly at dawn. Tell them they must open fire with the howitzer whether they can range the hostiles or not."

Olsen wigwagged steadily, flourishing the flag from side to side. There was a short wait, and then the white cloth appeared and waved vigorously.

"Acknowledge, sir," said Olsen.

Doug nodded. The stubby gun couldn't do much material damage, but it might do some psychological damage. He was clutching at straws now.

Kelly lipped into Stable Call. Men moved about the post and headed for the stables.

Doug passed the word around for the garrison and the women to get into the magazine. There was no use in placing sentries on the walls. They would be lost if the Sioux attacked, and Doug needed every man.

Doug stood outside of the magazine as the last of the people entered it. They did not seem excited, but he knew fear was gnawing steadily within them.

The door was left open for the last breath of air. Dust motes danced giddily in the shafts of light from the western loopholes. Doug watched the shafts move slowly across the earth floor of the building. He stepped outside and looked west. The sun was tipping the western range. Sweat began to trickle down his sides.

There was an overwhelming quiet when the trumpet should have sounded Assembly for Retreat. The flag flapped idly on the pole. Long shadows crept leisurely down the seared slopes of the hills and ridges. There was no outpouring of men from their barracks. Not a horse was led out onto the parade ground. The hills seemed to brood under the lengthening shadows.

Minutes dragged past with agonizing slowness. Doug could almost feel the silent approach of the warriors as they crept down the coulees and wriggled through the dry grass. *They knew now...*

Doug heard rifle and carbine hammers being placed at half-cock. Someone cleared his throat and was the target for angry words from the others.

Tobe came up beside Doug. "Look," he said.

A tall warrior had ridden out on a shoulder of the ridge to look down at the fort. It was Spotted Tail in the magnificent regalia of a fighting Sioux chief. The feathers of his war bonnet and his coup stick fluttered in the breeze. Scalps waved at his horse's bit. The dying sun shone on the hair-pipe breastplate he wore. It was time for the Long Knives to hold their evening ceremony to their medicine flag, but the flag still slapped softly against the pole.

Spotted Tail had guessed right. None of his scouts had seen the soldiers leave the fort. Spotted Tail himself had not believed the soldiers had left, but he knew it now. There was only a handful of men down there, soft for the killing.

He raised his coup stick and shook it four times, the Sioux good medicine number.

Sioux, Cheyenne's, and Arapahoe's began to close in on foot. There was no time for a full attack, for the sun would be gone in a matter of minutes, but they had all night to forge their ring about the defenders for the dawn attack.

———

Doug Boyd closed the door, and just as it clicked shut, a rifle cracked from a loophole in the wall beyond the magazine. The slug slapped into the thick wood of the door. A woman screamed.

Lead whistled past the magazine or screamed crazily from the thick walls. An infantryman fumbled with his rifle and thrust it through a loophole. "Hold your fire!" roared Doug.

There was a sound like a stick being whipped into thick mud. The infantryman dropped his rifle and turned away. Where his face had been, there was a red mass where a chewed slug had struck him; he pitched forward across Diane Rochelle's knees. She screamed again and again in a rising frenzy.

Louise ran to her sister, but Diane's mouth was squared like a Grecian tragedy mask, and she did not stop screaming until Louise's hand struck her hard across the face.

"They're after the flag!" yelled a soldier from a post facing the parade ground.

"Burgess!" snapped Locke Holmes. "Get them!"

Tobe made his way through the crowd to the loophole and thrust his long Sharps through it. Doug pushed up beside him and looked through the next loophole. A young buck wearing a headdress of yellow-stained buffalo horns was lashing his pony toward the flagpole. An older buck was close behind him. The young warrior slid from his mount and gripped the halyards. It was an easy shot for Tobe, a little less than two hundred yards. Tobe thumbed back the hammer and sighted. His finger tightened on the trigger. He fired, and the big rifle kicked back. A splinter flew from the pole a good two feet above the young warrior's head.

"Jesus," said Holleschied in disgust. "I thought you could shoot, Burgess!"

Tobe spat to one side. He lowered the breechblock and slid in another linen-covered cartridge. He raised the block, shearing off the rear of the cartridge and then capping the nipple.

The young buck was struggling with the halyards. Tobe raised the rifle and shot as swiftly as he sighted. The big .54 caliber 475-grain slug hit the older warrior squarely in the head, driving him back as though struck by a sledge. Tobe spat again as he reloaded.

"Give me that rifle!" said Holleschied. "I'll get the other one." He placed his hands on the Sharps.

"Leave me," said Tobe quietly.

"Damn you! Give it to me!"

Tobe shrugged. "All right, Holleschied." He jerked the rifle free, reversed it, and drove the steel-shod butt against the sergeant's head, felling him like an ox.

"Damn you," said Locke Holmes.

Tobe grounded his rifle. "He wanted it," he said simply.

The young buck had given up his struggle with the halyards. He lifted his dead companion to his horse and lashed the horse toward the open gateway.

Doug looked at Tobe. The scout was reloading. Tobe could have killed the young warrior easily enough.

Tobe rested the rifle on the loophole ledge and fired upward. He fired three times. The flagpole slowly tilted over three feet below the flag, but it did not snap. No one could get that flag down now without cutting the pole at the base. Tobe stowed a fresh chew into his mouth, stepped over Holleschied, and walked toward the front of the magazine.

The building was rifted with stinking powder. Slugs still slapped against the walls. Five horses had been brought into the magazine, and they were panicky. Corporal Olsen and four other men were holding the bridles. A hoof lashed out and drove a cursing quartermaster against the wall with a broken arm.

"They've got the horses from the corral," said a trooper.

"The enlisted men's mess is burning," said another.

Up on the butte across the creek, there was a distant coughing noise as the howitzer banged off. The projectile plunged into the creek a few feet from the fort side of the creek.

The sun was gone now, but the burning mess hall gave sufficient light to show warriors moving about between the buildings. The crash of breaking crockery and glass added to the noise of shooting.

Doug wiped the sweat from his face and looked about the crowded interior of his improvised citadel. "It isn't likely they'll attack at night. But they *will* harass as much as they can. The fools have given us light to shoot by. Get as much rest as you can. Men at loopholes to be relieved every hour. No shooting unless you get a fair target."

"Rest is it?" said Dandy Kelly. "There's hardly room to swing a cat by the tail in here."

The light from the burning building showed through the loopholes, and the heat from the day's sun still hovered in the place. Body heat began to raise the temperature still higher.

"Salt, pepper, and gravel in the grease," said Tobe dryly.

Doug watched the women settle down. Louise sat with Diane, cradling the younger woman's head in her lap. She looked at Doug as he walked behind a row of boxes. He knelt to examine the fuse he had laid to the powder kegs. He had told three reliable men to touch it off if it became necessary. Doug meant to do it himself, providing he was still alive.

She smiled at him as he came to her. "We'll make it," she said bravely.

"Yes. How is she?"

"Asleep."

"Keep her quiet."

"Don't worry."

"You have your pistol?" he asked.

"Yes."

There was nothing more to say. A woman sobbed somewhere in the background. Now and then, one of the soldiers fired from a loophole. There was a constant pattering of leaden rain against the stone walls. They had until dawn. Spotted Tail was a man of initiative and imagination. Not for him would there be a desperate frontal assault. He would think of something. It was the one sure thing in the whole bloody business.

CHAPTER TWENTY-THREE

The Forty-ninth United States Infantry, leg-weary and burned raw by the sun, was bivouacked without fires along the bottoms of Fortification Creek, a long day's march from Fort Purcell. The men lay sprawled in sleep. Sentries paced back and forth, peering into the darkness.

Colonel Manning Rochelle sat in his tent with a shielded candle lantern, poring over his inadequate map. His scouts hadn't seen a single warrior. They had brought in the word that the hostile encampment on Wildhorse Creek had vanished. The trail led to the southwest, trending toward Fort Purcell.

Manning Rochelle bit off the end of a cigar and lighted the tobacco. There was only one thing for him to do return to Fort Purcell and wash out the whole damned futile business. But the regiment was dead-beat. He'd have to let them rest the next day and then make it in easy stages to the fort.

A sentry's voice was raised not a hundred yards from the tent. "Halt! Who goes there?"

Colonel Rochelle stood up and reached for his holstered Colt. He turned the shield on the lantern to cut off the light.

Feet thudded against the hard-baked earth as men moved toward the sound of the challenge.

Rochelle stepped out of his tent and walked toward the sentry. The sentry challenged again, then cocked his piece.

A figure stood on the far side of the dry creek, silhouetted against the sky. The sentry raised his rifle.

"Wait!" commanded the colonel.

The figure raised both arms. "Forty-ninth?" he croaked.

"Who are you?" called out Rochelle.

"Trooper Ballard J. Smith, Boyd's Provisional Company, Third Cavalry."

"That's Walk-along," said a trooper. "I'd know his voice anywhere."

"Come on in, Smith!" called out the colonel.

Walk-along stumbled down the slope and across the creek bed. He stared wearily at the colonel. "The hostiles are in the hills about Fort Purcell, sir," he said.

Rochelle felt a cold wave of fear creep over him. "Did they attack?"

"Not when I was there. Lieutenant Boyd sent me to find the regiment, sir."

"Lieutenant Boyd?"

Smith nodded. "Captain Ledbetter was killed near the fort. Mr. Boyd took over the command."

Officers and men closed up about the colonel as he stood there. "My wife is there," said Sergeant Major Webster.

"And my Katie," said Farrier Corporal Dennis McGuire.

Manning Rochelle looked to the west. They could make it with a forced march, but what would they find when they got there?

Not a man was asleep now in the bivouac. They stood there looking at their colonel, the man who had led them away from the post on a wild goose chase.

The colonel looked at Walk-along. "You are sure there was no attack?"

"Yes, sir. Mr. Boyd expected one at dawn, though."

"That was this morning."

"Yes, sir."

Thoughts tumbled over each other in the colonel's mind. The Forty-ninth had the makings of a good combat regiment. They had shaken down fairly well on the hard marches, but it might be asking too much to expect them to march all that night to reach the besieged post. If the post had been taken, it was the end of everything for him and for others in the regiment.

"Orders, sir?" asked Captain Talbot.

The colonel's head jerked up. "Eh? Orders? Yes, yes, of course, Captain." Rochelle turned to face the command. "Men," he said, "you all know what has happened. We are needed at Fort Purcell. I know you are tired, but I propose to start at once for the fort and hope to God we make it in time to save those who are there."

There was a low murmuring among the men.

Rochelle looked at his watch. "We can make it before dawn by forced marching. We will leave the wagons and the artillery to follow us, guarded by those unable to make such a hard march. Strip down to marching gear. Rifle, forty rounds, canteen, haversack, and the will to make it in time. Captain Kohl will command the train and will follow us as quickly as possible."

The men began to move about.

Rochelle held up a hand. "They say infantry fights where it stands. Then we'll stand at Fort Purcell on the Crazy Woman! *March order!*"

They pulled out in less than ten minutes. They left the shelter of the willows and looked to the west. The warm wind swept across the open country. The column stretched out, led by an advance party of veterans who marched easily in the long, free, swinging stride of the infantryman. The Walk-a-heaps were on the move.

Manning Rochelle strode along at the head of the main party, his spirit striving to get ahead of him while his long legs thrust themselves one ahead of the other. Stonewall Jackson's famous Foot Cavalry had been able to make thirty miles a day. The Forty-ninth had only part of that distance to make, and they *would* make it.

The main party passed, leaving a wraith of dust in the air for the slogging rear guard to eat. There was a long gap behind the rear guard, and then a lone figure appeared, forcing one short leg ahead of the other. Walk-along Smith was going to see the end of the drama.

Walk-along felt the alkali dust cut into his throat. He lifted one of his two canteens and drank deeply. Then he began to sing in a low, deep voice:

"There was Sergeant John McCaffery and Captain Donahue,

Oh, they made us march and toe the mark in gallant Company 'Q.'

Oh, the drums would roll. Upon my soul, this is the style we'd go: Forty miles a day on beans and hay in the Regular Army O!"

The dust settled behind Walk-along as he followed the Forty-ninth United States Infantry—the Halt, the Lame, and the Blind.

CHAPTER TWENTY-FOUR

The stench in the magazine was terrific—mingled odors of horses, sweat, powder smoke, and wood smoke. The mess hall had collapsed and was now a huge bed of ashes from which the red eyes of embers glowed dully. Smoke hung over the parade ground and along the bottoms of the Crazy Woman, mingling with the light mist which had risen with the evening.

Men nodded at their loopholes. A woman sat aimlessly, ripping a rag into tiny shreds.

Doug Boyd placed his hand on the door bar. A few minutes of fresh air might clear some of the foul miasma from the magazine.

He eased up the bar and gently pulled on the door. It swung open a little on greased hinges. Doug waited. There was no sound from outside. Most of the warriors had vanished from sight, leaving a few bucks behind to keep an eye on the magazine.

He pulled on the door, and there was a quick movement from beside it. A knife rose and fell, but Doug caught the warrior's sinewy wrist and forced it up. He thrust his right arm under the warrior's upper arm and locked his own right hand on his left wrist, forcing the warrior's arm back in a vicious bending motion. Something snapped. The buck grunted.

Another warrior closed in on silent feet, swinging a pipe axe. There was a crashing explosion just beside Doug, and the second warrior staggered back with a bullet in his belly.

Doug threw his opponent back and drew his Starr in a fluid motion. He cocked and fired it at hip level. The warrior died with a smashed face.

Doug pulled the door shut. His ears were ringing, and he was half-blinded by the flash and powder smoke of the rifle. He dropped the bar into place and looked at Tobe. "Close," he said.

"You're slipping. I knew they was out there. Smelled them."

"Over this stink?"

Tobe spat. "I kept alive more than once smelling 'em."

Doug shook his head to clear the ringing. Rifles cracked, and bullets thudded into the thick door.

"Not long until dawn," said Tobe.

"No."

The night was wearing out. The stars were dim. The wind shifted to come down the valley of the Crazy Woman.

"Stand to," said Doug.

Something was jabbed against Doug's back. He looked over his shoulder into Locke Holmes' taut face. Sergeant Holleschied had his carbine against Tobe's back. The man named Gipson had his pistol on Corporal Olsen.

Holmes jerked his head. "Get out of the way," he said.

"What do you want?" asked Doug.

"I'm not staying here to die like a rat."

"Where do you figure on going?" asked Doug dryly.

"The Sioux are in the hills. There aren't enough of them to stop me from making a break for the outpost."

"Go ahead then."

Holmes smiled. "I'm taking Diane and Louise with me."

There was no need for him to say what was in his mind. He knew Doug would die in the magazine along with the others. If he saved the Rochelle sisters, he would be a hero again.

The sweat worked down Doug's face, making white runnels in the grime. "You'll never make it, Holmes."

"Let me be the judge of that."

There seemed to be a mist of madness in the man's light eyes. Tobe Burgess moved a little, and Holleschied, with a grin, raised his carbine and smashed the barrel alongside Tobe's head, driving the scout to the floor. Tobe moved once and then lay still.

There was no one asleep in the magazine now. They were watching the drama being played out before them.

"You'll not take my sister nor me," said Louise Rochelle. She held her pistol in a slim hand.

"Get into that cell," said Locke Holmes to Doug.

Doug did not move but heard the clicking of the pistol hammer behind his back. He walked to the cell. Holmes jerked Doug's Starr from its holster and threw it on the magazine floor. He kicked the door shut behind Doug and snapped the lock. Doug looked through the narrow peephole.

Gipson and Holleschied led the horses to the wide door. The two men were nervous. Sweat dewed their dirty faces. Now and then, they glanced at the door as though wondering what would happen to them out there in the deathly quiet.

Soft gray light filtered through the loopholes. Cool tendrils of the dawn breeze crept through the loopholes with the light.

Holmes gestured to the two young women. Louise raised her pistol. "Stand back," she warned quietly.

"Don't be a fool," he said quickly. "I'm going to save your life."

"You haven't a chance, Locke!"

"To hell with her," said Holleschied. "Let's go while we still got time."

Diane's face was deathly white. She passed a hand across her trembling mouth. She looked from Locke to Louise and back again.

Louise gripped her sister by the arm to draw her away from Holmes—and that was her mistake. Holmes moved swiftly, striking up her pistol. He jerked his head at Holleschied, and the sergeant dragged Louise toward the door while Holmes took Diane. Gipson opened the door.

Several men moved to stop them, but Doug yelled at them from the peephole. "Don't take a chance!"

The two enlisted men led the horses outside. Holmes forced Louise and Diane ahead of him and closed the door behind him.

Corporal Olsen opened the cell door. Doug snatched up his pistol and peered through a loophole. The five of them had mounted. In the dimness, he could see no sign of the Sioux. Then a rifle spat, and Gipson jerked in the saddle and went down. Holleschied cursed. He led Louise's horse while Holmes led Diane's. They spurred toward the wide opening in the palisade.

Doug ripped the bar from the door. He was outside before he could be stopped. He jumped over Gipson's body and swung up on the dead man's horse. He turned it around the side of the magazine, seeing dim shapes close in behind him.

Rifles barked from the loopholes, giving Doug covering fire. Sioux rifles winked from the dimness near the creek as Locke Holmes made his desperate try for freedom.

Hoofs thudded on the baked earth of the parade ground. A crescent of warriors raced toward the four riders, but they did not see the lone horseman coming up fast behind them. Doug ripped Gipson's Chicopee saber from the saddle sheath and thrust forward his heavy Starr revolver.

He was in among them so fast and furious they hardly knew what had hit them. He swung the saber viciously in a slashing figure-eight pattern, cutting down two shrieking warriors. Another buck thrust at him with a lance, and the saber cut through the tough ash shaft and across the face of the Sioux.

Holleschied broke free and drove toward the main gateway, but an arrow was faster than his dun, and the broad head struck him between the shoulder blades.

The firing had died away because of the close conflict, and white man and red stared in fascination at the deadly joust on the dusty parade ground.

Louise broke free and turned back toward Doug. Locke Holmes was standing in his stirrups, fighting like a madman, forcing even the bravest of the warriors back foot by foot while Diane screamed insanely in her gross fear.

Doug thrust hard at a naked chest, withdrew the blood-glittering blade, parried the slash of a pipe axe, and laid about him with the blade until he was near Louise. Three shots from the Starr cleared the way for them.

The light was growing fast. Dust and powder smoke drifted over the miniature battlefield. Louise's horse went down, and Doug dropped the saber to pull her free and onto his dun.

Diane had vanished through the wide gap in the palisade, followed by three whooping warriors.

Locke Holmes had cleared a path. He had two choices—one, to follow the woman he had claimed he loved; the other, to turn back toward the magazine. He chose the latter.

Holmes spurred up alongside Doug. For a fraction of a second, Doug thought the man would help him fight his way to safety, but then he saw Holmes thrust at him with his bloody saber. Doug fired and missed. The saber skinned over his head, and the force of the vicious blow sent him off balance. Holmes leaned forward, and the Starr exploded inches from his chest. He was dead as the horse turned away, bearing him full into the pursuing warriors, his shell jacket afire and his sightless eyes staring around him wildly. The warriors broke away from the dead man, yelling in superstitious fear as his big cavalry mount crashed through them.

Doug kicked at the tiring dun. There was one warrior in his way, the same young buck who had tried so hard to gain a coup by tearing down the flag. He thrust forward a heavy carbine, aiming at Doug's chest. Doug fired his last round and missed. It was all over, he realized.

A man jumped around the corner of the magazine and raised a long rifle. It was Tobe Burgess. He yelled at the young warrior in Cheyenne. The warrior turned, and as he did so, the Sharps flashed. The slug struck the buck in the chest and drove him from his horse.

As Doug reached the front of the magazine, he looked at Tobe. The scout was standing there looking at the dead warrior. "Get in!" yelled Doug.

Tobe shook his head. He reloaded swiftly. Doug dismounted and pulled Louise down beside him. "Tobe!" he yelled.

Tobe smiled faintly. "That young buck I just killed was Iron Shield," he said. He touched his fingers to his forehead in a mark of deep respect for Doug. "This is a good day to die," he said quietly. Then he started running swiftly toward the Sioux, who were massing together in the wide gap of the palisade.

Doug looked away as the rifles exploded.

The hills were covered with Sioux, Cheyenne, and Arapahoe. Spotted Tail was leading them down toward the creek to make his final attack through the gap in the palisade. It was getting light enough now.

The howitzer cracked futilely from the outpost.

The main body of the Sioux and their allies passed

just below a low ridge that ran at right angles to the
creek. As they did so, a small body of soldiers appeared
on foot, looking down at the warriors.

This was too much for the volatile and unstable
warriors. This was better than trying to pry the white
eyes from the stone magazine. They swung up toward the
ridge, lashing their painted ponies.

The mass of them was now fifty yards below the ridge
crest. Other warriors were streaming from the fort to
help out in the slaughter. This would be like Lodge Trail
Ridge near Fort Kearney—a bloody slaughter with few
losses. *Hoka hey!*

CHAPTER TWENTY-FIVE

The ridge seemed suddenly to rise a little at the top. A line of dark uniformed men powdered with dust stood there, and at the ringing commands of their leader, they raised their heavy rifles. A crashing volley sheeted them in flame and smoke. The heavy slugs chewed into the mass of astounded hostiles. The Forty-ninth United States Infantry had made it just in time.

It was all over in five minutes. Infantry fights where it stands. It is an old maxim of war. The trick is to have them stand in the right place at the right time, and this Manning Rochelle had managed to do—with the grace of God and the muscular legs of his once-green regiment.

The Forty-ninth stood there, be-grimed, be-whiskered, and stinking to high heaven on their blistered feet—and fired volley after volley until the ridge was strewn with thrashing horses and dying warriors. The sun tipped the eastern ranges and painted the heavy drifting clouds of powder smoke with a magic brush. It rose a little higher and glistened on the blood-stained ridge—the ridge which would become known to history as Forty-ninth Ridge.

The Forty-ninth had its losses, too. They buried them

all together in the once empty post cemetery. Locke Holmes, Tobe Burgess, Diane Rochelle, and the men of the garrison who had died to save Fort Purcell. They buried the dead hostiles in a common grave on Forty-ninth Ridge, with one exception, made after Lieutenant Douglas Boyd had had a private interview with Colonel Rochelle. They buried Iron Shield, the courageous young Cheyenne half blood, beside his father, Tobe Burgess— and the name they put on his headboard was not Iron Shield, but Samuel Burgess.

CHAPTER TWENTY-SIX

Boyd's Provisional Company of the Third Cavalry topped the low ridge which overlooked the Laramie River. The wide parade ground was lined with the garrison, ready to stand Retreat Parade.

Doug turned in his saddle. "Kelly!" he called out.

Dandy Kelly rode forward and saluted. "Yes, sir!"

"Trumpeter, we'll go in on the horn. Sound the Trot!"

Kelly grinned as he swung his trumpet on its yellow worsted cord. He raised it to his lips and blew softly into it to warm it up. That was Mr. Boyd's way, provisional company or no, he wanted the walk-a-heaps at Laramie to know *his* company was coming in from the bloody Bozeman Trail with credit for saving Fort Purcell or at least a damned good portion of that credit.

The garrison looked up as the cavalry company came smartly down the ridge with the brazen notes of the trumpet effectively halting Retreat Parade.

Louise Boyd swayed on the ambulance seat. She looked at the grinning face of First Sergeant Hector MacKenzie, who drove with dash despite the fact that his leg was still in a thick cast.

They were all there. Olsen, MacKenzie, Walk-along Smith and the others, and it seemed to Doug as he looked back along the dusty column that other dim horsemen rode in the cloud of dust at the rear of the column—Adam Morrisey, Tobe Burgess, Darnell Stevens, Miles Hendricks and all the others who would never ride with the company again.

"The Brave Rifles," said Doug.

Dandy Kelly flourished his trumpet. "Aye, sir. Ali Baba and the Forty Thieves."

TAKE A LOOK AT TOO TOUGH TO DIE AND THE VALIANT BUGLES:

Two Full Length Western Novels

Gordon D. Shirreffs was an award-winning author of incredible tales of the old American West. In this volume, readers will be delighted with two such action-filled stories.

In **Too Tough To Die**, Buck Ruffin, a righteous gunfighting lawman on a mission, stalks four vicious outlaws across the desert and through an abandoned mining town where snares and pitfalls threaten around every corner. Even against the odds, Ruffin is determined to see justice done for their victims —even if some of the dead might have deserved their fate. In Ruffin's mind, no man was above the law—or above the swift justice of death.

In **The Valiant Bugles**, Captain Holt Downey had vowed upon pain of death to kill the Apache brave known as "The Butcher," the unconscionable savage who had murdered Downey's brother and subjected his fiancée to a fate worse than death.

It takes time and many miles, but eventually Holt catches up to The Butcher, setting up a showdown between two able and determined fighters that will leave one victorious and alive, and the other dead in a shallow grave...

"Gordon Shirreffs, who has written extensively both for teen-agers and adults, does a professional job of merging history, Americana, and virile action..." — **Kirkus Reviews**

AVAILABLE NOW

ABOUT THE AUTHOR

Gordon D. Shirreffs published more than 80 western novels, 20 of them juvenile books, and John Wayne bought his book title, Rio Bravo, during the 1950s for a motion picture, which Shirreffs said constituted *"the most money I ever earned for two words."* Four of his novels were adapted to motion pictures, and he wrote a Playhouse 90 and the Boots and Saddles TV series pilot in 1957.

A former pulp magazine writer, he survived the transition to western novels without undue trauma, earning the admiration of his peers along the way. The novelist saw life a bit cynically from the edge of his funny bone and described himself as looking like a slightly parboiled owl. Despite his multifarious quips, he was dead serious about the writing profession.

Gordon D. Shirreffs was the 1995 recipient of the Owen Wister Award, given by the Western Writers of America for "a living individual who has made an outstanding contribution to the American West."

He passed in 1996.